PENGUIN BOOKS

ALL THE TEA IN CHINA

Kyril Bonfiglioli was born in Eastbourne in 1928 of an English mother and Italo-Slovene father, and after studying at Oxford University and spending five years in the army, took up a career as an art dealer, the same career as his eccentric creation, Charlie Mortdecai. He lived in Ireland and then in Jersey, where he died in 1985. Penguin publish all three Mortdecai novels (*Don't Point That Thing at Me, After You with the Pistol* and *Something Nasty in the Woodshed*) as well as *All the Tea in China*, a historical novel featuring a disreputable ancestor of Mortdecai, and *The Great Mortdecai Moustache Mystery*, which was left unfinished at his death and was completed by Craig Brown.

An accomplished fencer, a fair shot with most weapons and a serial marrier of beautiful women, Bonfiglioli claimed to be 'abstemious in all things except drink, food, tobacco and talking' and 'loved and respected by all who knew him slightly'.

Kyril Bonfiglioli

All the
Tea in China

WHICH TELLS HOW CAROLUS MORTDECAI VAN CLEEF
SET OUT TO SEEK HIS FORTUNE IN LONDON TOWN;
ON THE HIGH SEAS, IN INDIA, THE TREATY
PORTS OF CHINA AND EVEN IN DARKEST
AFRICA; AND HOW HE FOUND IT,
PREDICTABLY, IN A PLACE WHICH
HAS NO LONGITUDE AND
PRECIOUS LITTLE
LATITUDE

PENGUIN BOOKS

PENGUIN BOOKS

Published by the Penguin Group
Penguin Books Ltd, 80 Strand, London WC2R 0RL, England
Penguin Group (USA) Inc., 375 Hudson Street, New York, New York 10014, USA
Penguin Group (Canada), 90 Eglinton Avenue East, Suite 700, Toronto, Ontario, Canada M4P 2Y3
(a division of Pearson Penguin Canada Inc.)
Penguin Ireland, 25 St Stephen's Green, Dublin 2, Ireland (a division of Penguin Books Ltd)
Penguin Group (Australia), 707 Collins Street, Melbourne, Victoria 3008, Australia
(a division of Pearson Australia Group Pty Ltd)
Penguin Books India Pvt Ltd, 11 Community Centre, Panchsheel Park, New Delhi – 110 017, India
Penguin Group (NZ), 67 Apollo Drive, Rosedale, Auckland 0632, New Zealand
(a division of Pearson New Zealand Ltd)
Penguin Books (South Africa) (Pty) Ltd, Block D, Rosebank Office Park,
181 Jan Smuts Avenue, Parktown North, Gauteng 2193, South Africa

Penguin Books Ltd, Registered Offices: 80 Strand, London WC2R 0RL, England

www.penguin.com

First published by Secker & Warburg Ltd 1978
Published in Penguin Books 2002
Reissued in this edition 2014
002

Printed in Great Britain by Clays Ltd, St Ives plc

ISBN: 978–0–241–97176–5

www.greenpenguin.co.uk

MIX
Paper from
responsible sources
FSC
www.fsc.org   FSC™ C018179

Penguin Books is committed to a sustainable
future for our business, our readers and our planet.
This book is made from Forest Stewardship
Council™ certified paper.

For Rubincrantz and Rosenstern –
two princes without a Hamlet

I could not sit seriously down to write a serious romance under any other motive than to save my life; and if it were indispensable for me to keep it up and never relax into laughing at myself or other people, I am sure I should be hung before I had finished the first chapter. No, I must keep to my own style and go on in my own way; and though I may never succeed in that, I am convinced that I should totally fail in any other.

JANE AUSTEN

A Bloody Foretaste

I had been frightened many times since I started my sea-voyage but always by the rage of winds and waters, dangers I could not properly comprehend and which I could do nothing about. Moreover, the Captain and the ship's company clearly could comprehend and partly govern them, so even when I was most terrified I had some comfort and knew that I was not alone.

This, now, was different. I was very much alone. Never before had I seen, glaring from the eyes of another man, the clear intention to kill me and the certain knowledge that he could. There is no lonelier terror.

The belaying-pin – fourteen inches of greenheart – whirred past my ear and ripped through the mizzen course with a noise like a pistol-shot. Lubbock moved along the rail, his eyes fastened on me, his hand feeling for another pin.

The Captain's voice rasped from the poop: "Fined one shilling for damage to sails, Mister Mate, and eightpence for wantonly losing one belaying-pin overboard."

Utterly taken aback, Lubbock stared over my head at the quarter-deck. For my part, I kept my eyes on Lubbock. The end of my life was very close: I could not afford to lose one halfpenny-worth of advantage.

The Mate's jaw was open; his eyes glared dully at the Captain.

"Aye aye, Sir," he said thickly, "I'll pay presently but first I'm about to kill this little Dutchie yid, by the Holy I am!"

"You'll do no such thing, Mister," snapped the Captain. "Mr Van Cleef, whatever his race, is a supernumerary officer: if you do him a mischief I swear you shall stand trial for murder."

"But he called me a cowardly bastard!"

1

"He will apologise, will you not, Mr Van Cleef? You spoke in haste, I dare say?"

I knew that if I stood down now I would lose all standing and be unable to protect my young friend.

"No Sir, I shall not apologise," I said, "for he is no other than what I called him."

"Then Mr Lubbock has a remedy open to him. A gentlemanly one." There was a sneer in his voice.

"Stand there then," bawled Lubbock, "while I fetch a pair of barkers – I'll see daylight through your guts in three minutes!"

"No, damme, you shan't," cried the Captain. "I'll have no pistol-popping in this bucket, it's too killing and too chancy. Mr Lord Stevenage, take the key, serve out two cutlasses and see that they be of a length."

Peter Stevenage walked unhappily to the main-mast and unlocked the chain which ran through the guards of the glittering skirt of cutlasses and boarding-pikes at its base.

This was "all to the gravy" for me, an unexpected hope. I had been Dux of my school at single-sticks and, although Lubbock was big and strong, his arms were short: I had the reach, the speed and the skill. He would, I felt sure, rely on smashing through my guard and I knew how to deal with that sort of play.

"Canvas frocks and hats!" ordered the Captain, and these stout garments, commonly used for tarring or going aloft in the very wildest weather, were brought. My frock proved to be stiff with tar – another small point to me. I worked the right shoulder free as I felt the edge of my cutlass. It was keen.

"Mind now," the Captain shouted again, "it's first blood only; no hacking after. The instant claret is tapped you'll lay your arms on the deck!" Ostentatiously he drew out a little Bulldog pistol and cocked it.

"Ready? Begin!" he cried.

I fumbled my sword as though I had never handled anything of the sort and the Mate, grinning like a shark, rushed in with a great smash at my head, which I met with the high St George's guard. The force of his blow made my very shoulder tingle and despite my parry his blade dented the crown of my canvas hat. I looked as stupid as I could and as frightened as, indeed, I was. His next attack was a slow, clumsy *molinello*, commencing with a feint at my side under the sword-arm, another at my head which carried no conviction at all

2

and finishing with a slice at my breast. I performed a *salto in dietro* – the elegant leap backwards – at the latest possible moment and he missed by a foot; then I pretended to stumble and, as he rushed in to destroy me, dropped into the long Italian lunge, knuckles on the deck. He ran straight into it and, instantly, the front of his frock was a terrifying mess of blood.

"Swords down!" roared the Captain – needlessly, because Lubbock's had clattered to the deck and mine had been wrenched out of my hand by his collapsing body.

"Fined ten shillings, Mr Van Cleef," yelled the Captain, "for fouling the decks! Bosun, get that mess swabbed up; the watch is idling! Doctor, is the First Mate alive?"

The cook strode up and peeled off the blood-drenched frock and shirt. A great, slippery flap of flesh fell free. My blade had passed outside his ribs, sawing off a pound or two of muscle and fat. The "doctor" looked up.

"Yazzuh, he alive. He good as new two, three weeks."

"*Weeks*?" shrieked the Captain.

"Yazzuh. 'Less it foosters up, then maybe ten weeks, or maybe die."

The Captain breathed hard for a full minute.

"Fined two guineas, Mr Van Cleef. Interfering with the working of the ship."

"Aye aye, Sir," I said.

As they carried Lubbock below to the cook's kindly needle and thread, the rest of the watch was already swabbing and holy-stoning his blood from the snow-white deck. It seemed to me that they were, for once, smiling as they worked.

I have told you, my heirs-expectant, this ugly little episode to whet your appetites, for I know how you love to dwell on scenes of carnage; I have seen you snatch at the newspaper for reports of the latest slaughters between Boers and British and I recall how, even as children, you doted on the frightfulnesses of Grimm's so-called fairy-tales, tales which it shocked me to hear your mother reading to you.

Before I regale you more, however, with blood-curdling accounts of peril upon the high sea, I must write the first part of my tale, which is how a young and headstrong Dutch Jew – yes, me, the grandfather you profess to love so well and whose health you watch so narrowly – ran away from his native land and had adventures in the great city of London; adventures quite as thrilling and, to the sensible mind, far more instructive. I speak, of course, about a time some sixty years ago, when our portly, disapproving little Victoria was a beautiful young girl, not yet married to her half-bred German prig; a time when London was gay and wicked – before the man Albert laid his cold, dead hand upon English manners and taste.

If you cannot profit from this relation of my early adventures in London, then you are all unfit to traffic in the porcelains, the tapestries and the paintings for which our House is famous – our House which you may or may not inherit on my death. I am sure I make myself clear . . .

PART ONE

The Running Away

CHAPTER ONE

I was running, running, fit to burst my breast; the shot-gun pellets in my left buttock burning like a foretaste of hell. It is hard for a man to run after a vigorous passage of lechery with a young woman, harder still to do so when he is holding up his breeches. I stopped to draw breath, and to attend to the buttons of my small-clothes – and to listen. I could hear nothing behind me; in particular I could not hear the baying of my uncle's great dogs, thank God. Why he should have been so upset at finding me in an embarrassing posture with my own cousin is a mystery to me: we were, after all, engaged to be married, he knew that.

After a while I started to run again, but more slowly now for I had a tryst with another young lady that evening and I felt that in all fairness to her, I should husband my strength. She, this other one, was there: in the shadow of the great magnolia tree in the north-west corner of the knot-garden beside her father's castle. We embraced passionately.

"Karli," she murmured as we drew apart after our first frantic embrace, "why does your heart thump so?"

"For love of you," I lied valiantly. "It always thumps so when you are near, dearest one."

"I am so happy that you feel so," she said, still murmuring, "because I have such a wonderful piece of news for us." My heart missed a thump. I cocked an ear for the baying of hounds but there was only the rustle of magnolia leaves and two hearts beating as one, although for different reasons.

"Tell me this fine news, my sweet and only love," I said, furtively feeling the back of my breeches on the left side, "tell me it all, my Eve with the sweet little apples."

"Karli, you have given me a baby, I am so happy I could cry!" Naturally, she started to cry. My heart now began to thump in earnest. I collected my wits.

"And have you told your father the Ridder, dearest love?" I asked diffidently.

"Of course not, Karli, he would kill you, you know that. No, we shall say nothing to him nor to Mama, we shall run away. We shall be very poor but you can work on the canal and I shall take in washing and we shall be so happy with our baby and our love in some tiny cottage far, far away from here."

To speak plainly, this was far, far away from the future I had planned: my courtship of the Ridder's horse-faced daughter had been an attempt to better my station in life: the thought of toiling on a canal-dredge all day and returning at night to a red-wristed washerwoman and a brat in a squalid cottage was not at all what I had had in mind for myself.

"I shall lie down now, dearest one of all," she said, "and you shall have your will of me, you bad, shameless, wonderful boy."

Love – physical love in those organs designated for it – vanished and shrivelled with an almost audible rustle.

"No, heart of my heart," I whispered, "not tonight. Tonight is too sacred. I must be strong for both of us – I shall go home and pray for our happiness in store, in store for us three. You must go to your bed and take great care of yourself and of the little fruit of our love." I was a wonderful liar in those days.

She meekly agreed. I have often observed that women, in some matters, are almost as stupid as men. After many a perfunctory kiss, I was running again. This time, home to my mother was where I was running.

I did not cry "Oy veh!" as I ran, because on my father's side I am a Jew of the Sephardim, the aristocrats and scholars: our private language is *Ladina*, not the *Yüddisch* of the base Ashkenazim of the East. I have, of course, some smattering of *Yüddisch* but, frankly, I had no breath to cry "Oy veh!" or anything else. With my mother was where I needed to be, even if I had to take a bowl of her strong chicken broth.

You must understand that I was then a young – and am now an almost elderly – Dutch Jew, so of course I must be a liar. I understand that: it is of no importance. Words are words; truth is something precious you share only with your family. So do not burst a

8

kishka trying to believe what I am writing: just enjoy. You will learn nothing of importance from this story except, perhaps, how to die; but then, you were born knowing that and in any case it only has to be done once. It is easy: ask anyone who has done it.

My nose was dragging on the ground by the time I reached my mother's house: she must have been waiting, for the door opened before I could rattle the pin. She looked me up and down. I opened my mouth.

"First eat," she said firmly.

"But Mama–"

"Eat!" she said and steered me to a chair. I yelped as I sat down to the table and, in the twinkling of an eye, my mother had hoisted me up and bent me over. She is – was, now, I think perhaps – a little woman and fat but strong. She put her hands to her cheeks and started to keen, but quietly, so as not to waken my father.

"Mama, *please*," I said, "I am not badly hurt, I tell you truly."

"Your great bottom I'm not crying about – but who made you those beautiful broadcloth breeches not two years ago, and who now has to wash the blood off and maybe darn twenty little holes?"

Still bent over the table, my face among the knives and forks and plates, I answered with dignity.

"Mama, I'm hungry. *Yet*."

Without a word she flitted to the big iron kitchen-range and, by the time that I had adjusted myself to sitting on the right cheek of my bottom, there was a bowl of her best chicken broth steaming in front of me, scattered with those little crisp things; I forget the English word for them.

Five minutes later I wiped my mouth politely and she set before me a plate of delicate chopped liver, such as only she can – could – make.

When I had dealt honestly with that she asked me whether I was ready for my supper.

"I am sorry, Mama," I said sheepishly, "but tonight I seem to have no appetite. And my bottom hurts."

"Ah, yes," she said, a trifle piqued, "the bottom I had almost forgotten. Get the breeches off, I shall look."

"Mama, I am almost twenty – *please*!"

"That bottom I have washed a thousand times before you even knew it *was* a bottom. And men I've seen before – relatives I mean, naturally. Now quick, down with the breeches before they are spoiled."

A few minutes later she said, "Such a baby, I never heard such squealing. And it's not buckshot, the gamekeeper loaded his gun with rock-salt only."

"Mama."

"Yes, son?"

"This wasn't a gamekeeper. It was your brother, my uncle; my Oom Kaspar."

She didn't say anything, she stood back and folded her arms. While I was explaining, delicately, how things had been when my uncle burst in upon us, she pursed her mouth in a way which was not wholly condemnatory. I could see that she was thinking of how things could be arranged with decency. Before she could give a verdict I said, "Mama?"

"Yes, son?"

"Mama, there is a little something else." I told her about the Ridder's daughter at the castle. She did not clap her hands to her cheeks, she did not moan; she gave me a long, blank look, so careful not to be frightened that it frightened me.

"Just like your father," she said at last. "A stallion, a mad stallion."

I gaped at her amazedly. My father, slight, silver-haired, gentle, a bookworm, was snoring gently upstairs over his treasured copy of Jakob Böhme's *Mysterium Magnum*, that great and ridiculous work by another philosophical cobbler. (The sign over our door read *"Jooss v. Cleef, Saddler and Maker of Riding-Boots to the Nobility and Gentry"* but my father was, in effect, a cobbler.) To speak of my father as a mad stallion was purely absurd: he was, as I have said, snoring gently upstairs over his book of recondite philosophy.

Except that, at the moment I am writing of, he was standing in the doorway.

He nodded courteously at me and then looked at my mother.

"Give the boy some money, Annike," he said. "Give him as much as we can afford, get him to Rotterdam and England. I am not proud, but I will have no son of mine flogged in public."

Again, he nodded kindly at me and vanished. Before I had drawn three deep breaths, before even my mother could begin to speak, he reappeared and thrust a fat volume into my hands.

"Read," he said. "Then read again. Get it into your mind."

I have the book in front of me as I write: it is Flavius Josephus on the History of the Jews, printed by Marten Schagen in Amsterdam in 1736; Haverkamp's edition, bound in speckled calf. I must read it one day, to appease a gentle ghost who was once the best and kindest cobbler in our Province.

My mother finished dressing my wounds in haste, then bustled about, putting all my good clothes into a bag made of carpet and filling up a little canvas bag with food.

"Now," she said, "quick. Down to the wharf. Old Gerrit's barge is tied up there for the night and he will be at the inn, drunken old fool that he is and a shame to his wife. Get under the tarpaulin and sleep. Not in the middle part of the boat, it is full of German coal; in the forepeak there is a cargo of Delft, your clothes will not get so dirty. Mind, when I say Delft, I talk of the rubbish they call Delft nowadays."

Her eyes roved the room, as did mine; this time, perhaps, for the last time. From every wall and dresser, interspersed with lustrous copper-ware, twinkled the finest accumulation of blue-and-white Delft in Gelderland – and Noord Brabant. My mother had a passion for it; she would walk twenty miles through our flat countryside, divided by canals like rulers, to haggle for a fine old piece she had heard of. In the diamond-glazed corner-press were perhaps twenty pieces of the real Ming blue-and-white porcelain, some of them were of the true eggshell-ware, quite different from the so-called eggshell sold to common sailors, which my mother contemptuously called "dock-ware". She had often told me of the long journeys by camel along the Silk Road from China of the real porcelains; their arrival in Venice (where some of the plainer pieces were "klobbered" with gilt and Venetian red over the original glaze, obscuring the simple blue brush-strokes) and so to our United Holland Provinces where the clever men of Delft had long ago imitated them almost to perfection – except that the "body" (they called it the *arcanum*, the secret matter) long remained a mystery, for the Chinese were as secretive about their China clay paste as they had been about the silkworm hundreds of years before; and except, too, that the slick miracle of the Chinese glazes was never quite repeatable. The old *plateelschilders* of Delft did wonders (and by 1720 they had winkled out the secret *arcanum*) but they could never quite re-create the ringing body, the succulent glazes, the delicate, off-hand brush-work of the Chinese. And they could not fool people like my

11

mother, much as she loved the work of *De Paeuw* (The Peacock), *Het Jonge Moriaenshooft* (The Young Moor's Head), *De Dobbelde Schenkkan* (The Double Jug) and all the other fine little workshops (named after the breweries they took over after the great fire of 1654 when the gunpowder-boat almost destroyed the town of Delft). Fortunately for them, there were few people like my mother. Fortunately for me, I was one of those few because, from my very childhood, she had played games with me and her treasures until I could tell pottery from porcelain with one flip of the back of my finger-nail, soft-paste from hard-paste with one nibble of the tooth, lead-glaze from tin-glaze with one caress of a wetted finger. Blindfold.

To speak plainly, I was not over-interested and had at times almost suspected that her preoccupation with pots was unwholesome, especially since my remote father sometimes gave me a moment of his time to explain that earthly treasures were but ordure and the only true riches were in the mind, where heaven existed. At my age, of course, I knew that heaven was neither earthly treasures such as Ming porcelain nor the recesses of my spiritual mind, but was contained in the bodices and drawers of young women. I am older now but I shall not pretend that I am much wiser.

"In the morning, early," my mother continued, "I shall go down to Gerrit's barge in the neighbour's cart and shall explain things to him and give him some money. I shall give you some money too; not very much but enough to get you to England. I shall bring, in the cart, a chest of Delft – not of the choicest but good enough for the English. My sister's cousin writes that in London today they are crazy for blue-and-white wares and cannot tell Wan-Li from *De Metalen Pot*. You shall walk around and about and listen without talking and so find out what the English will pay, then you shall take a little shop to sell the Delft from. Slowly, patiently; don't push, don't hawk; they will hear about you and they will come to you. The money I bring tomorrow will be enough for you to get established. If you do not whore too much, that is."

"Such a mother as I have!" I cried with real affection, clasping her in my arms so far as the fatness of her little body permitted.

"Such a son as *I* have," she said, without expression on her face, pushing me away. "Some more of this good chicken broth? No? You are a fool, where will you get such broth in England, where they eat beef rolled in suet every day? Now go, quickly, before the angry fathers arrive with dogs and whips. Go. I have to spend the whole night packing pieces of Delft in soft cloth, there is no time to listen to bad sons talking from the fronts of their mouths."

I kissed her, picked up my bag of clothes and my bag of food and went out of the door, closing it gently. It opened again in an instant and my mother thrust a soft bundle inside my coat. Before I could ask what it was she was telling me.

"It is the blanket your grandmother wove for you before you were born. You well know that you have never been able to sleep without it. People you don't need, not even me after the milk in my breasts dried. I understand you, my son; I looked into your eyes ten minutes after you came out of my belly. You will never understand yourself, thank God. Take the blanket and run."

Then once again I was running, but now very gently and quietly; listening and running, running. All the dog I could hear barking was the *Schipperke* – "the Little Skipper" on Old Gerrit's barge at the wharf ahead of me – and he would know me as soon as I drew near enough to speak to him and give him the piece of bread, dipped in chicken-broth, which I had thoughtfully slipped into my pocket.

He bit me gently about the ankles as I stepped aboard, then he ate the piece of bread and remembered that he liked me. I crept forward and undid enough lashings of the tarpaulin to enable me to creep in amongst the cases of pottery. The little dog, Kees – all *Schipperkes* are called Kees just as all dachshunds are called Waldmann – came in with me and licked my nose, while I rummaged in the food-bag. There was a little bundle of the greenish, twisted Sumatra cheroots such as my mother knew I loved, along with a box of waxed lucifer splints. I bit the end off a cheroot, moistened it carefully, relishing the treacly taste of the outer leaf, and struck a lucifer. The little dog, as quick as lightning, reached forward and patted it out. I had forgotten that all barge-dogs learn to put out sparks before they learn anything else. I tied him up with my neckerchief and fed him morsels of smoked eel while I lit another splint. There are few things nicer than smoked eel eaten with a green, sticky Sumatra cheroot.

When I had finished I pushed the little Kees out from under the tarpaulin and rested my head upon the bag of clothes. I did not hear Old Gerrit come aboard.

13

CHAPTER TWO

There was a gentle but vexing *schlipp-schlopping* noise which annoyed me into wakefulness. "Piss off!" I said in Dutch but in a friendly way to little Kees, already intent as I was to become a dog-loving Englishman, my new life.

The noise did not piss off, nor the little *Schipperke* was not there licking my nose or stealing my mother's good smoked eel. The *schlipp-schlopp* came from outside the fusty cell of crates and tarpaulin in which I had spent the night; indeed, it came from outside the very boat itself. We were, that is to say Old Gerrit, Kees and I were under way; we were moving down the canal under sail and as I became awake I found that I needed to be sick. Quickly. I fought my way out of the fore-peak, found a side and achieved the sickness. It was the *wrong* side that I had found. The side from which the wind was blowing. This was unpleasant. I made my way aft, stumbling over things. Old Gerrit – who else? – was at the tiller with a nasty old pipe upside down in his toothless mouth. (His barge was one which still had the steer-board but he preferred to use the tiller for he was lazy, lazy.) He flicked an eye at me. His only eye.

"There is the bucket, there," he said, pointing with his chin. I streamed the bucket over the side, cleansed myself as best I could and sat down upon the *taffarel*. "Taffrail" I later learned to call it: it means the rail enclosing the aftermost part of a vessel.

I had known Old Gerrit since I was a little child – say, ten years – and had always liked him: he looked like all the pictures in all the story-books. His chin almost touched his nose; he had no teeth at all in front but some, I think, at the back, for there he clenched his pipe and often, when we children teased him, munched and crunched off the end in fury and spat out a spray of clay pieces. His pipes were always very short. One of his eyes was covered with a shiny pink patch, tied on with a piece of ribbon; he once let us look underneath and wonder at the tiny wrinkled hole. The other eye was not nearly so nice: the eyeball was a rich chestnut-brown and the iris wobbled about in it like a raw egg in a bucket of blood.

"Your mother was here this morning," he snarled. "We talked. Talked as best we could over you snoring like a sow pigging. Here." And he kicked towards me a paper packet, a heavy one. I picked it up, looked it over carefully. It was sealed with my father's ring and the wafers had not been disturbed.

"Why do you look so carefully?" he said. "Am I a thief to steal stivers from babies?"

"Are you?" I answered.

"Go and do something nameless to your sister."

"I do not have a sister, Old Gerrit."

"You are sure of that? Your father has sworn to that?"

I undid the packet. It contained one thousand gulden. I stowed them about my person, while Old Gerrit spat noisily over the side. A woman on the canal-bank berated him, calling him a disgusting old man, for the colourful spittle had landed upon her bleaching-lawn. Old Gerrit shrieked back that he had been a disgusting *young* man and that he saw no reason to change at the behest of fat, adulterous laundresses. Her reply, interestingly narrating his intimacies with his dog, was mercifully borne away by the wind as our boat drew a little wind and passed out of earshot. Dutch ladies are very clean and, except for laundresses, modest of speech.

"What else did my mother leave, Old Gerrit?" I asked.

"A chest of old pots for you. A few stivers for me: not nearly enough for conveying a nasty young fornicator to Rotterdam but I am no man for arguing with women."

"No," I said.

"Especially women like your mother."

"Yes," I said. "But what else did she leave?"

His eye wobbled at me menacingly for a moment and then, snarling and farting, he reached under a pile of nameless rubbish in the cockpit and fished out a big stoneware bottle of the true Z. O. Genever: this is a kind of gin but not at all like what is sold for gin in England.

"It was for *me*," he said.

"Yes," I said, gently taking it from his hand. I drank thirstily,

15

thrust the bottle back into his hand, ran to the side and made another offering to the Lord of the Canal.

"Waste," he said.

I drank some more; this time I kept it down and felt better.

"What is there to eat, Old Gerrit?"

What he said is not usually considered edible.

"No, seriously Old Gerrit, I am hungry – aren't you?"

"There is a jack-pike and a perch, only a couple of days old; cook them, never mind the smell. Also some onions, you will find them."

I found the fish – they took little finding, they almost found themselves – and the onions. Spitefully, I did not throw them over the side, I cooked them up for Old Gerrit, who grudgingly praised my deftness with the skillet. I myself ate smoked eel on good rye bread from my mother's bag of food; capped it with another mouthful of the good Hollands and lit one of the Sumatra cheroots. Suddenly it was a good morning to be alive in; the sun sparkled on the little waves of the canal, crowning each one with a golden star, the sky was as blue as the finest Ming hawthorn-pattern jar; I had a thousand gulden in my pockets, my boots rested on a case of good Delft and before me lay adventure: London and London girls – *city* girls, not fat cousins and the pregnant, pudding-faced daughters of country Ridders.

Life was good. It is still pretty good but not good in the way that it was at that moment.

I was so happy that I gave Old Gerrit a cheroot: not one of the Sumatras of course but an old one from my pocket, good but a little cracked. He eyed it with disgust, crumbled it up and stuffed it into his nasty old pipe. He was famous for his ill manners.

After Hertogenbosch ("Bois-le-Duc" they still called it in those days) we had a fair fresh breeze for the Willemstad Hollandsch Diep – the nose of the barge positively "cut a feather" – and by evening we were tied up at Willemsdorp. Old Gerrit said that we would do the last leg, to Rotterdam, on the following day; he was tired and thirsty, thirsty, for I had been doling out the gin in small portions for his own good and because I, too, liked it.

I helped him with the brails – pieces of string which secured the big sail – then raced him to the inn and ordered something hot, which proved to be disgusting: sour cabbage and the belly-fat of a pig. I stayed my hunger with the speciality of the house which everyone else seemed to be drinking: rum stolen from the British

16

Navy, served hot and spiced and with a little baked apple in every jug.

I fell in with good company at that inn; one young fellow of about my own age took my uneaten dinner and scoffed it greedily while his brother told jokes of a dirtiness then unknown to me. The jokes were very funny. When I told these brothers that I was bound for England they said that they and their father were sailing there too, on the next morning's tide, very early. They were for Harwich but they reckoned that for a consideration they could take me to the Pool of London first. We haggled all evening, I pretending to be near destitute, and finally settled on six gulden (nearly half an English sovereign) for the passage, ten stivers (almost a shilling) for each hot meal and two stivers for every refreshment in between. I was right to trust them: thieves would not have asked such high prices – indeed, they would probably have offered to take me free, and robbed and perhaps murdered me.

By first light we three young fellows had drunk ourselves sober again and made our way to the wharf where their little ship lay, anchor a-cockbill, their father pacing up and down. To me the ship looked like the ordinary kettle-bottomed Dutch smack but they told me it was an English craft, built on the Humber: what the Yorkshiremen call a "billy-boy". Years later I came to realise that their trade was probably that of a hoveller: one who ranges about in bad waters in hopes of finding ships in distress. Sometimes, it was rumoured, helping ships to get *into* distress. But they were kind to me and kept their word faithfully and I remember them with much friendship.

We got my crate of Delft aboard with exaggerated care, then my dunnage. I bade farewell to Kees and left a silver coin – perhaps I was not so sober after all – for Old Gerrit. I also gave him the old blanket of my childhood – such things were foolishness now. It would make a bed for Kees, the little dog.

To my surprise, on board the old round-ended, ketch-rigged "buss" there was the lads' Mama: a Mama just like mine but bigger and with a better-grown moustache. She gave me a pot of coffee all to myself and a big slab of honey-cake and a smile. As I bit into the honey-cake I heard a squeal behind me and jumped around, but it was only the Mama scratching "St II" on the slate. Such coffee and honey-cake I would cheerfully give two stivers for today; indeed, I think I would give more if I had to.

17

All I knew about ships in those days was to do as I was told – and quickly – not to meddle helpfully without being told and, in between that, to keep out of the way, with my head low because of the boom. A man could go through his life with three such basic pieces of wisdom; I sometimes wish I had never learned more.

Well, I did all these things: I helped with the brails and gaskets and the rest, then crouched low against the windward rail. The old-fashioned, flat-bottomed smack bounced on the water rather than floated and, when we came to the "gatt" of the Diep, and the wind was almost dead foul, she heeled over so far that I thought we were about to founder. The lads and their parents had oilskins but I had none: soon I was so drenched and cold that my chattering teeth would not have let me pray even if I could have recalled a prayer. The Mama was singing cheerily but this was of no help. After a while I crept into the "*kajuit*" or cuddy – a little sleeping-shed forward where my gear was stowed – and delved into my clothes-bag for some dry breeches. I also found a smelly old blanket in a hammock and wrapped myself up, feeling homesick, heartsick and, simply, sick.

Later, as I was almost becoming warm, the motion of the vessel abated and the deck became once more nearly horizontal. I came to believe that I would perhaps after all survive. One of the lads came in and hung up his streaming oilskins.

"We are clear of the Diep now," he said cheerfully, "and we have a fair beam wind. We shall make a fast crossing. Have you been sick? No? Good. Have you any gin? You have? *Very* good!"

We drank a little. I had not realised that it was what I had been needing. We drank a little more. The sun began to shine, or at least it seemed so.

Later still the Mama came in with a splendid pot of coffee for me, this time with some thick slices of rye bread covered with thin, tasty slices of smoked beef. I made a face; a polite face, but a face.

"Eat!" she commanded in the very accents of my own Mama. I ate. To my surprise – and her satisfaction – I ate it all.

"That was good, mevrouw," I said as I captured the last, errant crumb.

"For two stivers, *jonge*, it was *very* good. We are not thieves in this ship." Seeing that I was somewhat abashed, she leaned forward and planted a great, noisy kiss on my mouth. Courteously, I did not wipe it off until she had left the "*kajuit*". In a little while I went out

18

onto the deck, where I smelled for the first time the true smell of the open sea, carried by a fresh breeze and enriched by a clean sunshine. Once again, it was good to be Carolus Van Cleef at that moment and in that year.

Dinner, early in the afternoon, was capital: it was the last old-fashioned Dutch dinner I ever ate. It was of thick pea-soup, so thick you could have built castles with it, served in pewter bowls. In each of our bowls there was a good piece of beef sausage, the trotter of a pig and all sorts of little bits of salted pork. Half a century later my mouth still waters at the memory of that simple meal. To tell the truth, so do my eyes, for I have grown sentimental and silly. (But not so silly as to be deceived when certain grandchildren and distant cousins kiss me sweetly because a rich old man may soon be writing a will.)

Dinner, as I have said, was very good and we all gobbled and belched in honest Dutch style, then lay back in the sunshine, listening to our bellies chuckling with the pleasure of it.

The wind backed into the East and soon we had almost a following wind; every stitch of sail filled and drawing to it. Now it was a lovely day; the Mama made me more pots of coffee, brought me more honey-cake and squeaked away at her slate.

Whenever she was out of earshot the lads told me more wonderfully dirty stories; some I can remember to this day, I am ashamed to say. (It is strange that only the English and the Dutch can tell stories which are both dirty and funny; the Germans and the Americans can only tell dirty ones, the French only funny ones, the Italians only pitifully bad ones. I have never heard a good story from an Italian. The Irish, the Scotch and the Jews are in a different category: they can only tell Irish, Scotch and Jewish stories.)

Towards the evening of that day everyone agreed that we had indeed made a splendidly fast passage and that, because the tide was foul for working up the Thames, we would drop our hook outside the town of Ramsgate. Soon we three lads were in the pram – a kind of a dinghy – and the elder cried "Vaart!", a word which strikes strangely on an English ear but simply means "give way". However, no sooner were we a cable's length from the ship than the father hailed us to come back. A nasty, lumpy little lop was growing up in the sea and he feared that the anchor would not hold. He was vexed about this: he explained that to go into the inner harbour was

19

expensive and I realised that this would cost him a good little piece out of my passage-money.

"Of course," he mused aloud, "we could go round the North Foreland and get inside the Hook of Margate. There is a good jetty there, but we could not tie up for the night . . ."

They all looked at me. I was at first puzzled, then I understood. I was not, in those days, the ruthless old bugger who now writes these lines; that family had been kind to me and it seemed a small thing to accommodate them. I generously offered that, if they would put me and my crate and dunnage ashore in that beautiful city of Margate and buy me something hot and nice for supper, I would pay them the agreed passage-money in full and make my own way up-river to London Town in the morning. They all beamed at me, every one, and the Mama embraced me warmly and we all struck hands on the bargain.

Almost as soon as we had rounded the Foreland and were turning Margate's Hook, the Margate itself appeared as a wondrous aurora of light which, as we drew in, resolved itself into a pearl-necklace of gas-lights: I had never seen anything so entrancing in my life, it seemed to be one of the fabled Cities of the Plain. Such a place was sure to be bursting with tasty dinners and young, sinful women: the sea-voyage, although short, had sharpened my appetite for both.

The father decided not to go ashore and, in lieu of the promised hot supper, gave me back thirty of my stivers, explaining that he preferred to take advantage of the fair wind to try to be off Harwich by dawn, because of the Margate dues and the lop of the sea. I think now that, speaking plainly, he did not want to have to buy costly suppers for the lads and their mother as well as me; also, I think that he may have fancied that on such a night there might well be coasters in difficulties who would be glad of his kindly assistance. When he and the lads had lumped my gear onto the jetty and had made their farewells and were busy about the work of the boat, the Mama gave me another of her big, succulent kisses; not, this time, of the motherly sort. I think I have already told you that in those days I was a fine-looking young fellow and still had both of my hands. (Indeed, even at my present advanced age, which I do not propose to divulge, some of my friends are kind enough to tell me that I could still easily find another pretty young wife and beget a son. But do not be afraid, my loving grandchildren and distant cousins: I have long ago realised that it is cheaper to buy rashers of bacon than to keep a pig – more hygienic, too. Indeed, who, in these dreadful days when good Englishmen are fighting brave Dutch Boers in Suid Afrika, would want to push more babies into the bellies of women?)

CHAPTER THREE

Margate Jetty was bewildering and my carefully-learned English Language and Literature deserted me quite. As soon as I set foot upon it I was besieged by a throng of ribald porters competing for the lucrative privilege of carrying my light bags, although none of them seemed so concerned about my exceedingly heavy chest of Delft. Also, there were lodging-house ladies, touts for inns, genteel persons offering me the programmes of circulating libraries, bathing-women thrusting their cards into my pockets, fly-men importuning me in words quite incomprehensible and one saucy young – or almost young – woman who pretended to know me and shouted "Holloa! My young brockley-sprout, now then for the tizzy you owe me from last Easter?" The platform of the jetty was very low and the crowds on the shingly, gas-lit beach added to the uproar with more coarse comments upon me, my breeches, boots and general appearance until I was on the point of tears – or of punching some of them upon their noses.

At that moment there was a sort of eddy at the far end of the jetty and the crowd parted in a respectful way. A little round gentleman emerged, laying about him with his elbows until he had cleared a space around me.

"Vy, vot's this," he bellowed, "carn't a poor foreign young chap pitch up on a British shore without being mocked and jostled? Leave him be, I say, and you two take his box to the shipping-shed." With that he turned to me and lifted his huge white hat, bowing as well as his roundness would permit.

"John Jorrocks, M.F.H.," he said. "Merchant of Great Coram Street."

"Tea-grocer," said someone in the crowd.

"I *glories* in the name of tea-grocer," he retorted magnificently. "I imports none but the finest, both green and black, and has them earlier than anyone helse in the City."

"My name is Carolus Van Cleef, Sir," I said when he had finished, "and I am travelling to London to start a business selling Delft-ware."

"Vy," he cried, "ve're practically in the same perfession: I sells the scandal-water and you sells the cups for the old tabbies to drink it from!" He seized my hand and shook my arm like the handle of a pump. "Come to the White Hart and share my 'umble repast, for the inner man tells me it's supper time. You might as vell put up there, too; best beds in Margate and does you proud in the matter of wittles." So saying, he linked arms with me and, having bidden two ragamuffins to carry my bags, marched me off to the inn. I studied him surreptitiously as we walked. He wore a rough-napped, unshorn-looking white hat, a blue coat with metal buttons, ample laps and outside pockets bulging like those of a Dutch burgomaster, a handsome buff kerseymere waistcoat and the tightest pair of dark-blue, stocking-net pantaloons you can imagine: they might have been painted onto his splendid thighs. The costume was completed by a pair of great Hessian boots with tassels, and a white tie around his neck with a gold pin in the form of the head of a fox – a most bizarre touch, it seemed to me.

"This is most kind of you, Mr, ah, Emmeffetch," I said diffidently. He looked at me puzzledly, then roared with laughter, shaking and wheezing and slapping the splendid thighs.

"No, no," he cried at last, "*Jorrocks* is the name, 'M.F.H.' is but the title, 'the guinea stamp' as Nimrod says. It is mere hinitials and means Master of Fox-hounds: the finest handle anyone could lay to his name. Fox 'unting, my dear young Sir, is my werry life: the himage of war with none of the guilt and only five and twenty percent of the risk to life and limb. If ever I am wisited with the last infirmity of noble minds I fears it will be caused by my ungovernable passion for the chase." He jingled the silver in his pockets moodily. I was greatly puzzled: his words seemed irrational but the other English seemed to hold him in deep respect. Clearly, I had much to learn. However, I was just old enough to know that I should hold my tongue: some people learn this too late, some never learn it. It was a good thing that I did not speak, for Mr Jorrocks had not done.

"When there's neither hunting nor shooting going on," he cried,

23

waving his arms about in a prodigal fashion, "what's a man to do with himself? I'm sure you'd despise me if I went fishing: the werry word's a sickener."

"Yes, perhaps," I said, "but fish are good to eat, no?"

"You're a most persuasive young cock!" he cried, slapping his great thigh again, "and I daresay that our host, Mr Creed, may have something of the sort fit for our supper. And, even as I says it, here we are!"

Mr Creed, the landlord of the White Hart, greeted my new friend in an obsequious way and promptly agreed to find me a room – it was, it seemed, merely a matter of turning two bagmen out. They could, he was sure, find lodgings more suitable to their purses and condition in a "flea-trap" further down the street, for he explained that they were but "glass-of-water-and-a-toothpick gents" who "fought every threepence on the bill".

It was a snug room and the little maid who came to change the sheets whilst I was washing flirted her eyelashes at me in the most promising way. She seemed to be overworked and tired, but contrived to give the impression to me that she was not *too* tired. When I pinched her tight little bottom she smacked my face so gently that it was almost a caress. For the time being, however, my thoughts were on higher things. *Supper*, to be exact. When she had gone – after having promised to bring in a warming-pan as I retired – I concealed my store of gulden in various parts of the room, locked the door and made my way downstairs to the coffee-room where my excellent Mr Jorrocks awaited me. We were soon joined by a friend of his whom he addressed variously as "The Yorkshireman", "Mr York", "Mr Stubbs" and "Sir Tees". I could make nothing of all this but I held my tongue for my Mama had often told me that the English were, to speak plainly, not quite like other men.

"Now then, my young cock," cried Mr Jorrocks, clapping me on the shoulder (this is the mark of an Englishman: Prussians punch you in the ribs to show their friendship, Italians pinch you cruelly on the cheek), "now then!" he cried, "let's see if a row of Dutch grinders can out-do a British set!"

I was hungry. I was also a Dutchman. Also, I had studied the English Language and Literature.

"Lay on, Macduff!" I cried, "and cursed be he that first cries 'hold enough'."

"A werry noble sentiment, worthy of Nimrod himself. Vy, I

declares I could eat a helephant stuffed with grenadiers and wash them down with a hocean of malt liquor!"

We settled down at the table and squared our elbows. Mr Jorrocks had been boiling, on the coffee-room fire, an Imperial Quart and a half of Mr Creed's stoutest draught port, with the orthodox proportion of lemon, cloves, sugar and cinnamon: it was perfection. The table was adorned with beautifully-dressed dishes of shrimps, lobsters, broiled bones, a cold knuckle of veal, an aitch-bone of beef, fried ham, a few grouses and some poached eggs. Having trifled with the shellfish a while to tickle our appetites – there was but one lobster each, although large – Mr Creed brought in a dish of Dover soles which vanished like the dew upon a rose. Now ready for a real gullet-tickler, I speared a grouse and called for a plate so that I might pass it to the good Jorrocks.

"No *no*, my young Sir," he cried – but civilly – "Ve don't do that here, alvays eat the farmer before the gentlemen." Whereupon he drew the aitch-bone of beef towards him and helped me generously to the lovely, bloody slices encircled with marbled fat. Then we ate the grouses. Then we tried the fried ham with some poached eggs. Then Mr Jorrocks called for "three bottoms of brandy, hot, with" and we took the broiled bones in our fingers and gnawed happily.

Mr Jorrocks and the Yorkshireman seemed content but I wanted cheese. I asked diffidently for some of it, not being sure that the British used such things.

"Cheese?" cried Mr Jorrocks, "Cheese? Vy, wot a young Trojan you are, to be sure. Cheese you shall have, and in habundance. Mr Creed, I say Mr Creed, bring this young fighting-cock one of your Stiltons – the werry ripest, for he deserves no less!"

A strange thing, shaped like a bucket, was brought in and reverently placed upon the table. It stunk very nicely, not as rich as a Limberger but strong. There were little things burrowing busily in it but Mr Creed quietened them with a soup-ladle of hot port. No one else was hungry any more but I ate great store of it, spread upon strange biscuit-like things called Thick Captains. The others, I think, admired my appetite, for they applauded every mouthful. I do not think that they were making fun of me; they were kind, kind. Then we concocted a bowl of some hot drink of which I forget the name, which we drank, saying many a kind word one to another. Then we were given a chamber-candlestick apiece and made our ways upstairs to bed. Mr Jorrocks and Mr York, climbing the stairs ahead of me, seemed to be a little random in their choice of steps.

When I had stripped to my shirt and washed, the little maid came in with the promised warming-pan and spoke to me reproachfully.

"How late you are, Sir," she said. "Some of you gentlemen have no consideration for a poor girl. Why, see, I've already changed into my night-shift, all fresh-washed, and am shivering with cold!"

"So you have, child," I said compassionately, "and so you are. Come, let me warm you."

"Oh *Sir*!" she cried a few moments later.

"Yes," I said.

"No," she said, "You mistake me. I am not frightened. It is just that . . . well, have you been *wounded*? There, I mean?"

I thought for a moment. I *realised*.

"No my little love," I murmured, "all of us, ah, Dutchmen are born like this."

"Goodness gracious," she said. "But, does it not make any *difference*?"

"Let us see," I said.

Some twenty minutes later she was agreeing fervently that the difference, if any, was for the better. But women are notoriously feather-brained and she awoke me at least twice – I forget – in the night to reassure herself that my "novelty", as she coyly described it, was as adept as she had seemed to remember. I contrived to reassure her, for in those days I was even younger than I now am.

From that day to this I have firmly believed in the properties of the excellent English Stilton Cheese: my table is never without it.

I was awakened in the dark before dawn by certain young persons scrambling out of my bed, giving me a sleepy kiss and fending-off my sleepy advances.

"It's all right for some," she cried, "who have nothing to do but take advantage of poor innocent girls and then slug a'bed half the day themselves!"

I made placatory noises, grasped her and danced her lovingly round the room while I ascertained with finger and toe that my various little stores of *gulden*, concealed here and there, were intact. They were. She, I need scarcely say, was not: a further three-minutes' romp made sure of that, her protests making the interlude the more enjoyable. Before she left, frantic about the work she had

26

to do, I gave her a whole *gulden*; I was young in those days and foolish.

Washed, dressed and shaven, I sought out Mr Jorrocks's room – "you can tell it by 'is snoring," said the other, *uglier* chamber-maid – and entered after a series of knocks, each one louder than the other.

"Come, my good friend!" I cried cheerily, "be stirring! Dawn is breaking!"

The shapeless lump under the bed-clothes wriggled in an irritable fashion.

"Let it break," came the grumpy answer, "for it owes me nothing as I knows of."

"But I had hoped, Mr Jorrocks, that you might join me at breakfast, as my guest, unless you are feeling, how is it, *below the weather . . .?*"

"Below the weather?" he bellowed, bounding out of bed with a thump which must have shaken the whole inn, "*under* the weather? Wot a imperent young game-cock you are, to be sure!" He smoothed out those parts of his ample nightshirt which had become entrapped in the folds of his person, his good temper quickly restoring itself. "No man shall say that John Jorrocks could not face his breakfast, come what may. Now, let me adwise you to take a restorative dip into Mother Hocean whilst I perform my ablutions and attend to my toilet. I shall look for you in the coffee-room in one hour precise, when we shall see who can eat most of that Macduff you spoke of so freely last night."

Even at that hour the shingly shore of Margate was a heaving mass of bathing-women who came rushing towards me, avid for my patronage. I turned tail and fled. With one of the White Hart's towels in my pocket I crossed to the Ramsgate side and found a stretch of deserted beach below the Preventive Service Station. I found that it was easier to swim in the sea than in the fresh water of the canals of my native land, but the water tasted curiously salt. A quick towelling and a brisk run brought me back to the White Hart at just the moment that Mr Jorrocks emerged from the inn's kitchen, where he had been giving final directions for our breakfast. He rubbed his hands as he sat down. I, too, sat down, rubbing mine.

In the end I had to give him best. He had, after all, had a great deal more sleep than me and, you see, the appetite which my dips – one into Mother Hocean – had afforded me could not discount the healthy fatigue and strain upon the digestive organs.

"Wot?" he cried, dexterously trapping the last fourth of a muffin from my defeated plate, "Wot? 'Ave I made you cry *'capivi'*, my young prize-fighter? Vell, it's nothing to be ashamed of; ask anyone in the Surrey 'Unt vether they've ever seen John Jorrocks outfaced when his knees are under a breakfast-table. Indeed, you're the finest contender I've ever squared up against . . . consider Mr York, there," and he pointed with his triumphant fork to a pallid apparition in the coffee-room doorway, "consider him, I say. I'll wager you a hat – a *guinea* hat, not a 6/8d Goss – that he can get down no more than a pint of porter and a pair of ripe bloaters!" The apparition turned greenish and vanished.

"There you are!" he cried, "Wot did I say? Wot is 'appening to the youth of Old England when a slight breakfast daunts them? Where are the 'earts of hoak? Waiter, pray fetch me a few more of these capital prawns and another slice of that delicate Cambridge brawn, for I vows that my muffin-mill is almost stopped – needs hoiling – and I have promised Mrs J. that I shall not eat butter, lest I spoil the trimness of my figure."

"Do you stay here long, Mr Jorrocks?" I asked, with some trepidation.

"Vy, no; I and Mr York came but to stay a five pound note in Margate this delightful weather (plus eighteenpence vich Mr York furnished) and it is now all but spent. We leaves on the steamer at eleven o'clock sharp."

I summoned the waiter and asked for my bill. Mr Jorrocks took it from me but not, as I had hoped, to settle it. He took out a silver pencil-case and scrutinised the slip of paper carefully.

"Wot did you use by way of candles?" he asked.

"One," I said. "For perhaps five minutes."

"Imperence!" he cried, scratching out the item on the bill. "Now, 'hearly call in the morning'?"

"Well, I do not think so." He scratched some more.

"Wails for the vaiter – left blank."

"Vails?"

"Perquisites, honorariumbs, *tips* as the bagmen call 'em."

"Ah, I see. A shilling, do you think?"

"Fourpence is werry ample." He scratched again. "And the chambermaid?"

28

"I think," I said carefully, "that she has already been availed."
He handed me back the bill and I made great show of rummaging in
all my pockets to find enough silver to make up the sum.

"My word," said Mr J. as I rummaged, "I believe I am getting
oldish. I fancy a true fork-breakfast would have made a stiff 'un of
me. It's all werry well for you great Dutch cormorants but I has a
thriving warehouse and a great red-faced wife to see to." I did not
understand but I made polite noises as I gathered together the
amount of the bill.

"See here, young spadger," he said, presently, "if you should be a
little short of tin, by vich I means swag; since I have taken a fancy to
the way you can deal with your prog, by vich I means your wittles,
pray come and spend a night or two at Great Coram Street. Mrs J.
vill be delighted to see you" – his voice lost a little conviction at this
point – "and you shall have a h'aired bed, good wear and tear for
your teeth and all that sort of thing found you. Pray do me this
kindness, do. The steam-packet leaves at eleven prompt and it will
be strange if I cannot persuade the Captain to take your chest of
tea-cups aboard, although he has no cargo-bottomry."

I found this puzzling. First, I had been assured that the British
were not an hospitable folk. Second, I was well aware that this day
was the Sunday.

"But today is Sunday," I said, diffidently. "Is it thought proper
here to make so long a journey on this day?"

He chuckled fatly.

"My dear young sir," he said, "in England ve sees no more sin in
taking a journey on a Sunday than in cheating one another on the
Monday!"

"Mr J., I cried, "I feel that I have come home."

"Werry obliged," he said, "I'm sure. Now, pack your traps and
we'll retrieve your box of ware from the shipping-shed, for there's
little enough time left before the steamer commences its wulgar
'ooting."

Indeed, by the time that I had made a small, sentimental farewell
to the little chambermaid, packed my traps, met Mr Jorrocks on
Margate's far-famed jetty and struck a bargain with two surly longshoremen over the movement of my chest of Delft into the steamer,
the 'ooting was, indeed, becoming urgent. It was a beautiful
steamer, named the *Royal Adelaide* – after the Queen before this
one, you understand – painted magnificently in pea-green and

white; flags flying, decks swarming with smart bonnets and bodices: I had never seen anything so fine. Well might Britannia rule the waves; I felt my heart swelling with new-found patriotism, for I am easily moved.

Mr Jorrocks and I found a corner of the deck on which to settle; our various possessions firmly ensconced beneath our bottoms. He was nursing on his lap a great wicker hamper, at which I stole a glance once in a while.

"Prowisions," he said, patting the lid. "Breakfast is all werry well but – 'ow keen the sea air is! I 'ave brought but a knuckle of weal, half a ham, some genuine Dorking sarsingers (made in Drury Lane), a few plovers' eggs and some sherry white. Yes, and I believe some chickens. Werry acceptable they'll be before we gets to the Savoy Stairs, you may depend upon it."

He was right, I have never met a man of so much acumen. The sea air was, indeed, keen, keen. The knuckle of weal and the other little snacks were, indeed, welcome. I gained, I think, his respect, by agreeing that he should have the last chicken if I might have the last few plovers' eggs.

There was a sort of orchestra on the steamer, comprising one flute, one lute, one long and one short horn, also a harp played by a fat lady in a puce gown. They played quadrilles and other things to which I could not master the steps but it was pleasing to be taught them by young ladies who giggled. One of the young ladies had a gentlemen friend who tried to hit me with his knuckles. I made his nose bleed. When I lifted him up and apologised, he tried again to hit me and I had to make his nose bleed afresh.

"'E wos a beauty before you put the paint on!" cried the young lady, still giggling.

"'E is an uncommon fine young warbler," said Mr Jorrocks gravely, "now where shall we turn for a song?"

In default of the young gentleman with the bloody nose I sang a song in my own language, then, emboldened, another, with words which I was tolerably sure no one on board would understand. After this, I was besieged with more lessons in dancing by other and more desirable young ladies; at least one of which, I fancy, took place behind a ballast-box, but I forget, for I am old now, old.

PART TWO

The Great and Sinful City

CHAPTER FOUR

As we chugged up London River the wind shifted and I wrinkled my nose in puzzlement for suddenly the air was full of a stifling stench of horses. I remarked on this to Mr J., who sniffed the breeze appreciatively and told me that this was the very scent of London itself. "More 'osses to the square mile than anywhere helse in the civilised world," he told me. "You'll soon be relishing it as the homeliest smell in the world."

I found this hard to credit at the time but there is no doubt that within a very few days the stench became first inoffensive, then unnoticeable. It took me longer, fresh as I was from cleanly Holland, to reconcile myself to the human odours which reeked from every street-kennel.

Too soon the dancing on board stopped and there was a frantic search for children and other parcels as we drew up to London Bridge.

"Ease her! Stop her!" bellowed the Captain. "Now, Sir, yes, you Sir, in the wherry! Are you going to sleep there?"

Within a little while my chest of ware was on a tax-cart – an open, one-horse, farmer-like vehicle without springs – and Mr Jorrocks and I were following in a hansom cab to his warehouse in St Botolph-Lane, where my Delft was to be stored for the time being and where Mr Jorrocks hoped to catch his work-people napping.

"My vord!" he said contentedly as we jolted and trundled through the evil-smelling streets – "Easy over the pimples, barber!" he cried once or twice in his jocose fashion – "My vord, I wows I feels mightily refreshed of my jaunt, quite renowated: as fresh as an old hat after a shower of rain! But I fears there is nothing liquid left in the hamper and my gullet is dry as a bone."

"Shall I ask the cabbie to stop," I asked anxiously, "so that I can find you a drink of water?" He looked at me strangely.

"Water! Haven't surprised my stomach with a drink of water for fifteen years and that was a haccident, for I thought it gin. 'Ave you seen what water does to boot-leather?"

"And perhaps," I murmured diffidently – my first essay at an English joke – "perhaps it might rust your iron constitution?"

"Haw, haw, haw!" he bellowed, slapping my thigh quite painfully, "Werry good indeed, Mr Dutch, werry good indeed. Owes you one for that, owes you one!"

I blushed and sweated with pride.

"Cabbie!" shouted Mr Jorrocks, pulling a little string which was designed to attract the cab-driver's notice, "Cabbie, I say, pray stop at the Cock and Pullet when we gets there, for my young friend is feeling poorly. Yes, and you shall have a fancy four for yourself, in course, and a quart of stale vollop for your old screw, vich might have been a 'unter once, judging by his rat-tail."

This bore no relation to the English Language I had so sedulously learned at school, but the dissipated driver understood every word: he whipped up his sad nag and soon grated his wheels against a kerbstone at what Mr J. called "the werry spot".

I was puzzled that the "Cock and Pullet" was called, on its signboard, the "Mother Redcap". There we "baited" ourselves on sausages and salt herrings, washed down with a basin of new milk infused with "sticking-powder" – which proved to mean rum. I had never drunk rum in this way before. It was very good and stunk most agreeably.

We left soon, although the salt herrings, too, were good, because I was concerned about my case of Delft, although Mr J. assured me that no one in all London dared deliver goods clumsily at his warehouse.

In view of the respect with which he was treated by one and all, I had prepared myself for a palatial emporium with vast mahogany counters and liveried flunkies bowing at the head of a great flight of marble stairs. I did not in those days understand about Britain, still less about London which is almost a separate state. (Indeed, Queen Victoria herself has to use courtesy when entering London City, so proud and strange it is!)

It was no palatial emporium: a great, grubby, slab-sided building bore, on the door-post in dirty white letters, "JORROCKS & CO'S

WHOLESALE TEA WAREHOUSE". I later learned that this a British trait, a sort of upside-down boasting: you are supposed to *know* where such places as Jorrocks's are, on the principle that "good wine needs no bush". Only the "flash bucket-shops" spend money on display at their premises; when an English tradesman wants to "put on dog" as he calls it, he spends money on his horseflesh and "rigs" – and, indeed, outside this warehouse stood a magnificent errand-cart with "Jorrocks" blazoned upon it in great gold letters, surrounded by many a coat of arms of satisfied royal persons. This conveyance was pulled by a glossy bay Hackney gelding of blood, and driven by a superb person wearing, I should think, forty pounds' worth of livery-clothes upon his back.

"I daresay I shan't catch the warmints," said Mr Jorrocks as he leaped out of the hansom (leaving me to be cheated by the cabbie), "but venever I'm away they prig enough pewter out of the till – by pewter I means cash – to take their lasses to the Sadler's Wells theatre at the werry least, damn their teeth and toenails."

Inside, the warehouse was, to a Dutch eye and nose, disgusting. (We Dutch are a cleanly folk and the British at that time were still famous for their dirtiness. Now, as I write in this bad first year of the Twentieth Century, they have taken to scrubbing themselves and their houses but half a century ago, when all this took place, they had no such notion.)

The floor of the warehouse, huge, gloomy and dingy, was covered with dirt quite half an inch deep and seemed to be sown, as though for planting, with rice, currants, raisins, cardamoms and many another grocery.

Mr Jorrocks snuffed the air appreciatively.

"The werry scent of British commerce!" he cried. "Where would the vorld be without it?" I did not remark that we Hollanders, too, were arranging our affairs quite well, for in those days I was a civil youth, supple to my elders.

He darted towards a sort of office, like a sheep-fold, in one corner of the echoing warehouse, from which, through a couple of squares of grimy glass, he could survey all that was going on. I do not think that he found anyone prigging his pewter. I wandered here and there amongst the hogsheads, casks, flasks, sugar-loaves, jars, bags, bottles and bales and boxes, until I was quite lost, and my boots were caked with the exotic detritus upon the floor. I saw a person in his shirt-sleeves and a white apron, a brown-paper hat upon his head, leaning over a little vessel as though he had the nose-bleeds. I hurried over to him and offered assistance, but it proved to be my excellent Mr J. himself, sniffing and sipping from a tray of teacups, trying a newly-arrived consignment of teas for strength, flavour and other virtues. When he had finished he conducted me around this temple of commerce, pointing out and pricing the commodities in which he dealt until my head reeled at the mercantile wealth contained within that echoing, smelly cellar-above-ground. At last we came to the "werry backbone of the consarn" – the teas.

With many a spacious gesture he named these treasures in their great, mat-covered chests.

"There!" he cried proudly, "Red Mocho, superior Twankay, Lapsang, Souchong, Oolong (werry soothing that, will be all the go with the swells one day, had an order from a Honourable Wooster only last week) and the true Gunpowder, a tea werry hard to come by."

"And these?" I asked, pointing to a pile of chests he had not named.

"Vell, that's what we calls 'Toolong', for it is last season's tea, unsold. A trifle long in the tooth, but none the worse for that. 'Too long' – you twig?"

"Haw, haw!" I cried, for I was ever a quick learner, "werry good. Owes you one for that, Mr J.!" He clapped me on the shoulder.

"Make a Henglishman of you yet!" he cried happily. "Now, these here are the werry latest, the new season's green teas, wot I was just tasting and a werry level lot they are. Am thinking of offering the ship-captings a premium of a sovereign per ton if they can get them to me before the other merchants, for there is wicious competition to be first in the market with them and the rewards are great. Could I but vipe the eye of young Charlie Harrod I'd die content, I swears I would. But I fears all the fast brigs are more taken up with the opium trade today."

"The opium trade?" I asked idly.

"Vy, yes. A most lucrative branch of British enterprise. 'Undreds of thousands of acres are under opium poppies in India; 'John Company' – by vich I means the Honourable East India ditto – positively thrives upon it. The patent medicine trade here swallows up great quantities of it and many leading citizens take it regular to sooth their stummicks. Mr Villiam Vilberforce, the tireless abolisher of slavery who died but a few years ago, took it every day for forty-five years and many a wexed nursemaid infuses a little in the baby's milk to calm its passions. Every true-born Britisher, man, woman and child, takes, on the haverage, a quarter of an ounce per annum and that, for so precious a grocery, amounts to a great deal of tin indeed."

I stifled a yawn. The new milk, I believe, had made me sleepy. I did not mean to be rude and Mr Jorrocks did not notice my lapse.

"Get your great dirty 'oofs out of that fruit!" he bellowed at a "light porter" who was shifting currants from a bin with a wooden shovel. " 'Untouched by human hand' is wot we boasts and 'human foot' is hunderstood as well. I'm sure you considers yourself a human," he added, in a kinder voice.

"Yes," he went on, addressing me again, "hopium is a most lucrative trade, often thought of having a wenture in it myself but doesn't like the risk, would prefer dipping my toes into the cow-heel and tripe trade but Mrs Jorrocks considers it low. A pity, for there's a nice little consarn in that line going for a song not a furlong from this 'ouse."

He became moody and jingled the change in his pockets, for this was a habit of his.

"Joe!" he shouted suddenly to his foreman, "Make up two pounds of superior black for this gentleman and one of the newest lot of green, from the lot I rated 'Hextra' ven I wos a-tasting just now. And see if the errand-cart is outside, or send the boy for a hansom."

As we were jolting and jingling towards his house I recalled his words about opium trade.

"What are these risks you were speaking of, Mr Jorrocks?"

"Storm and tempest," he replied. "Crack-brained captings. Pirates – and mandarins, who are much the same article."

I did not understand.

"Vell, you see, the Henglish part of the trade is mostly in the hands of a few old firms which has a Nelson-hold on it and there's no breaking into it. But John Company grows more of the weed each year and there is a great new market growing up in China: there lies the richest rewards, for the heathen will buy at any price. It is but a question of getting it to their hongs and go-downs and there's the rub, for it is illegal by their quaint pagan laws although the sitivation is somewhat heased now that Jack Tar has won the glorious Hopium War. But the whole coast is a seething nest of pirates and immoral mandarins; the cargo is precious and the payments in bar-silver:

every man's hand is against them. Moreover, the prime rates is to be got from being the first to the Treaty Ports with the new season's crop from the Calcutta auctions and the captings – broken Royal Navy men, most of them – fairly goes insane to outsail the others."

"Yes?"

"Hindeed yes. And I means 'insane' to the letter. A capting in that line can be rich in three voyages, for he has a huge share and there is much to share, but my actuary friend at Lloyd's puts his expectation of surwival at precisely two and seven-eighth voyages, haw haw! And even as I says it we are at the end of our own perilous woyage: Great Coram Street, home and beauty!"

To speak plainly, Mrs Jorrocks was not pleasing to look at, nor did she seem over-pleased to see us. She looked askance at my baggage until Mr J. whispered loudly to her that I was a great Dutch merchant-prince "travelling incog", whereupon she creased her huge ham-like face into a smile and called me "Moungseer" each time she addressed me.

A shifty, snot-nosed boy was told off to carry my bags upstairs.

"And wash your hands first, Binjamin!" roared Jorrocks, "for I'm sure your thumb has been in my marmalade-pot as ever, you cupboard-headed little warmint!"

A pink, jolly maid called Batsay brought me hot water and a tin hip-bath. I did not look at her lasciviously for I thought it possible that she might furnish Mr J.'s own diversion in those times of the year when it is not permitted to chase foxes in England.

Scrubbed all over and wearing a change of linen, I went downstairs to find Mr Jorrocks pacing up and down, peering at a great gold watch in his hand. I read his mind for I, too, was ready for dinner.

"It will be but a snack, I fears," he said apologetically, "for Mrs J. knew not when I was to return, nor that I would have the pleasure of your company and, indeed, she is but a few hours back from her mother's in Tooting. But she has found a few prowisions in the cold larder – cheese, cold ham, cold beef, cold mutton – all the delicacies of the season as the sailor said, haw, haw! – and I daresay we shall make shift to tighten our weskit-buttons somewhat."

Indeed, the repast was plentiful. First came a great tureen of gravy soup, a new thing for me but strong and appetising, into which Mr J. splashed quite the third of a bottle of brown sherry.

"Bristol Milk," he chuckled. "I often lies avake vondering wot they feeds the cows on in Bristol!"

"Haw, haw," I said politely.

Then we attacked the cold meats, of which there was great store: the round of beef was the size of a trap-drum and the other things were to the same scale. In between, we drank prime stout from the Marquess of Cornwallis hard by (he proved to be a tavern, not a nobleman, it was very puzzling) and toasted each other again and again with something called Crane's Particklar ("hot and strong, real black-strap stuff, none of your French rot-gut," Mr J. explained).

There was also a dish of hot buttered parsnips; they were very good. I ate them all, for Mr J. declared they spoiled his appetite for the meats. Then Batsay brought in a dish of things called "Poor Knights of Windsor": these were pieces of bread and jam fried. They do not sound good but they are. Mr Jorrocks's Stilton cheese was even better than Mr Creed's; he pretended that it was "so werry frisky" that he had to hold it down on the table as I scooped, lest it walk away. This was a British joke, of course. We were by then, I think, a little drunk. He helped me to my bedroom, then I helped him to his, then he again to mine; this went on until Mrs J. appeared in a splendid *déshabillé* and coughed meaningfully.

In the morning – rather *late* in the morning – he and I breakfasted frugally off some cold mutton and bloaters and rich, dark marmalade from Oxford (where the English make capital sausages and also have a famous college called Belial) and then he lent me a curious little vehicle called a tub-trap, with the child Binjamin to drive, and a list of addresses of people who might have a shop-premise to let. By dinner-time I had made a bargain for a little shop with snug living-quarters above it, between a street called Strand and the cabbage-exchange of the Convent Gardens. We collected my Delft the next day and laid some of it out in an attractive fashion, using some good shop-fittings of the true San Domingo mahogany, racks and shelves and drawers, which I had seen lying in the back of Mr J.'s warehouse and which he let me have for one sovereign. This was not dear, for they were well-made, although dirty. The windows of the shop I washed myself, for in those days I had no stinking pride and Binjamin refused to do it for less than threepence. Then I put the shutters up and, on the way back to Great Coram Street, struck a bargain with a sign-writer to paint "C. VAN CLEEF & CO., WHOLESALE

39

CHINA WAREHOUSE" in dirty white letters on the door-post, for I was learning how these things are done in England.

The next day Mrs J. condescended to come a-marketing with me: I bought a nice brass bedstead, a genuine hair mattress and a feather one to go on top of it, some bolsters and pillows and sheets and things of that kind, a little round-bellied stove, a kettle, a tea-pot and some drink. Yes, and some food. Then we went to a Foundling School and I bought a boy for a year to keep the place clean. I could have had a girl but I was wise, *wise*. The boy looked honest and stupid and, for his age, strong; when I showed him the place under the counter where he was to sleep, he was so happy he wept: he had never seen anything so comfortable. I could never quite make out his name so I called him "You"; he answered to it cheerfully. He was a good boy.

I took my leave, with much gratitude, of the good Jorrockses, kissing the hand of Mrs J., which made her even redder and to cry "Vell, I do declare!" I gave Batsay a shilling but nothing to Binjamin for I knew he had stolen quite so much as that from my breeches while pretending to brush them.

I did not open my shop the first day I entered it; I was sleepy; I slept all day and, to speak plainly, spent the evening whoring. You may depend upon it, there is no woman in the world to compare with a street-bred, fourteen-year-old London girl – and I speak as one who has sailed the Seven Seas and whored in most of their ports. Only the Japanese can compare. The one I selected was clean, well-finished at all points of her charming little body and, she told me, "new to the game". She explained that she had taken up this profession because the food at home was meagre and she had an insatiable lust for little meat pies. The thought of them, it seemed, maddened her like wine. I bought her an abundance of these pies, hot; but only a little gin, for I had already long known that a girl full of food is flushed and beset with carnal thoughts, while a girl flushed with wine is often little more than a nuisance.

Certainly, when we got to bed she went about her work with unfeigned enthusiasm; I had never known such an indefatigable gymnast, she was gifted, gifted. Never have I laid out a few little meat pies so profitably.

At dawn, as the free-roaming roosters who live in the thick dung of the Strand commenced to crow hideously, I opened one eye and was sorry to see the child investigating the pockets of my breeches. I had taken the breeches off, you understand. I had of course hidden my money, too. She explained, quite unabashed, that she had been merely seeking the price of a little hot meat pie to stay her on the journey home to Tooley Street, where her father, who would beat her, was a tailor's cutter, and that she would have taken no more. I think she was telling the truth although I was not a credulous man, even in those days.

I gave her the price of six twopenny pies and promised to give her the same – and her supper – whenever she was hungry. She visited me often after that, often. Sometimes she brought her little sister, who would sit in the corner, fascinated, and from time to time would make us a pot of Mr J.'s delicious tea, or run to the shop on the corner for a little, hot meat pie for her sister. Sometimes we let her come into the bed; she was charmingly inquisitive.

I wish I could remember their names but I am old now and can only recall the deeds. She – the older one – used to call me her "dear little Suffolk Punch" although I am not little and often told her that my home was in Holland, not Suffolk, which is a flat, rainy Province in the East of England.

After that first night with the girl whose name I cannot recall I was so tired that I lay in bed all day again, with the shutters of the shop still up. In the late afternoon the boy "You" came upstairs and rapped on my door, saying excitedly that "a right, prime, bang-up, slap-dash, out-and-out swell cove" was hammering on the shop-door with a "cane with a 'orse's 'ead 'andle". I considered this carefully, wondering how the child could have learned such language in a Charity School.

"Tell him," I said at last, "that your master will be happy to wait upon him should he care to call again tomorrow."

When I arose in the late evening, dressed to go out for supper and any other entertainment the night might afford, the boy "You" told me that the swell cove had cursed most dreadfully and said that he would by no means again venture into so vile a part of the town. I accepted this philosophically.

It was quite two afternoons before he – the swell cove – came back. The shop was now open and the shutters down. He was, indeed, a very swell cove: his hat shone like a looking-glass, his coachman-like *surtout* bore countless frogs, lappets and capes (the topmost of which was trimmed with the curly black fur from Afghanistan) and a glance out of the window told me that the

41

phaeton he had arrived in was of the very finest, with a coat of arms on the panel of the door and a monogram embroidered on the hammer-cloth.

"Good afternoon, milord," I said civilly, rubbing my hands in a tradesmanly way, as I supposed he would expect. "You are interested in old blue-and-white wares?"

He stared at me. I stared back, for I was not an Englishman and did not understand the niceties of class.

"I might be and then again I might not," he said at last and, turning his back, began to examine such of the stock as I had chosen to lay out.

"How much," he asked languidly, "is *that*?" pointing with the littlest finger of his gloved hand to a rather good small pot with an impeccable glaze.

"*That*?" I asked, raising an amused eyebrow. "That toy is a shilling. If you really want it you may pay me next time you are passing."

He glowered at me. I picked up the piece and sneered at it, as though it were a mere pottery cow-creamer. "The piece to the right of it is thirty guineas, the piece to the left is fifty. This piece, since you are my first customer, and since it is of no value, you may have as a gift."

His face darkened horridly.

"You are an insolent rascal," he said quietly and dangerously.

I opened my fingers and let the little pot fall to the floor, where it was dashed to a thousand fragments. I snapped my fingers; the boy "You" crept out with a broom and swept the fragments away. The lord continued to glare at me. I looked back at him, not uncivilly. At last he turned on his heel and strode out of the shop. *My* shop, that is to say.

The boy, as I turned towards the stairs, gazed at me with saucer-eyes.

"Beg pardon, Sir," he said, "but had you ought to have done that, Sir? 'Im being a *lord*, I mean?"

"Time will tell," I said enigmatically, "and the end justifies the means."

"Yes Sir, I'm sure Sir," he said. I mounted the first two stairs, then a thought struck me. "Are you warm enough at night, 'You'?" I asked.

"Oh, Sir, yes Sir, warm as toast."

42

"Because there is a great deal of sacking and soft rags in the chest from which the Delft came."

"Yes Sir, thankyou, Sir, beg pardon Sir, I have already used it for bedding, but it is as good as new, Sir, I swears."

"Good boy. Now, all I ask is that, each week, when the weather is sunny, you shall spread it all out in the backyard to air it and to prevent smells. On the same day you shall go to the public fountain in the Convent Gardens vegetable-market and wash yourself all over with yellow soap. Here is twopence for the soap. You shall have the same each week unless I can smell you. The first smelliness and I shall beat you cruelly. You should make quite a halfpenny a week out of the soap-money if you are careful. But mind: no smells!"

"Yes Sir, thankyou Sir, I swear you shall not have the least annoyance." He was a well-spoken child for a charity-bastard although thin, thin.

I trudged up to my brass bedstead feeling all the noble emotions of an English gentleman, while he, no doubt, scuttled in to his cosy rat's-nest under the counter. A moment later I was at the head of the stairs.

"You!" I roared. He was there in a twinkling.

"Why have I fresh long candles in my chamber-sticks? What has been done with last night's snuff-ends?" The child quaked, with terror but not, I think, with guilt.

"Sir," he said, "there was but a quarter-inch of tallow left in each stick, so I recharged them. I scraped out the ends and have melted the into the lid of a tin box, thinking to use them with a rag wick so as to read my *Pilgrim's Progress* each night, as the Charity-school master bade me. I truly thought, Sir, that they were my perquisites: I am no thief, I swear."

"Hrrumph," I said, as I had heard Englishmen say. "Well, be that as it may, put some clothes on and run to the shop on the corner and fetch me three little fourpenny mutton pies, hot, for my supper. Aye, and a pennyworth of fried peas. Here is a shilling and a penny. And look *sharp!*"

When he returned I had changed into my better clothes and told him that I had, after all, decided to sup out.

"Do what you will with the pies," I said in a gruff, *English* voice, "I do not care. And, listen, 'You', each week you may have one penny-dip candle for reading by. This is no kindness, it is because I cannot afford to support little *blind* bastards."

I spent the next few days chiefly in bed, plucking up my strength for the battle before me, whoring a little but also thinking a great deal about how a dealer in Delft should go about becoming rich. Once or twice I sent for a hansom cab and prowled about that area between St James's Palace and Regent Street where, in those day, the serious dealers in old pottery and porcelain held their state. I was shocked – and, of course, pleased – to find how ignorant most of them were. One or two – and they had Jewish names – knew something: not as much as me, but something. The others filled their windows with flashy rubbish. What I did learn from all of them, however, was the prices that could be asked; they amazed me. I, in turn, was amazed that my mama, who had never left her native Province, should have given me such good advice in respect of "walking around and about".

I did not go into the shops of the dealers with Jewish names and no ignorance; I went into the shops where the goods in the window were laughably over-priced, for I reasoned (and this is still good reasoning) that a man who over-prices foolishly will make mistakes in the other direction, too. I spent a few pounds carefully in such shops. Later in my life I made a great many lamentable mistakes but in those early days I made only one, for I seemed to bear a charmed life. This was it, and I tell it without shame for it was beautifully done. So was I.

Walking into a nasty little mud-pie of a shop, far from Bond Street, I noticed on the floor an incomparable saucer, polychromed, yet from the very earliest part of the Ming Dynasty, when such wares were made with great difficulty and then only for the Emperor himself and his concubines. I kicked the saucer gently as I passed it. It rang true. It was a jewel, a jewel, unflawed. Better, it was dirty and crusted with tide-marks of old milk and a great, horrid, ginger pussy-cat was schlipp-schlopping some sour milk from it.

I walked around the shop, pretending to look at his pitiful stock, then said: "There is nothing here quite in my line, but I have taken a fancy to your pussy-cat, for my little daughter has begged me again and again to buy her just such a pussy-cat."

"Aarrgh," said the shop-keeper, "aarrgh. My own liddle daughter loves that there pussy-cat better than life itself. I vouldn't sell that pussy-cat for a fi'-pound note, I swear I vouldn't, for I could never look my little girl in the face agin."

"You are trying to say that this pussy-cat costs *six* pounds?" I asked.

"Yes, Sir."

I dealt out six good English pounds, scooped the noxious beast into my arms and, as though it were an after-thought, bent over to pick up the saucer.

"The pussy-cat will be accustomed to its own milk-bowl," I said off-handedly. "It is dirty but I shall take it with me."

"Oh no, no, *no*, Sir," he cried. "No, not by no means. Vy, that saucer there 'as sold me three pussy-cats in as many months!"

I looked at him without expression.

"Would you care," I asked "to buy this pussy-cat back for one pound? I have just noticed that it is not precisely the colour of pussy-cat my daughter pines for."

"No, Sir, thankyou, Sir," he said, "for to tell you the truth, the moment you discards that cat, were it in John O'Groats or even Hampstead itself, it will be back here by nightfall, shit or bust, for I gives it a little catnip and hopium in its milk each night; it has grown accustomed to it, you see."

Anyone who has ever fenced knows the feeling of scraping his foil tentatively along the blade of a professor of arms. There is an authority about the resistance, an especial *timbre* to the ring of the steel which tells the almost-good swordsman that he is paired against a master of the art.

"Good day," I said.

"Good day, Sir. Pray call again."

Every day the boy "You" took down the shutters at noon, having made the floor, the mahogany shop-fittings and the Delft glow, for he was, it proved, a cleanly and diligent boy. He was handy, too, for he neatly pierced for me a little Judas window in the private door, so that I could observe customers unseen. Only four came into the shop in as many days: two were dealers on the prowl, I could tell this by their casual, flickering glances. The boy told them that all the stock was spoken for, as I had instructed. One was a poor old woman with some blue-and-white to sell; it was all rubbish except for a little, sparrow-beaked jug from the English factory of Worcester, for which I gave her a few pennies.

The fourth was the person I had been praying for: the angry milord. He stamped about the shop, glaring at things and pretending, in a childish way, not to be aware of my presence. At last he picked up a small and beautiful vase and walked out of the shop with it. I made no move. He stood outside the shop holding the vase up to the sun, looking through it to see the colour of the paste. I went upstairs to make a pot of Mr Jorrocks's tea. When I came down the lord was back in the shop, walking moodily up and down, whacking his boot-leg with his cane. He rounded on me.

"See here," he said. "The piece I looked at the other day, the piece you dropped on the floor. Was it really rubbish?"

"No, it was worth about fifteen guineas."

"Why did you smash it, then, eh? Come now, let's be frank."

"Because I am a Dutchman," I said. "Which is like an Englishman only more pig-headed." He stared at me for several long seconds, then suddenly began to roar with laughter, raising his head and bellowing with mirth, so that little "You" crept out of the shop in fright.

"Oh, *stap* me!" he cried at last, when he had finished laughing, "but you're a cool 'un. Vewwy cool, stap me if you ain't!"

(It was strange: I pronounced the "very" as it is spelled and as I had been taught but people of Jorrocks's class said "*werry*" while gentlemen and lords, especially if they had served in the cavalry, pronounced it "vewwy". I did not understand the English in those days. To speak plainly, they seemed all to be mad. They still seem so to me but I am now wise enough to have stopped trying to understand them.)

"Windermere," he said, extending two fingers. I shook the fingers lightly. "How do you do, Lord Windermere," I said. "My name is Carolus Van Cleef. Do you drink tea?"

"Tay? Tay? Depends whose it is, weally."

"Jorrocks's," I said. "Of course. His new season's superior Twankay."

"'Pon my soul," he said, "you are a high-flier. Man of taste, man of taste. Yes, by all means, let's have some."

I locked the door; we propped our behinds on the counter and drank tea.

"Now, Meneer Van Cleef," he said, "show me something I should buy. Something choice. Rare and choice."

"No," I said. "For I do not know how advanced a collector you are. But I will tell you what *not* to buy, if you will be guided by me."

He stared, then roared with laughter again.

46

"Rot me, but you're a sportsman, damme if you ain't!"

This was a compliment, I could tell.

"Tell you what," he said, "tell you what, tell you what. Come and call on me this evening, see my bits of pots, drink a glass of port, eh?"

"Thankyou, Lord Windermere, but tonight I am, to speak plainly, whoring. Perhaps another night?"

Again he roared with laughter – I do not know why – cracking his cane against his boot most loudly and uttering many a strange oath. In the end we agreed upon an engagement for the following night and he left, still full of mirth, wishing me good sport and urging me not to catch anything I wasn't fishin' for. I do not know what that meant but it was clearly a British joke.

I dined in the Strand, eating a great many chops and a pigeon pie, then went to bed alone, for I was not, in truth, in the mood for whoring; I wanted to think. I thought a great deal that night, chiefly about the predictability, or otherwise, of mad English lords but also, a little, about opium and the way it could make surly pussy-cats trudge all the way from very Hampstead itself. I had read something of how the British Colonials had secured the best part of the North American Continent by judiciously selling Demon Rum to the Redskins; perhaps something of the sort might be happening in China with opium; it was a kinder thing to sell to the heathen for it took longer to kill them, it did not inflame them to massacres and, most of all, there were a great many more customers in China than in America.

When I at last went to sleep, my head was buzzing with ambition.

In the morning, to my great satisfaction, smart errand-carts began to arrive from the tailor, shirt-maker, boot-maker and other people with whom I had placed orders. This was good because of my engagement with Lord Windermere that night. I had ordered a blue coat very like that of Mr Jorrocks and a buff kerseymere waistcoat, too, but had stopped short of the dark-blue, stocking-net pantaloons and the great Hessian boots. Instead, I had ordered what the breeches-maker called "drab shorts and continuations" which more fitted my station in life, yet still lent a sportsmanlike relish to my outfit.

While I was trying on my new fineries, a large, fat, happy man came into the shop; I peeped at him through the peephole at the

47

bottom of the stairs. His belly stuck out in front, so did his magnificent moustache which was of the sort the English call "walrus" but was not in fashion in England at that time. I was sure that he was either a German or a Hollander and, certainly, had some good, strong, Jewish blood in his veins. He did not mind when the boy "You" told him that I was out and that all the stock was, for the time being, spoken for; he chuckled happily and went on looking, occasionally picking up a piece and nodding, chuckling. Then he left the shop, telling "You" that he was "a good boy" and giving him a halfpenny, telling him that he was to tell me that he would see me very soon.

"You" looked at the halfpenny in his hand for a long time – I watched him through the peep-hole – then put it into the till. He was, indeed, a good boy. After a little while I stamped noisily downstairs, examined the till and made the first credit entry in the ledger.

"½d," I wrote. Then I called for hammer and nail and solemnly nailed the coin to the counter. I said nothing to "You", nor he to me.

When I went out that evening I bade him buy ten pennyworth of tincture of opium. I handed him a shilling.

"With the change," I said, "you may buy yourself two fresh penny buns or, if you are sensible, three stale ones, which are better for you. If they are very stale and the baker a kindly man you might well get four."

He looked at me as though I were kind, which was far from the truth, although not so far as it would be today.

I realised, as I climbed into the cab, that I did not know Lord Windermere's address. The cabby however, did.

"You means the mad toff wot buys old junk?"

"That will be he," I said stiffly.

He whipped up his mare, a fine old black who looked as though she had known better days – he called her "Beauty" although he treated her ill – and soon we pitched up at a Square called Eaton; a fine neighbourhood, one could see that it was bursting with toffs. He tried to cheat me, of course, but I had, by then, at Mr Jorrocks's advice, acquired a copy of that inestimable work: *Mogg's Guide to 10,000 London Cab Fares*.

Lord Windermere's fine house was bursting with antiques and works of art and *vertu* of every description, some of them mistakes, I could see that, but all most valuable. He roared with laughter when he saw me in my new clothes, it was his way of putting me at my ease, you understand.

"Now," he cried, thrusting a bumper of fine port into my hand, "now, let's try you. Eh? D'you see these two pots? Uncle Henry here tells me I've been had, diddled. One of them's a ringer, d'you see, not right. *Wrong*," he added in the way the English explain things to foreigners.

I peered about the room for the Uncle Henry he spoke of. From a deep wing-chair emerged the large, fat, happy man who had visited my shop that afternoon. He beamed and we offered each other two fingers to shake.

"Duveen," he said happily. "Henry Duveen. Everyone calls me Uncle Henry pecoss I look like an uncle, ja?"

"Yes indeed, Sir," I said carefully. I liked this man but he was strong and dangerous and I was disturbed to find that my mad toff was already on friendly terms with a Dutch Jew who knew how to feel the glazes on pottery and porcelain. (Who would have guessed that I was facing the first of that great House of Duveen, that House with whom ours was to be locked in a death-grapple – and still is – for mastery of the art trade?)

I turned to the table upon which stood the pair of suspect pots. They were supremely beautiful hawthorn-pattern ginger-jars from the period when, briefly, generations of experiment, using up a thousand camel-loads of pigment from Arabia, had led to the discovery of the true Celestial Blue, the Blue of Blues.

I did not even touch the glaze with a wet finger, I simply looked at them narrowly. On one, the glaze had drawn away from the pigment during the firing, just as my mother had once told me, although she herself had never owned such a pot.

"Will you tell me what you gave for these, Lord Windermere?" I asked diffidently.

"Six hundred guineas."

"The genuine one is worth quite that and more by itself. As for the other, the wrong one, I will give you five pounds for it as a curiosity. Even so clever a fake as this should not be in a nobleman's collection."

"Done!" he cried, roaring with laughter again, "but which is which, eh? *Which*? What?"

I put five golden sovereigns on the table, fetched the poker from the fireplace and brought it down smartly on the bad pot, praying, as it fell to flinders, that I was right.

"Stap me!" bellowed Windermere, "oh *stap* me, I say! Said you were a cool card from the first – from the first! Oh, curse me, d'you never tire of smashing pots?"

"So clever a forgery," I said solemnly, "capable of deceiving even you, should not be allowed to survive. You see, it might have fallen into the hands of an unscrupulous dealer."

Now Uncle Henry, too, was shaking with laughter.

"Bot if you had zmoshed der *right* pot," he wheezed, "Vot den, my jonge, vot den?"

"Of course," I said modestly, jingling in my breeches pocket the few sovereigns remaining to me, "I would have given Lord Windermere the six hundred guineas. Less, of course, the five pounds."

Windermere swept up my five sovereigns and forced them into my unreluctant hand.

"Buy a suit of duds for that little bastard you keep," he cried. "It was well worth it to watch your face as you lifted the poker!"

He and Uncle Henry and I became firm friends that night, I think. We also became a little drunk: I recall that they had some difficulty in lifting me into my hansom, we all fell over again and again but my new coat was not damaged, only muddied.

CHAPTER FIVE

〓〓〓

The next day Lord Windermere called to see me early in the afternoon. I was setting about a pudding which the boy "You" had fetched me in from a place nearby in the Strand. It was called "Simpson's" and still is, for all I know. It is long since I was able to digest such a pudding, made of beefsteak and kidneys and oysters and sparrows; *very* good.

I offered to send out for just such another pudding for Lord Windermere but he seemed to be in no mood for eating.

"Pudding?" he cried, "*pudding*! Damme, you're not *eating*, Van Cleef; you *can't* be!"

"But in my country everyone eats a little something at this hour of the day, it is to keep our strength up. Do you not do so? Come, I have seen English gentlemen eating puddings in Simpson's as early as half-past noon!"

His face turned a strange colour, almost as though he had the "hot coppers", which is an English expression for how you feel at noon when you have drunk some good port the night before. When Englishmen's faces turn strange colours you must give them tea. I made him a pot of Mr J.'s "superior black", he drank with relish and seemed to be the better for it.

"Well, now, have you got the little merry-begot his suit of duds yet?" he asked, kicking the boy "You" up the arse in a condescending and friendly fashion.

"The suit," I said "is even now being cut and stitched by a fellow in Tooley Street, whose daughter I happen to know."

"Capital. Capital. Keep the little bugger warm. Got to look after the lower classes, d'you see. Don't want a revolution on our hands, do we?"

51

I thought of – and emulated – William the Silent, a great Dutch revolutionary of whom it was said "while he lived he was the guiding-star of a whole great nation; and when he died the little children cried in the streets."

"No," I said.

"Now," he said, handing his empty cup to "You", whose name he seemed to have guessed, "let us do a little business, if you are not in your pig-headed vein today. Uncle Henry tells me that some of your stock is not bad and that you are too demmed smart to wob me."

"Later, I might rob you," I said, "but just now it would, indeed, be foolishness to do so. Uncle Henry is *slim*, as we say in Holland. That means, not slim around the belly but '*slim*' in his head." This was my second English joke but I do not think Lord Windermere twigged, for "*slim*" is a Dutch word. But he guffawed politely, because he could tell that it was meant as a joke.

"Don't care about Nanking stuff," he went on, "only the best Chinese and vewwy finest Delft. Sell me some."

"'You'," I cried to the boy "You", "there is some pudding on my plate upstairs. Eat it up while it is still hot, then wash the plate carefully, because it is of the best Nanking ware."

Lord Windermere beat his boot with his cane happily, he took everything as a joke except, as I learned later, duelling with pistols, which was his third most favourite occupation and his only outdoor one for, in those days, fox-'unting was reserved for farmers, petty land-owners, tea-grocers and newly-landed people.

"Come," he said, "sell me something, I long to own something today."

"To be frank, Lord Windermere," I said, "I am beginning to be a little sleepy: your port last night was strong, strong, and the pudding of steak, kidneys, sparrows and oysters has made me lazy in the head. I make you a sporting offer: for five hundred pounds you may take your pick of the stock. When you have done so, if you have picked well, for another five hundred you shall have the pick of what is in the locked cabinet there."

He bellowed with laughter again. I love the English but would love them more if they did not make so much noise, especially when people have been drinking strong port the night before.

"Tell you what," he cried, "tell you what, tell you what! You're a sportsman, I can tell that: let's trust each other; here's a scrap of paper, I'll exchange it for the key to the locked cabinet – and no come-backs? Shall we strike hands on it?"

I did not think very long. I was either made or ruined.

We struck hands, not the limp two fingers this time but a proper hand-shake. The key was in my hand, the paper in his: we exchanged.

"When you have made your choice," I said, "send the boy up to me. I shall have a little folding of the hands to sleep, so that you may decide without being distracted by my chewing of the fingernails."

On the stairs I looked at the "scrap of paper". It was a draft on Mr Coutts's bank for £1,250. Lord Windermere cannot have been so *slim* by himself – I think he had discussed things with Uncle Henry. I went to sleep, happily, in most of my clothes. One hour later "You" roused me and helped me into my coat, which he had brushed nicely, and I went downstairs. I looked at what Lord Windermere had chosen, which was all laid out on the counter. I told "You" to make some green tea. The lord was not a fool, he had chosen well. Well, not wholly well, but well enough: he had had good value and I had made many hundreds per centum profit even if I had paid my Mama for the goods, which, of course, I had not. I made a wry face. He studied this wry face, then smiled.

"Have I turned you over a bit, eh? Turned you over? Picked too well, perhaps? Eh? Still, left you plenty, haven't I, even if I've skimmed the cream a bit, what?"

I made a show of examining what he had selected, still wearing the wry face of a good loser.

"You have not *quite* ruined me," I said at last. "You have left me a few pieces which may, for a couple of weeks, keep me out of the House of Correction. You have only made one mistake: this piece, this little sparrow-beaked jug with the crescent mark, is only English, although pretty. It is from the factory of Worcester and less than a hundred years old. Ask Uncle Henry, he will tell you."

He thrust the little jug away with the back of a finger as though it were infested with small, biting insects.

"Give you that back, then. Can't have Uncle Henry laughing at me. Call it your back-hander, what?"

"Hold it up to the light," I went on; "you will see that the paste is of a pleasing, light sea-green, but there are always little 'moons' in it and the glaze stretches away from the foot, it took them a long time to overcome these faults, just as it took your Chelsea factory years

53

to discover that their rich lead glaze was killing their workmen faster than they could train them."

"Vewwy likely," he said, taking no pains to simulate interest. "D'you have a water-closet here or anything of that sort?"

"I am sorry, Lord Windermere, there is no such refinement, I'm a poor man, but the boy will fetch a chamber-pot."

"Pray tell him to do so, for if I don't piss, I swear I'll burst like a frog."

The boy "You" held the pot while his Lordship genteelly eased the pressure of his bladder, throwing, with the last musical cadence of piddle, a couple of pennies into the vessel.

"Not kindness," he explained, securing his tight unmentionables, "never spoil another man's servants, matter of hygiene, really. Makes certain that the child – good boy, that, for a bastard – empties the 'Jerry' directly, d'you see."

"Yes," I said.

When he had gone – he was not driving his phaeton today but was in an odd-looking Clarence, driven by an under-coachman with a gold-laced cocked hat and a splendid grog-blossom of a nose – I retired to bed, having written "1,250*l* and 2*d*" in the ledger. I mused about the happenings of the day and sipped experimentally at the tincture of opium which the boy had fetched. It was not unpleasant, it gave me an agreeable sensation of being not quite drunk. When "You" rapped upon my door, asking whether I wished supper or a whore, or both, I said that, for the time being, I needed nothing.

"There should be twopence in the till," I added; "You may lay it out on jellied eels for yourself, and here is another penny for fried peas. See that you lock the door when you come in, there are thieves everywhere, thieves."

While he was out I sipped some more of the tincture of opium. I heard little whatever-her-name-was from Tooley Street giving her distinctive tap-tapping upon the shop-door but I paid her no heed: my head was awhirl with the most delightful fantasies, many of them salacious but not of the sort which a smelly little guttersnipe girl, however inventive, could augment.

I sipped away at the bottle, each sip sending me to a higher realm of ecstasy. The night was beautiful with colour, strange beasts, deliciously vile and lovely women and music beyond compare. I took the last drops with the bottle clamped between my lips, imagining that it was one of the multiplex teats of Diana of Ephesus.

One thousand years later a savage blow across the face brought me back to this base and venal world. I opened a languorous eye. The afternoon sun was entering the window: clearly, it was tomorrow. Above me towered a huge, angry man with whiskers. Behind him whimpered and cowered the boy "You". "Fetched a doctor, Sir," he squeaked, "I fought you was a stiff'un, I swear I did. I hope I did right."

I mumbled something in Dutch which I forget now and, in any case, could not commit to paper; then I sank back into delicious sleep.

Another savage blow lashed my face; I scarcely winced, reasoning that to ignore it would make it stop. It did not stop. The doctor had a wet towel in his hand and, when I finally opened an eye, seemed ready to use it again. And again.

"If he dares to strike me again," I thought, happily, "I shall rise up like an avenging angel and tear his throat out with my long, red, jewel-encrusted finger-nails, then feed him to my leash of dragon-dogs, to the tinkling laughter of my hundred odalisques."

He hit me again with the wet towel. His fate was sealed. Alas, though, I found that I could not get up: each time I attempted to do so the stately pleasure-domes of my inflamed mind gave place to an intense desire to vomit. I decided to give him best, he was but a mere mortal. I went back to sleep. He hit me again. There are few ecstasies which can withstand repeated blows with a wet towel. I commenced to weep. He yanked me to my feet and shouted to "You" to bring some hot, strong coffee.

"Couldn't drink it," I mumbled.

"You are not going to *drink* it," he said with some satisfaction, walking me up and down the bedroom and flicking my behind and, once, my privates, with the cold, wet towel. When I grew tired he put a bottle of smelling-salts under my nose, which made my head explode into coloured lights like the fireworks at a Holland Kermesse. Hooking my arm about his neck, so that I could not lie down, he opened his bag and drew out a hideous object, all nozzles and tubes and a gutta-percha bulb. Then "You" brought the hot coffee and the doctor threw me on the bed, face down. I went gratefully to sleep but, within a moment, something dreadful happened to me from behind; an invasion and a scalding influx.

You do not wish to learn more, nor I to recount it.

Later, I do not know how much later, he was pulling open

my eyelids, studying my pupils, *waking me up*. This was too much.

"Go away, or I shall kill you," I said.

"Six and eightpence," he said. I was by now awake enough to offer him six shillings for prompt cash; he took it, but the expression on his face did not make me feel brave and clever.

"How long have you been swilling this filth?" he asked, as he packed his bag.

"This is my first time," I answered.

"Then you're a damned imbecile. Ten grains of opium in that bottle, the dose for a confirmed addict. Lucky to be alive. If that's the way you want to die, don't call me in again; if you think I enjoy clystering out your back passage you're mistaken, I promise you. Even for six shillings, ready cash. Next time, get your brat to call in the Chinee quack in Villiers Street, probably do it for half a crown."

He left without saying "good-day" and I sank back under the blankets and wept bitterly. I was stricken with home-sickness for that beautiful, hot, swinish land where the opium had transported me; it was better to be dead there, there amongst the colours, the vile ladies and the strange music, than to be alive above a shop near the street called Strand in London, hundreds of miles from my Mama. It seemed sensible to me to obtain some more opium, nothing else would do. I banged upon the floor, perhaps feebly.

In a little while the boy "You" entered, carrying a bowl which steamed, smelling of rich meat.

"Out," I screamed, "OUT!"

"Yes, Sir, but, please Sir, the doctor give me thruppence to buy gravy-meat for to make you this beef-tea; pray drink it, Sir, do; he made me swear to get it down you. It's for your health, you see Sir."

I gagged it down with but ill grace. To be candid, I wished to beat someone painfully but I had not the strength to beat even "You".

"What is in that other basin?" I asked sternly.

"Nothing Sir, not yet, Sir. The doctor said that your stomach was weak and that you might not keep the beef-tea down first time."

"My stomach is *strong*," I replied, "and the doctor is an impudent fellow. If there is any *unused* coffee left, you may bring me some; it was but a momentary weakness." He brought me some coffee, which I drank, in the ordinary way that one takes coffee. The desire for the absurdly beautiful lands of opium-eating was dwindling: I knew that I must never travel those wondrous jungle-paths again unless I was prepared to eschew all the more solid pleasures of this fat and splendid real world, where a clever man may become rich and famous, if he keeps his head clear. I cleared my head peremptorily.

"Bring me my breeches!" I cried. He brought them. I felt in the pockets.

"Do you see these two sixpences? Now, hold, one of them is for you, to spend upon nourishing food. The other you are to hide, 'You', and the next time I bid you go out and buy me opium, either tincture or in the lump, you are to take that sixpence into the street and hire a hulking carter, drayman or vegetable porter from the market and bid him come in here and beat me about the head until I fall unconscious. This will be both cheaper and better for my health. Is that clear?"

He did not like this, he shifted from foot to foot, but in the end his intelligence grasped him, for he was not really a stupid boy.

"Yes, Sir," he said.

I told him that I was going to sleep and that I wished to be called early.

"Finish the beef-tea," I added, "for it will make you big and strong."

I did not sleep at once, however; I lay awake considering what had happened to me and wondering at the power of this opium, which could almost kill me yet make me lust for more of it, even as I quaked and retched. Clearly it was a more powerful commodity than Demon Rum and one that could be dealt with profitably if the vendor abstained from it himself.

My thoughts turned to Lord Windermere and the twelve hundred and fifty pounds – some sixteen thousand gulden. His selection of my stock had been strongly in favour of Ming and Kang H'si wares and their finest imitators: I did not know where I could get more, of that quality, short of going to China myself and I could not envisage a future of picking a living as a dealer in the commoner pottery. My thoughts went round in a circle. The opium dreams had been delicious. I fell asleep.

I spent the whole of the next morning virtuously; I rearranged what was left of my stock to its best advantage and stuck little numbered pieces of paper onto everything and wrote descriptions and prices in a "Long Tom" ledger so that "You" would be able to sell when I was out. Then I drank some glasses of sherry white and walked to the "Piazza" where I found my good Mr Jorrocks and his friend Sir Tees, in the Corner box arguing about the relative merits of skylarks and wheatears. Mr Jorrocks, it seemed, thought nothing of driving all the way to Brighton to eat wheatears at the Star and Garter when they were in season (the shepherds on the South Downs catch these little birds in horsehair snares) but Sir Tees scoffed at this, saying that they were no better than pudding-sparrows. I quietened this argument (for we do not eat such things in Holland) by inviting them both to see whether they could eat as many mutton chops as I could.

"A trifle early for me," said the Yorkshireman, pulling out a silver half-hunter.

"*Werry* early," agreed Mr J, pulling out a gold half-hunter.

"But . . .?" I said, fumbling in my waistcoat but not pulling out my gun-metal "turnip" watch.

The mutton chops were very good, although the boiled potatoes and cabbage were not: the British do strange and disgusting things to their vegetables. We all fortified ourselves heroically. Our little dinner was only marred when a barrel-organ outside struck up the popular air "If I Had a Donkey Vot Vouldn't Go". Mr Jorrocks rose to his feet, tore off his wig and dashed it to the floor.

"By all that's impure!" he bellowed, "shall I never be free of the warmint? I swears he follows me all over London! Waiter, *waiter* I say, take this penny and implore that pernicious dinner-spoiler to move into the next street before I does him a mischief."

"You are not, then, fond of music, Mr J.?" I asked carefully, when the music had stopped.

"Knows only two tunes," he grunted. "One of them is 'God Save The King' and the other – hisn't."

We called for more chops, again and again; my Mama would have been proud of me. Then we went into the reading-room to snooze a little. (I should explain that in England you sleep in the reading-room, just as you eat in the coffee-room, smoke in the study, spend the afternoon in the morning-room, drink tea in the drawing-room and, unless you happen to be in love with your wife, sleep in the dressing-room whilst your wife, quite likely, is committing adultery in her sewing-room. It is all very strange. There is now a book called *Alice in Wonderland* which explains how the English system works, although in veiled language.)

This snoozing of mine was not long, for my friends snored like Dutchmen. I crept out without awakening them, paid the bill and took a cab to the dealers' part of London which in those days was a few mean streets to the South of Piccadilly Road, near the Palace of St James's. I sauntered about, for I was in my fine new coat, a coat in which one could saunter with confidence, looking carefully at things in windows and even more carefully at their prices. Whilst I was looking carefully into such a window, of a shop kept by someone of a Jewish name and no ignorance, the proprietor opened the door of the back room and came into the shop. While that door was briefly open I had a brief vision, in the back room, of what seemed to be an incomparable set of five "*Lange Lyzen*" vases, quite beautiful. Although the dealer was, from his goods and their prices, not a man of ignorance, I felt drawn into his shop as though by invisible cords. We looked at each other, then nodded perfunctorily as people of our religion do when we meet each other but not in the bosom of our families.

I browsed around the shop, looking at this and that, while he pottered in and out, he knew I would not steal anything. I chaffered for, and bought, a fine eggshell cup and saucer of the real Imperial Yellow; also a good rice-bowl with the "leaping boy" decoration. They were not too dear, for it was a slack season; also, he was overstocked (which is the besetting vice of us Jews) and, at that time of the afternoon, neither of us was in the mood for protracted bargaining: we both knew what I would pay and we did not care to go through the usual long agony – or ecstasy – of reaching that figure.

As I was leaving I said "Ah, by the way . . ."

He did not say "*Oy veh!*" and he only sketched out the gesture of slapping the palms of his hands to the forehead. What he said was: "So. A 'by-the-way' asker, already. You have perhaps an expensive mistake you wish to pass on to a fellow-dealer? Or you have heard of my beautiful daughter with the large dowry?"

"Neither of those," I said politely; "I just wished to say that I might be interested to buy a set of good *Lange Lyzen* if the price were right." He shuffled his feet, avoiding my gaze. "Only the ones in the window," he said at last.

"They are pretty," I said politely, "but they are not quite as good as I require; moreover, they are but three and I wish for a full set of five, such as those I chanced to notice in your back room when you opened the door."

"Not for sale," he said gruffly.

"A pity. But perhaps, all the same, I might be permitted to look?" He hesitated, then agreed. "But you will promise to keep your mouth shut, eh?"

I promised, thinking that perhaps the person he had bought them from might not have been quite entitled to sell them. He read my thoughts.

"They are honestly come by," he growled. "If you are as clever as you think you may be able to guess why I cannot sell them."

The more I looked at the beautiful vases – the finest I had ever seen – the more puzzled I became. They bore a fine set of six-character marks and there was no visible flaw. When I made as though to pick up the last one the old dealer lifted an admonitory finger.

"Look only," he said; "don't lift." I thought about that, then lifted up one of the others, looked at the bottom again, felt it. The glaze there was very odd to the touch. I took it to the light: there was no doubt, it was not glaze but a clear varnish over white paint on which the marks had been forged. But why? It was baffling, for the pots themselves were as genuine as golden sovereigns.

"Forged marks on genuine vases," I said to the shopkeeper. "What was the need? And why does this prevent you from selling them? You have but to scrape off the paint."

He laughed bitterly.

"I scraped; oy, I scraped. See." He handed me the fifth pot. He had indeed scraped to good purpose: half-revealed on the bottom was a beautiful, delicate, detailed painting under the glaze. It depicted five most gifted Chinese persons engaged in a complicated act of quite unbelievable indecency; I found it entrancing: my face and neck became hot. He took the vase out of my hands.

"Don't enjoy!" he said sternly. "Two hundred pounds I gave for these *paskudnyaks* – you are a *mavin*, you know that was a *metsieh* but not robbery – and now I dare not show them at all. Even if the police did not send me to prison, who would buy? Collectors of porcelain are respectable people, ladies and gentlemen; noblemen some of them."

"Yes," I said reflectively. "How much of a loss would you take? I think I know a *meshuggener* who might take them."

"Loss?" he asked suspiciously, "loss? Who's talking of loss? Maybe only a small trifle of a profit . . ."

We settled down to haggle in earnest. He was an old man much frightened of the authorities, for in those unenlightened days our race was much persecuted; every time I slipped the word "prison" into my talk he covered his eyes and said either *"Zeeser Gottenyu!"* or *"Gevald!"*

It was half an hour before I saw that his price was hardening at one hundred and ten guineas. I trimmed the shillings off and paid one hundred and ten pounds, leaving him keening at the loss but, clearly, relieved to be rid of the dangerous vases.

I told my cabbie to take me home via Eaton Square, where I left a note for Lord Windermere, urging him to call on me as soon as might be, lest he miss an incomparable purchase.

At the shop, the boy "You" told me that he had sold his first pot, for five-and-seventy shillings. He was very proud. Also, his new suit of "duds" had arrived and he asked me shyly whether he might put them on and go to the Foundling Hospital to visit his little mates there, for it was the first Friday of the month, when such visits are permitted to the little "come-by-chance" inmates. I agreed.

"But first," I told him, "you are to climb onto the roof and break off a little piece of lead, about *so* big, for I wish to scrape a bottom." He sped off on this mission without question, for he had long ago decided that I was insane.

"You" was out, scrubbed and shining, and I had almost finished scraping the varnish and paint off the bottom of the second pot when Lord Windermere arrived in his Clarence. The Clarence was, I thought, a sign that he was in a buying mood, for it is a roomy rather than a dashing vehicle.

"Well now, what's all this, what's all this, burst me? Can't a man enjoy his whore and his bottle of port without being summoned like a footman by every Jew hawker in London?"

He was not being rude; in those days when an Englishman wished to make it clear that you were accepted he called you terrible names, it meant that he thought you were British enough to take British jokes. They were quite mad. Now they are still mad but more polite; I think I liked them better when they were mad and rude. I truly believe that Lord Windermere thought Holland a possession of Great Britain; they teach them Horace and Virgil at school, scarcely any of them knows that the Dutch Navy once smashed its way up the Thames Valley to London and then sailed out again unscathed. The

61

only Britishers with a sense of history are the Irish, but with them it is a disease.

I laid out the *"Lange Lyzen"* on the gleaming mahogany counter. He looked at them hungrily.

"These," I said, "are one thousand and one hundred and ten pounds. To you, that is, of course."

He gaped.

"Are you out of your senses?" he said at last. "Curse me, you said you'd rob me one day but you're coming on too fast, too fast; they'd be dear at seven hundred and you know it."

I showed him one of the bottoms. He gaped again, then roared with delight and laughter. "Done!" he bellowed, "done! Rot me, you knew I'd have to have 'em, you sod."

He gave me a draft on Mr Coutts's excellent bank and I showed him how to scrape with the piece of lead. We spent a happy evening, drinking three bottles of Madeira between us and scraping, scraping; hooting with pleasure as each lubricious scene became manifest.

"Smash me!" he cried at one point, "oh I say smash my eyes, d'you see this feller's rump-splitter? Demme, it's a good thing I'm a bachelor, couldn't keep all these nudgers and fannies if there was a Lady Windermere about the house, could I?"

When all five of the vases' bottoms were clean – if that is an appropriate word – and blazing in all their wonderful filthiness, Lord Windermere clapped me on the shoulder in the friendliest fashion, said that he'd never done a better day's work in his life and vowed to send me a dozen of his prime Sercial as a "sweetener", first thing in the morning.

After he had left I called for paper and pens and wrote to my mother like a good son. "This London is a fine place," I wrote, "and I think I shall do good business here. Please send more pots so that I may make all our fortunes. Tell my father that I read the Josephus whenever I am not too tired with my incessant labour."

Then I went to bed, replete with virtuous feelings and contentment.

I lay awake for quite an hour, for my head was buzzing with half-formed plans, plans only indirectly concerned with pottery and porcelain.

I did not have a reply from my Mama until eight days later for the posts in those days were bad and slow: sometimes a letter posted in the afternoon just to another part of London would not be delivered until the next morning; it was disgraceful.

Her letter was loving but crisp. She hoped I was well and that I was not conversing with bad girls from whom I might catch a disease. She was ready to send me more Delft and Chinese wares so soon as I remitted the money for the first lot. My father, she said, sent his love. She, for her part, sent me hers and hoped that I was eating properly, eschewing the notorious English puddings and pies.

I considered this letter carefully for many an hour. Honesty and filial affection ruled my actions in the end: I went to Coutts's excellent bank and arranged for two hundred and three pounds and fifteen shillings to be sent to my mother: she would, I knew be delighted. It shewed her a handsome profit on the wares for I knew her buying habits well.

Then I went to find my good Mr Jorrocks.

"Vy!" he cried "'Ow delighted I am to see you! Binjamin! I say *Binjamin* you young warmint! Fetch a pair of bottles of the strong stout from under the sideboard and two clean rummers, mind, *clean* not viped with the tail of your shirt, for I knows your 'abits! Now, my dear young friend, 'ow can I serve you? Delighted to do anything in my power. The Surrey Subscription 'Unt meets at Croydon tomorrow, perhaps you'd care for a day with the 'ounds? Would do you a power of good, for you looks a little peaked – not quite the plump currant – 'opes it's only dewotion to business," he added, looking at me keenly, "and not wicious living? *Mens sane in Corporal saner*' as my illustrious friend Nimrod says."

I reassured him; vowed that I was in bed by ten each night (which was, in fact, true, so lustful I was in those days) and swallowed the strong, nourishing stout with many an appreciative smack of the lips, for this was his way of drinking and it seemed civil to emulate him.

"Compliments you on your tog, Mr Dutch," he said, wiping the froth from his upper lip, "looks quite the thing, werry gentleman-like." (My coat, you may recall, was modelled upon his.) "But I feels the kickseys – for trowsers I shall not call them – is somewhat below your station in life – have a kind of groomish look. Pantaloons is the harticle; pantaloons and boots. Marks you out as a sportsman of quality."

"Yes," I said humbly.

63

"Now, 'ow can I serve you?"

"Mr J., I have been thinking about your edifying remarks on the opium trade and your statement that, had you been free to do so, you would have had a venture in it yourself."

"True, true. But it's werry risky."

"I understand that, but, if you will forgive me, I am still a young man and the riskishness appeals to me; moreover, it seems to me that on such a voyage I would have the opportunity of buying superior Chinese porcelains of a kind for which there seems to be a brisk demand in London Town and which I cannot obtain in sufficient quantity either here or, indeed, in Holland."

"My dear young Sir, the hopium-carrying trade is almost hentirely in the hands of a most reputable firm vich we calls Jardine Matheson (although Dent & Co. is bursting into the market), because the Hon. East India Co itself does not vish to sully its hands with so noxious a trade except for growing the poppies and taking the profits. Also, I understands that warious American colonial upstarts is carving themselves a knotch of the loaf and coming back with it buttered. But there is also wot they calls the country-trade, vich does not much frequent the treaty-ports, choosing rather to range up and down the Hokken Coast, running the goods in where they can and obtaining higher prices, despite the depperedations of pirates and wenal mandarins, then running back to the River to lay out the bar-silver on the new teas and bolts of silk."

I thought about this as best I could, because I was not, in those days, clever, only avaricious.

"Mr Jorrocks," I said at last, "could you introduce me to a person engaged in the country-trade part of this commerce, in order that I might buy a share in such a venture?"

He shifted his bottom uneasily in the capacious chair.

"I am not asking you to guarantee my credit," I said, perhaps a little stiffly. He raised both hands protestingly.

"Nothink was further from my mind, Mr Dutch, pray do not for a hinstant think that my mind was dwelling on anything of the kind. Wot consarned me was the thought of a innocent young cock like you inwesting your tin in so werry perilous a wenture."

"Well, Mr J.," I said mildly, "I shall be there myself to look after my tin, do you see."

He gaped at me in a droll way, then inserted a finger under his wig and scratched his pate.

"The risks," he said at last, "are hatrocious; 'opes I've made that clear?"

"Oh, yes," I said in an off-hand way, for I was young then and brave, brave.

"Werry well, since I sees you're intent on fetching up at the 'cold cook-shop', I'll do my best for you."

He fished out a great pen-knife, went to his scrutoire, as he called it, mended one pen after another, settled on one which would drop ink to his satisfaction and scratched and spluttered away with it until he had drafted some letters of introduction for me. I thanked him cordially but he wagged his great pink head with some sadness.

"Vishes you safe," he said. "Leave your gear in my ware-'ouse – it'll be there when you return." It showed a rare and grateful sensitivity on his part to say "when" rather than "if".

"Thankyou, Mr J."

It was to be a long time indeed before I again saw my good friend, who had fostered in me a great love for England and all things English.

PART THREE

The High Seas

CHAPTER SIX

" 'You'," I said to "You" two days later, "have you never longed for a life on the ocean wave, a home on the bounding deep? Does not the blood of your sea-faring ancestors surge in your veins at the very words?" His reaction was piteous: he fell upon his knees, cowering and quaking.

"Oh Sir, pray Sir, do not send me off to one of those floating hells to be flogged and keel-hauled and worse; I have been a good boy and kept myself clean as you bade me, I do not deserve such a fate, indeed I do not!"

"Come," I said sternly, "pull yourself together. There is no talk of hell-ships and floating orphan-asylums: I am newly appointed a supernumerary officer in a fine, lavishly-fitted opium clipper, all mahogany and brass and famed for comfort and lavish food. Why, they call it the 'Coffee Ship' because of the generosity with which its people are treated. All officers are expected to have a servant; the Captain keeps a butler, two Chinese boys and a wife to boot, the owners tell me. Moreover, I have just purchased a share in the venture, subject to my being able to come to terms with the Captain: my only duties are to supervise the *'schroff's'* and the *'comprador's'* accounts; yours are to keep my linen clean, fetch my victuals from the galley at suitable times and, when there is a grand dinner in the Captain's Cabin, to help wait at table. I would not have thought this too arduous for a biddable foundling such as you. However, if the spirit of adventure does not stir in your breast, if you have no lust to sniff the scented breezes of tropic isles, if, in short, you pine to return to the Foundling Hospital . . .?"

"Sir," he cried, "I shall follow you to the ends of the earth, I swear I shall, for you are a good and kind master, no boy could ask for a better. Let me, I beg you, go a-seafaring in your service."

"Very well," I said.

"May God bless you, Sir!" he said.

I could not, at that moment, recall the useful English word *'hrrumph'*, but I made a non-committal grunt which sounded quite like it. Even in those days, long ago, I was hard, hard and had no affection to waste on little charity-school bastards.

"Tell me your name," I said curtly, "for I have never mastered it and I need to inscribe it upon the ship's papers this afternoon."

He sneezed.

"Good luck," I said civilly, "but now, the name."

He seemed to sneeze again. My patience ebbed.

"The name, if you have one!" I cried. "Sneeze later, in your leisure time. At present, give me your name."

He scuttled under the counter, scrabbled there a while, fished out a wax-bespattered copy of *Pilgrim's Progress*. There on the fly-leaf, many times repeated, was the name "Horace Ashley Urquhart". Clearly, there could be no such name. I looked at him sternly.

"Do you realise, 'You', that boys who mock their masters are often whipped?"

"Sir, it is my name, I swear." He sneezed again. In a little while I could say it myself, in a sneezing fashion, while 'You' kept his face solemn.

After a while we agreed that his name was Orace, which I could pronounce without seeming ridiculous, and off we went to the East India Docks.

The East India Docks presented a scene of indescribable confusion; it was as though the Tower of Babel had collapsed alongside the Slough of Despond. A turmoil of cursing stevedores, ship's chandlers, longshoremen, wharfingers, slop-slop touts and other desperate wastrels jostled and reviled the decent money-lenders, lodging-house crimps and pickpockets who were about their lawful occasions, while the sewage-enriched waters of the Thames flopped fatly against the filthy sides of the ships. The snarlings and shrieking of obscene words were horrifying, deafening; it was like the Stock Exchange on a hot afternoon with gilt-edged shares tumbling, I was quite "taken aback", as sailors say. "You" – Orace, I should say – seemed not to mind, he felt at home, he had survived countless dinner-times at his charity-school.

We fought our way along our particular Dock towards the good ship *John Coram*, with whose master, Captain Knatchbull, I had made a tentative compact, although not yet his acquaintance. He had a forty-five per-centum share of the venture and was ready to sell me a morsel of it for £1,750, along with the right to sail as a supernumerary officer, unpaid but with merely nominal duties, the right to officer's food for myself and ship's rations for my servant, and, above all, the concession to buy a chest or two of opium at the Calcutta auctions on my own account and to ship home the proceeds in the form of some fine Chinese porcelains.

As we approached the *John Coram* we were halted by a mob of fellows who were plainly salt-water seamen, staring at a huge notice, painted on a square of old sail-cloth and displayed beside the brig next before our vessel. "THIS SHIP, THE YANKEE CLIPPER 'MARTHA WASHINGTON' WILL BE FIRST THIS SEASON IN THE CANTON RIVER. A FEW PRIME HANDS MIGHT STILL BE TAKEN ON: COGMEN & SEA-LAWYERS NEED NOT APPLY. FREE SLOP-CHEST & FINEST GRUB ON THE 7 SEAS".

On the next ship – our *John Coram* – a little, bearded man was dancing up and down and raving through a shouting-trumpet. As he finished, the captain of the Yankee ship appeared on his bridge, spread his arms open wide in the most confidential fashion and roared in turn.

"By Gosh and by Golly, are you bully-boys about to swallow that slop? Ask that old turtle-back to show you his holds: why, they're spading the goddam dry-rot out of her with shovels and her keelson's as soft as a dad-blamed cabbage!"

"By thunder!" bellowed back our Captain Knatchbull, "that's all roly-moly and Yankee spit! Just cast your eye on his bottom, that's all I ask, his *bottom*!" The seamen and I walked to the edge of the dock and, to be sure, there was something like a kitchen-garden growing on the planks of the Yankee ship, for all its gleaming brasswork at the rails.

"Now," roared on the little British captain, "come aboard a good British ship like brave British tarpaulins and make your marks on my watch-bill and your fortunes, likely enough! I'll warrant my ship's heart of oak is as sound as your own!"

The men shuffled and mumbled; a few of the younger ones sidled up the gang-plank of the *Martha Washington*, the rest put their heads together then went aboard the *John Coram*.

71

I looked at Orace. He was quaking a little.

"Be of good cheer," I said kindly, confidently, "no one shall hurt you." I was young then and foolish, you see, foolish.

We went aboard. At the break of the poop we were met by a great, coarse bear-like man who addressed me in a strange accent which I later learned was that of the former American Colonies of Great Britain. He was wearing a sort of uniform and so I touched the brim of my hat in a civil fashion, at which he sketched out a gesture towards the brim of his.

"Carolus Van Cleef," I said. "Calling on Captain Knatchbull. With my servant."

"He's swearing in new hands," he said curtly. "Wait here." I thought about that. It did not seem to me a courteous reply.

"No," I said. "I shall come back tomorrow. Pray tell him that I called." With that I turned on my heel.

"Just a minute, brother," he called, "don't be so all-fired tetchy; suppose you go to Dirty Annie's on the wharf there and get a mouthful of maw-wallop – Captain Knatchbull will be free in half an hour, I guess."

"Very well," I said. "Thankyou."

Dirty Annie's was a filthy shanty on the wharf-side: it was full of rough sailor-folk. I ordered some "Blind Scouse" for that was what was chalked on the "Ordinary" board – it proved to be a tasty and nourishing sort of vegetable stew – and some porter. There was no porter, I had to drink something called "cold four", a thin, sour ale; I gave most of it to Orace to drink with his bread and cheese, telling him that it would make a man of him. He drank it gratefully, he was a good boy.

When we returned to the *John Coram* the American officer – he was, it turned out, the First Mate and named Lubbock – greeted me with a grudging civility and shewed me into the Captain's cabin, telling Orace to remain outside the door. The cabin was sumptuously furnished; a *comprador* with a brown face but splendid livery gave me a chair and a glass of brown sherry or perhaps Marsala; I was young and green, I could not tell the difference. After a little while the inner door opened and the most beautiful woman I have ever seen in my life came in. Her breasts were trained on me like twin carronades, her hair was the colour of a lion's mane, her mouth was a moist invitation to sin and her eyes were languorous, drowsy. My loins stirred. It seemed an age before I could collect myself and

72

rise to my feet: she did not seem to mind, she was, perhaps, used to such an effect. Indeed, it may even have pleased her.

"Carolus Van Cleef," I mumbled, bowing stiffly.

"I am Mrs Knatchbull. You may *not* call me Blanche, for you are to be only a supernumerary officer, I believe." Her accent was not quite British, nor were her mannerisms.

"How do you do?" I said.

"Captain Knatchbull will be with you presently," she said, "he is praying just now. He always prays after he has had his will of me; I wonder why that is?" With great sang-froid I offered her a chair and watched entranced the sinuosity with which she settled her person into it. Her great, violet eyes were fixed on me, as though awaiting an answer to her question.

"The weather is fine, is it not," I said carefully, "for the time of the year?"

"Why do you speak of the weather?" she asked. "You are clearly not an Englishman. Who else remarks on these matters?"

I thought of saying "hrrumph" but could not, at that moment, command the pronunciation of the word. I was saved by the opening of the inner door and the entry of the small, bearded Captain.

"Carolus Van Cleef," I said, rising to my feet again. "Supernumerary officer."

"Queen Anne's dead and her bum's cold," he retorted. "Have you any other news from the Indies?"

Clearly, this was an English joke.

"No, Captain," I said, "except that I have come aboard."

"Don't trifle with me, Sir, and you call me 'Sir', not 'Captain'."

"Yes, Sir," I said.

"No, damme! You don't say 'yes', you say 'aye aye'!"

"Aye aye," I said, anxious to please in so small a matter.

"SIR!" he shouted.

"Sir," I agreed. He simmered awhile, like a kedgeree-pot.

"You shall have a drink with me," he said at last.

"Aye aye, Sir," I said.

"Boy! Bring a jug of piss-quick, and look sharp!"

In the twinkling of an eye a smartly-liveried Chinese boy appeared with a tray. "Piss-quick" proved to be gin with marmalade stirred in and topped up with hot water. It was not very good to drink, but better than Dirty Annie's "cold four". Indeed, at that moment the Captain cocked an ear, leaped up and strode to the door.

73

"Your servant's spewed across two square yards of my deck!" he thundered. "Fined two shillings, Mr Van Cleef!" And then, in an even greater voice: "Mr Mate! The watch is idling, get this deck swabbed if any of your quinsied cripples and quim-stickers' touts are on their feet!" He had a fine command of language, I could not understand one half of what he said, but it was fine to hear, fine.

"Now, Sir," he said, swallowing his glass of "piss-quick" and munching the pieces of orange-peel, "I hear you're ready to take up a piece of my share in this venture. How's this?"

"I have heard you well-spoken of, Sir," I said carefully, "and that your ship is a fast and happy one. I have decided to join the venture, subject to my being satisfied that what I have heard is correct."

. "Satisfied?" he cried, raising his voice thunderously again (I could not understand how so little a man could command so great a volume of sound). "*Satisfied*, Sir? Does it not occur to you that this interview is so that I can determine whether I am satisfied with *you*?"

I thought this over carefully for in those days I was not sure how clever I was.

"Of course, Sir," I said at last, "but you will appreciate that the money I am venturing is the whole of my fortune and I am sure that you admire prudence in so young a man as myself . . . who was once an entered apprentice."

He made that English "hrrumphing" noise which I have never properly mastered, and poured himself another glass of the "Piss-quick". Perhaps, in pouring none for me, he was admiring a young man's prudence: for my part, I applied myself to finishing the remainder of the brown sherry which the *comprador* had poured for me ten minutes before.

The way I had phrased my remark about having been taught prudence was tentatively Freemasonic. Guardedly, he asked me another question. I breathed a sigh of relief to the Great Architect and answered, translating freely from the Dutch. He sent his wife out of the cabin and invited me to share a certain word with him. I demurely suggested he begin, as I had been taught, and we lettered-and-halved it. He did not like my Dutch version of the last letter, so I wrote it down on the corner of a scrap of paper. This satisfied him, especially when I tore off the scrap of paper on which I had written and swallowed it. This made him a little benign, although no less severe, and it soon became evident that he had

74

made great progress in certain things and had passed under a certain architectural feature whilst I, because of my youth, had still to make my Mark. I hope I make myself clear but if I do not it is of no possible interest to you.

He drank some more of his nasty drink, patted his beard dry with a great pocket-handkerchief and gazed at me sternly and a little benignly.

"Well, now, young Lewis," he said (if you are good grand-children you will one day understand why he called me that), "I daresay you wish to look over my ship?"

"Do you think I should, Sir? I know nothing of ships," I answered diffidently.

"Then learn, Sir, *learn! Mr Mate!* Pray give my compliments to the Third Officer and say that I should esteem it a courtesy if he could spare the time to wait upon me at some time during this watch." I could hear the First Mate bellowing incomprehensibly dirty words from the quarter-deck, none of which seemed to echo the sardonic civilities of the Captain.

"My first mate," said Captain Knatchbull almost apologetically, "is invaluable. He is, as you have seen, or will see, a mere anthropoid ape who swings himself along on his knuckles, but there is none like him for coaxing a recalcitrant watch aloft to shorten sail on a black and stormy night. His principle is that the men should be more afraid of him than of death; it seems to serve well, for the men are even less intelligent than him and are good Christians every one: they have to attest to this before signing Ship's Articles."

In the time that it took him to say this, the Third Mate appeared in the cabin doorway, panting for breath and tugging at a last button on his tunic.

"Ah, Mr Lord Stevenage," said the Captain with heavy and, as it seemed to me, over-stressed civility, "pray allow me to apologise for disturbing your doubtless well-earned repose."

The Third Mate was a young and well-enough looking fellow, perhaps five years older than me but not so well set up and at first glance seeming older still because of the lines of dissipation or illness which marked his well-bred features.

"I was not asleep, Sir," he replied stiffly; "you will recall that I am standing both anchor watches at call until we sail."

"So you are," said the Captain, "so you are, to be sure. Now, let me present Mr Van Cleef, who proposes to do us the honour of

75

sailing with us as supernumerary officer; his appointment is that of, ah, let us say, Paymaster. I know that you will be glad to share your commodious cabin with him. His servant shall sling his hammock in the disused pantry next along. Perhaps now you will favour me by showing Mr Van Cleef over and around the ship."

The young officer opened his mouth then closed it again.

"Thankyou Mr Lord Stevenage," said the Captain. "That will be all."

Outside the cabin we looked at each other with entirely straight faces, silently challenging each other to display an emotion. One of us wanted to laugh, the other to curse; neither of us was sure which was which. Perhaps both for both things, I do not know now, it was long ago.

"Follow me, if you please," he said at last. We went down the gangplank and onto the dock. I flicked an eye in the direction of Dirty Annie's. His eye, too, flicked there momentarily but he was on duty, you understand, and British. Moreover, the Captain could have seen us through the scuttle.

"Mr Lord Stevenage," I began.

"I say," he said, "look, my name is Lord Peter Stevenage; it amuses the captain to address me in the droll way you have heard but I'm afraid I don't much care about it. In front of him or the other officers you'd better call me Mister Stevenage; in private you may call me what you will."

I looked at him. He had many pimples but in all other respects his face was frank and open, despite the marks of dissipation.

"Peter?" I said, diffidently.

"That will do very well," he said, suddenly smiling in the most engaging way. "And what am I to call you?"

"It is some while since anyone called me Karli," I said.

"Then Karli it shall be. Now, to our task. I have brought you onto the dock so that you may see our little ship from the outside."

It looked an enormous ship to me but I had no experience of such things in those days. In fact it looked like a man-of-war, for there was a long line of gunports down its side.

"Yes," he said following my gaze, "my father had her built almost like a Royal Navy corvette by old List of Wootton Creek, near Cowes, for in those days the Royal Yacht Squadron was an auxiliary fighting force. Indeed, the *John Coram* – although that was not her name then – fought well at Navarino in 1827. She mounted a broad-

76

side of eleven guns as well as a long brass piece amidships but now half of the ports are empty and rigged for sweeps."

"*Sweeps?*"

"Long oars. Damn' useful if you're becalmed and drifting, especially if there's a *lorcha* full of pirates about to swarm over you."

"Ah, yes," I said, my stomach jerking uneasily. "And your *father* . . .?"

"Had her built, yes. I lost her at cards. Now, you'd better pay attention, for the Captain may quiz you about her. She's the only ship-rigged vessel in the opium trade; the rest are brigs and schooners and a couple of barquentines. She's of 330 tons burthen but has little cargo-space: opium takes up very little room and, homeward bound, we carry nothing but a specie-room full of silver and a few chops of the new teas if we're in Canton River at the right time.

"That is why, d'you see, the officers' and crew's quarters are so ah, *commodious*." There was a note of bitterness in his voice.

"I am sorry," I said, "that I have been foisted upon you."

"Oh, damme, that's all right. Glad of your company. D'you snore much?"

"I do not think so."

"Oh, good. Now, pray observe the lines of the ship." For quite five minutes he described and rhapsodised about the ship's shape, using rare and wonderful words which at that time meant nothing whatever to me. "You see that, I'm sure?" he finished.

"Yes," I said. "Or at least, I think I remember most of what you have said so far." He made that engaging smile again.

"That's the spirit. When we're at sea I shall point out other, coarser vessels to you and you will understand when you compare them with what you are looking at now, from here."

He paused for two or three minutes while I dutifully etched the image of the *John Coram* onto my mind's eye – not a difficult task for one who had already learned to memorise some two hundred cryptic marks on Delft and porcelain.

"Now," he went on, "notice her breadth of beam: this allows her to carry a great press of canvas – and her heavy armament, which you may be glad of when we find ourselves amongst the *lorchas* of Hok-keen and the Ladrones."

"There cannot be too many guns for my taste," I said frankly.

"Quite right; well said. The buggers must, at all costs, be kept at a distance, for once they're aboard you may as well count yourself a

77

dead man and clap a pistol to your temple, for they are fiends incarnate."

I thought that he was trying, in a jocular, English way, to frighten me, so I said something brave and carefree, I forget what. He looked at me strangely, then changed the subject.

"The new owners have made a bad mistake, to my mind. This yacht – ship – was designed for spread of sail, not hoist. By that I mean that she was not built to carry sky-scrapers."

"Sky-scrapers?"

"Yes. Extra sails on extension masts – moonsails, skysails and so forth. In my father's day our masts seldom rose more than a few inches beyond the rigging that supported them; although, in exceptional summer-like weather, we sent up topgallant and royal masts in one."

"Really?" I said without comprehension.

"Yes. But Captain Knatchbull has contracted the new Yankee disease of flying kites far above the royals on spars the weight of salmon rods, his nature is such that he can brook no rival, he would send us all to Davy Jones's locker rather than let another ship eat the wind out of him, still less pass him."

"These skysails and so forth are, then, a bad thing?" I asked carefully, so as to make sure. He made a sort of exploding noise.

"God's teeth and trowsers!" he shouted. "Isn't that just what I've been telling you? Damme, look at the rake of her masts! Would any sane man send up skyscrapers to top 'em? Can't you see she's built for *spread*?" Then, in a kinder voice, he added "No, I forgot, pray forgive me; no doubt you'll see what I mean by the end of the voyage. If any of us are still alive."

"Is the venture so desperate as that?" I asked. He recovered himself, breathed deeply.

"This is Captain Knatchbull's fourth voyage in the country trade. He is living on borrowed time, for he is already rich; his motive now is only to excel all other captains in the trade, he cares nothing for his life or the lives of those he commands."

"And you?" I asked.

"I? I am a ruined man. The family fortune's entailed; the houses are mortgaged to the hilt; I cannot lie with my wife because I have the syphilis, d'you see – the Great Pox. In any case, she lies with another. And to me. Before I am thirty the signs and symptoms will become excruciating: I'd far rather take a Celestial Chinee knife in my liver then fetch up in the Incurables Hospital, sans teeth, sans nose, sans everything."

"I am sorry," I said, lamely.

"I'm not."

We went up the gangplank again, he whistling merrily or so it seemed; I rather glum and wishing myself well out of this perilous enterprise.

"Cheerily now, Karli!" he cried, clapping me upon the shoulder, "don't let me take the wind from your sails: there's many a worse ship afloat – aye, and many a worse skipper – and this one will make your fortune if ever a ship can!" I sketched out a smile.

"That's the thing!" he cried, "if we're to be messmates we must keep each other jolly, don't you see?"

He took me forward to the fo'c'sle and threw open the door. Several open-faced, clean, smiling fellows jumped to their feet with alacrity: it was clear that Peter Stevenage was popular with the crew.

"Here are our hearts of oak, Karli; at least, those who have finished wenching and come aboard. Some of them served under my father when this ship had another name and 'RYS' after it, eh, Tom Transom?"

"Yes indeed Mr Peter," grinned a capable-looking old shell-back, knuckling his forehead.

"Pray get on with your scrimshaw and make-and-mend, lads," said Peter, "but first say how d'ye do to Mr Van Cleef, our new supercargo, who will be bunking and messing along with me. He is new to the sea so I look to you all to show him the ropes and spars and to cover up his mistakes until he finds his sea-legs, what?"

"That we shall, Sir." they growled, some "making a leg", some tugging a forelock (but in no servile way), some bobbing their heads awkwardly.

"I had thought a fo'c'sle to be a kind of hell-hole," I remarked as we made our way aft. The place had surprised me by its roomy comfort and warmth.

"Most of them are," he replied, "many are little better than Mayfair tenements. But this one was designed for a crack yacht, you recall, and has been enlarged by throwing into it the former officers' quarters; we officers now live in the passengers' staterooms aft and the captain occupies the former owners' quarters." He did not say this at all bitterly; my respect for him grew every minute.

79

"We carry a double crew, d'you see, for we need so little cargo-space; in fact we muster three strong watches so that even in the wildest weather there can always be a watch below. We are one of the few ships that can weather the Cape and every man a dry suit of slops to his back. Depend upon it, that's a rarity!"

"I am sure of it," I said politely.

"Moreover, every man-jack is an able-bodied seaman, salted and dried, who can hand, reef and steer and heave the lead, turn in a dead-eye, gammon a bowsprit, fish a broken spar, rig a purchase, knot, point, splice, parcel and serve as well as spin his own yarns and lines in our ropewalk."

"Upon my word!" I murmured.

"Yes," he went on enthusiastically – this was clearly a topic close to his heart – "I'm bound to say this for Knatchbull – Captain Knatchbull, I should say – he has kept up my father's standards so far as crew is concerned, no cogsmen and fakers in this ship. Some of the Yankee ships that are coming into the trade now prefer to sign on a gaggle of waterfront rats, wasters, the scum of the seas who can get no other work, then break their spirits with brass knuckles and the rope's-end until they will do anything – feats no true seaman in his senses would attempt – for fear of losing their rations, their tot of rum – or their front teeth. 'Bully' Lubbock, our 'bucko' first officer, used to command such a ship until he was arraigned for triple manslaughter on the Barbary Coast of San Francisco."

"He did not, I confess, strike me as a wholly cultivated gentleman," I said.

"He is not a gentleman of any sort," said Peter sharply. "He is a boor, and a dangerous one. Steer clear of him, give him a wide berth and for God's sake do not let him anger you: one proud retort from you and he will find ways of making your life a hell upon the waters." My spirits, so recently raised, sank again. Peter, once again, clapped me upon the shoulder.

"Come, cheer up, I did not mean to daunt you. He is a well enough fellow in a rough way. Pretend to admire him and you will have no trouble. Now come and meet the doctor, the mainstay of our little ship."

"You carry a surgeon?" I asked, surprised.

"See for yourself," he replied, kicking hard at the door of a curious sort of round-house shed a little aft of the main-mast and roaring, in a voice new to me, "Come out of there, you black-enamelled bastard, we've come to hang you!" On the instant, the door burst open and a monstrous blackamoor appeared, almost naked and brandishing a meat-cleaver. On seeing Peter his face split open like a melon, displaying an inordinate number of exceedingly white teeth. He hid the cleaver behind him and spoke in a sheepish, high-pitched whine.

"Knowed it was you Maz Peter; cain't fool ole doctor after all thiz years; anyways, I hain't got nuthin on ma conshequence that's hanging stuff."

"Not even in Alabama?" asked my friend quizzically.

"Now hesh, Maz Peter; thass ole stuff, and Alabama's a million miles away I reckon."

"'But that was in another country, and, besides, the wench is dead.'" This was a quotation, I could tell. Perhaps from Nimrod himself, for all I knew. "Be that as it may," Peter went on, "this is Mr Van Cleef. He will be your friend, for he is well versed in the works of Captain Marryat, and you, in turn, are to treat him with respect – by which I mean that you are not to poison him or I shall flog you myself." The negro cook drew himself up, so far as the galley-door allowed.

"P'ison, Maz Peter? Why, you know I haint p'isoned nobody this ten years, 'cept accidental."

"Precisely. Let there be no accidents. By the same token, what hell's brew is that on the mess-kid bench, smelling so vilely?"

"That hain't no hell-brew, Maz Peter, that my famous portable soup an' mighty glad you'll be of it, soon as we clear the Cap Verdies." I looked at the curious, toffee-like slabs which were cooling in shallow trays. Peter explained that this was, indeed, highly concentrated soup which would set into a tough jelly: a piece no larger than the joint of a thumb would, he promised me, make a pint of nourishing soup and was scarcely poisonous at all except for a marked laxative effect which was often welcome during a long voyage. The "doctor" gazed at it proudly, ever and again scooping off a handful of the blowflies which were revelling upon its surface and squashing them in his huge, pink palm.

Peter jingled the coins in his pocket and looked at me in a meaningful way. I understood in a moment and slipped a half-sovereign into the doctor's hand. The hand closed upon it then opened again: the gold piece was gone! The next moment he retrieved just such a piece from my ear, with a merry chuckle.

Clearly, the fellow was versed in the ancient African magic, although now I am inclined to believe that it was mere legerdemain. Be that as it may, I never laid out a piece of money so fruitfully: throughout the voyage that cook saw to it that my Dutch belly never wanted for plentiful and delicate fare. (Indeed, the whole ship's company ate uncommonly well: the owners had the good sense – rare then and just as rare today – to know that an extra £100 laid out on galley-stuff over and above the usual rate of provisioning made for a sturdy and concentrated crew.)

From the galley we descended to the gun-deck, cable-tier and finally the hold, which was sparsely filled with cases and packages consigned to gentlemen in the East India Company's service – much of it fowling-pieces, pistols and rifles – as well as boxes of bibles for *colporteurs* at the Cape and in India, crates of bottled India Pale Ale, fashionable mantle-makers' rubbish for nabob's ladies, china and silver-ware for their tables, hams, brandy, a few barrels of whisky (scarcely worth the carriage at 2/6d a gallon but there are Scotch officers who positively *prefer* it to brandy!), whalebone splints for the stay-makers, hats from Mr Lock, boots from Mr Lobb and umbrellas from Mr Briggs. My new friend explained that the vacant spaces in the hold would be filled at the Cape, for we were to take aboard a great deal of fiery African brandy, many cases of the delicious Constantia and Stellenbosch wines, bales of ostrich feathers which, although light, take up much space for they cannot be compressed, as much ivory as the owners' agents would have been able to purchase and, with luck, some rhinoceros horns. The Chinese, he assured me with a solemn countenance, prize these last mightily: a cup made of such a horn will turn colour the moment poison is poured into it – no mandarin dares be without one – and the powder produced during the turning of the cup is worth its exact weight in gold because of its aphrodisiac properties. (I have seen rhinoceros horns as tall as a man.)

All the time Lord Peter was pouring facts and measurements into my ears; I coiled these away into my memory like a jolly jack-tar stowing an anchor-cable. At last he said that for the moment we were at the end of our task.

"Have you any questions?"

"Well, I should like to know why the ship is named the *John Coram*? Who was he?"

"Sir," piped up Orace from his respectful place at my heels,

"Please Sir, I know!" We turned and stared at him; for my part I had forgotten that he was there.

"Well, boy?" said Peter, not unkindly.

"Sir, John Coram was a great merchant in the City of London and Great Coram Street where your friend Mr J. lives is named after him and amongst his other philanthropical works he founded the Foundling Hospital where I was fortunate enough to receive a good education and before that he was a master ship-builder in the American Colonies please Sir."

The extent of the child's knowledge was less amazing than the speed at which he rattled off his lore.

"Very well!" cried Peter, giving him a halfpenny.

"You are a good boy," I said, patting him upon the head. He did not flinch, as he would have done a few weeks before.

"Now," said Peter, fishing out a beautiful gold repeater from his fob, "it is my watch below and I fear I must take advantage of it, for I am standing watch and watch about and ready to swoon with fatigue."

"Why is this?" I asked, puzzled.

"Oh, I came aboard drunk three nights ago and forgot to tip my hat to the quarter-deck. Re-living old times, d'you see; had forgotten I was no longer the owner's son. It's of no consequence. Now, you'd better make haste and report to the old – ah, to the Captain's cabin; he sometimes becomes a touch querulous at about this time of day. I'll see to it that your portion of my cabin is cleared for you by tomorrow noon: I'd count it a favour if you didn't rouse me till then. Delighted to make your acquaintance. Sure we shall get on famously."

With that he walked away, using a sort of wooden gait which betrayed the extreme fatigue which he had hitherto concealed. I looked at Orace.

"Poor gentleman," he said, respectfully. I said nothing; Orace probably knew more about such states than I did in those days.

In the cabin, the Captain seemed quite a different man from the irate person he had seemed to be earlier, but I was not deceived.

"Well, Sir," he said heavily, jovially, "what d'you think of my ship? Does she please you? Could you support the tedium of a profitable pleasure-cruise with us, d'you suppose?"

My mind started framing an English sentence which would tell him to go to the devil and perform curious acts with him, but at that

83

very moment the inner door opened a crack and Mrs Knatchbull's lovely face appeared, wearing an expression which delicately mingled humour, exasperation and a certain, well, a certain invitation. I was vexed to find myself answering the Captain in a civil – indeed an amiable – voice.

"I shall esteem it an honour to serve under you, Sir," is what I heard myself saying.

"Good," he said, "*good*." He said it again once or twice, as though he approved of the word "good". Then he pulled some papers toward him and from them rattled off at great speed some antique gibberish which I could not comprehend but which, I realised later, comprised the Ship's Articles.

"You are, of course, a practising Christian," he muttered, dipping a great pen into an inkpot and not meeting my eye, still less my nose. I opened my mouth. He peered up at me through the thickest of his eyebrows. The faintest rustle of silken petticoats filtered through the inner door.

"Aye aye, Sir!" I said staunchly.

"Sign here," he said.

CHAPTER SEVEN

That last evening of my life ashore I spent in the street called Strand: curiously, this word means "shore" – was that not apt?

I ate a great quantity of turbot, some boiled mutton and a few nicely-dressed woodcocks, each set upon a toast which had been spread with the bird's "trails", peppered. "Trails" means guts. I also drank some wine.

Then I bade a prolonged and salty farewell to the tailor's daughter whose name I forget and, as an especial treat, to her little sister also, for who knew when next I would find such charming and biddable girls? Then I drank some more wine, I believe. (I do not remember this wine but I recall a trifling sense of *malaise* the next day, which convinces me that I did drink a little something.)

That next day, *malaise* or no, I looked to all my small business affairs, made a bargain with my landlord about the lease, sent my stock-in-trade to Mr Jorrocks' warehouse and my new sea-chest, replete with sensible clothes and improving books, to the *John Coram* at the Docks. Then I went to a shop in Jermyn Street where two genial partners called Mr Paxton and Mr Whitfield selected for me one black Bradenham ham, one pink York ditto, an incomparable Stilton cheese, three salted tongues, a monstrous Bologna sausage which they assured me would travel to the Indies and be none the worse for it after a year and a tinned box of delicate sea-bread called "Thin Captain's Biscuits". (They assured me that, but for a printer's error, the name would have been "Captain's Thin Biscuits".) When I told them that I was a friend of John Jorrocks himself and that I would pay in coined gold, there and then, they cheerfully deducted seven and one half per centum from my score. Most of their business was with the nobility, you see.

85

Then, on advice, I took a cab to Number 205, Regent Street, where a Mr Beattie sold me a large revolving pistol made expressly for him by J. Lang himself. It was in a mahogany case, complete with moulds for both ball and bullet, a wad cutter, powder-measures and everything else proper to such a weapon. It was very costly, but the best that money could buy. I felt something of a fool as I walked out of the shop, my pockets lighter by so many guineas. It was to be several months before I congratulated myself upon buying so reliable a weapon.

Lord Peter Stevenage roared with laughter as he saw Orace staggering up the gangplank that afternoon; the child was so heavily burdened that I was having to push from behind to keep him upright. Had I not so recently become an English gentleman I believe I would have carried some of the parcels myself.

"You luxurious bugger!" cried Peter merrily, "is this the last of your stores? Your dunnage has been streaming aboard all day, quite altered the ship's trim, burst me if it hasn't! Come to the cabin, if that child can still walk, and let's overhaul this gear of yours."

He seemed taken aback at my choice of clothing and, since he was now free of the watch, offered to take me to a ship-chandler's slop-shop. There were many such places within a stonesthrow of the docks but Peter led me unerringly to one where, he said, the proprietor was too intelligent to rob one more than was reasonable. He made me buy two suits of oilskins, two pairs of sea-boots and some huge slabs of smelly, greasy wool which he said would prove, when unfolded, to be warm underclothing. I protested that my duties were to be mercantile rather than maritime and that I had no intention of scrambling up and down masts and riggings in the wind and weather-oh – why then should I need such things?

He looked at me strangely.

"Well," he said, "you never know. It might come on to rain or something, d'you see. Now, you'd better have a couple of 'thousand-milers' – and one for the little bastard, too." A "thousand-miler" turned out to be a sort of durable shirt made of black twill; so-called, Peter solemnly assured me, because it should be washed and changed after every thousand miles of the voyage, whether it was dirty or not. These shirts did not appear comfortable at all but Peter explained that I must ask the Doctor to put them in the copper for me when next he was boiling a "duff" or pudding:

this would make the garment supple and kindly to the skin, because of the suet-grease in the water.

I made a few other purchases at his suggestion, such as spermaceti candles, sticks of coarse barley-sugar, a pocket compass with folding sun-dial attached and some strong soap containing the biniodide of mercury to combat an infestation called "the crabs" by sailor-folk.

Our cabin, when we had brought in this final consignment of my goods, seemed quite full – "something of a Hoorah's nest" Peter called it – but he soon shewed Orace how and where to stow everything in ship-shape and seaman-like fashion and we were snug in next to no time. It was by no means a squalid little room – the fittings of brass and mahogany reminded me that this had once been the yacht of a Lord – and the hard mattress of my bunk was of good horsehair and not smelly. Peter's possessions were few: a sea-chest of clothes, a brass-bound mahogany chest of arms, a shelf of books. Some of these last were by heathen authors, some by a person writing under the nom-de-plume of "Jane Austen" – I came to know his work well during the voyage, he had a wonderful insight into the female mind, wonderful.

Peter and I cracked a bottle of Lord Windermere's Sercial before settling down for the night; it was rich and strong. He dowsed the candle early for we were to sail with the tide at first light.

Ships, in these nasty nowadays, are made of iron and propelled by coal. This may be a good thing, I cannot say. What I do know is that the ships of those days, real ships, wooden ships, were alive: they manifested their life in a thousand ways which at first irked – sometimes frightened – me, but later became a reassuring cradle-song when I had learned to single out each noise and understand its origin. The gurgle of the running tide past the ship's strakes, the gentle schlipp-schlopping of the wavelets created by a passing vessel, the soft, grinding bump, more felt than heard, of a fender nudging the quay-side and the moan of standing rigging set vi-brating by the wind – all these I had heard before, although on a smaller scale, but now there were countless other noises new to me. In particular I recall from that first night the placid straining and grunting of great timbers which had learned to live and work together, the rattle of the gangplank and boom of feet on the deck-planks which told of Johnny-tars rejoining ship at the last moment before midnight, the sudden clangour of the ship's bell marking the watches and, once, the squalling scream of the ship's cat locked in a death-struggle with some unhappy rat.

The smells, too, remain with me, although I have long since, and often, smelled worse. Peter's hair-lotion was sharp and agreeable; it reminded me of the verbena plant in my mother's window. Tar and timber and paint are good smells; so were the mingled richnesses of our cabin-stores, especially the Stilton cheese. The London River, laden with sewage, was less good and, when the ship pitched a little as another vessel passed, our bilges, disturbed, offered up a stench of graveyards. The ship's cat had pissed somewhere within range of my nose: I resolved to take the first opportunity to boot it overside, for I do not love such creatures. Dogs, yes, within reason. Overriding all, strange to say, was the smell of horses from London town. It was to be a long time until I again sniffed that smell – and with pleasure.

I slept a little towards dawn, but uneasily because of the strangeness of these noises and smells, and it was soon awakened by Peter's turning out, washing his face and dressing. His sense of time, like that of all good sea-faring men, was acute, he was ready for duty at the precise moment that three bells of the second watch sounded (this means half-past five in the morning) and a seaman thumped upon our door, calling out "Mister Stevenage to stir himself if you please, Sir!" Seeing that I was awake, Peter gave me a grimace of apology and a friendly wink as he left the cabin. He looked cheerful but old and ill.

There was no more attempt at sleeping for me: the ship resounded to the trampling. I huddled on some clothes and went on deck. A flat-footed but elaborate ballet was taking place, performed with what seemed random precision by the ship's people, guided by strange words in a clarion voice from the Captain, repeated in even stranger language by the First Mate and retailed by Peter in some part and also by the Second, whose voice was shrill and agitated. I was pushed and trodden upon by many a seaman who had eyes only for his incomprehensible task; scuttling for refuge I narrowly escaped being sent up the foremast by a purple-visaged boatswain.

"Mr Van Cleef fined two shillings," came the captain's roar from the bridge, "for interfering with the working of the ship. Fined a further three shillings for being on deck without a neck-cloth and with his breeches unbuttoned." I slunk aft through the throng of intent sailors. As I slunk I heard the Captain cry "Mr Lubbock! *Mister*, I say! Pray contain yourself with that down-East starter of yours, the men are working well enough." I continued to slink. I did not, you understand, "*know the ropes*" at that time.

All this hubbub and bawling and trampling was of course quite incomprehensible to me, but it was not many weeks before I could tell what the men were about simply by cocking an ear out of my bunk, and could bandy such words as "garboard" and "halyard" with the best of them. At this particular time, all we were doing was hauling the ship out into the stream, heaving up the great anchor, singling-up and casting-off the shore lines and setting the fore-topsail, so that we could drop down-river to the Pool with accuracy and without feeing a pilot.

I, meanwhile, climbed sulkily back into my bunk and fell asleep again, only to start up, cracking my pate cruelly against the upper bunk, when a rattling shriek from the best-bower anchor chain betokened – to those who understood such things – that we were in the Pool of London and swinging round into the tideway.

Peter popped his head round the cabin door with a haggard grin and began to explain that – here he was interrupted by a bellow of "Cangcoxnlarbdquarboscrew" in Lubbock's grating Yankee yell – the Mate was, in fact, summoning the Captain's Coxswain and the crew of the larboard quarter-boat – Peter, I say, began to explain that the Captain and the First Officer would now be rowed around and around the ship and would study the trim of it. This was important, he said, for the phrase "on an even keel" is no mere form of words: a vessel down by the head is ill to steer and dangerous in heavy weather, while if it is down by the stern its sailing properties are impaired. A list to one side, too, however slight, can also slow the craft down and be a danger in heavy seas, especially when close-hauled. I nodded sagely.

Our *John Coram*, you understand, was a dainty and responsive ship, the men swore that she could almost talk and had a sweet and willing temperament, responding gaily to any little attentions but becoming unhappy if her trim was neglected. The consumption of stores, particularly water, as the voyage wore on, would call for many another of these rowings around the ship whenever we were in port or a dead calm.

Peter went on to give me astonishing figures about the weight of water a ship's company can consume in a given period but I fear I must have yawned in his face for suddenly he laughed and went back to his duties.

I must have dozed. Peter aroused me in seamanlike fashion by kicking the edge of my bunk so vigorously that I started up and again cracked my head. He brought, in his own hands, our breakfast or nuncheon. It consisted of the sounds, cheeks and other delicate tidbits of fishes, fried up with pieces of onions and potatoes and anointed with the Doctor's famous ketchup. Peter watched me narrowly, I could tell he expected me to display the signs of sea-sickness but I disappointed him. The sea is one of the few things which has never made me sick. I ate in an almost greedy fashion, wiping up the gravy with one or two little hot rolls which the Doctor had made. Peter, who was a poor eater, watched me with admiration.

"Well, now," he cried when I had done, "come up on deck, there's a place called Margate on our starboard beam and you needn't go below again until we wear ship to round the North Foreland."

I waved sentimentally to Margate in case the little chambermaid should be watching our bonny ship go sailing by: I much hoped that she had not foolishly allowed herself to become pregnant, because I had no recollection of her name except that it began with a "d" or perhaps a "b" and was therefore unable to help her.

Peter gave me a rude awakening the next day by emptying part of his shaving-water in a friendly fashion onto my sleeping face. I cried out many an obscene word in Dutch (and some in English which certain young persons had taught me) but when I could open my eyes I saw the pleasant, dissipated face of my friend, who was tying his neck-cloth and beaming at me kindly.

"Come, Karli," he cried, "five minutes to wash, shave, dress and be on deck. Bustle about, do!"

"Is it pirates?" I mumbled, "Mutiny?" He laughed.

"Worse than that," he scoffed. "It's Sunday! Five minutes to be at the break of the poop or God forgive you, for the Captain won't."

I could make nothing of this, nor could I ask for explanations for he had whisked out of the cabin, but I took him at his word, except that I did not shave for my beard was light – I only needed to shave twice a week. I achieved the break of the poop in the very nick of time. The ship's people were lined up in ranks and wearing their best slops; wearing looks, also, of pious respectability such as are proper to the English when worshipping their God, who speaks English Himself and prizes such clothes and looks. The Captain intoned many a resounding phrase, commending our voyage on this, its first Sunday, to both God and Her Britannic Majesty, but it seemed to me that his voice carried a certain irony, a want of true fervour. I observed, whilst his voice boomed sonorously over my bared head, that neither the First nor the Second Mate was present. Since the ship was hove-to this seemed strange to me but I was, of course, ignorant of the ways of sailormen. The Captain, his tone even more ironic, commanded the men to sing a certain hymn, calling for a man named Evans to "fugle a note". The man Evans, sure enough, stepped forth from the ranks, threw back his head and delivered himself of a note approximating to that of "G" with all the brio of a barnyard fowl. He then turned about and waved his arms in such a way that the men instantly began to bellow

"All things bright and beautiful,
    All creatures great and small"

with every appearance of pleasure. It was, for me, a most unhappy experience for I have ever been a lover of music.

At the very moment that the hymn finished – the men had derived great comfort from it and, who knows, perhaps a tone-deaf God in an English heaven may have been relishing it, too – the First and Second Mates tramped aft, each carrying a cloth bundle.

"Searched forrard, Sir," bawled Lubbock; "found one flint-lock, one cap-fire and three Bulldog pistols, several spring-loaded knives, three filthy books (one illustrated), eight flat and three square-face bottles of spirit-liquor and one copy of *The Seaman's Friend* by Dana."

The Captain's visage took on a most convincing expression of sorrow and disgust. He raised his head to the heavens.

"Oh Lord," he roared, "look down in mercy, we implore Thee, upon our erring brethren – chuck it all over the side, Mr Mate – and help us to shew them the paths of Thy witness – yes, chuck the liquor over too, Mister – and guide their steps to Thine ineffable salvation – hold your tongues, you dogs! – Amen. I said *AMEN!*" he added in a voice of thunder.

"Amen," mumbled the crew, not too surlily.

"As to those of you who have broken the Laws of God and the Ship's Articles by bringing aboard these devil's toys, you are pardoned, like sheep who have gone astray." There was a gentle susurrus of relief. "All but one: the accursed sea-lawyer who owned the vile *Seaman's Friend* by Dana, that primer for mutineers; he signed, as you all did, a declaration that he would be bound by King's-ship discipline. I sentence him to a dozen with the cat but this sentence will only be carried out when next he errs. Only the First Mate and I shall know his name and there will be no victimisation – make a note, Mister Mate, if you please – but if I hear a breath of sedition from the forecastle the man will feel the sword of the Lord and of Gideon about his shoulders." There was a long pause. I was not facing the men but I could hear the slight shuffling sound of their bare feet.

"Dismissed!" cried the Captain at last.

"Get forrard!" bellowed the mate.

They got – suddenly no longer surly nor Godly but laughing and skylarking and cheerily kicking the bums of those of their comrades whose contraband had been sequestered. Well could I see how Britannia might rule the waves for ever and that Britons never shall be slaves.

The Second Mate and I were to dine with the Captain and Mrs Knatchbull – whom I was not to call Blanche – and I presented myself at the cabin promptly at six bells of the second watch; that is three o'clock in the afternoon. This seemed unconscionably late to me but amongst Englishmen it is a matter of dignity: the later you dine, the more genteel. As I write, half a century after these things occurred, some fashionable idiots are dining as late as six o'clock in the evening and supping after the theatre by candle-light, like Spaniards. The English are quite mad, from the lowest to the highest, but I think they will conquer the world for they are the only folk (excepting the brash Americans who do not count) who *know* that they are right in all things. For my part, I like them, except the few clever ones.

Dinner was very good, there was a sucking pig. I had never eaten pig before and – not because the Captain was watching me narrowly – I ate copiously of it, for I am not a religious man. It was entertaining, too, to watch the Second Mate gaping at Blanche Knatchbull's bosom as she leaned over her plate across the table from him. I sympathised; indeed, I stole a glance myself from time to time. Her nipples were of an intense terra-cotta colour and large, large. After dinner, at the Captain's request, she favoured us with a song. It was called "Sweet Afton". She had a splendid, rich contralto voice, exactly one semi-tone flat. The young pork in my stomach would have curdled had I not been entranced by the charming way she had of filling her lungs from time to time, for her gown was flimsy for so robust a young woman. All too soon the Captain apologised for keeping us from our duties, fishing out his great golden chronometer. As we closed the cabin door, with many a thank and bow, we heard him say, "Be ready in four and one half minutes, Blanche." No doubt the beauty of the song had inflamed his animal passions. He was a strange man. For my part, I strode the deck for a while, admiring the often-described patterns of the scend of the sea, as well as the various kinds of blue which the sky exhibited, until I was cool enough to go below, or "downstairs" as a landlobble would say. In my bunk I began to read a book of verses by three people called Bell – one of them was called Acton, I forget the others – which had appeared in the bookseller's just before I set out on my travels. It was abominable rubbish; a trio of thwarted virgin ladies could have written it. With their unemployed left hands.

I snoozed over this trash until awakened by Peter coming off watch and telling me that we were under all plain sail and on the larboard tack, making best use of light airs from the south-west.

"Does this mean anything?" I asked querulously. He smiled amiably.

"No, not really. What I should have said is, we're going along the English Channel – you've heard of that, I'm sure? – but the wind isn't quite behind us, so we're sort of pointing at the South coast of England for the time being."

"Is that a good thing?"

"It isn't a *bad* thing," he said. "We're getting along, d'you see, but in a sort of zig-zag fashion."

"I understand you perfectly," I lied, "but, more to the point, will there be anything for supper?" He must have heard footsteps for he flung open our cabin door dramatically and waved in the boy Orace, who was clutching a napkin-ful of hot bread under his left arm and carrying a mess-kid full of something wonderfully savoury-smelling in his right hand. As he laid out the forks and spoons I questioned the child, as a good master should.

"Have you eaten, Orace?"

"Oh, yes, indeed, Sir. I helped the doctor for two or three hours this afternoon, peeling roots and such, and he has been most generous, giving me roasted gobbets of meat, little patties and other good things. I am quite full to the brim, Sir."

"Good," I said, gruffly and not without a tincture of jealousy. "But, pray, what is this mess?"

"Sir, the Doctor calls it Kari: it is a stew much liked in the Indies, he says. Pieces of mutton simmered along with rare, hot spices. There is a pot of rice underneath: you must put some of this on your plate along with the Kari but, when the Kari stings your mouth, on no account must you drink water, the Doctor says, for this will worsen the stinging."

"Get out," I said.

This rare, fiery dish was good. At first I was alarmed when the sweat burst out of my scalp and my teeth seemed to be loosening, but Peter, who had eaten it before, laughed merrily and told me to be of good cheer: the only evil effect might be a certain flux of the bowels next morning. As I ate, the ferocity of the spices seemed to lessen and all sorts of subtle flavours made themselves manifest. It was – is – a wonderful dish and there are many forms of it, as I learned later. (You, my grandchildren, may scoff when I say that a man might do very well if he opened an eating-house in London itself offering such exotic stews; but give the matter some thought. This suggestion may be the only legacy you will receive.)

We seemed to spend an unconscionably long time in the English Channel (I call it that because I am writing in the English language, to my best ability, and because the English have more ships of war than the French); at one time we had to cast anchor or heave-to in the shelter of the lee of an island called Wight, because the wind had veered further into the west and was now what Peter called "dead foul" for our voyage.

"Dead foul?" I asked, alarmed, for the phrase seemed an ill-omened one.

"Cheer up, Karli," he laughed, "That's just a sailor's term meaning it's blowing exactly from where we'd like to sail. It's not worth tacking long boards in the Channel, the Captain's decided we may as well wait for the wind to change; there's lots of things for the men to do meantime."

There were indeed lots to do. The sailmaker was given some handy old seamen to help him overhaul the sail-locker and to make a start on some new-fangled studding-sails; the carpenter and his mates were to make a huge ballast-box which would be lashed to the deck, full of pig-iron, and moved from port to starboard when the ship needed trimming (the Captain, meanwhile, was forever being rowed around and about the ship, squinting and glaring at her trim); I was, without being ordered so to do, peering at the trim of the Captain's wife while pretending to check the *comprador*'s accounts and manifests – a hopeless task, I realised at once (the accounts, naturally) because I could tell that he was my master. A simple, gently-nurtured Jew of Holland is but a child when confronted with an experienced half-Asian *comprador*. I wasted no time on trying to find his small deceits – I sleep more easily without a knife between my ribs. I had already, quite against my will, earned his grave dislike when the Captain, seeking for light tasks with which I might earn my supernumerary officer's status, had ordered me to take over the keys of the slop-chest from the *comprador*. The slop-chest was in fact a small room or lazarette 'tween-decks, from which, under my eagle eye, a bosun's-mate (whom they jokingly called the "pusser") dispensed shirts, canvas trowsers, kerchiefs, chunks of pigtail-twist tobacco, soap, lucifer matches, bandages and other comforts such as tiny packages of tea, coffee and sugar; all set against the sailors' pay-warrants. The slop-chest did but little business so early in the voyage, for all of those tarry-breeks who could afford to do so had stocked up with such things before they came aboard, but I was shocked at the prices – and I am not one who is easily shocked at prices, as many people know to their cost. Being young and fearless, I sought an interview with the Captain – this also gave me an opportunity to eye Blanche, who seemed never wholly to close the door to her sleeping-cabin, nor ever to be more than thinly-clad during her flittings to and fro across the aperture.

The Captain listened with a face difficult to read whilst I made my case against the exploitation of his sailor-folk. My eloquence was, I need not say, marred from time to time by the fleeting apparition of Blanche across the half-opened door. When I had finished he sat for some minutes with his bearded chin sunk upon his breast. I waited respectfully, hoping that he had not fallen asleep. At last he broke silence, gave judgment.

"No piss-quick, Mr Van Cleef," he said, "that's an indulgence I only allow myself in port. But you'll take a glass of schnapps with me." It was not a question. The schnapps was good and fiery, fiery.

"Now, Mr Van Cleef," he said, "in the ordinary way I would

rebuke you for bringing into question the running of the ship, every particle of which is my responsibility and under my ceaseless surveillance. Every splinter and thread of it. Nothing escapes me."

"Aye aye, Sir," I replied stoutly, wondering whether his words or my sailor-like response were the more absurd.

"On the other hand," he went on, tucking his hands behind the tails of his coat and commencing to pace both up and down the stateroom, "on the other hand you have, as an officer, an obligation, nay a duty, to bring to my attention any venalities and tergiversations on the part of your subordinates, have you not?"

"Aye aye, Sir," I said, but his glare told me that this was, for once, the wrong thing to say. I tried "Indeed, Sir", which seemed more palatable.

"You will therefore ascertain from the *comprador*," he went on, resuming his pacing, "the exact cost price of all articles in the slop-chest. From this you will deduct ten per centum, which will be pretty well the extent to which the *comprador* will have lied to you." He seemed splendidly unaware of the *comprador*'s presence at that very moment, refilling our schnapps glasses. "You will then add twenty per centum to the corrected cost-figure to allow for spoilage and handling and so forth. This will be the price at which the ship's people will buy the goods. Is that clear?" Blanche's charming form was passing and re-passing the half-opened door to the sleeping cabin; she seemed to be clad in black stockings and a petticoat of pale-green gossamer. A phrase sprang usefully to mind.

"Abundantly, Sir," I said.

The wind remained foul and there was much to do, so we tarried another while in the bay or bight of Sandown. It rained very much as it always does near that Isle when the wind comes from the southwest. The common sailor-folk were too busy to be allowed to go ashore – indeed, they were still recovering from having been ashore before joining the ship – but we officers were told that we might take a quarter-boat to Bonchurch. Lubbock and the Second and Lord Stevenage were eager to sample the delights of the little town; I hung back, offering to look after the ship in their absence. My deeper, chivalrous reason was the thought that the Captain, too, might go ashore, leaving Blanche unprotected except for me. In the event, it was Blanche who, at the last moment, decided on a jaunt to the shore, leaving me alone with Captain Knatchbull. I strode the deck moodily, gazing at the feeble lights of land and wondering when next I would have such another opportunity to throw away. Orace found me and gave me "the Captain's compliments and he'd esteem it a favour if you'd sup with him and play after."

"Play after?" I asked, concealing my terror.

"Sir, yes Sir, those were his very words. He will have meant a game of chance or skill, will he not, Sir?"

"To be sure," I said. "To be sure."

Supper was simple but wholesome: only some ham, some pressed silverside of beef, half of a handsome game-pie, a salad of warm, vinegary slices of potatoes and watercress, a savoury morsel of toast with a strange thing upon it which looked like a cat's turd but tasted delicious, and some of the wonderfully smelly Stilton cheese which I had learned to love. I ate well; the Captain beamed upon me.

"You play backgammon, of course?" he said. I was at a loss and mumbled that I had never heard of it but was keen to learn. When the Chinese boy brought the board in I recognised it instantly: it was the game which we call tric-trac in the Netherlands, every idle, shiftless, loafing wastrel plays it incessantly in our taverns. I was very good at it indeed, as you can imagine.

"Sir," I said, "I now realise that I know this game a little, it was the English name which confused me."

"Good," he said, eying me narrowly, "I was beginning to fear that you were one of those fellows who ask to be taught a game then, having won because of the indulgence of their opponent, puts his success down to 'beginner's luck' while he pockets the guineas."

I drew myself up angrily. "Sir!" I said, for he had described the behaviour of a *schnorrer*, "Sir, I shall not . . ." He raised a hand and spoke in the friendliest fashion.

"Calm yourself, young man, I spoke provocatively to unsettle your nerves, so that you would play badly, which makes me as venal as I thought you, does it not?" I knew not what to say. "Moreover, Mr Van Cleef, pray remember that no officer may challenge the master of a ship on a point of honour – if that were permitted promotion would be too rapid and too chancy." He laughed shrilly, as though at some memory, then collected himself. "Perhaps," he added, soberly and, it seemed to me a little slyly, "I also made that *last* remark to add to your confusion, eh? Eh?"

97

Confused I was, and angry, but my head was clear enough to decide that it would be prudent to let the Captain win. The stakes he named were trifling, you see, and it seemed to me clear that he loved to win, since he prepared the ground so thoroughly. This art of winning games without cheating will one day be erected into a science, depend upon it. To the English, bloody war is a game but a game is bloody war.

In the event I had no need to let him win: the dice fell foul for me again and again, while for him they seemed anxious to please. Even he admitted that Lady Luck had smiled upon him and he agreed to doubling the small stakes so that my revenge might be sweetened. This next game, try as I might, I could not lose; everything fell right for me and he glared suspiciously at every clumsy move I made. I won. As a concession to my youth and poverty we had not been using the big doubling-die but now it was brought out.

From then on I fell upon evil times; try as I might I could make no headway against the cunning Captain and the malevolent dice. Every blot of mine was hit; I could re-enter not one of my stones from the bar; he blocked me, made primes again and again and, in the last game, shut me out utterly.

When it came to the reckoning I was shocked at how much I had lost: it took all my aplomb to crank onto my face the careless smile of the English milord who has lost a country estate on a hand of écarté.

"You play a capital game of backgammon, Mr Van Cleef," he said, clapping the board shut. "I trust you will indulge me in this innocent pastime again. And here, I fancy, is my dear spouse, refreshed with such innocent dissipations as the town of Bonchurch has had to offer." Sure enough, Blanche entered, throwing off her boat-cloak, smoothing her rumpled hair and astonishing me with a smile so unguardedly amorous, yet so enigmatic, that I stumbled as I rose, then stumbled worse over my polite goodnights.

"Yes," said Peter, as we tumbled into our bunks, "there was a little something of a subscription ball and a dice-raffle – it was quite diverting after ship-board life but the women, oh, burst me, the women, they were like so many poll-parrots swathed in last year's organdie. A sorry sight. No, I didn't dance with Mrs Knatchbull; indeed, I don't remember seeing her after the first few minutes. I have the impression that Lubbock carried her off to call on some friends in Ventnor, just down the coast."

"Goodnight," I said. He sat up.

"Have I said something to vex you?"

"Of course not, Peter. Goodnight."

"Goodnight."

If the wind in the English channel veers far enough to the west you may be sure that it will back again just so soon as the barometer rises. The Second Mate told me this while I nodded sagely, for, clearly, it meant something. What happened in the event was that the rain stopped the next day, the wind changed from the SW to the S and then to the SSE and soon we were battering our way down-Channel, close-hauled on the larboard tack, the sails booming and rigging screaming and sheets of spray knifing across the deck. It seemed a frightful storm to me, a very act of God; I did not want to drown like a rat in my cabin, I fled out. From the Second's cabin, next door, came a noise of snoring – should I rouse him and give him time to make his peace with his Maker? The crash of a sea hitting our side made me selfish: I rushed on deck, looking wildly about me, threaded my way between thinly-clad sailors who, all oblivous of their peril, were heaving at various ropes, chanting strange words as they stamped the deck with their bare feet; and after many a drenching with spray fetched up in the shelter of the galley. Inside, the doctor was fisting out great lumps of salt pork from a keg and roughly slicing them into a pan full of frying onions. He was braced against the side or bulwark of his galley and deftly tilting the pan each time it threatened to spill over, singing a deep-voiced and barbarous song.

He rolled a kindly yellow eyeball at me.

"Hot roll in the oven, Mr Cleef, sah. Only jess the one, *if* yo please; rest's fo' the Captain's table – Maz Lubbock's supping in de Cabin tonight."

This gave me two other things to think about beside a watery grave: Lubbock and a hot roll. Unwilling to offend the Doctor, I fished one out, dancing it between my fingers until I could split it open. As I did so the Doctor reached over and spooned some hot onion and pork gravy onto it; I clapped the roll together and, feeling like a schoolboy, crept out of the galley and braved the wild winds and the weather-oh until I was back in the cabin. Peter was there, towelling his naked body, some dry clothes ready beside him, the soaked ones dripping from a piece of cod-line he had rigged from the edge of my bunk to a nail in the bulkhead.

"How uncommonly thoughtful of you, my dear chap," he said, twitching the roll from my fingers, "you are clearly learning the ways of the sea, for you know enough to greet a mess-mate coming off watch with a bite of something hot and tasty." I did not rob him of his illusions; I fumbled in my tin box for a Thin Captain's biscuit to gnaw while I asked him whether our frail barque would survive the dreadful tempest. He spluttered a little: I believe that, had his mouth not been full of hot bread crammed with fried onions and delicious pork gravy, he would have laughed.

"I think," he said gravely, having swallowed the last exquisite morsel and pulled on a fresh pair of drawers, "I *think* that we have ridden out this particular Act of God. Indeed, for some twenty or thirty hours we may have little more than a fresh wind until we sight Ushant."

"Ushant?" I quavered. "What is that? I supposed that we were bound for the Indies and the China Coast. Why are we going to this Ushant?"

"We are not going there, Karli, we are looking for it. So soon as we see it we shall know where we are and shall leave it, God willing, on our port quarter. It is merely a headland which we must weather, d'you see."

"Ah," I said in an intelligent way.

"After Ushant we shall drive sou'west across the skirts of the Bay, of course."

"Of course, Peter. This Bay is . . .?"

"Biscay," he said solemnly. "Biscay. The weather there is often calm, mild and a joy to sailors."

"Capital!" I cried.

"But never at this time of the year," he went on. "At just this season the seas are as high as mountains, the winds seem the bitter enemies of man and many a tall ship has sunk without trace, dragging all hands down with her to Davy Jones's Locker."

"But, surely . . ." I began.

"Yes, surely, our little ship is well-found, well-officered and well-manned: we shall probably cross Biscay with the loss of but a few of us – and we can replace the spars which will be carried away with a few weeks of labour."

"I see," I said nonchalantly, fumbling in the tin box for another Thin Captain's. My voice was perfectly steady.

"That is, of course, unless we fall in with the Portuguese sardinho-fishers," he said.

"And what might they be?" I asked, my voice still steady. He lowered his voice, leaned towards me, his eyes wide.

"*Fiends incarnate!*" he whispered. "Promise me, Karli, that you will put a bullet in my head rather than let me fall into the hands of those fiends!"

"I promise," I quavered, a fragment of Thin Captain's falling from my nerveless lips. He burst into laughter and staggered about the floor, incapacitated by mirth. Slowly I realised that this had been an English joke. I retrieved the piece of biscuit and munched it sternly. When Peter had recovered he saw my expression and was at once contrite, for he had a kindly nature, except in dealings with his own heart and health.

"Forgive me, Karli," he cried, "we sailors reckon that we have a right to tweak the tails of landsmen: It helps us to endure our hardships, don't you see, and it helps you to come to terms with the sea."

"Of course," I said stiffly. We *Sephardim* are proud people, you remember, we do not carney like the base *Ashkenazim* of the East. For my part, I have always been a supple man and slow to take offence, but I do not care to be made ridiculous. Except when I have chosen that rôle. There was a long silence, then Peter slipped out of the cabin. I remained standing up, anger and something else taking the place of my fear. My shoulders were braced against the edge of the upper bunk, for the ship was leaning over in that direction and was also pitching, rolling and yawing erratically. I no longer cared. A tear formed in my right eye; the room was smoky from the slush-lamp. I wiped it away with a corner of the blanket. I began to think of my mother, God knows why, and found that I needed the corner of the blanket again.

Peter came in, kicked the door shut and showed me the two hot rolls he had brought. They smelt ravishing. He proffered one but, like a fool, I jerked my head away and gazed in an absurd and dignified fashion at the ceiling.

"Karli," said Peter, "I had to give the Doctor a shilling for these. Is it so hard to take one from your mess-mate, who meant no harm?" It became clear to me that I was being what an Englishman would call a silly ass. I took a roll with mumbled thanks and bit into its hot, crusty edge gratefully. My face I still kept turned away from him, for I did not wish him to see the traces of tears upon it; he might not have realised that they were caused by the smoke from the lamp. He said nothing more, he was that rare kind of man who knows when to keep his mouth shut.

CHAPTER EIGHT

What I found remarkable about the English Channel as we tacked lustily down it towards the fabled lights of Ushant, was that it was by no means a waste of cruel waters: it was more like the Strand on a warm Saturday night. Every kind of craft was running eastward or clawing westward as though the life of England depended upon them: wallowing colliers; big, fat, important Indiamen; slovenly hoys from Cornwall dripping China Clay; Breton crabbers; smacks and hovellers without number; the entire Brixham trawler fleet, hove-to and dancing on the green waves; a dangerous, rakish Excise cutter slashing along on some desperate errand and, a sight I would give a hundred pounds to see again, the Channel Fleet majestically making its way to Spithead in line astern under all plain sail. The Second explained to me that the snowy whiteness of the sails was because, on entering the Channel, the old, brown sails would have been taken down and the best suits bent onto the yards. As I watched, entranced, a stream of signal flags rose to the main-truck of the flagship and, like magic, her yards swung – you could hear the rattling boom of the canvas from our distance of eight hundred yards – and she went about on the other tack, followed, with terrifying precision, by each ship in her wake: I swear that the stretch of water on which they went about, one after the other, was no greater than a tennis-court. That was, I think, the moment at which I stopped laughing at the English.

I had another lesson to learn, however. As we came abreast of the flagship our Captain Knatchbull grunted orders to the First Mate about dipping our ensign.

"To the flagship, Sir?"

"To each ship in turn, Mister."

"Aye aye, Sir."

I blushed with shame at this silly impertinence, for we were, surely, but a common trading vessel and these lordly ships the might of the British Queen. My blushes, however, turned to a blush at my own ignorance and, yes, a flush of pleasure, as the flagship's ensign dipped gravely to us in return, followed by the same civility from each man of war as she came abreast. Our men cheered heartily, swarming up the ratlines and waving hats and kerchiefs, but our Captain stalked to the other side and gazed fixedly at the coast. He was, I suppose, regretting something, as every sensible man must from time to time.

Hour upon hour I watched, entranced, the changing pageant of this English Channel, asking a hundred questions of anyone who could pause and explain to me. Some of the more spanking merchant-craft had, like the Royal ships, already bent on their best suits of sails, all snowy-white, but most were still under working canvas, brown and weathered, patches and discoloration telling wordless tales of thousands upon thousands of perilous sea-miles. The Second Mate pointed out to me, in one of his rare moments of fellowship, a particularly foul-seeming craft, its sails of an inexplicable filthiness. He explained that it was a whaler, wallowing back from the furthest Southern seas, and that the greasy grime was from the smoke of the "trying-out" fires which rendered down the blubber from the great beasts.

"A horrid trade, young man," he said in his lugubrious way. "Permit an older man to give you a word of advice. If ever you fall in with a whaler's man, buy him a pot of beer but quit his company as soon as you safely can. He will be fearfully strong, easily roused to anger and possessed of a long, sharp knife. Eschew his company; he will not be sane. These words of mine are worth a guinea a box." With that he turned away moodily. He was a strange man, not one of whom one could make a boon-companion. He was unflagging at his duties. I think that, when not on watch, he either slept or wept. Perhaps both. Certainly, I never saw him eat or smile.

The doctor respected him, which was strangely reassuring.

The lights of Ushant, when Peter dragged me out of my bunk to admire them, seemed no great thing – merely a distant twinkle on our port bow. The beauty of them, it seemed, the thing to be

104

admired, was that we had sighted them at just the time the Captain had predicted and at just such a distance as enabled us to "weather them with plenty of sea-room" as Peter lucidly put it. After an hour or so – but it seemed longer – they were on our beam and, finally, they were but a remote glimmer on our quarter. We did not tack to port for, I was told, that would have driven us deep into the dreaded Biscay Bay itself. (I did not complain: I had no especial longing to tack to port and would have had less had I known what the phrase meant.)

We braced our yards so that we were sailing as close to the wind as our yare little ship could stand, every scrap of canvas and cordage and timber booming and shrieking and groaning as though intent on frightening the very guts out of me. Since there seemed to be little I could do to help, I retired to my bunk with an air of philosophical detachment. Biscay held no terrors for me: I was *proud*. There was some small difficulty attached to staying in my bunk because of the ship's erratic and wanton motions: resourcefully, I fished out the absurd slabs of woollen underclothing from my chest and wedged them in such fashion that I could no longer fall out. I slept well.

In the dawn I was awakened by a curious dream in which I had been standing on my head. When I came to my senses I found that I was indeed doing so, although still flat on my back. My head was pressed firmly against the head-board of my bunk, taking the whole weight of my body. I realised that the ship was standing on its nose and that my last hour had come. Before I could decide what to do I found myself standing almost upright on the footboard of the bunk, although still flat upon my back. The ship was now, quite clearly, sitting on its stern. I was not to be seen at a disadvantage again and, in a few minutes, when Peter slid into the cabin, I was fully clothed and as nonchalant as any salted Jack Tar.

"Are we sinking yet?" I asked nonchalantly.

"Not yet," he replied. "But have you heard of mountainous waves? And dismissed them as poetic extravagance?"

"Of course."

"Then come on deck; I have a treat for you." At his suggestion I forced my way into some stiff and crackling yellow oilskins before venturing out. I felt absurd in these but so soon as I had, with Peter's help, fought my way like a drunken man onto deck, I was glad of them for the wind kicked me in the face, green water smashed at me from the whole length of the ship, compressed me against the bulwark of the quarter-deck and so overwhelmed me with its cold, fierce lust that I was ready to surrender my life. Peter had a firm grip of the left arm of my oilskins; he dragged me up and across the heeling deck to the weather side and fastened each of my hands around the rail. Then he took my head and rotated it towards the right, so that I was staring forrard.

My fingers clenched into the rail so hard that they must have scarred it: a mountain of a wave – I mean a mountain, there was no poetic licence about it – was reared dead ahead of us and our absurd little ship was aiming its bowsprit straight into the scend of it. It was no moment for terror: our extinction was inevitable. I watched as though mesmerised. Up and up went our bows until Peter and I were bent almost level with the deck and still the peak of the glassy green mountain was high above us. I prepared in my mind a few suitable words of gratitude and farewell to say to Peter but, before I could speak, I heard a great roar from the Captain, behind and above us on the quarter-deck.

"Mr Lubbock!" he bellowed, "*Mister*, I say! Your watch is idling; the lee-braces are as slack as a whore's stays. When your men have done picking their noses, pray get them to work or they'll suffer a fine of a shilling each. Yes, a *shilling* I say!"

I gazed aghast at Peter for, clearly, Captain Knatchbull was insane. Peter pursed his lips in a vexed way and, cupping his mouth, shouted in my ear "I know what you are thinking. A shilling *is* a little severe: the men were only sheltering in the lee of the main-mast bitts and yarning to pass the time away because there was no work on hand you see: it was Lubbock's fault that he did not keep them busy."

My gape of incomprehension was ill-timed for we had just then fought our way to the very top of the fearful mountain of water and its crest broke over us, sending a hundred tons of "green" the length of our deck, much of which I swallowed. When I had exuded it I glanced at Peter. His face was unnaturally straight and expressionless. Against the evidence of my senses I came to realise that these unspeakable demonstrations of Nature's violence were neither rare nor considered perilous by those who went down to the sea in ships. We were, at that moment, pitching down the further slope of the watery mountain at such a rate and such an angle that it took all my manhood to speak casually.

"Do you have the watch, Peter?" I asked.

"No, not yet."

106

"Then why are you here?"

"Fresh air, my boy, fresh air! Just fill your lungs, isn't it splendid? Many an invalid would give a fortune for such stuff."

I believe he said something else but it was smothered by another monstrous surge of water, bidding fair to sweep us overside. I noticed that he unobtrusively kept a firm grip of my oilskins: I appreciated this although I said nothing.

"Karli," he said.

"Yes?"

"I have to speak seriously to you."

"Yes, Peter?"

"We may never have the opportunity to speak in privacy again."

"I understand," I said fervently.

"D'you see, we shall soon be entering the Tropics, where the Lord's writ doesn't run, where the stars take on unfamiliar patterns and men can turn into beasts overnight. You will take my word for these things, will you not?"

"Indeed I shall, Peter," I quavered.

"Now, more to the point, these strange Tropic manifestations work equally upon cooked meat." He laid a friendly arm upon my shoulder. "What I am trying to say, my dear chap, is that the galley fire has been out for ten hours and that there will be but short commons for breakfast. You, however, have not one or two but, so you tell me, three salt ox-tongues in your tin shirt-box. Do you not think that you should broach one this morning, before the sands of time run out for us both?"

I boggled at this: I could not understand its relevance to our perilous state. His arm remained upon my shoulder in an avuncular fashion.

"First," he continued, "a slice or two of delicious cold tongue will do you a power of good, d'you see. Second, to break out one of your delicious cold tongues and share it with your mess-mate would be a generous, comradely action. Third, since we are about to sink into the cold abyss of the sea . . ."

"Oh, shut up," I said. "You are pulling my leg because I am but a poor foreigner. You are a five-letter man, Peter."

"Four," he said, diffidently.

"I meant four. And I happen to know that you have some sweet pickles in your dunnage . . ."

"True!" he cried happily. "What's more, I have the crusty bottom of a loaf inside my shirt, still hot from the galley, and, under my bunk, unless unscrupulous people have purloined them, there is a crock of butter and a pot of mustard."

"Then what the damnation are we standing here for, arguing and quaking with cold and wet?"

"Hold on to me Karli; I shall lead the way."

No one, in the face of Peter's good humour and careless courage, could have been so base as to fear the elements. At every instant there was sure evidence – at least, so it seemed to me – that our little craft – it seemed *very* little now amidst those monstrous seas – had not the least chance of living through the storm but I was shamed out of all cowardice by Peter's pleasant teasing whenever he ducked into the cabin for dry clothes and by the child-like way he fell asleep between watches. Indeed, the very fact that he *had* spells between watches at all was a sort of comfort: with the ship being shaken about like dice in a cup to the incessant bellowing of the gale and the crash of seas I should have thought that every able officer and man would have been on deck, shouting useful orders or pulling at ropes or making promises to his Maker. That men could be spared from the horrors of the deck and that, when so spared, they could fold their hands in sleep was to me both a marvel and a re-assurance.

Clearly, such weather could not continue: there was not enough wind on the globe nor enough rain in the firmament to sustain such savagery for many hours. I was wrong; the fury continued unabated until even I lost my fear of it and contrived to wash and shave and shift my under-linen, toppling about the cabin like a drunken man. Little Orace staggered in manfully from time to time, his face drawn and green, bearing a kid of cold food (for of course the galley fire was still dowsed) and taking away my clothes for washing. His courage helped to make an Englishman of me for the time being: it was not so much that I was loath to disgrace myself in front of him, more that I did not wish to make him unhappy at having an unworthy master. What irrational people we English are, to be sure. Perhaps you, who were born here, have not observed this but to me, born amongst the sensible Dutch canals, it is sharply apparent.

Our skirting of the Bay took an inordinate time because, as I have said, we durst not go about on the port tack and were constrained to sail close-hauled – the yards braced up, the sheets well home and the bowlines bowsed down so taut that they squealed. (This last, Peter explained, was to stop the sails shivering. I was too proud to ask him for a similar remedy for me.)

After an eternity – perhaps seventy-two hours – I awoke one morning to find that the ship was only rolling and yawing in a way which I might have thought alarming a week before but which was now no more than pleasantly lulling.

"Come along, Karli!" cried Peter, his eyes red and squinting with fatigue, "we are weathering Finisterre, and a deuced fine landfall the Captain has made, I must say, although a little close for comfort – a mere couple of cables from the breakers."

I closed my eyes.

"Tell me when we are clear of these breakers," I said. "It seems to me that the perils of the sea do not improve upon acquaintance. This Finisterre is just another Ushant, is it not?"

"Yes, Karli. But in Spain. It is of little interest, I agree."

"Good," I said.

"Of course," he added, "when I call you again, after we are clear of the breakers, there will be no breakfast left. The Doctor has had the galley fire alight for two hours now and he will be disappointed that you would not try his kedgeree: he prides himself upon it. But it is only a savoury mess of rice and little fragments of smoked haddock and onions and such stuff, made aromatic with his kari-sauce such as is famed all over the seven seas . . ."

"Peter, your blandishments do not move me at all. I am not one of those who live for their bellies."

"No, Karli."

"On the other hand, it is important that I should not affront the Doctor, wouldn't you say?"

"Yes, Karli."

"Then I shall make the sacrifice and pretend to own an appetite. For his sake and yours."

"What a splendid chap you are, to be sure."

I threw a book at him and, while I was laughing, he popped a slippery cake of soap into my open mouth.

Kedgeree is very good. I reserved some for later on in the morning, to ascertain whether it is also good when cold.

It is also very good when cold.

Venturing upon deck in the mid-morning, to take the air and aid digestion, I encountered the First Mate, Lubbock.

"Good morning, Mister," I cried airily. He stepped very close to me, I could smell the rank sweat of him.

"Only a Captain calls a First Officer 'Mister'," he snarled. "Nasty little snot-nosed lubbers of supercargoes call me 'Sir' or by the great horned toad I chew them up and spit out their gristly bits – if any."

I had a decision to make. With an effort I met his eyes; studied the gravy-coloured whites of them.

"Thankyou, Mr Lubbock," I said at last. "It is a fine morning, is it not?" I was ready to jump over the side if necessary, but I do not think that he recognised this. He, too, made a decision and an effort; decided to be jocular.

"Well," he said, "bully for you to make the deck: thought the sea-sickness had turned you clear inside-out; haven't heard the dad-blamed ship's bell for days on account of your retching and puking." I let that pass; it might have been an American sort of joke. Moreover, it became necessary for him at just that moment to rave and bellow at a number of seamen who were heaving at a fall – which is a kind of a rope – so I had ample time to prepare a rejoinder. He turned towards me again, affecting surprise to see me still there.

"Where are we?" I asked civilly, "Mr Lubbock?" He glared at first, then studied me intently. His small brain, I think, was puzzling out what to say to me. In the end, what he decided to say was "We are scudding south along the coast of Portugal, *Mister* Van Cleef. Jest as soon as the wind backs a little more we'll likely lay a course for the Grand Canary. That's an island, Mr Van Cleef; off the coast of Africky – belongs to the Portu-geeses." He broke off to roar dirty words at a small gang of seamen who were trying to snub a little more of a brace: they did not seem to mind, nor indeed to pay much attention, for they were intent upon their work and had ears only for their boatswain, a cheery fellow who knew just how much they could do and would press them no further.

"Thankyou, Sir," I said, for I was curious as to what he would think of this gratuitous form of address. He glared at me suspiciously: I gazed back amicably.

"You're welcome," he said, turning on his heel.

The weather ameliorated: before I was prepared for it we were entering the skirts of the Tropics; each hour of southward sailing seemed to call for the shedding of another article of clothing. Had it not been for the irksome presence of Lubbock, my worries about the Captain's sanity, and the fretful lust which Blanche's occasional appearances evoked in me, I swear I would have been as happy a man as my kind, careless, poxy Peter Stevenage. Only thrice a day did my horizons clear, for the Doctor's skill and invention did not abate: each succeeding meal was a new, often bizarre, delight and, in the interims, one could always be sure that there was a "tabnab" to be had in the galley for any poor, perished, half-drowned seaman or any supernumerary officer who had had the foresight to give the Doctor a half-sovereign. These "tabnabs" were little gullet-tickling confections which the Doctor threw together when he was doing nothing else, for it was not in his nature to refrain from cooking, it was his very life, nor could he bear to waste any little oddments of food. Furthermore, he was full of concern and compassion for us all, ever concerned to make us fat and contented. He was, in a way, somewhat like my mother. My favourite "tabnab" was, without question, a little fried potato-cake with a morsel of kari'd mutton inside or perhaps a tasty scrap of cod's sound. Sometimes, too, he would fill one's pocket with small, folded-over pieces of pastry, filled with all manner of things, so that, munching at random, one might make a surprising, Lilliputian luncheon of marmalade, then chicken, then apple and finally fish: each course but a mouthful, each mouthful a delightful shock to the palate. Although I have never allowed myself to become preoccupied with food and drink, I must confess that the Doctor's ministrations helped me to while away the time and forget the perils of the deep.

Meanwhile, the weather became more and more intent to please and light airs wafted us southward towards the fabled Grand Canary. Soon the sailor-folk had cast off their coarse weather-proof attire and had donned duck trowsers and straw hats, whilst we officers had our servants press our linen unmentionables and soon we revelled in the coolness of sea-island cotton shirts. Life became delicious except for those wretches who lusted after women.

CHAPTER NINE

∗∘∗

Again it was Sunday – how far apart the Sundays seem to those of us in peril on the sea – and the Captain conducted Divine Service as though he were chewing something unpleasant. His own, private religious notions comprised some sort of hysterical mysticism but I never quite understood what they were, although he made it clear that there was no place in them for the Established Church of England, which he called "a shabby, money-grubbing conspiracy against the layman". He had some personal agreement with God which was not clear to me. Blanche was constrained by him to attend Service, always in a light and seductive dress, "so as to give," the Captain said, "a bad example and to keep the ship's people's minds off the damned, blasphemous mummery."

After the service he read, in a high, clear voice, the Ship's Articles and then – strangely – the Articles of War, as though he were still in command of a Queen's Ship. This was one of his little eccentricities, I thought, but I learned later that every before-the-mast sailor had gladly signed a chit stating that he would be bound by man-o'war's rules – which included flogging for breaches of discipline – and that this was not uncommon in East Indiamen and crack China clippers. At that time, however, my blood ran cold as he read out these Articles, for they listed countless offences and the condign punishments attached to them: each paragraph seemed to end with the words ". . . death or such lesser punishment . . ." but the men appeared to be asleep on their feet in the drugging sunshine, their half-closed eyes furtively fixed on the charming effect of the sunbeams piercing through Blanche's clothes. She was not in the habit of standing demurely, her feet together.

When the ritual was finished and Blanche had disappeared into her cabin, the men ran back to the forecastle laughing and chattering like children released from school. One man from each mess was soon at the galley door to fill a bucket with the boiling water which the Doctor had readied; piggins were streamed overside on lines to raise sea-water and soon the ratlines were gay with the men's laundry-work, for sailors are cleanly folk when given the opportunity: a dirty seaman soon becomes infested with vermin and will be much persecuted by his mates. At sea, moreover, there is no telling when the next chance to wash – still less to dry – one's clothes will arrive, and a seasoned sailor loses no opportunity to fill his chest with clean, dry slops. Only those who have lived and worked and slept in sea-soaked clothes for ten days at a time can know what exquisite pleasure there is to be had from a clean, dry shirt and drawers. Later in the voyage, when the weather had been unremittingly foul and there was not a dry clout in the forecastle, the ever-kindly Doctor would often contrive to find room in his crowded galley to dry at least a strip of old cotton-goods for those who were courteous or generous towards him: these strips they would wrap about their private parts before going on watch so that at least those sensitive organs escaped, for a little while, the almost unendurable chill and chafing.

It was understood in those days that any women on board a ship would keep to their quarters after Service of a Sunday, so that the men might strip to the buff and, having washed every stitch they owned, romp naked in the sunshine. Peter and I strolled through the throng, exchanging genial and cheery words with the men. Some of these had their own little business concerns: one resourceful fellow, for instance, known to all as "Lousy", had a charcoal-filled tailor's ironing-goose which, for a trifling sum in coin or grog, he would run along the seams of any shirt or pair of drawers suspected by its owner of harbouring lice. Only this treatment, Peter assured me, would extirpate these small and pestilent inquilines.

Another, humbler practitioner had for his stock-in-trade only a piece of "pusser's green", which is a coarse yellow soap sold by purser. His practice was, having exacted a modest fee, to scrutinise his client from the soles to the scalp, dabbing deftly at fleas and other small deer. Each time he caught one he would carry the soap to his mouth, kill the flea or bed-bug with his teeth and, at the same time, re-moisten the soap with a flick of his tongue. The men did not much despise him, for it was a useful art and he was skilful at it.

Orace was in the thick of things, scrubbing away with the best of them and from time to time fending off the clumsy advances of a sexual pervert. The pervert would not, in fact, be allowed to corrupt him, Peter assured me, because Orace was liked by the crew for his sunny nature.

The sexual society of a ship's company was, you see, a delicate and tolerant arrangement because all experienced seamen knew that to live together in a forecastle for perhaps three long years calls for a spirit of live-and-let-live, so long as the eccentric's private habits do not interfere with those of his mates, with the safe working of the ship and, above all, with their right to sleep undisturbed. Thus, the few sodomites and catamites aboard were soon recognised and tolerated so long as they kept within their own circle, did not offend others and did not shirk their work. Onanism was as necessary as going to "the head" and had only to be conducted silently if others were trying to sleep. ("When I'm at home, my wife is my right hand," Bully Lubbock once said to me in his coarse fashion; "when I'm at sea my right hand is my wife.") Then, during a long spell between ports, a full-blooded fellow of normal tastes might well exchange a sodomitic practice with a chum, rather than go out of his mind. This has given rise to the British saying "any port in a storm, matey".

None of this, however, is to be taken as suggesting that ships – the *John Coram* in particular – were seething with animal lust. On the contrary, a good taut ship kept the men so cheerfully busy that there was neither the time nor the vitality to spare upon such trivia. It was the practice to see that the crew went to their hammocks so drugged with out-of-doors work and indigestible food that all they craved was sleep. A truly tired man, his muscles twitching with toil, his mind relaxing from perilous hours spent fighting sail-cloth in the dark, higher than a house on an icy yard and, now, his belly distended with hot burgoo or lobscouse, why, such a man wants no silken bosom to caress, he aches only for the ineffable delight of his coarse pillow and no other orgasm than that of blessed unconsciousness.

The effect is much the same with compulsory games in the English public schools, which is why they are famous for their lack of sodomy.

"Now then, my lads!" cried Peter suddenly, "all hands to skylark! Who'll be King Arthur?"

"King Arthur", it seemed, was a game much relished by these simple tarry-breeks. The one named to be King was soused and drenched with laundry-water by his fellows until he could contrive to make one of his persecutors laugh, whereupon he who had laughed became King in turn, and was, in turn, soused. The first to be picked was a toothless old wag who entered merrily into the sport, capering about the deck in the drollest way as he evaded the buckets of water. Cornered against the hen-coops lashed to the rail, he reached in and plucked a rooster's feather, which he stuck between the cheeks of his bottom. He then strutted about, his neck jerking back and forth in the very manner of a cockerel, crowing shrilly until one of the lads was forced to guffaw and was duly made King. This new king, who was possessed of an inordinately long, thin member, performed so many antics with it that he soon "got his laugh" and gave place to another. So the sport went on. I believe I have said before that I shall never understand the English, they are a race apart, a race apart.

Wonderfully savoury smells were drifting from the galley and after a dangerous romp through the rigging – which seemed to delight them although they took the same risks for pay every day and night of their lives – they put on clothes and soon the duty-man of each mess reported to the cook with a great mess-kid. That day's dinner was the Doctor's famous Kentucky Burgoo, invented by a Colonel in Kentucky long ago, made of unimaginable things. I tried a tin platter of it and found it very good indeed. It became my favourite and I still treasure the recipe, which I shall write out at the end of this book if I live so long.

While the men ate their dinner we officers took tea with Blanche. We were but a small company for Lubbock scorned such "poodle-faking", the Second had the watch and the Captain was "busy with his charts" – we could hear him snoring in the inner sleeping-cabin. Peter left the room for a moment to fetch a book of verses which Blanche pretended to want.

"Blanche," I said.

"You are to call me 'Mrs Knatchbull'."

"Blanche, you were watching the sailormen romping naked a little while ago, were you not?"

"How *dare* you?" she whispered furiously.

I merely smiled.

"How do you know?" she asked.

I continued to smile.

"Well," she murmured, "if you had been me and they were girls, would you not have watched?"

I nodded vehemently.

"Well, then. But I asked you how you knew."

"I did not know, but I know *you*, Blanche." She blushed, furious again, or pretending to be so.

"Oh no you do not, Sir! Nor shall you, if that is what you think!"

"Yes I do – and shall," I said laconically. She marched up so close to me that her breasts nearly touched my shirt; glared at me for a moment, then kicked me very hard just above the ankle. I smiled.

"What is the name of the coarse seaman with the long, absurd, ah, thing?" she asked.

"I do not know. Let us ask Lord Stevenage when he returns."

"I hate you."

Dinner for us officers, later that day, was sea pie. It is quite delicious. The proper sort, such as we had, was known as a "three-decker" because it was made of layers of salt junk (pork or beef), vegetables and fish, each separated by its own pie-crust. Thus one could deal with it *seriatim* as a primitive meal of three courses or, if one was a connoisseur and the pie made by a reliable cook, one could cut through all the strata and have all three things delightfully mingled upon one's plate and palate. Each of the crusts, too, had its own peculiar flavour; the pungency of that which separated the fish from the meat was particularly prized although it tasted a little rank on first acquaintance.

("Junk", I should explain, really meant old ropes and such stuff so hardened with salt and tar that it was cut into lengths and sold – or saved – for picking into oakum, with which ships' seams were caulked. Ships would often carry a quantity of it in the lazaretto to give occupation for prisoners and idle hands generally. This is why "marine-stores", which dealt in such redundant things, came to be called "junk-shops" – and why "junk-shop" has come to be a contemptuous term for an establishment purveying fine antique porcelains. Salt pork, towards the end of its long life in the barrel, develops a curious appearance and texture which irresistibly reminds one of this pensioned-off cable: hence the opprobrious but affectionate name "salt junk". "Irish Horse" and "King's Own" were other names which do not need explanation, I think.)

After the sea-pie we were brought duff, for it was Sunday. The men, too, had been given duff – "dog in a blanket" they called it or, if without currants, "dog's vomit" – and although it was but a dark heavy mess of flour and beef-fat boiled in the tail of a shirt they prized it greatly, for it was their Sabbath privilege. Indeed, when anointed with a syrup made of hot water and molasses it served very well to fill up the chinks of a healthy belly, especially after taking vigorous exercise.

That night, after reading a few pages of print, Peter and I agreed to take our bedding out onto the deck, for the night was warm and seductive. We settled by the taffrail, exactly at the end of the "lubber-line" or fore-and-aft axis of the ship, for there the rolling motion is least and so digestion least disturbed. I lay on my back, wondering at the sky.

It is hard to explain how different the sky is in the Tropics at night: it is never black but a kind of rich, velvet blue, like the ground-colour of a fine Ming jar, and the stars are not cold and remote but hot, fat and within reach of an outflung hand. Until you have seen it you cannot begin to understand. The tropic sea chuckled knowingly under the ship's counter below us and, below us too, the rudder sometimes squeaked and grunted in its pintles as the quartermaster corrected his course. With a twist of the body and a straining of the neck I could see our wake streaming out behind and flashing with phosphorus, blue and green and silver fire. I was reminded of the sequined front of the gown of a plump lady singer I had once admired in Gatti's Music Hall in Villiers Street, by Charing Cross: it moved me almost to tears.

Since these pages are intended for the eyes of grandchildren of varying degrees of innocence and – now that the St Elmo's Fire of authorship is, I must confess, commencing to sear my breast – it seems to me that I must eschew describing the less genteel adventures which befell me from Finisterre to Gran Canaria, lest this relation might raise a blush upon the cheek of childish purity or, worse, cause a bookseller to feel that my work was not likely to be acceptable to Mr Mudie's Circulating Library. Suffice it to say, then, that I learned a great deal during the passage but was not able to have my will of Mrs Knatchbull, who still stoutly resisted my attempts to call her "Blanche".

Indeed, this would have been exquisitely dangerous – having my will of her, I mean – because the ship was small, as I have said, and her husband stalked incessantly about in the course of his duties and, at the most unpredictable times, would make it clear to her that she was to be ready for his husbanding in four and one half minutes. I thought I might never learn what had to be done in this four-and-one-half minute interim but you may be sure that my imagination ran riot. Yours, too, I suspect, would also have run the same riot, for she was most desirable and, by the time I am speaking of, would make a charming grimace at me when he gave her these orders in my presence. Sometimes she would raise her eyebrows a little while looking at me enigmatically. It was quite enervating.

Peter used to look at me strangely in those days, as though marvelling at my ill temper. Fortunately, there was the ever-present spiritual consolation of the Doctor's food: who can dwell upon the evanescent delights of the female body ("*sacca stercoris, sacca vermorum*") when every few hours comes fresh and fresh some new delight to gladden the belly and fortify the animal tissues? I defy anyone to lie brooding over the bosom of his Captain's wife when his own bosom is crammed with a breast of young lamb, boned and rolled and stuffed with forcemeat and rosemary.

So we sped southward; each one of us, I am sure, wrapt in his own preoccupation. I remember Las Palmas, the port of Gran Canaria, only because there I caught from a young person a tiresome little infestation which is of no interest and also because I bought a canary-bird which sang so indefatigably that I felt obliged, on my way back to the ship, to cool its ardour in sea-water. I did not mean it to die; I have felt unhappy about it ever since. It must have been frail, frail.

At some time soon after the Gran Canaria – I am not certain when, for I was preoccupied with certain formidable headaches I had acquired there, as well as the slight infestation (which the excellent mercury soap which Peter had urged me to buy proved sovereign for) – at some time after quitting this island, I say, we fell in with the Trade Winds, which enabled our Captain to set every scrap of sail and run south and a little east at a rate which pleased everyone on board who knew about these matters.

Porpoises, dolphins and other engaging monsters of the deep played about the ship, as though welcoming us to these latitudes, and flying-fish continually threw themselves upon the deck as wil-

118

ling sacrifices to the Doctor's skillet. (They are also very good baked.)

The men were happy for, with three strong watches, there was little work: an occasional trimming of the sails and snubbing of the bowlines and, apart from that, a little painting and, of course, the continual burnishing of the bright brass-work.

The officers were happy because the men were happy and there was no wary eye to be kept upon them.

The Captain was happy because we were making wonderfully fast days' runs southward, which seemed to be what his God wanted of him.

I was happy, in a way, because as the weather grew warmer Blanche chose to don ever more diaphanous and revealing garments although, in another way, I was miserable, for I had long been used to the solaces which the other sex affords and there was no opportunity to work my will upon Blanche – although there was no doubt in my mind that I would, sooner or later, do so. Indeed, each day my imaginative fervour became more inflamed and each night I imagined an even more vigorous consummation between us when the time should be ripe.

I read a great deal in Jane Austen and some of Peter's heathen authors; I found one of the latter much to my taste, a poet, Catullus, who wrote a Latin that I could construe without great difficulty. One of his lines, so apt to my feelings towards Blanche, sticks in my mind to this day:

"*Odi et amo. Excrucior*." – "I hate her; I love her. It *hurts*."

That was not, I suppose, a novel sentiment even in ancient Rome but was expressed with a concision which few writers of our day could rival.

The days, as I have said, passed pleasantly enough and indeed uneventfully except for one diverting moment when we were close to the southernmost point of the Bight of Benin and the lookout man hailed the deck with news of a ship crossing our stern at the distance of a mile. Captain Knatchbull, to my surprise, seized his spy-glass and swarmed up the ratlines like a marmoset. In a moment he was down again, shouting a string of orders. The ship went about, the White Ensign – which we had no right to fly – was run up, powder and shot were broken out and soon a ball from our long brass carronade went screaming across the bows of the long, fast-looking vessel which was now on our starboard quarter. The vessel

119

paid no heed, except to shake out a reef or two of sail; our second ball fell short. Shaken and dazed by the noise and the suddenness of it, I asked Peter what on earth the Captain was about. He gave me a blank, expressionless gaze and I realised that the Captain was within earshot.

"What I am about, Mr Van Cleef," he said grimly, "is putting the fear of the Lord of Hosts into a vile slaver. Snuff the air, Sir, pray snuff it!" I snuffed. Indeed, even from that distance a loathsome stench was on the breeze.

"Those slaves are fresh from the barracoons," the Captain rasped on, "in a week they'll be puddled in their own excrement, and you'd smell the craft from five miles."

This range was short enough for me; I made polite excuses and strolled as fast as one can stroll to the nearest rail.

"Go to the loo, Mr Van Cleef!" shouted the Captain. I paused, turned, gritting my teeth hard against the bile rising in my stomach.

"The *loo*, Karli – the loo'ard rail: never spew into the wind!" cried Peter.

Because I was – am – nimble upon my feet I contrived to reach the leeward rail in time and presently understood the seaman-like logic of their advice. (Even now you clever grandchildren smirk – I have seen you – when I use this antiquated sailorman's word "loo" for what you genteely call the "water-closet": if you were ever to piddle over the windward side of a ship in the roaring forties I think you might find that old men are not altogether foolish.)

That was the first time I was ever sick on ship-board (except, naturally, after drinking unwholesome liquor in foreign ports) and there was only one other time afterward and that, too, was not caused by the motion of the ship.

When I had quite voided my excellent luncheon into the deep –no one laughed at me; some of the most seasoned of the watch on deck seemed to be almost as revolted as I was – the black, rakish slaver was already almost hull-down, making best speed on the notorious Middle Passage to the West Indies. Quite sixty percent of the slaves, I am assured, will have survived to find interesting and useful work in the Americas and, as I write, I am informed credibly that their descendants are now often taught to read and write and may well, one day, prove to be the equals of their former owners. This seems strange but by no means impossible to one who, like me, has seen strange things in every quarter of the globe. *Respice finem*, I say, and indeed, *experto crede*.

We charged on southwards and, although my duties were light, I became as bronzed and weatherbeaten as any shellbacked sailor, for I often went on deck and gazed at my crew-mates sprawled aloft upon the yards, setting or furling sails at heights which would have induced acute vertigo in me. The ship's people seemed to grumble a great deal when made to scramble up the masts to make these adjustments to the sails – the main course weighed quite one English ton when wet and there were few of the topmen who could boast a full count of finger-nails – but the Second assured me that this grumbling habit of theirs was a natural bent, it made them happy in some curious British way. They were over-fed and under-worked, the First Mate assured me: he was sometimes at his wits' end to think how to keep them occupied with a fair wind and fine weather. It is easier nowadays in iron ships: there is always rust to be chipped off and steel masts to be scoured with sand and sacking.

Why I refer, from time to time, to "the ship's people" rather than to "the sailors" is because "sailor" has a precise meaning at sea: it means a before-the-mast man who is making at least his second long passage – on his first he was but a "landsman". During this, or a later voyage, he might or might not be raised to the degree of *"seaman"*, of which there are two grades. If a man can perform every maritime task imaginable with skill and courage and conceal his crimes from his superiors he may well attain the excellence of being rated an "ordinary seaman". If he can add to these arts the art of surviving all perils, such as storms, bucko mates, syphilis and "nose-paint" (which means cheap liquor), he may one day reach the distinction of being called "Able-Bodied". Few achieve this peak and those who do can rarely claim to own an entire able body: they are old and often deficient in fingers, toes, eyes and so forth. The sea is a hard mistress.

So you see that our "ship's people" comprised landsmen, sailors, seamen, idlers (viz., carpenters, sailmakers and the like), officers, their servants and, sometimes, a supercargo such as I then was.

I cultivated, when I could, the companionship of the horniest-handed of the seamen, for these were great treasure-chests of "yarns" (this word means lovingly-polished lies). They promised me that everything on land had its counterpart in the seas: there was sea-weed, of course, a sea-devil, sea-eagles, sea-girdles, sea-dogs (but not, they assured me, sea-*bitches*, although I knew better), sea-hogs, sea-lions, sea-jellies, sea-horses and sea-holly, sea-mews and sea-otters, sea-snakes, sea-urchins and, needless to say, the dreaded sea-serpent itself. Every one of them had talked to a man who had seen the sea-serpent; not one claimed to have seen it himself. This disclaimer, universal amongst seafaring men, is an agreed ruse to disarm incredulity, of course.

In those long, sunny days, each one so like the other that one could not tell if one were in yesterday again or no, even an attack of flatulence brought on by the Doctor's "shot-skilligolee" (dried-pease soup) was a memorable event. (For my part, I have no quarrel with flatulence: it is a harmless enough recreation, provides an admirable commentary to novels such as *Northanger Abbey*, gives no offence to oneself and little to bystanders – although Peter called me Montgolfier – and has been much praised by the American B. Franklin, who also invented tram-conductors.)

But the first great relief from the bewildering monotony of sea and sun and steady wind was when we put in for water at Delagoa Bay. It seemed that sweet water was plentiful there and cheap: later in our voyage we might well be paying £1 a ton for the stuff! Even in those days I preferred richer fluids but the men needed to drink great quantities of it. It is good, too, for shaving and washing.

Delagoa Bay is not an interesting port-of-call. I found little to see, nothing good to eat and drab girls who were yellow of complexion, also ugly and tired, tired. An enterprising youth sold me his sister for the night, vowing that she was but fourteen and a virgin. I cannot be sure that he lied about her age but her virginity was less than plausible: she accepted my courteous attentions with all the sweet, coy diffidence of a sow who has too often been taken in a wheelbarrow to the boar. I did not spend the whole night with her, although I had paid for it; she made me feel "like a piece of string in a bucket of warm water" (as the rough sailormen say) and I was anxious to get back to my bar of mercury soap.

As I made my way to my cabin I encountered Blanche: she was lightly clad and seemed to be coming from the direction of the First Mate's quarters. She smiled enigmatically at me and was gone before I could select a suitable expression for my own face. I fancy I looked shifty, simply.

"Peter," I asked gloomily as I rolled into my bunk, "is there also such a thing as a sea-cow?"

"Indeed there is; it is also known as the dugong and many legends of mermaids are based upon . . ."

"Thankyou," I said. "I only wished for a plain 'yes' or 'no'. Goodnight."

"Goodnight, Karli." He spoke no more that night. As I fell into a fretful doze I scratched the beginnings of my first gurrey-sore. To be Able-Bodied one should have one's hands and forearms pocked and pitted with these sores. You will never know what they are, and you do not care to know.

I know what you care about.

CHAPTER TEN

≈≈≈≈

Watered, provisioned with fresh fruit and disenchanted with the dreams of sweet femininity which some of us had been foolishly harbouring, we set sail again for the Cape of Good Hope where, everyone assured me, things would be better. They were mistaken. Cape Town – called the Tavern of the Seas – is full of dishonest people; many of them claim to be Dutch but their language is quite barbarous to a true Hollander, their religion is preposterous and their women are devout and fat – excepting the whores, who are smelly and fat. Many of these Boers, Afrikaaners as they call themselves, are Jews: the women of these, of course, are *chaste* and fat.

In this Town the best bargain for a lusty young man is a Griqua girl, you may depend upon it. They are astonishing, quite astonishing; it puzzles me where they can have learned such sophisticated arts of love in a community so devoted to Jehovah and fat old ladies.

Soon the rich and rare cargo of ostrich plumes and rhinoceros horns was flowing aboard and my days were much taken up with writing these things into manifests, consulting Bills of Lading and applying the blessed mercury soap whenever my duties permitted me a little leisure. To this day I never travel without a cake of such soap; it is as sovereign as Dr Collis Browne's noted Chlorodyne, which is saving so many cholera-stricken soldiers in the Transvaal today.

There came a time when the last bale of cargo had been stowed away, the last official bribed and, for me, the last acceptable Griqua girl had revealed her most exhausting *tour de force*. We weighed anchor; none too soon for the crew's health, I may say: British sailors are like animals when they see a foreign woman, animals.

124

Clearing Cape Town when bound for the East is, or was in those days, something of a dangerous proceeding, not as dramatic as rounding Cape Horn but still dangerous. Davy Jones's locker there is well-stocked with the bones of fine ships and brave men. First one must fight round a thirty-mile projection of the Cape, usually against stubbornly adverse winds, then run east past Cape Agulhas, notorious for its fiendish winds, then parallel to the country's southern shore where there is a small patch of low-lying ground between Green Point and Mouillé Point over which the fog has an evilly misleading way of clinging. A mere passenger might have thought this part of our passage merely slow and tedious but I knew Peter well by now and could see that under his ordinary air of carelessness there was now a tense preoccupation and fatigue. I noticed, too, that both he and the Second did not, at this time, take advantage of all the sleeping-times to which they were entitled – and sleep, even more than rum and dry clothes, is the sailor's most coveted treat.

Peter Stevenage was a strange and valuable man and I often blame myself for not having prized him more at that time, when my character was being formed. He had the rarest and truest sort of charm: that is, he did not exude a charm of his own but gave you the certainty, simply with a special sort of silence, that you were charming him. This is not an art which can be learned by taking thought or by studying books; it is not an art at all, it is a gift from God, if you will pardon the expression. (There was a boy at my school who had this gift. He was neither tall nor strong nor handsome; at lessons he was always just half-way up, or down, the form. At games he was reliable but did not shine. He spoke little and never harmfully, even of us few Jews in the school, but he would listen intently to anyone who spoke to him, even the masters; this was his gift. When you had finished he would say "yes" or perhaps "no" and you would go away purged and happy, like a Papist from the confessional-box. All of us in my year would cheerfully have died for him, except that he would have thought this a bizarre thing to do. He is now, without a doubt, the teller in a bank, trusted by one and all, and goes home each evening to a fat wife in a house smelling of cabbage and children's urine.)

Peter had been born with this happy gift of listening as though each word you spoke was powerful; his only other gift was that of a gentle, solemn mockery which prevented one from admiring him too much. This was, I am sure, deliberate. Only the strongest of men

125

try, when they are ripe for death, to make themselves appear valueless. Peter was strong in just such a way.

The air in the Indian Ocean, when we were fairly into it, was hot and moist and cosy as the well-pissed bed of a sleepy child. There were little, desultory airs which sometimes made our sails rattle and shake but these scarcely did more than keep the quartermaster awake at his wheel.

There came a day when our diminutive Captain was pacing up and down, glaring aloft from under his chimney-pot hat in a fashion which made the more knowing of our crew suspect that a capful of wind might be signified by the barometer and that he would presently be ordering royal studding-sails, sky-sails and all the other "flying kites" that she had room for to be sent aloft, although there was small chance that any of our rivals in the trade would have found better winds.

Fate, however, was on the side of our top-men, for at noon, just as the Captain was chewing his beard in an agony of decision, the fellow at the mast-head holla'd the deck, crying a sail "fine on the port bow". Captain Knatchbull instantly sent Peter Stevenage up the shrouds with the best spy-glass in the ship. For his part, he strolled to the starboard side, affecting to study the scend of the sea.

Two minutes later Peter was reporting: "Large Aden dhow, Sir; at about three miles. Only a scrap of sail on her and a bucket at the main-truck. Distress, Sir. No sign of life. No one at the helm, I fancy."

"Thankyou, Mr Lord Stevenage; I am well acquainted with the meaning of a bucket at the main-truck in these waters. Pray tell the steersman to set a course to close with the, ah, distressed vessel and to heave to at one cable's length from her."

I followed Peter and intercepted him after he had delivered his orders.

"Why are you smiling, Peter?" I asked.

"Wait and see. And, oh, Karli, are your pistols primed, the charges dry and so forth?"

I looked at his grave face, decided that for once he was in deadly earnest, scuttled below and saw to my pistols. In a minute, one barker at each side of my belt, I sauntered on deck and joined the Captain in his scrutiny of the waves.

"Is it the plague, do you suppose, Sir?"

"They *are* the plague, Mr Van Cleef," he answered tersely. I said no more, for his manner invited silence.

When we were hove-to every glass in the ship was trained upon the unlucky vessel. The only living being observable was a man in a turban and a gaudy, night-shirt-like robe, lashed to the mast and waving feebly to us.

"Gunner," said the captain quietly, "can you put a ball through the mast?"

"I reckon I can that, Sir."

"Then pray do so."

"Aye aye, Sir."

I gazed aghast as the gunner ambled towards the long brass Armstrong 68-pounder mounted on a pivot between the mast and bustled about it, testing the lock and handling the balls in the net until he chose one of perfect roundness. One of his mates came running up in list slippers (for he had been in the magazine, where a spark from a nailed shoe would send the whole ship to glory) carrying a stout cylindrical package. The gunner bit off a fragment of the cartridge-paper and poured some of the powder into the touch-hole. His mate rammed the rest into the barrel, then a wad, then the ball and another wad, thumping all well home.

"The ship's company will wave," said the captain. "Cheerily, now, lads!" Everyone waved in a cheery fashion to the poor wretch so near to salvation, except for me, who waved in a mystified way. The heathen waved back vigorously. The captain nodded to the gunner, who fussed a little more with his piece then snapped the lock.

When I could open my eyes again the heathen was no longer waving. This was because his head had vanished, you see. He was still tied to the stump but the rest of the mast was toppling, infinitely slowly, overside. I turned to the Captain: in my horror and agitation at his barbarous conduct I believe I was on the very point of rebuking him but, at that moment, a horrid clamour of raging screams came over the water and from behind the dhow there emerged two long boats, crammed with heathens, rowing frantically towards us. Those who were not rowing were brandishing curved swords which glistered in the sun.

"Only two boats, Sir," said the First Mate laconically.

"Then I'll have two guns run out, Mister," grunted the Captain.

"Fire at will. But destroy them before they come too close. I want no blood on my decks, you understand? See to it."

The gunner was a master of his art, a master: his first shot from the carronade was a trifle high and only killed the heathen at the steering-oar but his next took her squarely in the bows and she opened out like a cabbage ready for stuffing – and, indeed, there was no want of minced meat to add kitchen-colour to the receipt. Our fellows on the gun-deck were less fortunate, or ill-trained, for their shots missed time and again so that the other boat, at which they were shooting, was soon so close that the guns would not depress low enough to bear.

"All gun crews to practise during their watches below for the next two days," said the Captain in a disgusted voice. "Break out cold shot, if you please, Gunner."

The next instant, it seemed, the shrieking horde were against our chains and grappling-hooks were flying – some lodged on our rail. Two of our men ambled forward nursing great cannon-balls and dropped them into the bottom of the boat. It was holed, filled and sunk in a moment but not before several of the Mahometan fiends were swarming up our side. One of our sturdy fellows sawed away at the grappling-lines with his great case-knife: he took a bullet from an ancient flintlock pistol in his shoulder but the lines were severed and the heathens fell screaming into the sea. Only one succeeded in boarding us; he rushed towards the Captain and me. There was a pistol in my hand. I aimed at his heart but my hand shook so that I shot him just above the private parts; he made an intolerable noise as he squirmed in the scuppers, voiding his bowels, his bladder and his blood most copiously. I had never killed a man before. I felt no distress, only a detached interest at how ignobly a brave man dies. I realised for the first time that Blanche was beside me, her lips parted, her eyes wide, her bosom heaving rapidly.

"Fined five shillings, Mr Van Cleef," said the Captain crossly. "You heard me say I'd have no blood on my decks, did you not?"

I opened my mouth and shut it again. After all, I had saved his life, although I confess that my preoccupation had been more with my own.

"Go to your cabin, Blanche," he went on. "Be ready in four and one half minutes." He pulled out his watch.

A bored, disgusted seaman lifted my victim, still jerking and squealing, and hove him over the rail. I gazed down in horror, for the water was already boiling with sharks and other rapacious scavengers of the deep. Peter appeared beside me, put his hand on my shoulder.

"Karli, if you ever go overside in Tropic waters, pray for a shark, do. They are quick, you see. The barracoutha takes his time, goes for the titbits first, if you take my meaning. A fellow might live for half an hour with a barracoutha at him. Now, I've just to see the guns swabbed and secured then I'll join you for dinner. Fish chowder today, you are fond of fish I believe?"

I think he was trying to hearten me. I forget what I said to him.

As we traversed the Indian Ocean the breezes became ever more warm and spiced. The doctor's dishes, too, became hotter and spicier as he weaned me, not unwillingly, onto such fare. Those karis, pilaffs and tarkeeans, you see, not only disguise the odour of meat which is past its youth, they also provoke the jaded appetite in the long, languorous days and induce a wholesome, cooling sweat. How different they were from the gross Dutch food of my childhood, yet how I learned to love them! The Doctor, it was evident, grew to love me for my appreciation of his victuals and Orace was kept busy running from the galley to our cabin, carrying each day new and more bizarre confections. Peter Stevenage had a poor appetite, ruined by liquor and the pox, I suppose, but he never ceased to marvel at my adroitness with the knife and fork. He often remarked, as he passed me his scarcely-touched plate, that to watch me at the trencher was as good as a feast. I am sure that he meant this in sincerity and kindness, for there was no malice in his whole body.

Blanche, too, became warmer and spicier in the sultry air; her clothing – I observed her narrowly – was now little more than a muslin gown no less explicit than a shift. She no longer bridled when I called her "Blanche" and sometimes, when we leaned on the rail together enjoying the first cool wafts of the tropic dusk, her naked arm would rest warmly against mine and once or twice, even, I would relish the incandescence of her flank through my cotton trowsers.

I made no move, for I had decided on this as a new tactic, and I was right. She was, perhaps, piqued or perhaps she had heard about the Griqua girls in the Cape Town and thought that my lust for her had been allayed. Be that as it may, one evening as we left the rail,

Blanche, inadvertently as it were or was meant to seem, brushed her splendid teats across my arm as she bade me goodnight.

Have you ever played the game where everyone holds hands and the instigator winds the handle of an electrical generating machine, in a little mahogany box, each terminal of which is held by the two people at the open end of the circle? The effect is quite formidable. One *jumps*. The sport has gone out of fashion, I am told, because there have been occasions when young ladies have wet themselves with the surprise and alarm of it.

The effect on me of the brief brushing of Blanche's breasts against me was just such a shock, but without the wetting, thank God. There was, you see, not the soft, goose-feather sensation that you or I might have expected. Her teats were hard, hard, as though swollen.

"Are you well, Mr Van Cleef?" she asked, looking over her shoulder as she left me.

I mumbled something valiantly although my head was reeling.

"I'm so glad," she said, her eyelashes flickering modestly as her large and lovely eyes rested for an instant on a territory just below my belt. "These tropic nights are replete with evil humours, are they not, and gentlemen's clothes are so constricting. I hope you will sleep well. My husband always sleeps well but then, he is used to . . . these tropic nights, you understand." I understood.

"Good night," I said. It seemed an inadequate rejoinder but I had not been given the time to think of a better and, in any case, my mind was on lower things.

Peter was reading in the cabin. He eyed me in a friendly way.

"Are you well?" he asked.

"Uncommonly well, thankyou," I replied evenly.

"Then why are you grinding your teeth, Karli?"

The world stood still while I decided whether to strike my mess-mate and only friend or to chew on my bile and swallow it. I made the right decision.

"It is because I am hungry, Peter," I said.

"Karli," he said in a grave voice.

"Yes?"

"There is something I must say to you." I sat down.

"Yes?" I said.

"Karli, when you were out on deck communing with the, ah, spiced breezes, I made a decision."

"Yes?" I said again.

130

"Yes. You see, I have been much disturbed. The long, hard, Italian sausage which has been hanging between our bunks was preying on my mind. You said, I know, that the grocer assured you that it would travel to the Indies but what do Italian warehousemen know of the Indies? In any case, we are, to speak strictly, already in the Indies. I *fear* for that sausage, Karli. Shall we cut it?"

He had the art, you see, of distracting a preoccupied mind.

The long, halcyon days span themselves out, each one much the same as another. It became, tacitly, an understood thing that Blanche would be at the weather rail a little before the short tropic dusk gathered and that I would be there, sometimes with Peter Stevenage, sometimes alone. We talked of many things and I found that she, too, was an admirer of "Jane Austen", although in her sweet womanly simplicity she firmly believed him to have been a woman. But little ignorances of this kind only endeared her the more to me. All one can ask for in a woman is that she have a soft voice, a firm body and a pretty, empty head. (You will remark that I do not demand that she be complacent – every woman is unchaste if one applies oneself with zeal and patience to making her so. If you are tongue-tied and maladroit, do *not* attempt to practise on an ugly woman: she will know that she is but a *pis-aller* and there will be difficulties. Attempt, rather, a beautiful one, for she may well have a compassionate heart and her experience as a beauty will have taught her curiosity and, perhaps, a relish for carnality. You will understand all these matters when you are older, like me. By then, of course, it will be too late.)

She had, too, a passion for the poems of one Wordsworthy; a man of small talent who chose to write simple verses about idiot children, wayside weeds and large geographical features in the cold Northern parts of England. His work bore no relation to life but appealed to her charming, silly head and I indulged her in this matter. Sometimes I would recite to her, in Dutch, the English play *Hamlet* which I had mastered at school, but, inexplicably, she could not take it seriously. Once, when I had reached the solemn moment when the ghost says *"Omlet, Omlet, ik ben je poppa's spook . . ."* she stuffed her handkerchief in her mouth and ran to her cabin. She was strange, strange.

Once, too, First Mate Lubbock joined us, making many an ironic remark to me. I drew the subject round to Great Circle Navigation, which I had been conning in one of Peter's books. It was clear that Lubbock had but little knowledge in this and he soon made off, snorting vehemently.

I taught Blanche a few phrases in Dutch – although these did not mean what I told her they meant: it was pleasant to hear her say them unwittingly but also *disturbing*. I remember, for instance, that she mastered perfectly a sentence which she believed meant "It is a fine night, is it not: only look at the stars!" but which, in fact, meant, "Loosen my bodice, I beg you, and cover my breasts with kisses until I swoon in your arms." When she at last pronounced it perfectly, I kissed her on the cheek, saying that this was a Dutch school-master's praise. She believed this, too, and the cheek-kissing became a normal part of our lessons. Better still, and more encouraging, her accidental brushing of her breasts against me became more frequent and once my hand was in the way. She pretended not to notice. But the ship was full of eyes – there is no privacy on so small a vessel – and I durst not make more explicit overtures.

Our first landfall for many weeks was hailed with absurd pleasure by the lookout, greeted with cheers by the jaded crew and with admiration by those of the officers who understood how skilful must have been the Captain's navigation. It was the island of Minicoy, the most southerly of the Laccadivhs. The Captain gave the quartermaster a correction of his course but, just then, the lookout bawled "Deck, there! Sail three points on the port quarter, tops'ls just over the horizon. Ship-rigged, looks to me Sir."

A grim glance and a nod from the Captain and Peter was swarming up the ratlines ("the lady's ladder" we called it on the *John Coram*, for the rope steps were set kindly close together) and soon we could see him in the wide-circling crows-nest, training his glass on what was invisible to us. Then we saw him almost vaulting out of the nest – scorning the lubber-hole – and slithering down the rigging like a toy monkey.

On deck, panting from his exertions (for he was not well, you recall) he reported "Not ship-rigged, Sir. A barque. Baltimore-built, I fancy. Carrying top-gallants, royals, sky-sails. Fore-reaching on us, I'm afraid, Sir."

Usually Peter spoke, even to the Captain, in a debonair, damn-your-eyes fashion: I had never before heard him use such a timid, almost cringing, tone.

The Captain's face went white and, through his closed teeth, he said "Cattermole." I did not understand.

Peter said, diffidently, "Yes, Sir, from what I could see of her she might well be the *Martha Washington*." I still did not understand.

"Belay that course, Quartermaster," snarled the Captain, "steer nor-nor'east until I give you a true course. Mister, kindly wear ship." He stumped off to the little chart-room in his sleeping-cabin. The quartermaster's face was blank as he span the wheel, the men went uncheerily about their business of wearing ship and even Lubbock seemed to have no heart for chivvying them in his usual coarse way.

"What in the devil's name . . .?" I murmured to Peter.

"The ship astern of us," he explained in an unhappy voice, "is almost certainly the *Martha Washington*, skippered by Micah Cattermole, Captain Knatchbull's most deadly rival. He is young and fearless and, if he has had her bottom scraped, she has the legs of us by quite two knots. If she rounds Cape Comorin before us she will be in Calcutta three tides before us."

"Is that important?"

"Very. The first at the opium auctions will pick up a raft of bargains and so will have cash to spare for the better quality chests at the end of the auctions. Worse, he will be in the Canton River before us and will skim the cream of the hungry market, have his bar-silver and new teas aboard and will be refitting for the voyage home before we have dropped our hook below the Two Islands."

"I see," I said vaguely. "And this change of course which seems to be so unwelcome to the crew?"

He took a deep breath.

"You see, Karli, in the ordinary way we would have taken the safe, comfortable, Eight Degree Channel, leaving Minicoy on our port and the Maldivhs on our starboard. But, now that we are being pressed by the *Martha Washington* our –" he looked about him cautiously "– our old maniac of a Captain is going to venture the Nine Degree Channel to the north of Minicoy Island. It is most hazardous. Captain Knatchbull reckons himself the only salt-water skipper who knows its little ways." He fished out his watch. "We should be entering it just as night falls – and the wind is strengthening from the sou'west."

I did not like the sound of any of this.

"Why is he doing this, do you suppose, Peter?"

"Because young Micah Cattermole is a dashing and hare-brained young fellow who will think that where one man can go another can follow. If he can win close enough to follow our lights he may succeed but our Captain is unlikely to help him in that way."

"But . . ."

"Wait and see, Karli, and above all make no comments in the Captain's hearing – he is a little, well, irrational, in matters concerning Micah Cattermole."

The Captain emerged onto the poop and we heard him giving a more precise course to the quartermaster at the wheel, then bidding Lubbock have two reefs shaken out of our top-sails – reefs which had been made only an hour before on account of the freshing wind. One of the watch, as he scrambled aloft, made an audible sound of displeasure and Lubbock snarled at him, but without his usual fury. The wind was rising fast and ever larger waves began to chase our poop. The rigging began to whine and thrum and dusk gathered with the rapidity I had become so used to in those latitudes. Our ordinary sea-lights were lit and the Captain, to everyone's mystification, ordered an extra light to be put at the mizzen-mast-head.

"And, *comprador*," he said, "I want lamps burning in all cabins aft; see to it."

I exchanged glances with Peter. He said nothing.

Soon the Captain gave a fresh course to the helmsman and the deck was an organised riot of men bracing the sails around. The wind was now, of course, on our starboard quarter and imparting an unpleasant roll and yaw to the vessel, which nevertheless flew on at unabated speed.

Peter was sent to the fore royal yard and reported that he descried the *Martha Washington*'s lights abaft and still, he thought, fore-reaching on us. This did not seem to displease the Captain.

The First Mate hovered, as though awaiting an order.

"Shorten sail, Sir?" he said at last, in a more diffident voice than I had ever heard him use. We were now, it was clear even to me, well into the perilous channel.

The Captain glared at him evilly. "Thankyou for your advice, Mister," he whispered, "but giving advice to the Master of a vessel is not part of a First Mate's duties. Pray call all hands on deck: I'll have both bower anchors cock-a-bill and six men at the bill-boards of the sheet anchor. In exactly eight minutes I shall give orders to bring the ship up into the wind and, at precisely that moment, I'll have every light in the ship dowsed."

The First Mate gaped.

"And Mister, I'll have all these manoeuvres carried out in silence, d'ye hear?"

"Aye aye, Sir."

In just seven and one half minutes the man in the chains with the lead sang out that he had "by the mark" eight fathoms "and shoaling fast".

To me, we were in the midst of a torrent of tearing waters buffetted by fearful winds but the Captain seemed as at home as if he were in his own parlour. Every light was dowsed in an instant; the ship came up into the wind and all three great anchors roared out together, bringing the ship up into the wind with a wrench which one would have thought would jar the very masts out of her.

There was, suddenly, no sound but the smash of the waves on our bows, no sight but the phosphorescence at our bows.

"A barrel of oil from the bows," growled the Captain. In a minute the phosphorescence had gone and the crashing of the seas onto our stem became a mere schlipp-schlopp. We waited. We waited perhaps an hour, I cannot tell at this remove of time. Suddenly, like a ghost, a tall and lovely ship came storming past, like a vision. Her creaming bow-wave and the radiance of her wake were the most beautiful thing I had ever seen: it was like looking at a lovely, naked woman in the prime of her beauty.

She did not see us and soon vanished into the dark, leaving a dwindling wake of phosphorescence. Later, the Captain ordered the galley-stove to be re-lit and the lamps in cabins and forecastle; but not the great riding lights. Soon the watch below was piped but they were already on deck, muttering in groups.

In a wonderfully short time the cook had hot supper ready for the watch relieved but there was not the usual rush of mess-men to the galley. Indeed, I had to send an "idler" to find Orace before I could get my supper: he, like most of the men, was far forward, still staring into the darkness where the *Martha Washington* had sailed. I was not in the least hungry, but those in peril on the sea have a natural duty to keep up their strength, you understand. The meal was, as I recall, a "bindalooh" or sour-pork kari; very good except that the rice was over-moist. I had become a connoisseur in these matters by then.

I was lying on my bunk, meditating on the frailty of the human spirit, especially in the fair sex, when Orace rushed into the cabin without rapping and said that Lord Stevenage sent his compliments and would I join him on deck. Sighing, I struggled into a pair of trowsers and a hat (the latter was essential: the Captain insisted on his "gentlemen" saluting the quarterdeck in a proper fashion) and sought out Peter. He was in what seemed to be a heated altercation with the Captain.

"No, Mr Lord Stevenage," the Captain was growling, "I shall not weigh anchor, nor set sail. You have, I fancy, enough seamanship to know that these waters are perilous at night and I know my duty to my owners and my crew. What you think you see may or may not be the *Martha Washington*: it is just as likely to be a lure set by wreckers for our destruction. If it were the *Martha*, we could not reach her until she were burned out and in this darkness and sea we could do nothing for survivors. You have now had more explanation than I commonly give to junior officers. Pray attend to your duties. Clear the decks of the watch below, who should be getting their sleep. Write on the watch-slate that the ship is to be ready to weigh anchor and set sail at first light."

Just as he turned on his heel I heard Peter whisper something to him of which I could hear nothing except, it seemed to me, the word *"murder"*. The Captain stood still. Then he said:

"I shall make an entry in the log that I have reprimanded you, Sir."

"Aye aye, Sir," said Peter. The words were commonplace but they fell slowly from his lips like a curse, or perhaps a challenge.

The Captain ignored his insubordinate tone and turned on his heel; as he entered his cabin I heard him say "Blanche!"

"What in the name of God . . .?" I began to say.

"Go forrard, Karli, go forrard," said Peter in a choked voice.

I jostled my way to the bows through the throng of men who had been ordered below. Over on the starboard bow there was a great glow in the sky – I could not tell how far off. Peter was at my elbow although, having the watch, he should have been aft.

"That *'may or may not be'*," he said bitterly, "the *Martha Washington*. Go to bed, Karli."

"But . . ."

"*No*, Karli. Go to bed."

I stirred in my sleep at the sound of the great anchors being weighed at first light and at the thunder and rush of bare feet on the deck above me as sail was made and set. I slept again until Orace brought me my morning drink: bitter coffee sweetened only with rum, for the cow had died some days before. I huddled on some clothes and went on deck. The whole ship's company, it seemed, was staring and peering at the breakers smashing and creaming on the reef outside a low-lying island. There was nothing to see.

Then, a bellow from the look-out: "Object one point on the port bow! Piece of flotsam and what looks like a corpus, Sir!"

The Captain, who had been staring fixedly aft, received this news from the Second Mate, who had the watch. He did not look up.

"Do your duty," he said, "take in sail, lower a boat, you know what to do, you have an Extra Master's ticket, I believe." He said it as though an Extra Master's Certificate was a token for a soup-kitchen.

Within ten minutes a half-charred timber was gently swayed aboard with a shockingly charred human being adhering to it – whether lashed to it or clinging by some primal rigour it was hard to say.

The man was alive; that is to say, he was not dead. One of our fellows cried his name as "Jack Cherry of Salem!" and the man's face split in what may well have been a smile. They brought him to the break of the poop and the Captain, for he was a Christian, came to look; bent down and asked, "What ship are you from, my man?"

The charred man eyed him with his left eye – the unroasted one – then raised himself with infinite difficulty on one elbow. A horrible noise came from his chest – I thought it was the death-rattle, but he was only gathering phlegm – then he spat full in the Captain's face.

Bully Lubbock reached to the back of his belt for his rope's end "starter" but the Captain checked him with a gesture.

"You'll not lay a finger on this man!" he cried. "Have him taken to an officer's cabin and see that the doctor and the loblolly-boy give him the best of food and care, for he is a brave fellow." He reached behind him for the napkin, which his Chinese servant had ready, and wiped the mucus from his face.

"When he is well he may sign with us at one rating higher than on his – ah – last ship" (he could not name the *Martha Washington*) "or we shall put him ashore at any place he chooses between Pondi-cherry and Calcutta with five golden guineas in his pocket. See to it, Mister."

They carried the man away with the tenderness which only coarse, rough men know how to exercise towards their mates. When he had gone, I looked up and saw Blanche smiling her enigmatic smile at me. That I found disgusting.

The Captain's charity and forbearance cost him little in guineas for the man died that very evening. Next morning he was sewn up in tarpaulin with a forty-pound lump of pig-iron ballast at his foot and the sailmaker, at the end, passed the ritual last stitch through his nose, lest he were not quite dead. The Captain, despite his desperate lust for making sea-miles, had the ship hove-to and the yards cock-billed and read the Service with some colour of sincerity. The sail-maker had cobbled up a Yankee flag and the canvas parcel slid out from under it in quite the proper fashion. But the men, I noticed, were not watching the committal to the deep; their eyes were on the Captain. I looked at Peter but could not catch his eye. I looked at the Second: he looked in my direction, certainly, but his eyes were fixed on something quite one hundred miles away. I detected an uncomfortable feeling throughout the ship's company. Even the Doctor, who, being but a black man, could not attend a Christian burial – if that is what it was – lurked plainly to be seen in the entrance of his galley and his big, red lips, which I had never before seen without a grin upon them, were pursed and puckered into an expression which I could not read at all.

That evening I was loafing on the quarterdeck and trying to draw the taciturn Second into conversation.

"Why," I asked pettishly after exchanging a few commonplaces, "are my toes so sore? I have never suffered from soreness of the toes in my life."

"Sleep in socks or sea-boots," he said and crossed to the weather-rail. Baffled, I followed him.

"I confess I do not understand," I said meekly. He did not turn his head but gave me a sidelong stare with his pale eyes. He was a sidelong sort of man.

"Cockroaches," he said. "They love the hard skin on a man's feet but, after a few days at sea, you're thoroughly pedicured and must protect your feet or the little buggers will munch their way up to your ankles."

I digested this revolting fact, then, since this was almost the longest sentence I had ever heard him utter, I was emboldened to confide that I was not wholly clear about the events of the previous night. Again he gave me that pallid stare; clearly, he was deciding whether to answer me or not. Finally he said,

"Mr Van Cleef, do you know what a vigia is?"

"No," I said unhesitatingly, because this was true.

"It is a mark on a map. A Portugee word, meaning 'watch out'. The Frogs call it an *'ouvre l'oeil'*, which amounts to the same thing. It means that there's a reef or shoal or some other hazard – or at least that the master of some ship, some time, has fancied that he's seen something of the sort. Nine times out of ten it was just a dead whale or a raffle of unsunk wreckage or the sea breaking on some heavy-heeled floating spar; further south it may have been the last of a 'berg; off the West Coast of Africa just a floating island that some river has spewed out. Often as not it's just the effect of too much rum." He fell silent. I prompted him, asking why these interesting facts were connected with what I wanted to know. He heaved a deep, patient breath.

"Our Captain," he said, "has a passion for these waters we are in; his charts are a mass of pencilled-in vigias – you may have observed this morning that he was tacking about like a spaniel in a turnip-field. Captain Cattermole – the *late* Captain Cattermole we must now call him – was a dashing young man who believed in nothing but survey-proven shoals on clean charts. Also, he believed that he could follow where Captain Knatchbull led. Furthermore, as you must have noticed, Captain Knatchbull was not, in fact, leading. R.I.P."

"I have the impression," I said carefully, "that Captain Cattermole was a well-liked man . . .?" But I had pushed too far.

"Mr Van Cleef, I have the watch and must ask you to delight me with your conversation at some time when the safety and the working of the ship are not in my hands. If you wish to hear an encomium on Captain Cattermole I suggest you offer a glass of spirits to O'Casey, the red-haired top-man, who sailed with him through three voyages. His watch is below and he will have eaten by now. Indeed, that is the fellow, there, lounging with his pipe in the lee of the foremast-bitts. Goodnight."

I began to believe that our chat was at an end so I returned his goodnight and, consumed now with curiosity, I did indeed procure a tin cup of rum and strolled forrard.

The man O'Casey was an Irish and so had a great gift for speech, although some of this was not always easy to comprehend. I listened politely for a while as he extolled the beauties and virtue of a place called Tralee, then delicately raised the subject of Captain Cattermole.

"Captain Cattermole?" he said, "Captain Cattermole? A fine raparee of a man: had he but been born in Kerry he would have been perfection itself." Two fat tears rolled down his weathered cheeks. "A brave bull of a man," he went on; "when he was in port you could see the women dancing round him like coopers round a cask. When the wind broke from his splendid, God-given arse it would part the thickest of thickets and topple the tallest forest tree. Did he but belch in a genteel fashion the foundations of the poorhouse would mutter and crumble and all the old and needy would bless themselves, thanking God for such rich enjoyment. Did he but pick his teeth, why, every cur and cat for miles around would scramble to the feast, leaving their dinners. As to his coupling, when he could bring his lovely mind to it, he was like one of them great steam locomotives working off a grudge against the buffers. I had that from one of his very wives herself."

"A bigamist, then?" I asked idly.

"God save ye, no, a good Cartholic, never more than one wife at the same time at all. It's just that he was hard on wives, wasn't I telling you? It might be four he wore out or it might be five and never a child could he get out of any one of them. There's little scraggy fellers that have their cabins so full of gossoons that they'd splash out between your toes but Jack Cattermole could never get one out of a woman, bump away as he might."

"Indeed," I said in a suitable voice.

" 'Indeed' is the very two words in it," he replied.

The Irish have a wonderful command of language, wonderful. If ever they learn to read and write there will, one day, be great literature from them, mark my words.

I bade O'Casey goodnight and repaired to my cabin, there to chew reflection's solitary cud until supper-time.

CHAPTER ELEVEN

※

We rounded Cape Comorin as neatly as any seaman could wish and were soon making long slants up the Coromandel Coast under all plain sail and sometimes with royals set, accordingly as the wind veered from the east through south to the west. It was an easy, leisurely time, even for the common sailor-folk, but it was plain even to me that they no longer went about their business with their usual "cheerily-oh".

One night, when we had left Madras's lights on our port quarter and had no landfall to look for until Vizagapatam, Peter fished out from under his bunk a black, fat-bellied bottle of something called "Van Der Hum's" which he had prudently laid in at the Cape. It was too sweet for my taste but rich, *rich*; also as strong as the thighs of a Griqua girl – Peter warned me to turn my head away from my glass when lighting a cheroot, lest my breath should ignite. I was, even in those my salad days, abstemious in all things, but on that night I felt his need to be joined by a friend in becoming a little drunk, and could not deny him so small an act of amity.

"The men," I said in an off-hand fashion, when Peter had drunk quite one third of the potent bottle, "the men seem to have lost some little of their, ah, *zest*. Is it not so?"

He looked at me owlishly.

"Seamanship, Karli, is a sort of Freemasonry – are you at all familiar with the word?"

"I have heard it," I answered guardedly, for I had long ago "tried" him in a veiled way and knew that he was not of our Craft.

"Well, d'you see, Karli, although those Yankees aboard the *Martha Washington* were, in a way, our deadly rivals, nevertheless many of our people had sailed with many of theirs and there is scarcely a man aboard who has not caroused or brawled with a *Martha Washington* man in one or another port of the Seven Seas."

He paused a long while, drinking some more of the villainous Van Der Hum. I did not, for once, say anything, although I wished to tell him about my talk with the Irishman O'Casey.

"So you see, Karli, they feel that our Captain's little ruse, which lured them onto a coral reef and sent them flaming down to hell, does not seem to them a legitimate *ruse de guerre*, for there is, you see, no war in progress – only a sordid struggle for commercial advantage in selling poison to heathens. Their sullenness probably arises from a belief that our Captain is a murderous, fucking little maniac."

I thought about this carefully; slowly, too, for I had drunk my share of the Van Der Hum. At last I said, "And Peter, *is* our Captain, in fact, a murderous, fucking little maniac?"

Peter rose to his feet, stoney-faced, his eyes like ice.

"Mr Van Cleef," he said, in a thin, unpleasant voice, "I shall, since you are my mess-mate, pretend that I did not hear that question. However, I cannot promise that I shall overlook any future impertinences of the kind."

After collecting my thoughts, I too rose. I bowed, but only from the neck, as I had seen Lord Windermere bow.

"I apologise, Lord Stevenage," I said stiffly. "Pray believe that it was the wine which spoke and not I."

"Sit down, Karli, there's a good fellow. And my name's Peter. And let us kill this bottle before it kills us."

We drank – in perfect friendship. I shall never understand the English. (There was a time when I thought that I would never understand *women*, but now, after having owned and trained perhaps twenty spaniels, the female mind is an open book to me. All they ask from life is something to adore and fear: it is as simple as that. But the English *men* – no one will ever understand them, least of all their women. It is, of course, possible that there is nothing to understand and perhaps, too, that is their great strength. Who can tell?)

By the time Orace entered to put me into my nightshirt I was in the mood to throw pieces of Italian sausage at him and he stalked out, looking very English although but a bastard and small of stature. Peter and I finished the bottle and fell asleep in our clothes. He probably washed his face first, for he was English, *English*.

The last leg of our passage to Calcutta was "sailed large" for we caught the first of the hot, south-west monsoon and snored up the Coromandel Coast in great style, the sea making a pleasing hiss under our forefoot as it shored through the swell. Not a reef would the Captain allow in her sails although, when the wind stiffened at nightfall, he would sometimes reluctantly have the royals stowed.

From time to time, when no one could observe, I made something of a friend of the strange Irish O'Casey. (I say "when no one could observe" because I was, you see, an officer and he but a common seaman and, to boot, not even English, although he spoke a tongue of which many of the words seemed to be English.) His gift of language was enviable; he could hold me spellbound by the hour although I did not understand one half of what he said. Better, he had great store of mournful ballads, all evincing a terrible homesickness for his land, which is an island off the coast of England, just as England is an island off the coast of Holland. Although, whenever he had a few pounds in his pocket after a voyage, he would go to his home and lord it as long as the money lasted, he would always sing of it as though he was an eternal exile. I remember, but indistinctly, many of these sad songs; in particular one in which he vowed to cross the sea to Ireland even at the closing of his days in order to see the women in the uplands dropping praties on the gossoons making water in the bog. I did not understand this wish but it never failed to bring tears to my eyes. There will one day be an Irish Empire, you may depend upon it.

There was, in truth, little else to keep my mental faculties awake: one day of scudding through a tropical sea is much like another; one balmy, breathless tropic eve, spangled with improbably large stars, is hard to distinguish from its fellows and one hot, tossing, sleepless night spent lusting after a woman who is in bed with a Sea-Captain a few yards above one's head is only a little more hellish than the last. Having exhausted the tepid pleasures of "Jane Austen" and vainly attempted to woo sleep with the incomprehensible logic of Norie's *Seamanship*, I was at last forced to borrow a tattered copy of the Bible from the fo'c'sle.

I learned to love this book. There is no finer compendium of factual and fictional lore to be had, with the possible exception of Captain Burton's translation of the *Arabian Nights*, which is unexpurgated. I took care to eschew the more inflammatory passages, such as the Song of Solomon and certain parts of Ezekiel, but my state was such that even when trying to drug myself with the lists of the ancestors of Abraham, I found myself not so much marvelling that Nahor begat Terah but wishing that I could be relishing the begetting-act myself. Such is the magic of the written word.

Our course often took us within sight of shore but this was rarely more than a smudge on the horizon to port, although sometimes we could glimpse white, sandy beaches and palm-trees. Once, when we were in shoaling water and about to change course to starboard, the look-out bellowed "Shipwrecked mariner clinging to wreckage, five cables distant, fine on the starboard bow!" The Captain used his telescope and held course until we came up with the wretched fellow, then had the yards backed and hove-to. This surprised me for by then it was evident that the mariner was by no means shipwrecked, but the master of the most primitive craft you can imagine: he was seated astride a log, half awash, which was attached to a smaller log by means of a sort of basket-work structure which supported a large stone and a length of line.

"A pearl-fisher, Mr Van Cleef," said the Second curtly, in answer to my question. "Ancient, pre-Dravidian race; *ugly*. The stone gets him down to the oyster-beds, d'ye see. Bad life. Never make old bones." The fellow was by now swarming up a rope which had been tossed to him and soon stood on our deck in a puddle of water. He was, indeed, notably ugly and of a deep, blue-black hue. His features could only have been acceptable to others of his race. He was entirely naked and, after one glance (which lasted quite five seconds) Blanche fled modestly from the scene. His male member was pitifully small, resembling nothing so much as a wrinkled hazel-nut but this, I supposed, was due to long immersion in the water. He wrung out his long hair onto the deck but this elicited no more than a low growling sound from Captain Knatchbull who, clearly, was determined to show the man civility.

"Greet him," he growled to the *comprador*, who addressed a few words of some *lingua franca* to the fisherman, with an air of great disdain such as you might see in the demeanour of an English parlourmaid bidden to do some task which was "not her work". The black man's face burst open into an enormous smile, made the more interesting by the lack of his front teeth and the fact that the remaining ones were of a rich scarlet colour.

He rattled off some words in what must have been a language because the *comprador* made shift to understand them. A pannikin

144

of fresh water was brought and the man drank it off with every sign of relish.

"No fresh water on this coast," vouchsafed the Second. "They have to catch the dew."

After more exchanges the man reached behind him and began to explore the terminus of his digestive tract, bestowing on us all the while that nightmare smile. One of the Captain's Chinese boys fetched a bucket of sea-water, into which the fisherman dropped the fruits of his rummaging. After rinsing, the nasty nuggets proved to be three pearls. I knew little of such things at the time, but still, perhaps, more than most Gentiles. One was a very fine rose-coloured stone, one a large one but of bad colour and the third smaller but of a most perfect roundness and luminosity. The Captain proffered a half-guinea, somewhat worn and bent. The pearl-fisher gazed at it, horror-stricken, then threw himself upon the deck, patting the Captain's boots and shrieking in a dignified fashion.

"Well?" asked the Captain of the *comprador*.

"He says, Sir, you are his father and mother and he is your dog." The Captain brushed aside the interesting suggestions, ignoring their implications.

"What does he want?"

"He says, Sir, that he wants two whole guineas and a piece of cloth. *Thick* guineas, he says and *new* cloth."

After more shrieking and growling a deal was struck: the black-amoor took two half-guineas, one of them thick, a sprinkle of small silver coins and a short yard of red flannel from the slop-chest. He also begged a wisp of cotton, in which he wrapped his bullion before committing it to the vault where he had kept the pearls. As soon as he was over side the Captain called all officers to the break of the poop. There was a custom in these affairs, it seems.

"Order of seniority," rasped the Captain. "I claim the pink pearl at half a guinea." He aimed his eyebrows at us. No one demurred.

Lubbock had next pick. He was, as I have told you, not clever and he claimed the large, ill-coloured stone at the cost of a guinea and a crown. The Second, with a gloomy air which, I fancy, concealed a certain pleasure, pouched the smaller, beautiful pearl for an outlay of half a guinea. The money was then ritually divided between the three, after deducting the initial outlay: each received six shillings and eightpence. It was a glum Carolus Van Cleef who sulked in his cabin that afternoon.

145

We took in sail and cruised slowly up that coast, taking soundings, for the rest of the day. Sure enough, just before evening another log-borne fisherman was sighted and taken aboard. He had four pearls. "Our turn this time, Karli," murmured Peter.

The Captain claimed the finest for a half guinea again but then it was "reverse order of seniority" which meant that I had first choice. To everyone's amusement I selected a large, misshapen pearl of varied colour and secured it for three half-crowns. Such "baroque" pearls are despised in England but I knew how much they were prized by jewellers in Augsburg and Amsterdam. (If ever you are privileged to call on my young friend Ferdinand de Rothschild at Waddesdon, his château, you will be shown wonderful examples, wonderful.) The remaining two might have been brothers, they were not large but perfectly matched. It was conceded that they might be considered a single lot and Peter gave two pounds. Dear fellow, he thought that I had stood back from them out of courtesy to him.

I supped heartily that night and with great contentment. I washed my pearl again, for I am a fastidious man, and admired it for an hour, while Orace sewed me a little bag made out of the tail of my silk shirt so that I could hang it about my neck. Pearls are happiest when close to the warmth and natural grease of the human skin, everyone knows that.

We reached the end of the pearling-coast and clapped on sail again until there came a day when we found ourselves at the Mouths of the Ganges and hove-to at the entrance to the Hooghly River awaiting a pilot, while our Captain paced up and down, munching his beard impatiently. Even he, let alone anyone in his senses, would not try to navigate the Hooghly unassisted, for the whole stretch of it is a treacherous maze of mud- and sand-banks, forever shifting. The pilot-cutter came dancing out to us the next morning and a little tea-coloured man skipped aboard, nodding and becking daintily but with a curious dignity, and introducing himself as "Mister Pilot D'Souza".

"Well, Mister Pilot D'Souza," growled our Captain, "pray take the conn and get this bucket up to Shalimar Point as soon as may be: I want my hook in Garden Reach before dark."

The little man was wonderfully skilful; he rapped out orders to the helmsman in an unending succession all day long, leading our ship in the most improbable directions along and across the vast, muddy river. The Captain stood behind him for much of the time, sometimes snorting but never once contradicting an order. The pilot asked for a new helmsman every hour or so, for the work was testing, and this was not denied him. Sure enough, we dropped our anchor just before dusk and the Captain immediately called away his gig to set the pilot ashore. At the last moment, he decided to join him and bade the First Mate to join the party. I think he wanted to make sure that no other skipper in the trade was there before him.

Peter Stevenage had the anchor-watch and, after having the boarding-nets spread (for there are *thieves* in Calcutta), he retired to the taffrail for a snooze. The Second was in his cabin as usual, moodily pulling the wings off flies, I fancy. In the circumstances, my usual little meeting at the rail with Blanche was in more darkness than usual and more private. I taught her a new Dutch sentence in which one or two words were so close to English that I think she must have suspected that it cannot *really* have meant "Where is there a good milliner in this town?" This night my schoolmasterly kiss strayed to her lips and was answered warmly although it was clear that she had never been taught to kiss in the way that lovers do. I taught her. She had misgivings at first but was soon an adept pupil, so engrossed in this new art that she seemed unaware that my hand had firmly captured one of her delightful breasts. Her breathing quickened but all of a sudden she broke away, bade me goodnight and fled to her cabin. I was puzzled and chagrined as I stood by the rail alone, until I heard what she must have heard sooner: a boat approaching, the oars propelled by the long Navy-stroke which our Captain always insisted on.

I, too, fled, but to the galley to see what was for supper. The doctor had bought from a bum-boat some hens and coconuts and was confecting a kari-stew of these which ravished my nostrils. (How strange it is that language has words for being deaf, dumb and blind but no word for the shocking deprivation of being without the sense of smell! To speak plainly, I would rather be dumb, although not *deaf*, because I love to hear what certain grandchildren murmur behind my back: I should not like to write an ill-considered will.)

I found Peter on the poop and we leaned and gazed in silence at the thousands of little flickering lights which flowered and died in the great heathen city, listened to the strange sounds of drums and wailing music which wafted across the water to us and, when a little off-shore breeze arose, snuffed the scented air – an air laden with

147

spices, woodsmoke, rotting fruit and shit. It was a magical moment and my spirits were exalted beyond the plane of mere human existence and its attendant lures of Captain's wives.

"Are there many whores in Calcutta?" I asked Peter at last.

"More than you could pleasure in a life-time, Karli. The best and safest are the temple-prostitutes: to them it is a religious rite."

"Do you mean that it is *free*?"

"Of course. But, of course, you must make a donation to the temple treasure, that is only civil. Besides, it does save your throat from being slit on the way home."

"That seems prudent," I said.

Later, I ate great store of the hens seethed in spices and coconut-milk but when I went to bed my thoughts turned again to Blanche and my supper lay surlily on my stomach like a hastily-chewed dead dog. Sleep was slow to come and, when it came, was visited with evil dreams. Peter woke me up once or twice, saying that I had been speaking unguardedly in my sleep. I took my bedding onto the deck but certain flies stang me so bitterly that I fled back to the hot and fusty cabin.

Promptly, as the ship's bell struck to signify the end of the watch at noon, next day, the Captain made his appearance on the deck in a splendid uniform, gallooned with gold braid, that I had never seen before. Lubbock was awaiting him, also clad in some sort of marine finery which made him look quite gentlemanlike. They were attended by the *comprador* and the Captain's two Chinese boys, all bedecked in silks and marvellous head-cloths. The Second glumly joined the glittering throng, wearing a rusty garb of antique cut, made all the more shabby-looking by the splendid sword at his hip. The Captain was off to inspect the first wares at the opium auction.

Peter, who once again had the anchor-watch – an undemanding chore – confided to me that he proposed to become a little drunk.

I do not much love to become drunk of an afternoon when the weather is hot, so I took but a glass with him before retiring to the lazaretto to check the slop-chest stores, the *comprador* being ashore, you see.

There Orace found me, fast asleep upon a pile of oilskins, an hour or two later. He looked at me curiously as I rubbed my eyes, for he was growing up fast, then delivered his message. "Mum" – by which

148

he meant the Captain's wife – "sends her compliments and wishes you to take a dish of tea with her in half an hour."

"Very well, Orace. Have I any clean linen?"

"In course, Sir."

"Then come to the cabin and dress me suitably for tea-parties."

Having shifted my linen and shaved, I gave Orace a pile of clothes for him to attend to and warned him that I wished to see them back spotless in precisely two hours: no more and *no less*.

"Aye aye, Sir," he replied smartly in the maritime fashion he was now affecting.

Blanche was sitting behind the tea-table primly – or as primly as a young woman can sit who is wearing a light tea-gown of a kind which makes it evident that she is, indeed, young and a woman.

"The servants are all ashore," she said, still primly, "and I do not make tea well. Perhaps you will be content to share a glass of white Cape wine with me?"

I mumbled assent and we drank the delicious wine. The English, particularly the English women, have a notion in their strange heads that slightly-sweet white wine is not an alcoholic beverage. I already knew that this was an error for I was not, in those days, a naturalised Englishman. I drank frugally.

After a little the conversation drew around to Dutch customs. She reminded me, in an off-hand fashion, that I had been telling her the night before that Dutchmen kissed in a different fashion from Englishmen. I did not, of course, refresh her memory that I had demonstrated this Continental practice, for that would have been uncivil. I walked around the table and lifted her in my arms. Laying her gently on the sofa I began to teach her how Dutchmen kiss desirable women. She had, I think, been considering the matter, for now she seemed quickly to master the art of it, so much so that at times I had difficulty in drawing breath. So engrossed was she that, when her silk gown slid away from her shoulders and my hands took both of her naked breasts and gently squeezed them, she seemed quite unconscious of the action but continued with her lesson. When she began to tremble and hold me fiercely I drew away and said, half-jokingly:

"Blanche, be ready in four and one half minutes."

To my astonishment she rose instantly and flew into the sleeping-cabin as I drew out my gun-metal watch. The four and one half minutes seemed long, long: I believe I could have recited the

149

whole of the Torah before the minute hand erected itself to the desired mark.

On that very instant I opened the door of the sleeping-cabin and stepped in, closing it behind me.

What met my eyes made me stagger back against the door in astonishment, not unmixed with salacious delight, to speak plainly.

Blanche was spread-eagled face down on the great, gaily-painted Indian bedstead, each ankle and wrist manacled to one of the corner-posts. She wore silk stockings but no drawers: this was plain, for her silk gown was hoisted up to her waist. There was a pillow under her loins which raised her rump in the most engaging fashion and another was under her face. This other pillow, as I realised when I saw the array of whips and canes on the little table beside the bed, was for her to scream into. I gazed, entranced, at her superb bottom and noticed that it was all traced and laced with long stripes and scars and cicatrices, some old, some fresh and pink.

"Please only use the little green one at first, Karli," she said in a voice muffled by the pillow. I found it: a beautiful little terrier-crop with a silver horse's-head handle and the lash bound with green velvet. In a spirit of experiment I laid it across her croup a few times in a sheepish fashion. She wriggled, as though impatiently. I have never much enjoyed giving pain (except to my own descendants) but the situation was so novel and picturesque that I laid on even harder, watching with undeniable interest the way her enviable nates blossomed into a deep rose-colour.

My interest – and the strokes of the whip – diminished after a while and she turned her head from the pillow and gazed at me wonderingly.

"Why are you not . . .?" she said, puzzledly.

"Not what?" I asked.

"Well," she said, in some confusion, her cheeks as pink now as her bottom, "you should be, well, your clothes should be unfastened and you should be, that is, ah, holding your *person*. Do you not *know* how to make love?"

I began to understand.

"Blanche," I said lovingly, passing a hand gently over her rosy bum, "Blanche, let us have a little lesson. Let me teach you how we make love in Holland?"

We unclasped the absurd manacles and fetters and I turned her the right way up. That is to say, upon her back. We rehearsed, for a while, that way of kissing which was so new to her, then I applied my attentions to her unusually fine teats. This, too, seemed something of a novelty to her but, after a token protest, she submitted to it.

"What are you doing?" she cried a little later, "it is you that must hold *that*, not I . . ." But she grew reconciled to this, too. The crux came presently.

"Karli, you must not touch me there, you must not, you must . . . my God, what are you doing, that is wicked, it is against religion, it is beastly, it is what horses do, I have seen them, it is abominable, stop, stop, it *hurts*; *stop*, I beg you!"

"*Stop*?" I asked, in a kindly, considerate way. She breathed deeply, perhaps three breaths.

"Stop *stopping* is what I meant, Karli." She said this in a small voice.

I stopped stopping. Incredibly, but demonstrably, she was – had been until that afternoon – a virgin. After some little time we both had need to stop. I explained certain things to her.

"And am I now deflowered, Karli?"

"I *think* so."

"Should we not make sure?"

We made sure; it was even better than the first time. Then we fell asleep. Then she awoke me, seeming concerned that the deflowerment might not have been permanent. This time, although it was perhaps a little uncomfortable for her, I made it very certain indeed. I left her in a deep sleep and went to the galley, for I was hungry, hungry. I have no recollection of what the food was except that it was good and that, for once, I ate greedily.

The Captain returned at dusk in a state of satisfaction equalling mine, although I would not have exchanged my reasons for gratification with his. He had indeed been the first Western buyer in the market – the auctions were due to begin within the week – and he had already set our Calcutta *schroff* to work at suborning everyone concerned and, in particular, the venal auctioneers. Also, he had contrived to buy for ready gold a few chests of the very primest opium – grown and dried by private horticulturalists of course, for the stuff grown under the aegis of the Honourable East India Company was not subject to unofficial dealings. (Unless your *schroff* had the ear of a penurious official and a bag of gold to chink into that ear, you understand.)

151

The Yankee clippers of Russell & Co., and those slower ships of Dent & Co. and Jardine Matheson, were evidently days behind us and, although the auctions would not commence until there was a decent quorum, we had our foot in the doorway first and your honest Oriental respects the first man to bribe him – especially when he has had to give a receipt. The Parsee firm of Bonajee were already there, of course, but at this time they were only dipping the toes of their mighty banking firm into the evil footbath of opium and their ships were few and old and ill-crewed.

As the Captain, having delivered his news with unwonted friendliness and condescension, bade us goodnight, he pulled out his great watch and I heard him say "Blanche, be ready in –" only to be cut off short, to my delight, with her snappish rejoinder that she had a severe headache.

In our little cabin, I rummaged in the tin shirt-box for some delicacies to augment our dinner that night: Peter was enchanted at my change of mood.

"Is it that you feel riches already within your grasp, Karli?" he asked with his mouth full.

I answered him ambiguously for my mouth, too, was as full as my wicked heart.

At dawn the next morning we made a full boat: Captain Knatch-bull and Blanche – who, indeed, may have had a headache for there were dark circles under her lovely eyes – Lubbock, Peter, me, the *comprador* and the Captain's servants and our new *schroff*, a base, ill-made looking little man who was clever. The lugubrious Second was left with the anchor-watch.

To speak plainly, Calcutta was a disappointment. There were some fine European buildings and some Indian temples adorned with carvings which were so explicit in their indecency that I might almost have averted my face, had it not occurred to me that Oriental ingenuity might well have a lesson for me, even me. A side-glance at Blanche shewed that she was averting her face so determinedly that she had clearly glimpsed these carvings and was now convinced that it was I, and not her husband, who had the right of it in such matters.

Nevertheless, the city was a disappointment. Where were the scented arbours, the jewelled birds, the shameless, bare-breasted, nard-anointed houris I had dreamed of? This city was a crammed turmoil of white-swathed figures, screaming and chaffering and jostling in a humid air laden with the stench of dead dogs and human excrement. To have walked those streets would have been unthinkable, but we were drawn in a small procession of little chariots like the bathing-machines of the wonderful Margate itself, each pulled by a horse of amazing thinness who could yet break wind again and again in the most striking manner. I recall wondering what such decayed horses could be fed upon in so stricken a city.

We were entertained in a huge, cool hall by some petty merchant princeling of John Company – the tea, we were assured, was cooled by snow brought two hundred miles from the Hills – then sauntered out into a great cloistered enclosure, shaded by awnings, where the very opium itself was laid out in neat batches. The fat, dark cakes of the Patna stuff, the lovely, polished balls of best Benares – oh, I came to know them all, all. And their values, you may be sure.

Peter was in a strange mood of bitter elation. "Look, Karli," he murmured, "here is England's greatness and the pride of commerce. Enough poison to corrupt and ruin a great Empire. (No, the *Chinese* Empire, Karli, do not be obtuse: how could the *British* Empire ever fall?) The Celestial One has banned opium from all his territories – he has heard of the havoc it has wrought in Formosa – but although he is well-informed, he is ill-served by a system of mandarins whose only concern is to become rich as quickly as may be. They send out a brace of war-junks as a sort of token; they fire off an antique cannon or two, we return fire in an aimless sort of way and, honour appeased, they make best speed for shelter. The Emperor receives reports of bloody battles in which the Western-Oceans devils were routed and we then comfortably make our bargains. It's a shabby business but everyone becomes rich. Honour is out of date, you see, Karli."

"I am sure you are right, Peter," I said.

"So am I," he said. Then he laughed but not merrily.

I liked Peter much but did not always understand him in those days. I understand now but, as in the matter of sex, such understanding comes too late in life. By the time that you, too, understand these things it will be too late for you, too. This gives me a wry pleasure similar to that which my poxy friend Peter exhibited to my imcomprehension that day.

The Captain strolled grandly about the courtyard, followed by his splendidly-clad entourage, and made some more illicit forward bargains. Being sure that he would recall that we had both been entered, passed and raised through certain Degrees of a Craft which I may have referred to before, I gladly allowed him to make similar bargains for me, to the limit of the sum I had set aside for this. His aspect towards the dusky vendors was implacable but I could tell, although not understanding the tongues, that he was shrewd, shrewd.

There is a strange repast called "Tiffin" in those climes which consists of pleasant cold curried dishes and a great deal of Dry London Gin with interesting sparkling waters added. Peter and I made a hearty meal. Indeed, so soon as we had returned to the ship, we found a compulsion to sing songs. Peter had learned his in a county called Harrow; mine were from Holland but, once translated, there seemed to be little difference in their content. I recall that we made many a protestation of undying friendship before we fell asleep and, for I wished to emulate these fine men from Harrow County, I too washed my face in a thorough, English way and removed all my clothes before donning the smocked, silken night-shirt which some generous soul had placed beneath my pillow.

We remained some days in Calcutta until the formalities of the auctions were over and our Captain had availed himself of all opportunities to twit the arriving skippers on their tardiness. He did this with much dignity and met their rebukes without ever raising his voice above a scream.

I essayed a little whoring but only half-heartedly. The brightest memory I carried away from Calcutta was of a young or youngish person (it is very hard to discern ages in those latitudes) who contrived to ingest, as it were, a pile of silver coins (she spurned copper) in the most improbable direction and then to receive the attentions of a donkey, after which she retrieved the coins from the donkey's ear. Clearly, this was sleight of hand. I can think of no other explanation.

When I say that my whoring was half-hearted I mean, of course, that I had by then fallen in love with Blanche. It is not every day that one has the delight of instructing a hearty, nubile virgin of nearly thirty into the raptures of adultery. She was an apt and eager pupil. Sometimes I feared that the Captain would catch us in the very act but more often, as she became more adept, I feared for my own health. Peter marvelled at how soundly I slept of nights.

The ship's people, who have a sort of scuttlebut telegraph, nudged and winked as I strolled the deck.

The day before we were due to drop down the Hooghly to commence the perilous part of our voyage, I was standing idly at the port rail, watching the lumpers fetch in the last of our stores (the chests of the drug were already safe stowed) and keeping half an eye on the *comprador* and *schroff* who were checking these incoming things against the bills and quietly snarling at each other. I knew that I could go over the bills at leisure, for these two hated each other and there was no likelihood of collusion; or, if there was, it would be at so rarefied and convoluted a level that my simple Dutch mind would never reach the bottom of it. Indeed, on that warm and languid morning, my simple Dutch mind was reaching more toward the charming bottom of Blanche than concerning itself with any petty cheatings that these two might be arranging in the matter of pigs and poultry and pigtail-twist tobacco.

My eye fell upon a group of sturdy seafaring men on the dock who were eyeing our ship with admiration.

"Sir!" cried one of them, "Sir?"

I realised that he was addressing me.

"Yes?" I cried in a haughty, officer-like way.

"Sir, this is the sweetest ship we have seen upon the seas and we beg permission to come aboard and admire of her, Sir."

I knew not what to say but Lubbock, who had the watch, saved me the decision.

"Come aboard, my bullies!" he bellowed sweetly, "I can tell at a glance that you are kernoozers of a vessel's lines. Come aboard and squinch at her from truck to keelson, for you'll never see a better – even in a Marblehead yard. Jest take your boots off at the head of the gangway for we dearly love our decks and don't like to work our men too hard a-scrubbing of them. There'll be a pannikin of something strong in the fo'c'sle for you when you've looked your fill."

They trooped aboard, doffing boots and caps. Their praise was boundless, although expressed in language of a dirtiness new to me. The costly mahogany and brass-work excited their fierce admiration, while the capacious fo'c'sle sent them into raptures. An hour later, three of them left with many a thankful word; the other five were in the cabin, signing not only the Ship's Articles but also the document which laid down that they realised the sovereign merits of flogging and were happy to submit to British Navy rules, waiving their rights as private mariners.

The First Mate was postively jocund when I next met him on deck.

"From here on out," he condescended to tell me, "we'd be glad of a double crew. Wait and see, sonny, wait and see. These five shagamores will be first-class topmen as soon as I've beaten the bug-juice out of them and now we'll have three strong watches. They were shanghaied here by Martin Churchill, or maybe Black Jack himself, the finest crimps in New York, and they've jumped ship. Cain't say as I blame them. They reckon this bucket will be a floating paradise after what they bin through. They reckon." He laughed a soft, unpleasing laugh.

"What is bug-juice?" I asked.

"Rum. Or something like it."

"And you have coaxed these sturdy shell-backs to sign on because they are capable seamen?" I asked. He gave me a look which was hard to interpret.

"I've took them, *Mr* Van Cleef, for the same reason the Kentucky thief took the hot stove: there was nothing else to be had that season. They're waterfront scum, two shades worse than bilge-rats and they don't fool me worth a nickel. They don't know timber from canvas and they don't want to learn."

"But you'll teach them, I daresay, Mr Lubbock?" I ventured.

"No. I ain't about to teach them. I'm going to bloody *learn* them. Before we're in the Canton River I'll have them dancing on the cro-jacks like Maggie May in scarlet drawers."

"Indeed," I said politely. He turned on his heel. I reflected that such a man ought not to be allowed to live.

156

PART FOUR

The Empire of the Dragon

CHAPTER TWELVE

〜〜〜

THE EIGHT REGULATIONS UNDER WHICH THE EAST INDIA COMPANY MAY TRADE IN CANTON
(Paraphrase and abridgment)

1. No ships of war are to enter the Pearl River of Canton.
2. Europeans are permitted to inhabit the Factories of the Canton suburb during the shipping season only; and no wives, children or weapons may be kept there.
3. No boatman, agent or any other subject of the Celestial One may work for a European without a licence.
4. No European may keep a household larger than the lowest grade of mandarin might employ.
5. No European may leave the factories in pleasure-boat or palanquin; no visits to the City or other suburbs are permitted. Each ten days a party of not more than ten may be *conducted* to the pleasure garden on Hanan Island; there they shall not mingle with the populace, become drunk or remain after dark.
6. All commerce and all communication with authority shall be carried out through the merchants of the Hong.
7. Smuggling and the giving or taking of credit are forbidden.
8. All ships must anchor, unload and load at Whampoa, thirteen miles below the City.

From the moment that we dropped our Pilot at the mouth of the Hooghly our voyage seemed to bear a charmed life. Every wind was in our favour and of the right force, every line cast overboard brought in a large and succulent fish, and our rate of passage was such that the Captain seemed often almost benevolent in his demeanour, despite Blanche's protracted headaches. Taking the perilous Malacca Strait without the least trouble – indeed, without shortening sail by a stitch – we found another favourable wind which sped us north and a little east at a splendid rate of knots. Captain Knatchbull appeared on deck precisely twenty minutes before the masthead sighted land – the Island of Hainan – then, without troubling to open his telescope, he gave a grunt of self-approval and vanished below. For all his faults, he was an inspired navigator. This made the crew admire him, although he had forfeited all claim to their affections. In the event, we raised Lin-Tin in the unheard-of time of eighteen days out of Calcutta. Grog was served out to all the fo'c'sle people and they romped and skylarked almost as cheerily as they had in the days before the dreadful *Martha Washington* affair. Almost but not quite. The more thoughtless and carefree lads seemed to be quite themselves again but Tom Transom and the other older salts were subdued and concerned, while Sean O'Casey, the Irish, professed to have some inner presage of disaster. This gift is not uncommon amongst folk of Celtic blood. The Doctor, too, muttered as he worked, although his concoctions, now that he had fresh Indian spices and herbs to conjure with, seemed to make memory a liar. He dedicated himself to teasing my appetite – which has always been small – into an interested state with ever new delicacies.

Before going up the Pearl River to Whampoa, where the Eight Rules said that we must unload and load, and, later, by boat to the European Factories and the Hongs, we put in at Macao, a lovely island, in order to learn the going prices of the various grades of the drug, the latest edicts of the Lord of the World sitting in his Court of Heaven, and to smarten the ship before proceeding to Lin Tin and Whampoa. Macao was enchanting: the Portuguese had been there for more than two centuries and their absurd baroque architecture seemed to grow naturally out of that Oriental soil. Our first view of it was a charming little bay with a crescent of old white houses fringing its waterfont and above them a maze of houses, churches and monasteries of every size and shape and style you can imagine. Highest above all were some ancient and imposing forts: there were cannon there still, but now only used, I was told, for ceremonial saluting.

This delightful place was the centre of European society in the Treaty Coast, for no families could go up to the Factories, nor could the merchants themselves inhabit the Factories except in the shipping season – that is to say, when the south-west Monsoon, which had sped us here, was blowing out.

It fell to Peter, the most junior watch-keeping officer, to go ashore and carry out the bribery necessary to obtain a pass for the ship from the resident Chinese official, also to buy a landing-permit which cost thirteen shillings and fourpence – although it cost quite that sum again to be passed into the presence of the scoundrel who issued it. We were carried ashore in an "egg-boat", a curious craft some eight feet long and six feet in the beam and half-roofed over with a hemisphere of matting. It was propelled by two bold and beddable girls wearing, if you can believe it, *trowsers* of some blue material. I asked Peter whether he thought they were chaste, to which he replied, cryptically, that they were of the female sex, a fact which was palpable.

We had leave until midnight and, our tiresome business done, we strolled along the Praya Grande, where there were many ancient and crumbling buildings and many lovely, strolling ladies. The Portuguese ones were accompanied by ancient, crumbling *dueñas*, but the English ones, although not so desirable, walked in pairs, glancing at us boldly. They seemed to be, for the most part, the neglected wives of merchants who were up at Whampoa or Canton, and impatient, in that tepid climate, with the enforced separation.

Peter carried me off to dinner with an old acquaintance of his, a strange, ugly little Irish with white curls and old-fashioned spectacles like those of my father. He had been in the Orient longer than I had been alive and was a painter much esteemed. His name was Chinnery and his talk was copious and enchanting. We were just becoming agreeably drunk when one of his servants came in and gabbled. It seemed that our ship was, inexplicably, flying the "Blue Peter" from the fore-topmast-head: this flag is blue with a square white centre and it means that everyone of that ship's company must be back aboard instantly, for it is about to sail. This was vexing, because I had promised myself that I would console a merchant's wife or two before midnight, and baffling, because I had heard the Captain dismiss our Ladrones pilot until the next afternoon's tide.

When we were outside Chinnery's house, climbing into a man-drawn vehicle, Peter pointed at the heavens. There was, indeed, a strange look to them, a kind of livid light which changed the colours of everything about; there was also an uncomfortable feeling to the air and a great stillness.

161

We scrambled across the "brow" between our ship and the sampan alongside it, under a glare from the Captain. In an instant the men at the sweeps were bending to it with a will and we were amongst a flock of vessels making best speed towards the open sea. I knew enough by now to keep out of the way. The men at the sweeps were pulling like galley-slaves and needed no whip to urge them. "Typhoon," snapped Peter as he ran past me, "get oilskins – and get below!" I got both.

Later I crept out to the break of the poop, for nothing seemed to be happening. On the poop stood the Captain and all three mates. Captain Knatchbull and Peter were discussing something heatedly, the First Mate was growling ignorantly and the Second was looking white but holding his peace.

(Afterwards, I pieced together the burden of their argument: a typhoon in the Northern Hemisphere moves north, you see, and rotates anti-clockwise. The western side or half-circle is navigable but, clearly, blows south – dead foul for us. The eastern semi-circle is dangerous, for the wind there blows at unimaginable speeds – few have attempted to measure these speeds and very few have survived to record them. But that side blows northwards, towards the "country-trade" part of the Coast where, sooner or later, we wished to be. The Captain's great experience and insanity told him that, by a dashing use of sail, we could make use of the south-western part of the rotatory storm, claw ourselves free on its eastern side and use the residual fringe winds to carry us safely north.)

I did not, thank God, understand anything of what was said, but I heard the Captain close the discussion with a roar of command, saw Peter throw up his hands in a gesture of despair and was jostled by the First Mate as he thrust by me, eyes terrified, to give orders for making sail. The sky was now a rich reddish-brown, full of bizarre menace. I crept below again. There was some cold food in the cabin but I could not touch it: I confess that I was alarmed.

This alarm was nothing to my feelings when the wind first hit us: the impact was such that I thought we had struck a great rock. But the blow was from *behind*: the ship leaped forward like a maddened horse, I could hear the water roaring against the skin of the ship, the yelling, then the screaming of the tortured rigging and above all the demented bellow of the prodigious wind. Again and again I was sure that this was the climax, that nothing could exceed such violence, no force on earth make a more deafening clamour, but again and again

162

I was proved wrong as the clamour grew more intolerable. At last, insane with the noise and the terror, I clapped my hands to my ears and rushed on deck, determined to confront death sooner than later – and not in that rat-trap of a cabin. As I emerged the hellish din was heightened by an explosion – or so it seemed – as the fore staysail burst into tatters. We lost steerage-way, yawed, and in an instant we were pooped by a cliff-like wave which had been pursuing us. A thousand tons of grey water thundered the length of the ship, lifting me as though I were a fragment of paper and burying me oceans deep. I knew that I was a dead man, there was no question of it, my eardrums cracked, water spurted into my nostrils and, as I opened my mouth to scream, my lungs were instantly so gorged that I could feel them begin to split with the pressure. In the few instants it took to die the whole of my past life flashed in review across my inner eye: this was a disgusting experience.

I awoke in hell, which did not surprise me, all things considered. A black, glistening demon, ten feet high, was tormenting me excruciatingly, crushing my agonised ribs with his great hands. I spewed a gallon of sea-water at him. He turned me over and attacked my chest from behind. It was intolerable – and I knew that the torments would continue through all eternity. I vomited another gallon.

"Din't eat yo' nice supper, did you, Maz Cleef," said the Doctor reproachfully, making me sit up and forcing my head between my knees. "Don' tell me different: I seen you brung up nothing but sea-water. Might a gone to glory on a empty stomach; ain't no sense in that now."

As my eyes cleared and the shards of my wits reassembled themselves I became amused at the sense of disappointment that I felt. I began to cry, then to giggle idiotically. The Doctor smacked me hard across the face and I sank into a happy sleep.

What had happened, it seemed, was this: the great mass of water had wedged me into the bowsprit-rigging – in the angle between the martingale-backstays and the dolphin-striker, to be exact – and, as the ship stood on her tail after the wave had passed, gravity had thrown me onto the fo'c'sle, along the deck, where I caromed off the mainmast bitts and fetched up against the galley. The Doctor had plucked me inside, just before the next pooping.

"Were many drowned?" I asked when I could speak again.

"Of course not," said Peter. "Everyone else had the sense to be lashed to something stout – or to stay below when told to. Do your bruises hurt much?"

"Yes" I said. "Very much."

"Good," he said. But he said it with a kindly grin.

Strangely enough, I slept through the last of the wind's fury and, two mornings later, went on deck to snuff the wonderfully clean air. It must, in fact, have been almost the end of the morning for the *comprador* was standing behind the Captain holding the mahogany box which contained his quadrant (for our Captain did not hold with the new-fangled sextants) and the ship's chronometer hung about his neck. (The sun is "shot" through the "hog-yoke" as Lubbock called the quadrant in his rough Yankee way, at noon, you understand.)

The sails were backed and, as Peter called out the time of noon, the Captain fiddled with the quadrant and soon gave Peter some figures. Peter scrambled to the chart-room and was back in less than a minute, handing the Captain a slip of paper which he gazed at with what seemed a kind of satisfaction.

"I'll have a sounding, if you please, Mister," he growled.

Lubbock – it was in fact his watch but Peter was usually on deck when there was a chance of a sun-sight because Lubbock's arithmetic was that of the beasts of the field – roared his orders.

"Transom, there, fly the blue pigeon! Smart you now!"

In a trice the deep-sea lead was out of its locker abaft the fo'c'sle and Transom was whirling it about his head. (Why "swinging the lead" has come to be a term for idling is a mystery to me for, even with the little six-pound hand-lead and twenty fathoms of line in a flat calm, taking soundings is an arduous and testing work enough; and casting and coiling in the full deep-sea lead again and again, while balanced in the chains in foul weather and, perhaps, darkness is a labour for Hercules himself.)

Transom sang out numbers of fathoms which now I forget but which seemed to gratify the Captain.

"Arm it!" he cried. Transom ran to the locker and stuffed some mutton-fat into the hollow of the lead and hove it again.

The Captain thumbed out the resulting mess and sniffed it, felt it, even chewed a morsel of it. He now seemed uncommonly elated and positively capered to the chartroom.

"Happy as a dog with two cocks," growled Lubbock.

164

"Why?" I asked civilly.

He shrugged. I suspect he did not know. The Captain emerged and gave Peter a course which Peter retailed to the steersman and soon there was much bracing of yards and hauling upon this and that rope until we were heading almost due west, with the wind on our starboard beam.

Within an hour we had raised an island, Namoa, which lies in the Bay of Swatow and was, so Peter assured me, a capital place for the selling of illegal opium of poor quality. When I say that this island is quite three hundred sea miles north of Macao you will begin to understand the ferocity of the typhoon which had driven us there in one day and a half.

"What a splendid seaman our Captain is, to be sure!" I murmured admiringly.

"Yes indeed, Karli," said Peter, smiling at me in a friendly way.

When we reached the anchorage at Namoa I was alarmed to see two large junks, clearly men-of-war and heavily armed, riding inshore of us. One flew an enormous silken pennant, embroidered with dragons: this, Peter told me, denoted a petty Admiral of the Chinese Navy.

"Will they fight?" I asked bravely.

Lubbock, who was leaning over the rail of the poop and had heard, answered for him.

"Will they *fuck*," he said in his coarse fashion.

No sooner were we swinging with the tide than a scow put off from the side of that junk which bore the imposing flag. Plainly to be seen in it, clothed in great finery and puffing at a long pipe, was a grossly fat man, surrounded by well-dressed servants who fanned him incessantly. In his cap was the button of a mandarin. I did not, at that time, know the insignia of the different grades of mandarin and at this time I have forgotten them.

Peter whistled.

"The Clam-Jandrum himself," he said, "Governor of the whole district."

"Has he come to arrest the ship?"

"Not he. Watch the Captain."

The Captain was at the gangway, clad in his best uniform and flanked by two miraculously-scrubbed seamen and, behind them, his two servant boys. The representative of the Court of Heaven was prised out of his armchair in the sternsheets of the scow by his rattan-hatted servants and our Captain himself, having bared his head, assisted the great bulk aboard. The party proceeded to the cabin with measured tread. A moment later I was sent for: I was to bring the *schroff* and a ledger. *Any* ledger.

In the cabin the mandarin reclined on the sofa at full length, sucking wetly at one of the Captain's biggest cigars and disdainfully sipping a tumbler of gin. The Captain was standing, a servant on each side. The *schroff* began to interpret.

"Fat old pig say why you doing here, no at Canton? He say he must cut off all heads by mercy of Emperor."

"Tell him," said the Captain, "that we have been blown here by terrible winds and that all we ask is to rest a while and to buy, with permission, some fresh food."

"He say Emperor's mercy bigger than all seas, perhaps give water, sell one-two pigs, one-two ducks. Then you go, chop-chop."

"Tell him his world-famed generosity reflects the infinite compassion of the Celestial One himself," said the Captain, grinding his teeth soundlessly.

The mandarin made a wonderfully elegant gesture with his third finger and all his people left the cabin. The Captain made an economic gesture with his head and one eyebrow and all *his* people left except for the *schroff* and me.

"Fat old pig say how many chests Western shit you get here in boat, Captain?"

"How many, Mr Van Cleef?" asked the Captain, staring at me meaningfully. "About a hundred and fifty, I fancy?"

I ran a diligent finger down the columns of a ledger-page which were, if the truth must be told, devoted to the sales of pigtail tobacco from the slop-chest.

"One hundred and forty nine, Sir," I said at last, brightly.

The *schroff* translated at such length and with such unction that I became certain that his words, although they sounded like a small dog being sick, meant something like: "Idiotic young officer pretends only 150 chests but I, being a poor man, supporting many grandparents who display an undignified reluctance to die, throw myself upon the richly-embroidered slippers of the august one, confident of his famous generosity to the poor and ancestor-encumbered, and declare that from my hunger-shrivelled breast I have plucked a number closer to three hundred."

The mandarin drew an exquisite little abacus from the depths of a sleeve and made its jade and cornelian beads flicker with a silver-encased fingernail until he had worked out, one supposed, some little problem of percentage, such as used to trouble us lads at school. (The Chinese and the Arabians will one day inherit the earth because of their mastery of the abacus, mark my words.)

Fatigued with this, he let the abacus lie on his lap. No, this is not accurate, for he *had* no lap. He let the little instrument lie on the point of one knee, where the splendid folds of his belly had left, as if by design, just enough space for it.

The Captain squinted at the position of the abacus-beads on their golden wires, nodded courteously and went to his desk. He counted certain guineas into a bag and left the bag absently on a chair. The Chinaman pulled out a tiny whistle of gold from his infinitely resourceful sleeve and blew upon it. His secretary slipped in, bowed with different degrees of obsequiousness to everyone present except the *schroff* and vanished. He had not, it seemed to me, approached the chair whereon the guineas lay, but they were gone.

"Fat old pig say now he sorry to take sunshine of his face from your blinded eyes but too much light not good for common men. Means he now fucking off. Also, on order of Celestial One, must seize any Western Ocean strong waters in boat. Think he wants get pissy-pissy."

"Give him a case of the trade gin," growled the Captain, "the stuff with the cayenne and tobacco-juice in it."

No sooner had the mandarin's scow – now a little lower in the stern – returned to the war-junk, than all kinds of other scows, sampans and egg-boats emerged from their concealment on the shore and made towards us, pulling frantically. At the Captain's behest, I sent a small gang of sailors below decks to fetch up, under the schroff's supervision, exactly one hundred and forty-nine chests of the drug. These comprised nine chests of very superior Benares balls, forty cases of middling stuff and one hundred of the cheapest quality, including some of the *Madak* mixed with charred babul leaves and the dottles from opium already smoked. (Oddly to say, there are addicts to the drug who prefer the last: much of the virtue remains in it and is now more readily released. Strange, is it not?)

All these chests were laid out on each side of the break of the poop just as the first of the Chinese boats came alongside. One merchant from each vessel scrambled aboard and all were welcomed with copious words from the *schroff* and a false, greasy smile from Lubbock. They jostled and shouldered each other with every mark of courtesy, making cackling, splashy noises as they burrowed in the chests, smelling, scratching and prodding at the opium, dabbing little spots of red pigment here and there on the woodwork and flicking similar memoranda onto the little leaves of ivory they each held.

"Should there not be a guard over the chests?" I asked Peter anxiously. He stared at me.

"Good God, no. These are Chinese merchants, Karli, the only honest men in the world. The word of one of these fellows would be honoured by his grand-daughter's son-in-law fifty years from now. You could give any one of them a thousand in gold this moment; he'd give you a scrap of paper with a squiggle from his little paint-brush on it and a lick of his chop – that's their sort of personal seal – and a year from now you could cash it on the Barbary Coast, aye, and get the accrued interest to the nearest half cent as well as a dashed good meal."

This seemed strange to me, for I had hitherto believed that only we Jews had such standards and such international trust. I mused. The crowd around the chests thinned out and the merchants sauntered about the deck wearing polite expressions and taking care not to appear to be impressed by the marvels of Western civilisation evident thereon. Looking back, it occurs to me that perhaps they were, indeed, not impressed. They strolled everywhere. Sailors chuckled at them and hailed them with phrases of amiable obscenity, often using the word "plick". To each greeting the Chinamen would bow, civilly although not deeply, but their faces were masks, masks.

"Damn it, Peter," I said at one point, "three of the buggers are going into our cabin, don't you see them?"

"Karli, do you never listen to me? I'll give you a hundred pounds for every pin or penny you have missed when they've gone. They only wish to sneer politely at the poverty in which we barbarians live. If one of them asked you into his house it would be yours while you were there, except that part of it 'behind the curtain' where the women are. If you glanced more than once at their most treasured possession – again, I except the womenfolk – it would be pressed upon you. You would have to accept it. You would never be forgiven, of course. Not for accepting it, I mean, but for looking at it more than once. Do you begin to understand?"

168

I reflected a while.

"No," I said.

Had I understood and believed more, in those days when I was beginning to become clever, I might have become rich more quickly. Also, perhaps, dead. (Here, though, as you perceive, I am: both rich and *alive*. To be alive at my great age is pleasant for I love to indulge myself with eating, drinking and, from time to time, changing my will. There was a time when I thought that Bully Lubbock's rope's end "starter" could make men jump; now I understand that asking one of you to deliver a note to my solicitor has a much more enlivening effect. I am sure that you do not begrudge an old man his simple pleasures.)

After a proper interval to allow the Chinamen to exhibit their lack of interest in our ship and to make it clear that they had no vulgar, mercantile lust for our opium, the *schroff* passed among them, murmuring to such effect that they wandered, as if by chance, to the Captain's cabin, there to be plied with a mixture of gin, rum and warm water which they much relished and which befitted their station in life.

They lolled elegantly for quite half an hour, our Captain showing no sign of impatience. Then the senior of the merchants, an austere and venerable person, commenced to quack. I had been eyeing his features for some little while: the thin, implacable lips, sparsely moustached, had reminded me of the private parts of the Griqua girl I had patronised in Cape Town. When he commenced to quack, however, all fell silent. The *schroff* interpreted the duck-like noises as an insulting bid for the whole of the cargo at a price which would not have paid for its weight in toffee-apples. The *schroff*'s phrase for him was less kind than the "fat old pig" he had applied to the mandarin but, curiously, it somewhat bore out the comparison I had been making in my mind with the Griqua girl.

The Captain was no whit nonplussed. He gazed at the decanter before him for quite a minute, then delicately placed the stopper in its neck.

"Tell the old person," he said at last, "that although we Western Ocean barbarians are unable fully to comprehend the delicate spice of his wit, I would certainly allow myself to unbend in merriment were not so many of his juniors – his *richer* juniors – present."

The *schroff* took thought, then launched into an impassioned speech in the duck-like tongue which went on and on. The Captain seemed to doze. The senior merchant studied the colza-oil lamp hanging above the table as though it were a relic of the past; something his ancestors had invented a thousand years ago and discarded immediately. A silence fell. I yawned; I was sleepy, for reasons of my own. The Captain snapped at me:

"The diplomacy is *my* part, Mr Van Cleef!" Then, to the *schroff*, "Tell the old person that this ungifted step-child of mine comes from a country even more distant than mine and that there, because they know no better, to open the mouth widely, as though yawning, is a sign of admiration for those gifted in speech and riches."

The old person half-rose and half-bowed. I could do no less. I do not think my old rabbi would have rebuked me, for there are precedents for doing just so in the house of Rimmon. (Study, children, *study*; why do you think we support the Rebb?)

Quacking now broke forth unstemmed from every side; the *schroff* took notes – bribes, too, of course – and I, having been given a secret price-list by the Captain, said both this and that from time to time and with great dignity. In a surprisingly short time all our chests had been sold and, after one last glass each of the dreadful "bug-juice", the Chinamen left in order of seniority, becking and bowing. Their boatmen, cut-throats to a man, were then allowed aboard and these plucked out their masters' purchases unerringly and boated them. No money had changed hands but the Captain's mouth twitched visibly at the corners, almost as though he were on the point of smiling.

Within an hour, a frail and filthy sampan sculled toward us, a hideous half-man propelling it and three naked infants baling for their lives the water from its rotten bottom.

A line was lowered and a cloth bag was drawn up the side of our ship. The Captain turned to me.

"Have you an old garment, Mr Van Cleef?" he asked. I searched my mind.

"I have a pair of under-drawers," I said, "which the rats have got at. I had thought of giving them to my servant-boy, since they are beyond repair."

"Will you give them to me, Sir?"

"Of course," I stammered, "but they are quite gone at the gusset of the crotch, quite gone."

"All the better," he said, "all the better. Ventilation is the secret of hygiene. You will donate them to this child of nature, if you please."

Blushingly I sought out the small-clothes *in avisandum*. The Captain did not look at them, for he had been a gentleman once, you see; he dropped a half-handful of small copper coins into their noisome depths and tossed the parcel into the sampan. It was by way of being a gift or fee. The man was transported with gratitude.

The parcel which the fellow had delivered was exceedingly heavy; a seaman had to help the *schroff* to drag it into the Captain's cabin. There we counted it and weighed it: there were Maria Theresa thalers worn thin, slabs of bar-silver, Spanish dollars which betrayed the presence of Yanqui traders, old English spade-guineas bent in half twice and hammered into a lump, and a fragment of paper, so greasy that one could have read a gazette through it, which proved to be a draft on a Cairo bank by one of the Bonajee family, written out nine years before. In each separate sub-package within the bundle was a trifle wrapped in silk: a little lump of jade, a morsel of carved ivory or of rose quartz, the tooth of a shark. They were tokens of esteem, what O'Casey would have called "luck-pennies". Seeing my interest, Captain Knatchbull freely gave me all of them which were not made of precious metals. I prized them more than the lost, shameful under-drawers.

No sooner had we finished the counting and weighing but we heard a cry from the deck that various small craft were approaching us. No one save I was one whit alarmed at this news and, indeed, the craft proved to be nothing but egg-boats and sampans bringing out the promised pigs and ducks, along with hens, eggs and great store of a strange, cabbage-like vegetable much esteemed in those latitudes. Everything was absurdly dear at first asking, but the *comprador*, aided disdainfully by the *schroff* (for this was not *his* work), spoke so scornfully to the higglers that prices soon sank to a rocky bottom. The vendors shewed no bitterness; it was clear that they had set their prices at random, having no notion of how much we Western Ocean Barbarians might pay for the necessities of life.

The ducks were of a size and quality which I had never before seen: the Chinese may be a godless and illiterate race but in the matter of breeding ducks they have nothing to learn from the civilised world. Peter and I "clubbed" to buy a brace of these portly fowls for our own mess and talked seriously to the Doctor about how they should be dressed for the table. Greatly learned in all the cooking modes of the Seven Seas, he offered to make us a tidbit in the Manchu fashion. One coats the duck's feet in a sort of syrup, he told us, then persuades it to trot up and down upon the red-hot stove-top until the feet are puffed and crisp. This delicacy, he assured us, is much prized. I was interested but, having been brought up in a cleanly household, pointed out that the duck's toenails were dirty. Peter, too, demurred, saying that he preferred to save his appetite for the bird itself. The Doctor then prepared to pluck the first bird alive: this leaves the skin more perfect, he explained, and everyone accepts that the skin is the best part of the duck. To my surprise, Peter vehemently forbade this on the grounds that it would cause the duck – this *Chinese* duck – discomfort! I shall never understand the English, never. The Doctor smiled indulgently and, to prove that ducks feel no pain, held it between his knees and slit its throat gently. He stroked it and murmured soft words in some strange tongue while Orace collected the blood in a cup for the gravy. The duck, indeed, seemed perfectly complacent and, when the cup was full and the Doctor set it down, it waddled a few paces, opened its beak to quack, found that it could not and died tranquilly. It was most droll; the Doctor and I laughed and laughed.

At that moment we heard a succession of shouted orders, the thunder of sailors' feet upon the deck and then Bucko Lubbock's bellow of "Stamp and go!" told us that we were weighing anchor and setting sail: evidently our Captain had decided not to water at Namoa after all and had resolved to be clear of Swatow Bay before darkness fell.

Sure enough, as soon as we were in the open sea, we found a small but favourable wind – a false foretaste of the north-east monsoon – and the watch on deck was kept busy for much of the night setting more and more sail to it and sending light spars aloft until we were pretty well "a-taunto".

Peter and I, too, were kept busy for a good while with the first of our ducks, served with the Chinese cabbage and a spiced sauce of oranges.

While Orace cleared away the dishes I picked my teeth and eyed the child in a benign but critical way.

"Orace," I said.

"Sir?"

"You are a good enough boy."

"Sir, thankyou Sir."

"Your hands are always clean, despite the hazards of ship-board life. Your face, too, is spotless and I do not doubt that your ears and neck would bear the closest inspection."

"Sir, thankyou; I do my best to be a clean boy, as you have bid."

"Why then," I asked judicially – for I was in the sententious phase of drunkenness – "why then is your shirt stained? You know how delicate a digestion I own and you are clever enough to understand the dyspeptic effect of a stained shirt upon such a digestion. Explain this negligence!"

To my astonishment the child burst into tears. I started to say something but Peter gave me a glance of such startling authority that the words froze in my open mouth.

"Karli," he said evenly, "the boy's shirt is clean. The stains are blood. Look at his face." He crooked a finger and Orace bent his tearful face into the circle of lamplight. His nose was swollen and the nostrils crusted with blood. There was a little blood, too, at one corner of the mouth and an eye was puffed and discoloured. I was at a loss for words.

"Who struck you, boy?" asked Peter kindly. Orace, fighting back tears, answered manfully, standing to attention. It seemed that he had fallen out of his hammock. This was a plausible excuse and I was prepared to let the matter rest, but Peter told him to turn around. In his gentle, almost womanly way, he pulled the boy's shirt-tail out of his breeches and raised it to the arm-pits. Orace's ribs were black and blue. I rose, outraged, and was about to shout furiously but Peter quietened me with a gesture. He did not ask the boy who had brutalised him; he only asked whether it was any of the men before the mast.

"Oh, no, Sir!" cried the boy.

"Very well, run along. Ask the cook for some salve for your hurts. Your master will protect you from now on, you may depend upon him."

When the door had closed behind the boy Peter rested his chin upon his hands. His countenance was dark and bitter. I think that I was gaping foolishly.

"Lubbock," said Peter, as though it were a dirty word.

"Lubbock?"

"Oh, God, Karli; who else? He had set his heart, if you can call it that, on a certain lady, who now, for reasons I care to know nothing about, no longer welcomes his admiration." I looked at him sharply but he avoided my eye. "Then," he went on, "he will have tried to sodomise your boy, part lust, part spite. He will not have succeeded, for Orace is a good boy." Again I looked at him narrowly, again he preferred to fix his gaze on the bulkhead. "So he will now make the child's life a hell until, in a very short time, he will go over the side. I am not exaggerating, Karli, you may take me at my word. I have seen this sort of thing before. Too often."

I gazed at him dully, filled with guilt and trepidation.

"What, then, should I do, Peter?"

"A man doesn't tell another how to look after his servants," he said, a little stiffly. Then, seeing my face fall, he added in a kindlier voice, "You might try altering your rather regular sleeping habits. Lubbock has the second watch, from four until eight tomorrow morning. Your boy will be up at first light – say half-past six. Why not take the air on deck at, say, half past seven? Now I must turn in. Goodnight, Karli. You will know what to do in the event: you are a better man than you believe."

"Goodnight," I said.

My new silk nightshirt afforded me no sense of luxury that night, nor did sleep come readily.

Sure enough, I rose at the unheard-of hour that Peter had suggested. It was not cold. For some obscure reason I washed myself all over in cold water as though I were an Englishman. This had a tonic effect. I sauntered on deck. There was no one to be seen on the quarterdeck except the steersman, whose glazed eyes jerked from the compass-card to the leech of the sail and back to the compass-card. Two men were at the pump, watering down the deck; two more were dragging the "bear" – a large, weighted scrubbing-mat – to and fro in a drowsy fashion. The rest of the watch was clustered just abaft the fo'c'sle; they seemed to be staring up at something unpleasant. I followed their gaze. High up in the main-mast shrouds a tiny figure was picking its way even higher, clinging desperately at each hand-hold. Leaning against the halyard rail was Lubbock, a dirty smirk on his lips and the "starter" swinging like a fat serpent from his hand.

Peter was right: I knew what to do. Cupping my hands I shouted up to the boy, "Come down at once, Orace, and get about your chores." I had ignored Lubbock. From behind me he drawled, "*I* sent him aloft, Mr Van Cleef." I ignored him still. Orace was hesitating. "Come down at once!" I shouted, "you have no business there. Come down; no one shall hurt you."

The nasal drawl behind me was now menacing.

"I said *I* sent him aloft, mister. The little bastard was insolent to me." I rounded on him.

"If you have any complaints to make about my servant you may make them to me. You will not punish him, nor shall you ill-treat him. He has his duties; no doubt you, too, have yours."

The man stared at me, quite at a loss for the moment, as a fox might be if a rabbit cuffed him across the muzzle. His mouth opened and shut. Orace jumped the last few feet of the ratlines and scuttled between us. As he passed, the Mate's starter snaked out between the boy's legs, curling cruelly up at his groin. He squealed with pain and scrambled on all fours to the safety of the galley where the Doctor stood, arms folded, his face a mask. Lubbock stalked aft. My feet seemed nailed to the deck. I turned my head to the little group at the fo'c'sle: they were all looking at me curiously, not unkindly. Strangely, it came to me with great certainty that they were all recalling that I was a Jew. They knew just how Peter Stevenage would behave in such a case but they could not guess how a Jew would comport himself. This helped me. I strode after Lubbock.

"Mr Lubbock!" I called clearly. He did not falter in his progress aft. I called again, louder; still he did not pause. By now he was at the break of the poop, I was just abaft the mizzen mast. I stopped, put my hands on my hips and roared "LUBBOCK!" in a voice such as I did not know I could command.

This time he stopped in his tracks, slowly turned, crouching dangerously. He waited. The moment span itself out for half an eternity. I could hear my heart knocking at my ribs.

"Lubbock," I cried in a ringing voice, "you are a cowardly bastard!"

His face split open into an alligator-grin as he sidled to the rail, his hand outstretched for a belaying-pin.

I have already described that fight and how I won it. Afterwards I went to my cabin and lay down; as soon as my heart slowed a little I fell fast asleep, for I was not in the habit of rising early. When I awoke, towards noon, Peter was sitting on his bunk gazing at me morosely.

175

"Well," I asked, grinning idiotically I suppose, "did I do the right thing?" I expected praise, admiration, but all he said was that I was a bloody nuisance for now there were but two watch-keeping officers besides the Captain, which would be burdensome to all aft.

CHAPTER THIRTEEN

Peter's coolness, in the ensuing days, was reflected twofold by the Second, whose taciturnity changed to a complete unawareness of my presence. The Captain, too, chose to pretend that I was invisible and, when I appeared, would stump to the weather-rail and occupy himself with his telescope. It was otherwise with the common sailors of the crew: their smiles were broad and they tugged many a forelock as I strolled the deck. A proud, awe-struck Orace brought Peter and me a succession of splendid messes from the galley which made me confident that I had won the Doctor's approval. Blanche made frequent visits to where Lubbock lay groaning in delirium, as a woman should, but there was no cause for jealousy. Once, when she passed close to me and no one was in sight, she smiled at me enigmatically and made the most delightfully suggestive *moue* with her wet, red lips.

When we were eating Peter would relax a little unless I brought up the subject of the duel, whereupon he would become cold and distant again. Looking back in time, now that I am in the prime of life and have purged myself of all vice and vanity, it occurs to me that he was trying to stifle in me a certain overweening self-satisfaction which he may have wrongly believed I was exuding in those days.

Despite the light airs, our great press of canvas brought us in a very few days to within sight of the island of Lin Tin. This means "Single Nail Island" but the resemblance is only apparent to the Chinese. Many things were apparent to the Chinese at the time of which I speak, things which were apparent *only* to them. They held this truth self-evident, for example: The Emperor, The Son of

Heaven, The Dragon, bore the name Tau Kuang, which means Glorious Rectitude, and was, naturally, Lord of the World. It was serenely admitted that there were distant regions of his Empire, such as England, which had not yet been blessed with the ineffable radiance of The Heavenly Face, but this was a pardonable, childish ignorance and would be corrected when we grew old enough to learn. (This was comparable with the splendid common sense of the British Empire-builder when confronted with cannibalism and the feeding of worn-out old ladies to the crocodiles: get the beggars to understand hut-tax and road-making first, civilisation will follow. It was the missionaries who spoiled things with their prudery and prurience; to this day they cannot understand that making black women cover their breasts rehearsed the Fall – the key passage is at Genesis 3 vii – nor can they see that assuring the base savage that he is the equal, not only of his witch-doctor but also of his District Commissioner, is a source of bewilderment to the savage, resentment to the witch-doctor and a great nuisance to the D.C. I digress, but informatively: learn, *learn*.)

Our baseness – that of us Western Ocean Barbarians – was controlled by forbidding us to address anyone but the merchants of the Hong, or Ko'Hong, a venal body of contractors who purchased concessions to trade with us from the Hai Kwan Pu, a relative of the Emperor (who had in turn bought his unpaid but immensely lucrative appointment) and whose title was abbreviated in the usual, irreverent British way to "The Hoppo".

The breath-taking absurdity of these people's arrogance had been shown only a few years before – in 1834, I fancy – when Lord Napier himself, as Special Envoy of His Britannic Majesty, arrived at Canton and proposed to pay a visit of protocol on the Viceroy of the province. The first thing that happened was that the merchants of the Ko'Hong were terrifyingly rebuked for having allowed any person not a merchant to enter the Factories suburb. "Tremble!" the letter to them concluded, "Intensely tremble!" The next thing was that, finding it impossible to gain an audience of the Viceroy, Lord Napier sent a State Letter by his secretary to the Gate of the Petitions outside Canton. For hours this letter was proffered to one merchant or official after another, but none would touch it, for it was superscribed with a Chinese character which means "Letter". Had it borne the character for "Petition" someone might have dared to carry it to some petty clerk in the Viceroy's bureau. The third thing was that Lord Napier, addressed by a character which meant "elaborately nasty", was urged, then ordered, to return to Macao.

If you find that hard to believe, read this, which is just as true. As late as 1839 a Mandarin or Commissioner called Lin Tsê-hsü wrote to Queen Victoria herself (naturally, the Celestial One could not deign personally to recognise so piddling a tributary sovereign) and rebuked her roundly for base ingratitude at the Celestial Bounty, saying that punishment for her disobedience would be, for the time being, suspended, and suggesting ways in which she could show proper submission without losing too much face. Lin, by all accounts, was a man of great intelligence; it is hard to tell whether his tongue was in his cheek and, if so, how far. But then, it is hard to tell anything about Orientals. One might say that they are the English of the East.

Perhaps the best of all illustrations of the working of their minds is the well-recorded tale of the first steam-ship to appear at the Bogue. They picked up a pilot at the Grand Lemma (the largest of the Ladrone Islands) and were taken through the island channels to the Macao Roads without the least flicker of curiosity from the pilot. Dropping him at Macao, the Captain, unable to contain himself, asked the pilot what he thought of the new system of propulsion. The latter glanced back at the funnel without interest and replied that this way of driving a ship had been invented in the Celestial Empire some thousand years ago, but had been discarded as too dirty and extravagant.

When I first heard that story I laughed immoderately. Later, I came to wonder uneasily whether the pilot might not have been speaking the truth.

This island of Lin Tin is three miles long and is occupied chiefly by a mountain of some two thousand feet. Only the anchorage has interest. The first and finest sight was an ancient ship which, had you seen it in a storm in the Southern Seas, you would have taken for the *Flying Dutchman* itself. It was, I was told, an old "country wallah" – teak-built in India perhaps two hundred years ago and modelled on an even earlier design. As the name suggests, these ships were for the "country-trade" only and dabbled in all sorts of trading as well as opium. This one had been on the Coast since the end of the last shipping season so, despite our digression with the typhoon, we were still the first in the field.

Apart from a swarm of egg-boats, sampans and such Chinese craft, the only other vessels in the anchorage were the receiving ships: large, dismasted hulks which were nothing more or less than floating warehouses – although from the gay awnings, the stove-chimneys, the pots of flowering plants and the strings of laundry you might have thought them floating tenements. We laid alongside one of them and a "brow" was quickly laid from our deck to one of the many entry-ports. I was loafing at the entrance of the galley when four of our men laboured up from 'tween decks bearing a makeshift stretcher. I had known that Lubbock's wound was not healing well but was nevertheless startled at the change in his appearance: his face was yellow and the skin stretched tightly over his bones, his hands were like claws, plucking at the light sheet which covered him and his head rolled to and fro in a horrid way.

"Why does his head wag so?" I asked the Doctor. "Is it delirium?"

"No, Maz Cleef," he replied gravely. "I think he looking for *you*." Ever ready to receive an apology and give a forgiveness, I strode towards what had been Lubbock. So soon as I came within his range of vision the horrid wagging of the head ceased, sure enough. His lips, crusted with sordor, cracked open and he croaked something inaudible. I bent over him, so as to hear what might well be his dying words of repentance.

"I am going to live, Van Cleef," he rasped faintly, "*live*. Can you hear me?" I nodded, encouragingly.

"Live to make you wish you never had lived." I started back, but not before he had spat, feebly but disgustingly, into my ear. I should have known better: people of such vileness do not change, even in the presence of death. As the men carried him to the receiving ship he was making an ugly, gasping sort of titter which no doubt sounded to him like a bellow of ribald mirth.

(There was an excellently-appointed sick-bay on this receiving ship, I was assured, and if necessary Lubbock would be carried to Macao where a neat little hospital was maintained by a Pomeranian medical missionary called Gutzlaff who was one of only two Euro-peans who could speak, read and write the Chinese tongue and whose nimble intellect was able to reconcile the creation of twenty million opium addicts with the opportunity to distribute Protestant Bibles and Cockle's pills. This Prussian Christian and Lubbock deserved each other.)

Then our chests of opium were brought up and flowed into the receiving ship. Our *schroff*, and the grand *schroff* on the larger vessel, made a show of marking off each chest but there was little need: pilfering was unknown in that otherwise dishonest trade. Captain Knatchbull went, in his good uniform, to pay calls on old acquaintances aboard the receiving vessel, taking his *comprador*, servants and both remaining watch-keeping officers with him for the look of the thing.

The air of Lin Tin must have been sovereign, for Blanche's headache vanished like the dew upon a Dutch tulip as soon as we were alone together.

When the party returned after several hours – none too soon for me because the heavy climate was not conducive to prolonged lessons in venery, such as Blanche loved – the Captain's face was long and glum. Although we were the first at Lin Tin the Chinese were confident that other and larger vessels would soon be at the anchorage and therefore they would pay no more than an average of £185 per chest of the drug, the poorer grades making up for the better. (At Namoa we had taken an average of £210 per chest although the overall quality we had sold there had been lower.) Why, then, had we not sold all at Namoa? For one thing, the country trade, so early in the season, although glad to pay high prices to satisfy a craving market, had not the resources to buy large quantities until their retail profits came in. More important, each ship had to sell a plausible quantity of the drug at Lin Tin in order to keep the mandarins, the Hong merchants, the Hoppo (all of whom, of course, took large, illegal commissions on each transaction) and even the proprietors of the receiving ships, content.

To my surprise, we did not stay at Lin Tin to deal but set sail the next morning for Whampoa, the official unloading port, thirteen miles below Canton. It was explained to me that the people of the receiving ship would deal for us capably and honestly.

At Whampoa an absurd Chinese official, calling himself the port doctor, came aboard to give us *"pratique"*. This means that such an official should satisfy himself that there are not, and have not recently been, any cases of infectious disease aboard. In practice it meant that there was a long and bitter argument as to how much he would take to go away.

The cargo we unloaded there into crab-boats was scarcely plausible as the entire contents of a ship's hold: the rhinoceros horns and elephant tusks, a few bags of American ginseng (which the Chinese prized more than their own) a few tiger- and leopard-skins, a small but valuable box of tigers' whiskers, some furs and woollen goods and, for the European community, liquor, letters, journals, books, hats, corsets and the like. There would of course be no comment on the paucity of our cargo – everyone understood perfectly that the bulk of it had been discharged elsewhere.

Leaving in the *John Coram* only the Second (now acting-First) Mate, Blanche and a handful of teetotallers as skeleton crew, the rest of the ship's company followed the goods up the Pearl River to Canton, or rather to that suburb where the Factories were permitted to exist. (Why they were called "Factories" is a mystery to me for nothing was manufactured there but profits.) Long before we reached the Factories, however, we seemed to be in a city upon the water: I swear one could have walked for a mile at least across the tightly-packed boats without the least risk of a wetting. The racket and the stench were quite enervating. Our Chinese boatmen pointed our craft into a narrow alley between these floating houses, stowing the oars and using paddles and, finally, boathooks to squeeze a passage. I was gazing entranced at a wonderful houseboat full of charming young ladies when Peter nudged me. "Canton," he said, pointing. There it stood; a grim, thirty-foot wall, each side more than a mile long and pierced by imposing gates.

"They say there are more people inside those walls than in London," said Peter. "Add the population of the suburbs and of this water-city and the number cannot be much less than two millions." Much impressed by this, for large figures always make me think of money, my eyes nevertheless strayed back to the houseboat of the young ladies. It was a splendid building – wonderfully carved and gilded balconies with intricate railings sprouted from every part of it and each balcony held a richly-clad young lady or two, whispering, tittering and nodding at us.

"Calm yourself, Karli," said Peter, drily, "they are forbidden to admit you onto the Flower Boats."

"Then why are they at such pains to make themselves attractive?"

" 'Nightee time come'," he replied enigmatically.

"Which means?"

"It is a pidgin-English phrase of wide application: it means that, after dark, officials cannot see regulations being broken."

"Then . . .?"

"*No*, Karli. Below decks in that boat of sin there are quite half a dozen burly pimps. If you ventured aboard you would, at the very best, be beaten and robbed but, more likely, you would never be seen again. Small parcels of you, neatly wrapped, would be thrown overboard when the tide was running. If you must sample Chinese womanhood, contain yourself until we are back at Whampoa, where there are many complacent and hygienic young persons of fine quality. But I warn you, anything you may have heard about the, ah, eccentric arrangements of the Chinese women's anatomy is simply one of those 'bouncers' with which sailormen love to tease landsmen. They are exactly like English women in that area."

"Oh," I said, a little put out, for I had been looking forward to making love on a T-shaped bed.

"But somewhat smaller," he added thoughtfully, "although whether this is due to the application of alum-water I cannot say."

At that moment we bumped, at last, at the foot of the landing stairs to the English Factory's garden. In front of us, across an elegant shrubbery and garden, rose a flagstaff from which bravely waved the Union Jack. Over to the left, two more flagstaffs bore the flags of France and the United States of North America.

Meanwhile, our Captain's face was darkening with anger as the *schroff* bickered with the boatmaster over the price of our passage. This darkening or scowling arose from the evident fact that the *schroff* was having difficulty in making himself understood; he had done well at Namoa for his native tongue was Foo-Kien, but his command of Cantonese was clearly not as perfect as he had claimed. At last a bargain was struck and we poured off the boat and into the garden. At the top of the stairs my heart leaped up, for to my right, over a high wall, I saw the flag of Holland herself.

All the Factories were curiously dignified in a variety of European styles yet all bearing an indefinable Oriental flavour. The English Factory was enormous: forty yards wide and one hundred and forty yards deep, a maze of courtyards, treasuries, state reception rooms and even a church. It was as self-contained as a monastery.

Each of the common crewmen was now issued a small advance of pay: enough to buy a few trinkets and to become drunk for just less than the length of time we were to remain there. They were strictly enjoined to stay in parties of not less than five, each party to include, and be governed by, a senior rating who was familiar with the perils of the place. The boatswain "Tommy Pipes" was to make these arrangements. Finally, the Captain vowed that he would severely fine any man who allowed himself to be murdered. To this day I am not certain whether he meant this as a joke, for he was a humourless man.

Then, before he entered the factory proper, to pay his formal calls, he turned to me and thrust a slip of paper into my hand.

"Proceeds of your share, Mr Van Cleef," he growled. It was a brand-new draft on a Parsee bank.

I puzzled at the amount, for it represented a price of no less than £215 per chest – the price for the highest quality we had sold at Namoa. I opened my mouth to point out his error but he silenced me with a gesture.

"I sold all yours at Namoa, Mr Van Cleef. Lay it out carefully on your cups and saucers and fiddle-faddles. They'll not rob you but you'll not get the choicest wares unless you put on a little arrogance. That's a word to the wise, young Lewis."

I believe I have already suggested the reason why he had once before given me that name. He was, I suppose, not really a bad man, only sad and mad; this is like having a broken leg inside your brain – no splints can be applied and, since there are no physical signs, you get no sympathy nor any kindly nurses.

Dismissed, Peter and I joined forces and he offered to be my *cicerone*. I checked him.

"First," I said, "we eat."

"Well now," he began, "there are numerous . . ."

"No," I said. "Be guided by me." He gaped, then grinned sardonically and thrust his hands into his trowsers-pockets.

"Very well, Karli. Lead on, I am in your hands."

Taking a mental bearing on the flagstaff which I had seen over the wall, I soon found the entrance to the Dutch Factory and we sauntered into the great counting-house, where a dozen pairs of eyes, and as many eyebrows, rose from desks and ledgers to meet us. I studied these people rapidly and selected a youngish man who seemed to be of middle rank and, although his eyes were blue and his hair yellow, was clearly of my own race. Introducing myself courteously, I gave him some vague story of a long-lost uncle who had last been heard of on the China Coast. It was wonderfully

184

pleasant to speak – and to hear again – the good Dutch tongue and he seemed no less pleased to converse with someone fresh from home. Soon everyone in the room was gathered around the desk, gossiping freely. A gong sounded for dinner and we were carried in to a veritable feast, a wonderful blend of Dutch and Chinese food – and great store of it. Peter, at first a little huffed, soon succumbed, for his nature was generous, and winked at me across the mounds of *rijsstaffel*. Afterwards, for I had been at pains to make myself agreeable, a splendid bedroom was pressed upon us – the place at that time of the year was half empty – and I changed my draft for several smaller drafts and a little gold and silver for pocket money. It was arranged that a Chinese dealer in fine porcelains would be summoned to wait upon me that evening with his wares and that I should pay one half of one per centum on any transaction in exchange for the services of their interpreter.

"Now," I said, linking arms with Peter as we emerged into the sunlight and stink, "I have exhausted my little skills, please take command and let me follow."

"Do you mind if I call you a bastard, Karli?"

"Not in the least," I replied smugly, "for I know that it is not literally true and that you would not say it if you thought so." He roared with laughter, for he was as full of food and wine and schnapps as I was.

"You are a *pompous* bastard, then, Karli, a crafty bastard and, I suspect, a lucky bastard. Also, you are drunk."

"Not yet, but the suggestion is a good one. Where shall we go?"

First we went a-sightseeing the length of Thirteen Factories Street, past the English, Parsee, "Old" English, Swedish, Imperial and Paou Shun Factories until we came to the corner of Old China Street, where the American Factory and the Hong warehouses faced each other. To the right, Peter pointed out an elegant building which was the Consoo Hall, which was a sort of Council Chamber for the Hong and the office of their mutual-assistance-against-bankruptcy fund. (True to the quirkiness of Chinese humour, this was funded not by brotherly co-operation amongst themselves but by an arbitrary *ad valorem* charge of four or five per centum on all Western goods passing customs, so that the "Western Ocean Barbarians" were, willy-nilly, protecting the Hong merchants against their own rashness in business (God save the mark!) to the tune of some third of a million sterling each year.

Although I have no Chinese blood, I could relish the irony of this.)

Strolling a little further, so as to see the fine French Factory, we turned down New China Street between the Spanish and Danish Factories, which flew no flags because they were no longer staffed by Spaniards and Danes, but let out as offices and bedrooms to all sorts of minor commerce-venturers. At the end of this street we entered a sort of square called Respondentia Walk or, after the nearest feature of the river-bank, Jackass Point. This was an alarming place, thronged with pimps and pedlars, whore-masters and hucksters, beggars, loafers, cripples, madmen; drunken sailors from our own ship and a knot of a Chinese policemen who were laying about them with seven-foot staves in their twice-daily pretence of clearing this promenade of undesirables. We made haste to turn left into the thoroughfare between the English and Parsee Factories: this was called by a string of crack-jaw Chinese syllables which meant "Green Pea Street" but was known to all English-speakers as "Hog Lane".

It was indeed a hoggish place, devoted to drunkenness, the selling of caged birds, threatening demands by able-bodied beggars, the telling of fortunes by professional liars, carneying pleadings by shifty fellows who had failed to pass the examination for mandarin because of enemies in high places, pimps, ponces, perverts and minor civil servants with secrets to sell. Had the street been broader and the faces white, one would have thought oneself to be in Fleet Street.

We shouldered our way to Ben Backstay's establishment, a gin-shop where Peter was remembered and greeted rapturously. Enough drunken people were kicked and thrown into the street to make a table clear for us. Delicate little dishes of shrimp and duck-skin appeared as if by magic and, as we munched, Peter ordered a bottle of gin, a loaf of sugar, a lemon, and a pot of hot water. This was not to my taste and I signified to the proprietor that I would have what the happily-drunk fellows at the next table were enjoying. This came in a bottle shaped like an Indian club and proved to be "First Chop Rum Number One Curio", which promised well. Peter shook his head gravely.

"Better stick to gin, Karli, I promise you. That is not only a violent intoxicant but a most inflammatory genital vesicant. In other words, it will not only make you fearfully drunk but also desperately lustful."

It certainly commenced to make me drunk but as to the other property I cannot honestly vouch because, to speak plainly, I was in those days desperately lustful all the time. I should be most interested to try that drink again, now that I am a little less full of sap.

As I plied my glass with a will, Peter grew more concerned.

"Karli, I beg you, take advice: that is no common puggle-pawnee or nose-paint, it is like firing a charge of dismantling shot into the brain." I smiled at him reassuringly and sang a stave or two to show how little I had been affected.

"Listen, Karli. *Listen*, you booby. In an hour you have to do business with a Chinese dealer in porcelains. *Business*, Karli. *Porcelains*! For a great deal of *money*!"

That fetched me. With a magnificent gesture I swept everything off the table, gave Peter my purse and rose to my feet. After the third or fourth attempt I succeeded in rising to them. Peter lugged me to the booth of a Chinese apothecary, where they made me drink something to make me sick; then something else, hot and bitter, which cleared the fumes from my brain. I clearly recall that on the druggist's counter there was a glass jar full of curious objects and I continued to drink the bitter drench until I could focus my eyes on all the little scraps of ivory, amber, jade, roots and pebbles in the jar. Amongst them was a tooth. It was a human incisor, but half the size of a playing-card, a sure proof that giants had indeed once walked the earth. I longed to buy it but Peter hustled me out. To this day I still wish I had bought it.

At the Dutch Factory I was again quite sober although a little exalted. A fat, richly-clad merchant awaited me in a side-room, accompanied by the interpreter and a disdainful person sitting at a window with his back to us. This last was a merchant of the Hong, for no commerce could take place except through such a person. The porcelains laid out for my approval were good, several of them of a quality such as I had never handled. I picked up the very best piece of all, which I sensed had been included to test my knowledge; it was a plain, undecorated bowl of the richest, deepest ox-blood colour and could not have been later than the fourteenth Century. I put it down again and turned on my heel. I knew nothing of Chinese practice in these matters but I have a deep, inherited knowledge of how to deal with Gentile antique-dealers.

I lit a cheroot and addressed the interpreter.

"Tell this old person that he is under a misapprehension. I am not a drunken sailor looking for trinkets to take home as presents for whores. I have serious funds to dispose of and wish to buy serious wares. *Imperial* wares. Wares with six-character marks. If he has nothing better than these earthenware beggars' bowls, tell him to borrow some from a dealer of seriousness. I shall be here at ten o'clock tomorrow morning." He caught the small gold coin I flipped at him and bowed me out of the room. Peter was vastly impressed.

I was ill in the night, but not through trepidation.

The wares laid out the next morning were indeed of serious quality, I separated some two-thirds of them and asked a price. The dealer named one.

"Tell him," I said to the interpreter, "that, when I wish my gravity to be relaxed, I go to where some professional story-teller has unrolled his mat, but when I am conducting business a certain heaviness of the spirit makes it difficult for me to unbend in merriment." We began to deal. Twice the dealer began to re-pack his wares, thrice I began to walk out of the room with well-feigned impatience. At last we struck a bargain and the dealer put a little dab of ochre on my pieces. When I said that he should return that evening with more and better goods, his face went even blanker than it had been all through our chaffering.

"Wanchee see cash," explained the interpreter. I showed him enough to convince. By the end of the afternoon I owned porcelain of a quality and quantity beyond my wildest dreams, and still possessed £200 in notes and gold. I was well satisfied. The merchant's porters carried all away: it was explained to me that it would be at Whampoa, carefully packed and crated, before we sailed. Naturally, I hated to let it out of my sight, but I knew that no merchant with his knowledge would stoop to sharp practice once a deal had been struck.

As I left the room I heard the Hong merchant, who had stared silently out of the window for most of the day, stir in his chair and begin to click his abacus. He had made, no doubt, a pretty commission. For my part, I had made, at the smallest estimate, some twenty-five thousand per centum profit on my capital.

CHAPTER FOURTEEN

At Whampoa I found Blanche looking radiant, puzzlingly radiant. I could not help wondering whether she had been practising her late-found skill with one or another of the handsome young Europeans. I particularly wondered whether she had fallen in with any Dutchmen and perhaps tried on them the phrases I had taught her. But I was never a jealous man.

We made but a poor passage down towards the open sea: the winds were either dead foul – and often there was little sea-room for tacking – or else they were non-existent. The Captain's temper deteriorated hourly; it erupted when the cooper, hat in trembling hand, reported that many of the water-casks were foul.

"Some of 'em's salt, Sir, and some of 'em's foul; there's a liddle dead dog floating in one of 'em. I jest can't understand it, I watched every one of 'em filled with me own eyes and lidded 'em with me own hands." He held out his gnarled hands as though they were evidence.

The Captain's face changed in the most terrifying way: it darkened and swelled until all around expected him to fall to the ground in an apoplexy. But he stepped forward and smashed his fist into the Cooper's mouth. The Cooper scrambled to his feet and spat a bloody tooth into the scuppers.

"Begging your pardon, Sir," he mumbled with a sort of dignity, "I signed to be flogged, but I never signed to be struck in the face." The Captain was twitching all over, his face working, his hands clutching and clutching convulsively.

"Then flogged you shall be," he whispered at last. "Flogged you shall be. Yes; yes, you shall. Just as soon as we have re-watered, for after the flogging that you are to have you won't be fit to work for many a day. Oh, many and many a day."

I must say that I felt a little sympathy for the poor fellow; he was fond of rum and had doubtless been deceived by some Chinese sleight-of-hand, but on the other hand he knew very well that all our lives depended upon his care for the water-casks. Had the spoiled casks not been discovered until we were many miles from a landfall we might have been in grave trouble.

As it fell out, although we were close to many landfalls, we *were* in the gravest trouble, although we thought it no more at the time than a vexing delay in our race to bring the new season's teas to London.

A course was set for one of the smaller islands of the Ladrones group – but one where the Admiralty Directions said that there was a safe anchorage and sweet water. By manning the sweeps we reached this anchorage just at dusk and dropped our hook some six or eight cables'-length from the shore. There was nothing to see to landward except the glints of two or three driftwood fires, from the hearths of hovels pitched among the wind-stripped palms.

"Mister," growled Captain Knatchbull to the Second (who was now, as I have explained, entitled to that form of address since the First was at death's door and at Macao, whichever be the nearer), "Mister, I'll have all hands, idlers and all, ready at first light to go ashore to scour and refill water-casks. You'll see to it that every man who touches a cask will scratch his name or mark on a stave – and may Christ protect anyone who has handled a cask which proves foul, for he'll get no mercy from me."

"Aye aye, sir," said the Second in a thin voice. He leaned over and plucked up the end of the smouldering length of punk which lay coiled in the tub, meaning to light his cheroot. The Captain chose to take this as a piece of nonchalance which, in his mood at that time, was the same as insolence.

"And Mister, secure the ship, if you please. No lights of any kind" – the Second flipped his cheroot over the side – "the galley fire to be out in five minutes. Two lookouts at the mast-head, each responsible for the other's vigilance, on pain of flogging. I'll write that on the watch-keeper's slate and you'll be so good as to initial it."

"Aye aye, Sir," said the Second in the most expressionless voice I have ever heard.

"And, Mr Van Cleef," the Captain said to where I lurked in the shadows against the lee rail, "reassuring though it is to have your presence so continually on the quarter-deck, I fear we are depriving you of the opportunity to carry out your duties in the lazaretto and the specie-room."

"Aye aye, Sir," I said briskly. You cannot go far wrong on ship-board if you say "aye aye, Sir": almost any other remark can be misconstrued.

As I slipped below I heard the Captain, while still on the companion-way, rasping out an order to Blanche to be ready in four and one half minutes. I gritted my teeth a little, for I was in love with Blanche, as I think I have made clear; moreover, there had been no time in Whampoa to meet any of the adept young ladies Peter had spoken of. My hand on the brass handle of my cabin door, I heard Knatchbull raise the sky-light and address the Second yet again.

"Mister, you understand that 'secure ship' means that boarding-nets are to be rigged, do you not?"

"Aye aye, Sir. The nets are being broken out now. They should be in place in precisely four and one half minutes."

Who would have thought that the bloodless Second would have a sense of humour? It makes me happy to think that his last words were his first jest.

I closed the door of my cabin, kicked off my boots and reached for the plate of delicate eatables beside my bunk. I was at something of a loss as I lay down, for there was nothing to read except the Bible and nothing to think about except the Captain exercising his recondite connubial rites upon Blanche, a few feet above my head. As I munched the doctor's "tabnabs" I strained my ears for the crack of the lash, the stifled scream, but all was drowned in the patter of bare feet upon the deck as the watch rove the boarding-nets into place, the occasional muffled curse and thud as a seaman lost his footing and a strangled cry of anguish as some clumsy fellow caught his finger, I supposed, in the tackle.

At a loss for pastime, I reached under the bunk and fished out the fat, flat mahogany box which contained my expensive revolving pistol. I drew the charges and loads and cleaned each chamber carefully. The watch on deck seemed to be making a great deal of noise about their task of rigging the boarding-nettings, they were yelling and blundering about like drunken men – woe betide them, I thought, if they disturb the Captain at his pleasure.

Yes, sure enough, there was the sound of his cabin door flung open, and a crash as (I hoped) he tripped over a chair and fell heavily. As I finished reloading and fitted the first percussion-cap onto its nipple, Peter flung open our cabin door. I looked up idly. Peter proved to be a huge yellow man with a shining naked head and a shining naked sword in his hand. There was a blood-curdling screech – from both us I fancy – then I shot him in the face. Just such another fiend took his place in the doorway, waving an even larger sword above his head. Time seemed to stand still as I carefully fitted another cap and shot him in mid-spring. His sword bit deep into the foot of my bunk and his blood hosed out in three or four great gushes: I must have severed the aorta. I dragged the two of them right into the cabin (so that they would not attract attention) then bolted the door and sat on my bunk, shaking uncontrollably. When I could master the use of my fingers again I reloaded the two expended chambers, re-capped all with infinite care, span the cylinder. Above my head, from the Captain's cabin, came a frantic, rhythmical thumping and pounding, a sound that none but a nun could mistake for anything but what it was.

Inside my head the battle began: valour and honour strove to come to grips with and strangle slippery cowardice, who dodged and whined and hid behind the furniture of my mind. Was I a craven hound? Could I skulk behind a bolted door while the woman I loved was being abused and polluted by murderous savages?

Yes, I could. Yet there is some inner resource, deep inside us dastards, which rises up in times of terror and makes us ignore the commands of common sense. Somewhere, close by, a cannon roared; I was too bemused to wonder why or whence but the noise drove me to my feet. I unbolted the door, opened it a crack. Whooping, half-naked, blood-slobbered Chinese – some ten or a dozen – were pouring down the companion-way to the specie-room. I stole out and drew closed the water-tight teak door they had passed through and silently shot the great brass bolts. A-tiptoe, quaking, I mounted until I could just peer out, my nose at deck-level. Much of the tarry standing rigging of the main and foremasts was alight and by its gleam I could see a rabble of pirates forrard, crouched ready to storm the fo'c'sle and only held at bay by the occasional crack of a well-aimed pistol from its darkened recesses.

Behind and above me on the poop there was a stamping and shuffling and Peter's voice, cracked with desperation, screaming "Dogs! Dogs!" Now my cowardice had quite crept away and in a moment I was on the poop, where Peter stood astride the body of the Second Mate, his back to the binnacle, a Chinese sword in one hand and a pistol in the other, daring them to come on.

"Hold quite still for a second, Peter!" I shouted, and fired past his ear at a gigantic pirate who had stolen up behind him. The man fell, but Peter's assailants now turned to me – only to be dazzled by the blinding light of a dozen flare-rockets which turned the night into noon-tide. A speaking-trumpet blared from the sea: "All white men, flat on your faces on the word 'three'. One, two . . ." I stared at the loom of a great ship which was almost aboard us – on her deck was a double rank of scarlet-coated men, those in front kneeling, the others standing. I flung myself to the deck. ". . . THREE" blared the loud-hailer and a withering blast of musketry swept the decks clear of pirates.

"Boarders away!" came the stentorian bellow and, with a mighty cheer, a host of sturdy, cutlass-armed bluejackets jumped over the side of their ship and landed thunderously onto the pirate *lorcha* which was grappled to our side. In another instant they were swarming into our *John Coram*, our own men were joining them from the fo'c'sle and the pirates were being hunted down like rats. I seized a midshipman, perhaps fifteen years old, his eyes wild, his dirk bloody.

"Down there!" I yelled into his ear, pointing at the door I had bolted. "A dozen of the swine!" Then I rushed to the Captain's cabin.

As I burst in I stumbled over a hard, round object – the Captain's head. This stumble saved my life, for a pistol banged and the ball whirred over my head. Lying on the ground, I shot the man who had tried to kill me, then the man who was squatting, dazed or drugged, in a corner of the room, all passion spent. The man on the bed, hunkered between Blanche's out-spread thighs, was wearing the Captain's stove-pipe hat; he was oblivious of all around him as he pumped and pounded at her belly. It was necessary to walk beside him and clap the pistol to his temple so as to shoot him without danger to Blanche. His rapt convulsions did not falter until his brains were splashed onto the bulkhead.

I have often tried to recall in the mind's eye the precise expression Blanche's face wore when I dragged the corpse off her. It was a fleeting expression, for she fainted a moment later and was not, indeed, properly herself for several days afterwards.

I have only related the adventure as I heard – and mis-heard and saw scattered parts of it. To make things clear I should explain that the men rigging the boarding-nets were already too late, their throats were silently slit as they leaned over the side. The clumsy noises and the cries of annoyance, as I had thought them, were, in reality, the death-struggles of the watch on deck. One of them, thank God, had survived long enough to fire a distress-rocket, which had been seen by the frigate, *en route* from Macao to Lin Tin. The watch below, and a few other survivors, had succeeded in holding the fo'c'sle by virtue of a couple of little Bulldog pistols smuggled aboard by the Yankees we had recruited at Calcutta. The Second had succumbed to a ragged scalp-wound which laid him unconscious for days but from which he recovered. Peter had defended the poop with all the blithe ferocity of a man who does not care whether he lives or dies.

"Karli," he said that night, laying his hands on my shoulders, "you saved my life today."

"Oh really," I said, shuffling my feet in an embarrassed, British way, "I beg you to forget it, anyone would have done the same."

"Yes, I suppose they would," he said, disappointingly. "But Karli" – solemnly again – "there is one thing I cannot forget."

I kept a modest silence.

"Yes, Karli, I cannot erase from my memory that in your shirt-box there are quite eight inches of good Italian sausage, also a crock of wonderfully smelly cheese steeped in wine. I have a bottle of the best Constantia hidden away for just such an occasion as this. Shall we eat?"

"We shall indeed," I replied happily, "just so soon as Orace has scrubbed up the last of the blood from the cabin."

That was our last happy night.

CHAPTER FIFTEEN

The next two days were full of great business. Our depleted crew toiled mightily, some sewing our dead into their "tarpaulin jackets", some renewing the burned rigging, others rowing to and fro to the island refilling our water-casks under the supervision of the frigate's cooper – for our own had escaped his flogging by the valiant fight he had put up against the pirates. The hewn pieces of his body were even now forming part of the long line of packages which awaited consignment to the deep.

The frigate had in attendance an *aviso* boat in the form of a little, country-built, sloop-like vessel; this was dispatched at first light to ask orders from our owners' agent at Macao.

The frigate's Captain came aboard to carry out the burial services, a long and mournful task. He also lent us a bosun and a sail-maker's mate, together with a few old salts who could reeve and splice and a file of marines for the coarser tasks. Peter, now the only watch-keeping officer aboard (except of course the unconscious Second), had no time to eat or sleep, poor fellow, I have never seen anyone work so hard and so deftly in all my life, yet again and again he threw a laughing word over his shoulder to me or cracked a coarse jest for the labouring crew-men.

There was little I could do to help except check stores, make lists, set the specie-room to rights and write out receipts for the hundred-and-one things which we had to borrow from the frigate. It is quite amazing how much damage a few pirates can do in half an hour when they set their minds to it.

Late in the following afternoon our splendid little ship was again more or less fit for sea and the kindly frigate hastened off to its rendezvous, asking us to send off the *aviso* boat as soon as it returned with our orders. Every man-jack on the *John Coram* who could be spared was sent to his bunk or hammock; those who remained on deck, the barest anchor watch, were asleep on their feet. I could not, for very shame, repair to my bunk until Peter, my true, kindly-mocking, pox-ridden friend, could also find repose. He and I and the binnacle-post supported each other: I kept him awake and in good humour by proving to him, with many a cogent argument, that his so-called Jane Austen was clearly a German Jew called Shakespeare, going under the name of Göthe. We were both propped up, nine-tenths asleep, against the binnacle, giggling feebly, when a sleepy bellow from the mast-head announced that the little sloop was in sight. We kicked the deck-messenger from his hoggish slumber and bade him see that those few who should be on deck were awake. I bellowed wearily for Orace; good boy, he was with us in a trice and scampered below to fetch us clean neckcloths.

As we tied them, the fellow at the mast-head warned us that a boat had left the sloop and was pulling towards us. We went to the rail and, as soon as the boat was visible, Peter seized the trumpet and cried "Boat ahoy! What boat is that?"

"*John Coram*," came the answer, faint but clear. This did not seem to me to be an answer but Peter understood: it seems that, in the old navy, when a boat's coxswain named a ship, it was understood that his boat was carrying the Captain of that ship. Peter rapped out a filthy word, then a string of brusque orders. There was a bosun's mate trilling upon a pipe and two reasonably clean seamen pretending to be "sideboys" at the entry-port just one second before an ugly, shag-haired, purple-nosed old gentleman heaved himself aboard. He looked around with a disgust he made no effort to conceal. Then he sketched out a tipping of his hat to the quarterdeck, skipped up to the poop and glared at us.

"Where is the Officer of the Watch?" he snarled. Poor, unshaven, red-cyed Peter swept the hat off his tangled curls and made a dancing-master's bow.

"Your servant, Sir," he said, "but whom have I the pleasure to. . . ?"

"Jacob Dogg, Sir; Lieutenant R.N., retired. I have orders from your owners' agent appointing me Captain into this ship." He pulled a piece of paper from his pocket, snapped it open and thrust it away again. Peter touched his hat.

"Welcome aboard, Sir. I am Peter, Viscount Stevenage, third officer."

"Pray summon my other officers and present them to me, Mr Stevenage."

"I fear that is not possible, Sir. The First Officer is in Macao Hospital, the Second is in the sick-berth, still unconscious from a wound received in the engagement with the pirates. I am the only watch-keeping officer, although there is a capable sailing-master who could serve for the time being."

"Make it so, Mister. And this gentleman?"

"Carolus Van Cleef, supernumerary and shareholder."

"Very well. I'll take the larboard watch, you the starboard. You are temporary First until the Second regains his faculties, then he is promoted First, you Second and the sailing-master acting Third. Mr Van Cleef to take lessons in navigation three times a day. Now I'll have a sight of the watch-bill, if you please."

Peter drew out a tattered document and handed it over.

"The names crossed out are the dead," he explained. "Those underlined are wounded – a tick beside the name indicates that the man should be fit for duty in a few days; a cross means he's likely to survive. As you see, we could muster three strong watches before the fight: now we can scrape together two weak ones. We are desperately short of top-men. I have not yet sorted out the new watches."

"Why not, pray?"

"I had hoped that we might have picked up a few hands at Macao, Sir."

"My orders are to make all speed to London with the teas. Positively no recruiting. The men we have must work harder. They will have had an easy time up until now."

Peter opened his mouth, then shut it again.

"Now, Mister," growled the Captain, "how soon will the ship be ready to sail?"

"She *is* ready to sail, Sir. As soon as the men are rested, that is."

"Ready? *Ready?* Have you seen the state of the decks? Do you suppose I'm going to put to sea in a floating jakes, a stinking abattoir? Why are they not clean? Why are the men not at work?"

"Sir," said Peter flatly, wearily, "the frigate's Captain advised me to make the ship seaworthy first. We have completed with stores and water, sewn-up and buried our dead, repaired and renewed all burned and damaged rigging and done a hundred other necessary things. The decks, I was advised, could be properly cleansed when we were at sea, under plain sail."

"Advised," sneered Captain Dogg. "Ah, *advised*, Mr Stevenage, eh? You are one of those fellows, are you, always ready with someone to blame? I've met your sort before. I asked you, why are the men not at work on those abominable DECKS?"

Peter drew himself up and spoke in a languid and lordly voice I had not heard him use before.

"Sir, not a soul in this vessel has had a wink of sleep since fighting a bloody battle two nights ago. It is too dark to scrub decks, even if the men could be aroused from their exhaustion. I sent them to rest an hour ago. I gave these orders while in temporary command of this ship. So soon as you care to read me your orders I shall relinquish command to you and make an entry in the Ship's Log to that effect. From that moment I shall of course accept your reprimands for any errors of judgment I may make – *after that moment*."

Captain Dogg's nasty old face wreathed itself into a sly and malignant smile.

"A sea-lawyer, too, Mr Stevenage? Well, well, we shall have much to learn from each other in the next few months, shall we not?" He fished out his Orders again, gabbled them out and touched the brim of his hat. Peter touched the brim of his and, taking the log from the deck-messenger, solemnly inscribed the fact that Jacob Dogg R.N. (Ret'd) had assumed command of the *John Coram* at – he fished out his watch – such and such a time. When he had done, the new Captain, still smiling nastily, took the log from him and said that he, too, wished to pen a few remarks on coming aboard. Peter sauntered to the rail as he did so, as though he had not a care in the world.

"Now then, Mister," rapped the Captain as he closed the book, "If you've finished your promenade perhaps you'll be good enough to have someone shew me my quarters."

"Well, Sir, our late Captain's widow is still in the Great Cabin, prostrated with grief and shock and, ah, molestation."

"The First Officer's quarters are empty, are they not? Good. See that the bereaved lady is removed there at once, with all gentleness and solicitude – and speed. Her personal possessions, too, of course. The late Captain's stores, particularly in the way of wines and ardent spirits, to remain in the Cabin. Mr Van Cleef and the Comprador to be strictly accountable."

"Aye aye, Sir," said Peter with no expression in his voice.

"All hands – *all* hands – to be mustered at first light, yes, write that on the watch-slate, Mister; they will have the decks snow-white in one hour precisely, all falls flemished and coiled – you know what is expected. See to it. At the end of that hour we shall set sail."

"Aye aye, Sir. I formally request, Sir, that you enter in the Log that in my considered opinion, as an officer who has known this ship for several years, it is imprudent to put to sea without at least one more watch-keeping officer and ten more seamen, six of whom should be able top-men."

"It is your right to request that, Mister, as you know, and I shall do it. It is *my* right, and my duty, to make an entry at the same time stating that Lord Stevenage, from the moment I joined this ship, has put every obstacle in my path while I endeavoured to make this ship fit for sea."

Peter bowed.

"I shall be happy to initial that entry, Sir, and to record the time at which it was made – some four minutes after you assumed command."

He and Captain Dogg smiled politely at each other, like two Bengal tigers over a dead Hindoo. It seemed plain to me that our homeward voyage was not to be a cheery one.

PART FIVE

The Long Way Home

CHAPTER SIXTEEN

Uncheery, indeed, the voyage proved. No one could deny that Dogg was a gifted captain; by dint of merciless driving he contrived to work the ship efficiently. He divided our two weak watches into three pitifully weak ones, one of which was always on call: this meant that for much of the time two-thirds of the men were at work but, when the sailing was plain, two-thirds of them could be snatching some sleep. The men went about their tasks like sleep-walkers but did not, at first, properly comprehend the arithmetic of the thing. In any case, they were more pre-occupied with the question of whether Dogg's morose inhumanity when sober was worse than his merry savagery when drunk. On the whole, the men preferred him drunk, for he would then sometimes order double shares of grog to be served out at unexpected times.

Peter, of course, even after the Second recovered enough to be able to stand his watches, was overworked and persecuted in a thousand ways, great and petty, but all perfectly legal by the letter of the law of the sea. I, too, was hounded and mocked but there was comparatively little that Dogg could do to me until I was qualified to stand watches – and I was shrewd enough to take care that my mastery of navigation grew slowly, although, in fact, I found it a simple enough science for anyone with a head for figures and had already, on the outward voyage, picked up the elements from Peter.

Captain Dogg was unlovely to behold: his shaggy head seemed to exude a dirty dust and he was afflicted with the disease called "Devil in the Beard" which made his jaws as hideously colourful as his strawberry nose. There was no doubt but that he was a wonderfully able Master Mariner but this won not even grudging admiration from the men. One came across little knots of them, muttering –

falling silent whenever an officer or a warrant-rating drew near. In each of these knots, it seemed to me, there was always one of our Calcutta Yankees; our men dropped their eyes sheepishly at these times but the Yankee would stare at one boldly with a sort of a sneering smile. I caught glimpses of a little book passing from hand to hand.

Each day, as we ploughed through the island passages towards the Indian Ocean, I grew more uneasy. Strangely, whenever I tried to sympathise with Peter about some new imposition upon him or some fresh drunken outrage on the Captain's part, he silenced me curtly, reminding me that Dogg was our commanding officer. This made it harder for me: to worry without a friend to confide in is a lonely business and wearing, wearing. What it was like for Peter I cannot say, perhaps I cannot even guess, even now.

Sheer loneliness – for Peter was at this time too tired when off duty to exchange even the lightest pleasantries – drove me to seek the company of the Doctor but he, too, seemed to become more glum and taciturn each day, although I cannot pretend that the flow and quality of his eatables abated. The change in his nature may well have been due in part to the new Captain's base approach to the matter of eating. Long service in the Royal Navy had given him a morbid appetite for kinds of food which you or I would spread upon the rose-garden as a mulch. The demands he made upon the Doctor for weevily biscuits, smelly salt pork and the kind of nasty duff called "dog's vomit" and his scorn for "made dishes" and what he called "kickshaws" must sorely have tried the patience of my negro friend. But this cannot have been the whole of the story. No, the Doctor was, so to say, the ship's moral barometer and one could almost see the mercury slithering lower and lower in his Torricellian tube.

Blanche recovered but slowly and was less than eager to receive my caresses, nor would she often meet me at the rail for our twilight talks.

One evening, strolling past the main-mast bitts in search of a cooling breeze, I was accosted by the Irish O'Casey who pointed out to me the beauty of the evening, especially for those fortunate enough to have something to drink in such beauteous circumstances. Desperately lonely, I willingly fetched him a pannikin of what he called "the crater", which he emptied with many a "God bless yez, Sorr" before commencing to talk.

" 'Tis a shockin' tarror of a life dese times, is it not, Sorr?"

"I'm afraid," I said in a benign but Peter-like voice, "that I cannot discuss the failings of any of my superiors with you. Pray keep the conversation general."

"Of course, Sorr. I was just t'inking of a Lieutenant I sailed under wance. A great, drunken, red-nosed, rug-headed bastard he was and not a man in the ship but wouldn't have laughed to see him gibbeted. I t'ink his name was Catt or some such."

I made a non-committal noise, not wholly discouraging.

"And gibbeted he should have been, too, for didn't I see him murder three men in front of me own eyes? It was in these very waters, now I call it to mind. He was always a man to carry a press of canvas too long with a freshening wind, as you know."

I coughed warningly.

"I mean, you might well have come across the kind of a man I'm speaking of, Sorr."

"Just so."

"Well it was just one of them occasions; with the wind roaring like the Bull itself and shrieking like the Black Pig, up he sends the foretop men to shorten sail. They lay out along the yard, clinging on for very life, their bare feet clenching on the footropes like canary-birds on a perch, finger-nails torn and bleeding as they fight the bursting canvas – and bursting is the very thing the canvas is likely to do at any moment – while yer lieutenant is dancing on the deck and howling up at the men, calling them idle cowards and names I would be ashamed to hear even in me mother's mouth. He's as drunk as the eldest son at a Donegal wake, foaming at the mouth and a black bottle in his hand and at his lips every moment: he's as full as a Catholic School. Still the men cannot come to grips with the iron-hard canvas, it is as much as they can do to cling to life at all.

"The after-guard are standing by with axes, ready to clear away wreckage if the ship should be dismasted; the Lieutenant snatches an axe and with one mad, drunken blow, severs the sheet – the yard whips round and three top-men are twitched into the raging sea like musket-balls. No question of lowering a boat into that sea; no question of heaving-to, only a question of can the ship live, and every man working away like a dog at a bitch. But murder it was, black murder, and I seen it. I seen it in the Log, too, when I next had duty aft: 'Sudden storm this day,' he'd written, 'the men surly and

205

idle; I obliged to cut sheets to save the ship; three careless seamen drownd through their own inattention.' "

"But the Lieutenent you speak of was a young man then, O'Casey, and foolhardy, rash?"

"It was not dat terrible a lot of years ago, Sorr, and the only difference is that in them days he still had a few marks of the gentleman about him. Today he's a man that would tear Christ off the Cross."

"Goodnight, O'Casey," I said.

Naturally, I did not believe a word of all this, for he was an Irish, as I think I have said, but nevertheless I passed an uncomfortable night.

Strangely, while the men were being worked like slaves as we battered our way against contrary winds through the Island passages, continually making, shortening and furling sail, the sullenness did not seem to increase. It is hard for an exhausted man to brood on mutiny: the hardness of his lot cannot compete with the softness of his pillow. You, whose lot has never been hard, will probably not understand this until my death. (In politeness I must add: "You should live so long.")

It was later, when we were tearing west and south-west through the Indian Ocean toward the Cape of Good Hope, under all plain sail, that the men, with little to do and some sleep to prompt their appetites, commenced to become seriously surly, to reckon up the hours they spent on deck and to con over and over the little tattered book I had seen circulating, which must, of course, have been the dreaded *Seaman's Friend* by the American revolutionary Dana, the arch-sea-lawyer.

When the Captain was sober the men worked just well enough to escape punishment; when he was drunk they gauged his moods to a "T", idling when they knew it to be safe, hauling away with a "cheerily-ho!" when his eye was upon them and when they were confident that an issue of grog was in the offing.

I knew little of the sea and less of the world at that time but I knew enough to know that this was unwholesome. It seems strange to relate but it is true that, even when I held Blanche in my arms, I found myself wishing that Captain Knatchbull was still alive. (I could not – cannot – forget that moment when I stumbled over his head at the entrance to the Great Cabin and my remembrance that it – the head – was still attached to his trunk by a thick shred of the nape of his neck will never leave me. You may think it a small price to pay, but you have only dealt in money and goods: you have never seen a not-quite-severed head.)

Day followed day; it is impossible to explain to those who have never made a long sea-passage how tediously similar one day in an ocean is to another when the winds are fair, nor could you ever believe how the most trifling incidents can magnify themselves into calamities fit to set an entire ship's company a-buzz. Let me, simply, say again that the crew became less and less like the jolly Jacks with whom I had set sail from London River, that the Second changed from a taciturn to an utterly silent man, that my dear friend Peter became a stranger who wolfed his food and fell into his bunk with the briefest of "goodnights", that Orace carried out his duties in a perfunctory and timid way, and that the Captain grew more and more drunken and unpredictable. Sometimes he would not be seen for thirty or forty hours, other times he would rage about the vessel as though determined to make it a floating hell – and an hour later would be clapping every man upon the back, calling him a capital fellow and telling the Bosun to serve out rum to everyone in sight.

Even I could tell that this was no way to command a ship on the high seas.

Retribution came soon and arose from that very vice of Dogg's which O'Casey had spoken of, taking in sail at a minute after the last minute.

We were running before a fair wind but it was too light for the Captain's taste and all day long, as he grew drunker and drunker, he sent up more sail until we had staysails alow and aloft, water-sails and save-alls beneath the foot of the topsails; and, high above all, every "kite" that the sail-maker could find or improvise: moonrakers, a "Jamie Green" or jib-o-jib, even a Yankee-style Jolly Jumper and a "hope-in-heaven". Peter looked at all this press of canvas gloomily and I recalled his words when we first met: that the *John Coram* was built for spread, not hoist.

The Second had the watch; Peter and I were walking the deck in silence. The wind began to freshen and to shift a point here and then a point there. On the horizon there were tropical squalls plain to be seen, like dark-grey tree-trunks joining sea and sky. I noticed, with some uneasiness, that the watch on deck were all gazing aloft, where the extra masts looked no thicker than cabmen's whips – and were behaving like them.

At last the Second lifted the speaking-tube and called down to the Captain's cabin.

"Permission to shorten sail, Sir, and send down sky-sails."

We could clearly hear Dogg's answer.

"You have your orders on the watch-slate, Mister. Brace her up to the wind."

"Sir, I do not believe she can carry this press of sail much longer."

"What she can't carry she may drag!" came the drunken bellow.

I tried to catch Peter's eye, but without success. Looking around, I saw that many of the watch below had silently appeared on deck. There were ugly looks, both at the poop and at the weather. One or two of the squalls were approaching us fast, it seemed to me, and we were scudding along at a terrifying rate, shouldering the ocean aside like a constable shoving his way through a rabble. The Second drew a deep breath, like a man who expects it to be his last, and lifted the speaking-tube.

"Sir," he said flatly, "I formally request you to come on deck and judge the situation with your own eyes. I shall record this request of mine in the Log."

The Captain appeared, dishevelled and red-eyed, cursing foully. He looked at the weather, which worsened even as he looked. Then he looked at the sails.

"Send down all to the royals, Mister, and one reef in all plain canvas."

The Second picked up the "trumpet" – for the noise was now deafening – and relayed the order to the Bosun, who yelled it out piecemeal to the watch. Those who were to reef jumped to their work with alacrity but one gang shuffled their feet and did not otherwise move. The Bosun ranted at them but to no avail. He came to the break of the poop.

"Beggin' yer pardon, Sir, but the top-men won't go aloft."

"*Won't?*" roared the Captain, "*won't?* What kind of talk is that on ship-board?"

"Beggin' yer pardon again, Sir, but there's only one proper top-man in the gang, Sir, and he's got an 'and in bandages still."

"The men refuse to obey orders?" he whispered horridly.

"Not exackly, Sir. They just reckon it's suicide to attemp' it."

To everyone's astonishment, the ordinarily mute Second cleared his throat and spoke.

"Forgive me, Sir, but I consider that the men are within their rights. All that raffle of top-hamper will be carried away at any moment and an order which sends men to almost certain death in an effort to save a few light spars and rags of canvas is, by the laws of the sea, an improper order."

The Captain slowly turned and smiled at him. This was a disgusting sight, for his teeth were nastier than his face.

"Pray write your remarks in the Log," he said. With that he leaped at the futtock-shrouds and scrambled up like some great ape. Every eye in the ship was on him as he swayed and clung and fought the elements and canvas; but, by God, he took in and sent down all. No sane man would have attempted it, no sober man could have done it.

When he was back on deck, retching for breath and sucking his torn and bloody fingers, he glared about him with a kind of mad happiness.

"Line up the men who refused to obey orders," he croaked. "I have just shewn that the orders were reasonable, have I not? Line them up, I say, and bring the cat. I am about to flog every man-jack with my own hands."

"Oh no you ain't, mister bleeding Dogg," came a Yankee drawl. The Captain whirled about. One of our Calcutta recruits was pointing a little nickel-plated Bulldog pistol at his breast.

The Captain stood like a stone man for what seemed like a stone age. Wonderfully slowly, gently even, he reached out for the pistol. So persuasive was this gesture that even the coarse American faltered, spellbound until the last moment – but at this last moment he lashed out at the Captain's knuckles with the barrel of the weapon. Dogg recoiled, snarling, spitting like a cat.

"If you drop that weapon this instant," he said in the frightening whisper, "then I shall stretch a point and only have you flogged. If you do not, then I swear I shall stretch your neck. Unless, of course" – here he raised his voice – "any of your mates were so foolish as to support you, which would make it mutiny and hangings for one and all."

The American pointed his pistol into the air and fired a shot. This was a signal, clearly. The men who now crowded the deck shifted to and fro and arranged themselves hesitatingly into two groups. There were whispered curses, threats, promises, and several fellows shuffled first to one group, then to another.

At last all seemed settled.

"How many?" asked the American over his shoulder, never taking his eyes off the Captain and us other officers.

"Twenny-eight," replied one of his accomplices.

"Fine. Jest fine. *Mighty* fine. Mister Dogg, you are no longer in command here; I have placed you under arrest as a dangerous lunatic. You are free to leave this vessel, along with your shit-livered officers, who should have locked you up weeks ago. Any men who wish to stay and help work the ship, why, I'll write their names in the Log and say they had no part in this consarn."

There was a shuffling and a muttering from the uncommitted part of the crew; I was reminded perfectly of the crowd-scene in *Julius Caesar* by W. Shakespeare. Dogg leapt at the American with a strangled yell: he was, as they say, fit to be tied, and tied up is what he was, after some compassionate mutineer had hit him on the head often enough to calm him. Peter and the Second strode into the fray, unarmed, ordering the men to lay down their arms and accept their punishments like honest seamen, but their words carried little weight, for all knew that the only punishment was the stretching of the neck to which Dogg had referred. They, too, were bound.

I, as a thoughtful man, had reserved my judgment and, when the fellows wielding belaying-pins and pistols looked towards me I may well have been studying the horizon in an abstracted way. I was, after all, only a supernumerary officer.

There ensued a great deal of sordid bickering and bargaining, during which, to show my contempt for these proceedings, I strolled to the galley and filled my pockets with two double-handfuls of the Doctor's "tabnabs". I have always been a practical man.

Soon all arguments were settled. Dogg, the Second, Peter, the sailing-master and a few ancient mariners of warrant rank who had served Peter's father were to be set into the long-boat. Blanche was to remain aboard. The mutineers snickered at this. They asked me where I stood. I had been thinking.

"Where are you bound?" I asked haughtily, brushing a few crumbs from my lips.

"We're taking this hooker to the West Indies, brother. When we've sold the cargo, why, we'll jest go into business on our own account. Whole heap of work for a handy little ship in South Americky nowadays, 'spacially if she carries a few guns."

"And who, pray, is to navigate you to the West Indies?"

"You. We seen you taking lessons."

"And if I refuse?"

"Guess you kin take your chance in the open boat – but your fancy lady stays here. Calc'late we kin find a use for her."

I thought some more. A thousand miles in an open boat with Dogg held few attractions and the chances of survival seemed small in any case. Moreover I was, as I have explained, in love with Blanche.

"Very well," I said. "I'll navigate you to the West Indies; on conditions."

"Oh, yeah?" he said (this is how Americans speak, you understand – it means "indeed?").

"Yes. First, Mrs Knatchbull not to be molested, on your word as an honest seaman. Second, I am to be put ashore in the West Indies with Mrs Knatchbull and my private cargo. Third, I am to retain my pistol for self-protection – you shall have my *parole d'honneur* that I shall not attempt to seize the ship with it." I grinned disarmingly at this point. I am very good at grinning disarmingly – I *practise*. (*Verb. sap.*) "Fourth, the Captain, officers and seamen leaving in the boat are to be properly provisioned, watered, supplied with a boat's-compass and two firearms for use when they reach shore and to be given the ship's position and a sight of the charts before they leave."

The Yankee did not consider long, for he was an intelligent man.

"No," he said.

I reasoned with him, pointing out that behaving in the way I had suggested would lend a colour of legality to his assuming command from an insane Captain; otherwise they were mutineers and would spend all their days in the shadow of the rope. He agreed, at the urging of his accomplices.

The departure was unpleasant; Dogg raved and cursed, the Second looked at me as though I were something unpleasant he had noticed adhering to the sole of his shoe, Peter wrung my hand and gave me a long, anguished look which seemed more to indicate compassion for me than fear for his own survival.

The mutineers, ignorant fellows, made a trifling mistake which may well have cost them their lives one day. They seized the Second Officer's beautiful modern sextant for my use but contemptuously let the Captain take his old-fashioned quadrant or "hog-yoke" as they called it.

"'T'ain't no use without the star-book," said the leader knowledgeably, "and thet's right here on the chart-table." So it was. As

211

soon as the boat had left I stole to our cabin and studied Peter's little shelf of books. All his "Jane" Austens were there, also his Catullus and his Norie, but there was a gap at the end of the row where his own copy of the *Ephemerides* had used to stand. I was mightily comforted. A longitude and latitude, you see, and a course set by a boat's compass are but rough guides because of the set to leeward, the drift of the current and so forth, whereas with the quadrant, the *Ephemerides* and Peter's pocket-chronometer they would be able to fix their position with great accuracy each noon if the weather were clear, and at night, too. Moreover, I had seen the Second having the agreed "sight of the charts": he had stared at them for quite two minutes – Peter had long ago casually told me that the Second's brain was freakish, like Lord Macaulay's: he could memorise a page of print in the time it took to pass his eyes over it. Today we would say that he had a mind like a photographer's plate.

Their dangers were still unimaginable but now at least they could not be lost in the waste of waters. I pitied the mutineers if Dogg reached land; he was a man who would hound them to death if it took him all his life.

That he was not wholly insane was soon evident; when the boat was out of gunshot I saw the little lug-sail come down. Through the telescope I saw her begin to row as though towards us, then turn to port and to port again.

"Swinging his compass, the ole bastard," muttered one of the Yankees. "That's a shaggy wolf from 'way up where the river forks." I did not understand these words but I relished them, for they were spoken in a voice tinged with apprehension.

I popped a "tabnab" into my mouth and went to reassure Blanche.

CHAPTER SEVENTEEN

An evening or two later I was leaning on the rail at the waist of the ship, on the windward side, greedily snuffing what slight air wafted to me. There was the least shuffle of bare feet on the deck. I did not move except to put my hand upon the butt of the revolving pistol in my waistband. A shadowy form materialised beside me. It was on my left side, which gave me some reassurance, for I am right-handed. I drew back the hammer of the pistol, soundlessly, as I thought.

"Put it back to 'arf-cock, Sir," whispered the shadowy form, "for I means you no 'arm."

I lowered the hammer completely, then pulled it back to full-cock: I could afford to trust no one. The clicking seemed to satisfy the shadow.

"It's only old Tom Transom," it said. I almost put the hammer to half-cock, but at that time I would not have trusted my mother. My father, perhaps, yes.

"Mr Van Cleef, Sir," whispered Transom, "meaning no disrespect, but are you out of your sodding mind?" There were only two answers to this; "yes" or "no", and I could not find it in my heart to give either.

"Hrrumph," I said Britishly.

"Shh!" he whispered.

"Sorry!" I squeaked.

"Ssshhh!" he shushed, anguishedly. I shushed. He fell silent, peering and listening until he was sure that no one was a party to our conversation. It struck me that he was almost as afraid as I was.

"Listen, Mr Van Cleef, Sir," he whispered at last, "'aven't you wondered why you ain't in that boat with the other ossifers?"

To tell the truth I had not wondered much: perhaps in my vanity I had supposed that I was popular, perhaps I had thought, in a modesty more natural to me, that I was too insignificant to be awarded the dramatic casting-away. I did not answer, for I had no answer ready.

"Well, I'll tell you. First, they needs someone to take sights of the sun with that quadrant; them Yankees can 'andle the ship everywise but that. Second, they reckon that if we're cotched, you'll speak up for them at the trial. Third, you was the only one stupid enough, beggin' yer pardon, Sir, not to know that jest by staying aboard, let alone doing the navigationing, you was aiding and comforting mutiny on the high seas and you'll be 'ung 'igher than any on us if we're taken."

This sank in, painfully, terrifyingly.

"I see," I said. "What, then, can be done?"

"Dunno, Sir. 'Opes you'll come up with an idea. Smartly, Sir." Frantically, I clutched my wits together, tried to think as a Nelson.

"I do not see how we can attempt to re-take the ship," I said, "for they have every arm in the ship except my revolver."

"True enough, Sir, true."

"How many of the crew are of your turn of mind, Transom?"

"Well, Sir, there's a clear twenty on us served under Lord Stevenage's pa; I reckon I could trust a dozen of them, true as steel, the others is old or daft or plain frittened."

"Hm," I said. A plan commenced to glimmer in my frightened brain. "Meet me here at this time tomorrow night, Transom," I murmured. "I think something can be done but I must have a look at the charts."

"Aye aye, Sir," he said. This made me feel wise and responsible; no one had ever said "Aye aye Sir" to me before. It also reminded me, uncomfortably, that I was indeed an officer, however supernumerary, and an officer condoning mutiny. I had never witnessed a hanging and felt strongly that, if I should ever do so, it would be more interesting to be a spectator than the principal.

I spent a miserable night, slept a little in the morning and at noon, when it was my task to shoot the sun, my mind was a mere riot of half-digested plans. Alone in the chart-room, plotting our position and laying out a course, I took the opportunity of stuffing the chart for the coast between Knysna and Cape Town under my shirt and down my trousers. This chart I pored over agonisedly all afternoon, to some avail.

Transome and I met again in the dark.

"The day after tomorrow," I said, "at just about this time, we should be at Longitude 20° East."

"Arrh," he said, "Cape Agulhas. Nasty bank there and a famous place for dirty winds."

"Suppose I made a false reckoning at noon and laid a bad course and one of our party was quartermaster: we could run her aground, don't you think?"

"Yerss," he said bitterly, "that'd solve our little troubles for good, that would. Might as well jest jump over the side now an' be done with it."

"It's like that, is it?"

"Exackerly like that. An' if one or two on us got ashore alive, we'd still be mutineers, wouldn't we?"

"I hadn't thought of that."

"Well, I 'ad," he said, caressing his leathery neck affectionately, as though he liked it as it was. I was chagrined that he no longer called me "Sir"; clearly, I was no Nelson in his eyes.

"Never mind," I said briskly, "I am just testing my thoughts, you understand."

"Yerss. There's summink in it though. Make a wrong course so's we pass close to land on a rising tide in the dark and we could swim ashore."

"Mrs Knatchbull cannot swim," I said. I did not know this, but what I did know was that I could not.

"Oh," he said in a disinterested voice.

"Now then," I said, still briskly, "how long would it take to lower a boat, quietly, in the dark; one large enough to take us all?"

"Quarter-boat too small," he mused. "Lower the launch – fifteen minutes. In the dark – twenty. If we got everything cleared away, falls loosened and such, all before'and like, p'raps ten minutes in a flat calm."

"Excellent!"

"But *quietly*," he went on, remorselessly, "carn't be done. Arsk me to slaughter a pig quiet and I'd give it a try, but lower a long boat . . ." I think he would have laughed if the need for silence had not been so imperative.

"Don't jump to conclusions!" I rapped – but as quietly as it is

215

possible to rap. "I am examining the possibilities; your part is to make seaman-like comments. *When asked*."

"Aye aye, Sir," he replied, gratifyingly. There was no trace of surliness in his voice: I might not know wood from canvas but I was a gentleman and therefore capable of thought. All he had was knowledge. He could probably have made an ass of me at draughts but he would not have attempted to learn chess, for he knew his station in life. (This is the art of dealing with the lower orders: praise their mastery of the craft to which they are born but keep the chess-board locked up as you would your wine-cellar.)

"Now," I said, "suppose that the mutinous, self-appointed officers were locked in the cabin when they have dined and supped and one of our hearts of oak knocked the quartermaster's brains out quietly; would that give us time to lower the boat?"

He breathed deeply; one would have thought that he was thinking.

"No, Sir," he said. "You couldn't reckon they'd all be drunk enough; I've seen that crazy Boothcastle wide awake after a quart of rum. They got all the firearms in there, they could blow the lock off before you could say 'ow's yer farver."

"My pistol?"

"Might 'old 'em back, might not. Then, when we're in the boat?"

"Hm," I said, striving for a tone of "hm" which would convince him that this was what I had expected him to say.

"Anyways," he went on, "there's a fair lot in the fo'c'sle what would come raging out at us; they got their hearts set on South Americky and freedom. They'd reckon that if we got ashore a King's ship would be arter them in jig-time – and we knows their names and their destination. Which ain't 'Eaven," he added, obscurely. "You couldn't 'old off the cabin and the fo'c'sle both, not with that pistol – the men forrard still 'ave their case-knives, let alone the firearms aft. See?"

I saw, but preserved my feigned nonchalance.

"Quite right," I said. "Now, this gun," nudging the pivot-piece beside me, "I fancy this could be brought to bear on the fo'c'sle? There is a garland of shot beside it, a flexible rammer and sponge racked against the bulwarks, a flint in the lock and the expense-chest of powder cartridges under my very foot as I speak. What do you say to that, eh?"

"Wot I says, Sir, is: tap the expense-chest with your boot."

I tapped. It rang hollow. It seemed to me that just such a tap at my head would have produced a similar sound, for that had been the last of my ideas, my trump card. Never again would Transom call me "Sir". My hand stole to my collar and fingered the soft skin at my throat. Transome maintained a respectful silence, no doubt sure that I was elaborating some further part of a plan, but I was considering the technicalities of hanging. In the hands of a skilled craftsman, a well-calculated drop brings kindly oblivion in a twinkling of an eye, I am told, but to be hoisted aloft in a noose is a quite different matter: more prolonged, tediously uncomfortable and calculated to make the subject behave in various shameful and disgusting ways which I shall not trouble you with describing.

My craven musings were blown to pieces by a deep, *sotto voce* cough, six inches behind me, I did not quite jump over the side, nor did my heart altogether stop, but I must confess that I shuddered violently and, indeed, may have moistened myself a little.

In an instant I collected myself, realising that it was only the Doctor: a man to be trusted regardless of his creed or colour.

"Ah was wokened up by yo' thinkin', Mistuh Cleef," he rumbled softly in my ear, "so ah jes' naturally come out heah to heah what you was saying. 'T'warn't at all the same as what I heard you a-thinkin'." I looked over my shoulder at him: his grin was like the keyboard of a small piano-forte.

"Speak, thou apparition," I said.

"Cain't hex me, Mistuh Cleef; I hear't longer words nor that. Jes' wanted to tell you about my medicine chest."

"Yes, well, I did see it before," I mumbled, swallowing the blood from my bitten tongue. (It was, indeed, a beautiful chest, with double doors and sliding sides and back, all filled with little bottles of Gregory's powder, snake-oil and other useful jollops.)

"Didn't see the secret drawer in the bottom, Mistuh Cleef. Didn't see the big flat bottle of micky-o-flynn."

Transom, beside me, stiffened into attention; clearly this meant something. I raised an interested eyebrow: the doctor could see it in the dark, I was sure.

"Cheloral hyderate," he explained, " 'nuff to send a school o' whales to sleep."

My mind raced.

"Only trouble," went on the cook, "it don't keep too long. Bo't it two year ago. Still send ev'one to sleep but anyone ain't fit, well they jes' might not wake up agin."

"Tsk tsk," I said. "That is a risk we must take, is it not?"

Our plans were soon laid.

On the night, all went wonderfully well. Only the watch on deck had not drunk of the micky-o-flynn in their fish-chowder; only six of these were not of our persuasion and they were tapped upon the head and battened below hatches. I made a dutiful visit to see that all was well in the specie-room and took a little gold to cover travelling-expenses. Then I went onto the quarter-deck and showed the steersman my pistol. Without hesitation he agreed that it was better to be tied up than shot. I delivered him to Transom, set a course to take us as near to the mouth of False Bay as possible, slipped the becket over the spoke of the wheel and went to supervise the loading of my chests of porcelain. A whip had been rove to the main-mast yard-arm for this and all went as smoothly as a rabbi's wedding. Nothing was heard but the creaking of the tackle and the hoggish snores of those who had eaten of the fish-chowder. Yes, well, also the muffled sobs of Blanche, who had been obliged to abandon half her wardrobe. I had not troubled to explain to her the benefits of our action, for women, as you will learn when you are older, think only with that charming organ which is their third eye, second heart and only brain. For my part, being compassionate by nature, I was concerned for the crew we had left behind, mutinous dogs though they were, but a glance over my shoulder as I sat in the stern-sheets shewed me the ship pursuing an excellent course. If even half of them awoke by morning they should be able to round the Cape; after that they needed no navigator, any course west of north would pitch them up somewhere in South America where life, liberty and the pursuit of happiness awaited them.

At dawn we beached the boat somewhere south of Simonstown, emptied it, stove it in and shoved it back into the sea to sink. I gave each man a guinea to see him safe home to England and we dispersed, only Blanche, the doctor and Orace staying with me and the chests. We slept until noon, when the doctor, who had rambled off, arrived with a yellow-faced man, two thin, strong negroes and a spring-cart.

Arrived at the village of Simonstown, our bottoms blackened and blued with the jolting of the cart's hard seat, we were taken to a house where a fat woman gave us something nameless to eat and put us into a monstrous feather-bed. I do not know how long we slept. When I awoke I saw from the window some ships which clearly belonged to Her Majesty and I lost no time in hiring another cart to take us to the town of Cape Town, where we mingled with the motley crowd. We ate better there and slept as softly. After a day the doctor came to find us and announced that he was going off to seek his fortune at the digging of gold and diamonds, poor benighted heathen. I assured him that he would be safer working in one of the vineyards, such as the great Constantia, but he had been convinced by some plausible fellow that there was gold to be had for the digging and diamonds to boot. Sadly, I offered him a piece or two of gold but he refused these, explaining that, when I was about to leave the *John Coram*, I had carelessly left the key in the door of the specie-room. I bade him farewell with much feeling.

I occupied a few days thus: I discarded my surname of Van Cleef and retained my middle name of Mortdecai; I found a synagogue, stricken with poverty, which was prepared to marry me to Blanche without enquiring too strenuously into our antecedents. I found a similarly stricken Scotch church whose minister did more or less the same thing: this satisfied Blanche, who happily sewed both sets of marriage lines into her stays. Normal matrimony suited her: it was only rarely that she hinted at a nostalgic desire for the whip. I helped her through those times.

More important for our future was the necessity to get back to England, the home of the free and the brave. My first attempts to buy a map were baffling: the Dutch settlers (they liked to be called Afrikaaners – the word "Boer" in those days meant a rustic clown, perhaps rightly) had no faith in cartography, for they *knew* that the earth was flat. London was a few weeks' marches North; Holland a little further. One could not disagree with such men for each one carried a firearm and was fierce in his faith, fierce. Anything not explicitly spoken of in the Bible could not exist: it was so simple. I envied them their certainty. One Predikant or preacher harangued me for quite half an hour, his food-encrusted beard cracking like a whip as he spoke. Armageddon, he assured me, along with the end of the world, was positively to begin in the year 1914. I have every intention of seeing that year (for I am careful about choosing those who prepare my food) but I shall be surprised if anything Armageddon-like occurs.

219

No map was to be had, I learned, except by favour of the Clerk to the British Admiralty at the Royal Dockyard. This meant, for me, in my peculiar circumstances, that no map was to be had. While Blanche occupied herself with replenishing her wardrobe, I roved the town, making friends both here and there. The Afrikaaners were difficult to befriend: my clean Gelderland Dutch seemed affected to them and their yokel-patter grated upon my delicate ear. Many a time, when I had plucked up the appetite to attack a bowl of beef stewed with ginger and dried apricots, a monstrous she-Boer with breasts like pillows and moustaches which seemed to have strayed from her private parts would clap me heartily upon the shoulder and cry *"Smaaklike ete!"* into my ear. This never failed to destroy my appetite.

On one such night, famished and forlorn, I fell in with a rich young *smouse*, or Jewish pedlar, in a drinking-shop. He had been up-country many times, he said, and was indeed about to set forth again. I expressed interest. He studied my clothes, which were of good quality but not showy and decided that I was a man of some small substance. We began the elaborate, ritual dance of conversation which takes place when Greek meets Greek. He was, it appeared, tailing on to a caravan of farming settlers who were "trekking" north-westwards instead of taking the more usual route to the Orange River and the Vaal. This trek was to march parallel to the coast, through the Little Bushman Country, skirting the great Kalahari Desert and, it was hoped, joining a party of kinsmen who had gone that way a couple of years before.

"And how are these kinsmen faring?" I asked.

"Who knows?" he shrugged. "What is news? Who is going to ride through dangers for a month on a valuable horse just to tell that Oom Paul has the gout and the cow has calved? Maybe they are all dead, God forbid; more likely, they are wallowing in milk and honey in some new Canaan."

The *smouse* clearly believed, from his experience, that the gamble of taking his wares so far was a better-than-even chance: he was not a man to take odds worse than seven to three. If the trek found the community settled and prosperous, the contents of his pedlar-packs would be almost beyond price. Such a community, you see, might well be self-sufficient in the matter of meat and butter, corn and leather, even milk and honey – but no such community could make fine steel needles, gun-flints and powder, silk shawls, lead bars for the casting of bullets, ribbons, petticoats and delicate under-drawers for brides. (A Predikant would be in our trek and would have a busy time if we found the settlement: there would be a great *naagtmaal* with much hell-fire preaching and drunkenness, many informal marriages to be regularised, adulterers to be chastised and babies to be baptised.)

Yes, the *smouse* agreed, there was much room to spare in his wagon. The charges, of course, would be heavy, for this space could otherwise be used for valuable freight. Surely I could see that? I pressed many a glass of the excellent Van Der Hum drink upon him but the heaviness of the charges dwindled only a little. At last we struck hands on the bargain.

"By the way," I asked idly, "where will you sleep?"

"Why, in the wagon with you of course, where else? There are two pallets, each with a good palliasse of sweet hay."

"But my wife . . . ?"

He had not known that I had a wife. He did not quite rend his garments, nor tear his hair – indeed, the latter was so richly pomaded that I do not think he could have secured enough grip upon it for tearing purposes. Back and forth the argument swayed: twice he stormed out of the drinking-shop in disgust, only to return for something he had forgotten and to give me one last chance to be reasonable; three times I, too, stalked out, only to be dragged back in and implored to be reasonable. Being reasonable meant that I should either abandon Blanche – women, he assured me with many an anatomical detail, are much like each other and can be readily replaced – or pay a monstrous extra charge to compensate him for sleeping outside his wagon, away from his goods. We came, of course, to an agreement in the end. The other clients of the boozing-ken, listening avidly, may have believed that I had broken the *smouse*'s heart, for this is what he vowed; while he – for this is what I cried aloud – had reduced me to penury and consigned my unborn children to the poorhouse. Altogether, it was a most satisfactory and profitable evening. I would not be a Gentile for a knighthood – even for a peerage.

We – that is to say, Blanche, I and Orace – made rendezvous with the trek three afternoons later. The *smouse* made a great fuss about Orace, although I explained that he was only a bastard and would not need a bed. Then he complained about our baggage, which was more than had been agreed upon. Ever ready to meet a reasonable demand, I compromised by jettisoning one trunk of Blanche's clothes. I had bought a fine battery or chest of weapons for our protection and explained to her that these would prove more valuable than basques and drawers and stays. She was not an unreasonable woman. I had also, at the last moment, bought a fine saddle-horse: I fancy I cut a fine figure on it, although the Boers, inexplicably, laughed at me. Next morning – not a time that you or I would call morning, but at the "hour of the horns", when, before true dawn, a man with good eyesight can just discern the horns of the oxen against the sky – the whole cumbrous, complaining encampment of what was to be our trek roused itself, beat its oxen and blackamoors into activity and grated into a sort of motion. Northwards.

So eager were these Boers for the sight of long-lost kinsmen, not to mention land and profits, that the Predikant was left on his knees, still bellowing prayers, and had to scramble into his cart and whip up his sorry mule for a mile before he could bring up the tail of our strange caravan.

(I tried, from time to time, to discourse with this Predikant, hoping for intellectual stimulus, but I found that his learning was as narrow as his beliefs. He had a perfect knowledge of the more merciless parts of the Old Testament but was vague and evasive on the subject of Jesus Christ. I lost his friendship, I believe, when I postulated, simply as a point of argument, that the prophets Isaiah and Jeremiah must have been drunk when they wrote. He never spoke to me again but I did not regret this. One of the few things I have learned in life is that only a fool argues with bigots when he could be in bed with a lovely and lustful woman. And Blanche, at just this time, was coming into full blossom as a lover: all the years of misdirected passion burst forth like petals of an autumn rose and her inventiveness astonished and challenged my simple Dutch lechery.)

A trek is like a long sea-voyage but dusty. The dangers are as many but of a different nature: there is little danger of drowning, for instance. The boredom is exactly similar, day follows day in an unchanging pattern, one loses count of time, and after many days one can only recall trivial incidents, small oases in a desert of dullness. One such was the night when Orace was eaten by a lion. Poor child, he had failed to keep the fire bright and had fallen asleep. I was awakened by a gentle thudding, as though someone

222

were pounding the earth with fists. Peering out between the laces of the wagon-flap, I caught a glimpse of a great yellow beast trotting away with a large object between its jaws, then, despite its burden, clearing the thorn stockade or *bomah*, which closed the entry-gap between the semi-circle of wagons, with one bound. I called crossly for Orace to make up the fire but he did not reply. A search shewed that he was missing and must have been what the lion was carrying. I had half a mind to go out with my heavy rifle and pursue the cowardly beast, but I was readily persuaded that this would be both hopeless and dangerous.

I was quite cast down by the loss of this devoted child; indeed, I believe I shed a tear. Blanche comforted me, saying that she would learn to wash my linen, but she did not understand: I had become fond of Orace, foundling or no. *Fond*.

Another day which sticks in my memory is the day after we crossed the Olifants River, skirting the high ground to the west of the great Desert of Kali-Hari. It was my turn to be riding far ahead of the trek as *voorloper* and I was nodding in the saddle when I noticed that my horse had come to a halt. Looking up, I saw through sleep-filmed eyes what appeared to be a monstrous cloud of dust hazing the air a few miles ahead. I rubbed my eyes clear and looked again. As far as I could see, from east to west, this cloud of dust was still rising. I galloped back to the trek-leader – although I had been warned against galloping a horse in that climate – and reported that at least a regiment, probably a brigade, perhaps a division of cavalry was crossing our front.

He glared inscrutably at me from the forest of his brows and beard and said, although with little conviction, that everything was possible under God. Then he called up young Cloete, a man of fine breeding who had scouted as far as the Congo River itself, although not for gain, because he was one of the heirs of the great Constantia estate, where the finest wine in the world is made. (If you do not believe this last remark, I remind you that Napoleon Bonaparte himself, on his death-bed, called for a glass of Constantia.)

Young Cloete, reins slack, moved out on his beautiful half-bred Arab at a ground-eating single-step pace, the great broad brim of his hat over his eyes and only one foot in a stirrup, so sure he was of his mount. (This is also a useful way to ride over broken ground or if you fear an ambuscade.)

In twenty minutes he was back with us, smiling, but holding up his arm, palm out-stretched. The trek halted untidily, the men growling, the women squabbling, the children squealing and the oxen, horses, milch-cows, goats, mules, pigs, poultry and dogs each making noises proper to their kind.

"What is it?" I asked.

"*Bok*," said Cloete as he dismounted and lay down to rest.

"Is that offensive?" I asked the trek-leader.

"No. It is *bok*."

I walked my tired horse back to the wagon and gave him a hatful of water.

"Why have we stopped?" asked Blanche.

"*Bok*," I said.

"The same to you!" she replied with spirit.

Hours later our motley cavalcade ground into motion again and, before dusk, crossed the track of the great movement I had first seen. A thin film of the finest particles of dust still hung over it and for the breadth of quite half a mile, our wagon wheels pressed over a carpet of flattened corpses of little buck. Cloete told me later that this particular kind of antelope, once in a while, takes it into its head to migrate in unimaginable numbers, for no discernible reason. "They are almost human," he explained. If I used the words "one million" in respect of this exodus of buck you would only laugh, for you have seen little of the world and know less. Cloete used these words, prefixed by the words "at least".

The irrational nature of this business of the *bok* vexed me strangely, for I had already made a fool of myself the previous day, when I had suggested that I might leave the trek at the River Olifants and proceed down it to the sea, finding a ship at the Western Coast. The trek-leader, whose religion, I think, prohibited laughter, sank his great *bomah*-covered chin further into his breast and controlled his breathing carefully before pointing out to me that the Olifants, except in spate, was a series of disconnected lagoons and that its course was, in any case, opposite to the direction I named. These Boers have a name for us British: *rooinek* – it means red-neck. My neck became red.

In this business of the Afrikaaners' religion I found much to reflect on. Their "Reformed Church" was strict in its doctrine but easy to follow: the whole truth was to be found in the Bible, therefore nothing else could be true. So, the earth had four corners and was therefore flat. Nothing could be more logical. (They mar-

224

velled that I should want to take *ship* to London: it was only a couple of hundred marches to the north-west, just as Jerusalem was a similar number of marches to the north-east. Perhaps this was the cause of the continual treks northward from the Cape: they did not like to live so close to the southern edge of the world.)

There was no possibility of salvation for any but members of this Reformed Church – and, to judge by the rantings of the Predikant, precious little chance for them. One formed a mental picture of the Elysian fields, empty as the High Veldt except for an occasional Predikant wearing a justified look of righteousness and a few withered virgins wearing calico from hairy chin to scrawny ankle.

They had the inhabitants of this continent of Africa neatly docketed. The Kaffirs were partly educable and might be beaten and baptised. The Hottentots were sub-human: the very word comes from the Dutch word for a stutterer; the Hottentot does not speak but he *tries* to. So, he may be trained and charitably fed and beaten but not baptised. The little yellow Bushmen, with hair like a sprinkle of peppercorns and buttocks which, in a good season, protruded astonishingly but, in times of hardship, withered into a sort of flaccid apron, were clearly non-human. They had to be exterminated, for all sorts of excellent reasons which I cannot recall at this remove of time.

While we trudged at the maddeningly slow oxen-speed through giraffe country one of the skilled huntsmen in the trek would set out each Friday and kill a giraffe. This great, improbable beast would be skinned and the Kaffir "boys" would cut his hide, with infinite care, into one or perhaps two enormously long strips. On the Saturday all would fall to and grease this strip with the tallow from the creature's kidneys and guts. On the Sabbath, when all who had the slightest hope of salvation rested and would do no more than eat and journey no further than nature and decency demanded, the Hottentots would loop and sling the *riem*, as it was called, over the high branch of a tree and, having attached a heavy stone to the lower ends, twist and re-twist it until it became a stout and resilient rope. This took quite twenty hours and the "boys" became lazy, lazy, for they knew, intuitively, that no one would beat them on the Sabbath and to their untutored minds the Monday, when they could and certainly would be beaten, seemed infinitely far away. They were a cheery lot, with no memory of the past and no care for the morrow, but I did not envy them.

This beast, the giraffe, illustrates again the certainty of the Afrikaaners about the definitive nature of the Bible. There is no beast of that name in that Book so, clearly, it must be a camel – and *kameel* is what it was called. In the same way, the leopard was a *tijger* – what else could it be? One peculiarly ugly kind of antelope defied Biblical nomenclature, but the Reformed Church were not long at a loss: they called it the "wild animal": *wildebeeste*. I was proud to share Dutch blood with these people; their pig-headedness exceeded that of the English by far.

Inch by inch, day by day, the landscape changed: flat-topped trees gave way to scrub, earth became sand and sand soon became stones, then rocks; for days we might march towards a distant mountain which seemed but a few miles distant, then for days we might crunch through grass taller than a horseman's head, correcting our course at night when the stars came out. Some of us died, of course: snakes and crocodiles, buffalo and sickness all took their toll but my own little party were spared except for Orace, whose loss I think I have already mentioned, and my horse. He had been sold to me as "salted" – that is to say, he was supposed to have survived the fever which kills horses in Africa. This was not true. As soon as we entered the area where horses die, he died. I quarrelled bitterly with the *smouse* because he had introduced me to the horse-coper who had sold and vouched for the animal and I knew he must have drawn a commission but he would not part with a stiver as recompense. He was a bad Jew; he treated me as though I were a Gentile. "This is no way to conduct business," are the words I spoke to him from a full heart. He pretended to care nothing for them, but such words, spoken by a full-blooded Jew of the Sephardim to a mere son of the sons of Gomer is a terrible rebuke, terrible.

The next day, at the mid-day meal, he approached me in an ingratiating way and offered to sell me a riding-mule at cost-price. My buttocks were bruised blue (I speak from hearsay, of course) from riding on the tailgate of the wagon but I affected to ignore the *smouse*'s existence. "See, Blanche," I said, pointing at the sky, "a kite or vulture!"

"They call it an *aasvogel* here," she replied, smiling. I was not pleased with her. From women one wishes loyalty, not information.

CHAPTER EIGHTEEN

◁▷

Since I penned those last few words I have been thinking. Dozing a little, too, but also thinking. My difficulty is that this next episode, as well as being unpleasant, involves a matter to which the Statute of Limitations does not apply – I refer, of course, to murder – and also involves certain people with whose descendants I have a pleasant and profitable trade relationship.

I think that if I mention the name of the *smouse*, which was Oppenheimer, any of you who may inherit shares in this House will realise that it is in *no one's* interest to bruit the incident abroad. As to the other matter, that of the Statute of Limitations, I fear I can only surmount the difficulty by, for once, paltering with the truth a little. You may therefore treat the ensuing few folios as, in some sort, mere fiction.

The cruel sun, glaring blindingly down on human beings threading their weary way across South-Western Africa, takes its toll from each one in a different way. Members of the Reformed Church become confirmed in their belief that the world is flat; women spend most of their day in bed and yet spurn their husbands' attentions; little children grow old and wise overnight. The effect on me was that I dwelled more and more on the *smouse*'s perfidy in the matter of the horse until hatred filled and darkened my whole mind. Each time I set eyes on his accursed riding-mule I trembled with irrational rage. The *smouse*'s sickness from the sun took a curiously opposite form: he became obsessed with the notion that I hated him, and whispered to all who would listen that I had threatened his life. This was a monstrous mis-reading of my character, for I was then the mildest of men and had killed no more than six or perhaps seven men in my whole life – and always in self-defence, as I have related.

Silly though these phantasies were, they nevertheless poisoned our lives and many a curious glance was cast at both of us, especially when the *smouse* had occasion to go to our – his – wagon for supplies or fresh linen. I watched him narrowly on these occasions, for I believed, by then, that he was capable of everything base. I received the impression that, while I watched him, the men of the trek were watching me.

One day it fell to the men of our wagon – the *smouse* and me – to go out and shoot for the communal pot; it was the custom for each wagon to take its turn at this. I was bidden to ride eastward (on a borrowed horse), the *smouse* was to go west. Neither of us was skilled in the traversing of wild country and I suppose both of us must have unwittingly circled towards the north. After riding several miles without sighting any game, I tethered my horse just below the crest of a ridge and crept to the top, hoping that there might be a fertile valley, rich in game, on the other side. To my fury, all that was to be seen was that accursed riding-mule of the *smouse*, tied to a thorn-tree a bare hundred yards away.

With a chuckle which rang crazily even on my own ears, I levelled my rifle at the brute's hindquarters, confident that I could graze its backside enough to lame it without crippling. I cannot tell whether the sweat ran into my eyes or the heat-haze distorted my vision or whether some madness possessed me; all I can say is that, as I squeezed the trigger, the hated beast dropped dead, a bullet through its heart.

Something snapped in my brain: in a flash I saw what childish petulance had been inflaming my brain for days – and what a criminally stupid and unworthy thing I had now done. As the *smouse*'s head rose above the bush where he had been "still-hunting" I jumped to my feet, waving my gun and shouting, running towards him, longing to apologise and to repair our friendship.

Poor, craven fool, he quite misconstrued my actions; he fired both barrels wildly in my direction, threw away his gun and took to his heels as though the devil was after him. It was idle to pursue – he ran as fleetly as any *bok*.

I remounted and rode on sadly, taking little notice of my direction. Fortunately, I fell in with game: covey after covey of fat, mindless birds resembling guinea-fowls and a nice little *gemsbok*.

228

The westering sun startled me: I realised that the laager was now to my south-east. Soon I walked my laden horse in through the thorn zareba – *having approached from the direction in which the smouse had left*.

In an instant the laager was alive with activity: women's hands flew as they plucked the fat fowls, pots were a-boiling from the *gemsbok*'s flesh, while dogs snapped and snarled for its entrails.

There is little dusk in those latitudes: darkness falls from the air in minutes. It was in that brief dusk that the leader of the trek walked over to our fire. His face was grave and stern in the ruddy light.

"When shooting, did you see anything of Oppenheimer?" he asked.

I was exhausted in mind and in body and my mouth was full; I did a thoughtless, foolish thing: I shook my head. A moment later I choked on a fragment of bone and my mouthful sprayed out into the fire, almost as though I was suddenly overcome with laughter. He looked sombrely at me, then turned on his heel. Blanche went to bed. A fire was kindled outside the zareba to guide the *smouse* back.

He did not come back.

There was no in-spanning of oxen next morning; instead, the trek-leader, with young Cloete and four other men, rode out at first light in the direction from which I had returned. They rode in again at noon. I ran towards them, asking whether they had found any sign of the *smouse*. They did not look at me, much less answer. I began to understand. The trek in-spanned and made a short stage before evening. No one spoke to me that evening. I begged Blanche to gather news but she had few friends among the women, for she was young and beautiful and wore clothes which did not wholly conceal her breasts. It was not until the noontide halt of the next day that she was able to bring me information gleaned from a Kaffir woman in Cloete's service.

"They found Mr Oppenheimer, Karli. He was alive, but he died as they took him down from the cross."

"The *cross*? What cross?"

"The cross he was nailed to, Karli. He had been crucified."

I was speechless with dismay for quite a minute. Then I exploded with grief and rage.

"Those vile, accursed savages!" I cried.

"Yes, Karli, the savages, of course," she said quietly. "But they found the mule, too." There was nothing I could say: for the first

229

time I was tasting the bitter indignation of a wicked man charged with a wickedness which he has not committed.

"Karli, the killing is not so important; they believe that God will avenge that. It is the blasphemy of crucifying a *Jew*."

"But their *Christ* was a Jew!" I bellowed.

"Hush, Karli, they are listening." I could have bitten off my tongue.

The ensuing days do not bear speaking of, for I simply ceased to exist as far as the Boers were concerned. Blanche placidly drew our allowance of water and share of game without apparent embarrassment, for she had been more or less ostracised from the beginning of the trek, but I am a warm and companionable man: this rôle of Ishmael bit deeply into my soul.

Let it suffice to say that there came a day when the leader of our trek pointed to a river we had just forded and told me that it would lead us to the West Coast at a place where ships were said to call. He did not know how far the coast was. He would give us one Hottentot. Our baggage was my crates of precious porcelains, my chest of arms, my hamper of clothes, my tin shirt-box of delicate foods and medicine, two bundles of Blanche's clothes and necessaries – and Blanche herself, of course. I protested. The trek-leader – there are reasons why I cannot give his name, even if I wished to – told me that willing bearers would spring up out of the ground as soon as the trek had passed.

Blanche stood silent, as dignified as I, beside our heap of goods with the Hottentot squatting beside it. The horrible thing was when they left the *smouse*'s wagon with all his goods beside the road as they trudged away on their impossible journey. I shouted, then screamed after them until Blanche was hanging on my arms, begging me to calm myself. Young Cloete, who was a compassionate young man and quite liked me, rode back to ask what the matter was.

I could only mumble stupidly. He stared down at me from his fine horse with veiled contempt. I wiped away the sweat which threatened to fill my eyes and he looked at the gesture with interest. He asked me a certain question; then I sent Blanche away and repeated the gesture in a precise and formal way. This made things different. It did not, of course, make it possible to condone a crime, but it made things different. He said that there were enough men in

230

the trek who would understand and that the *smouse*'s wagon, beasts and goods could be distributed to those who most needed them. He would make all square. I thanked him. As he rode away, driving the beasts and the wagon, he bade me farewell and used the word "brother".

Our Hottentot absconded in the night of course but, sure enough, bearers sprang out of the ground, apparently, in the morning. I made some sort of a bargain with them and off we trudged, following this nurseling river to the distant sea.

The trek had in some sort hardened us to hardship but this next journey was more than hardship. After the first few hours of the first morning, every step was misery, every fold and crevice of our bodies an inflamed torment. By the third day I was vividly recalling those anatomical diagrams which depict each thread of muscle and tendon in the human body, neatly picked out in blue and red: there was no morsel of me which I could not have identified on such a diagram and expatiated on the agony it could cause. Blanche, too, I daresay, was in some discomfort but women are born to suffer, this is well known. Indeed, she did not complain.

Again, just as at sea or on trek, the days followed each other with a remorseless sameness, only diversified by different nastinesses. The torments were the same in kind but different in degree, while dangers and difficulties and diseases came fresh and fresh each day, so that we arose each morning dully wondering what our next tribulation was to be. If we achieved the noontide rest before some disaster struck we wondered, just as dully, what the afternoon march held in store for us, because no day could pass without some frightfulness. After the first few days our gang of bearers became sulky, then demanded money as an earnest of our solvency. I was foolish enough to pay them a little on account: they vanished in the night, not stealing anything of importance. The next day, sure enough, others of another tribe drifted out of the bush, offering their services. When they absconded, two or three days later, stealing a little more, others replaced them. Each gang demanded less pay but, on leaving, stole more. Luckily, they stole trash and items of Blanche's clothing; they had no judgment in matters of fine porcelain, thank God, and as to my chest of arms and box of foods and medicines, Blanche and I slept with our heads upon them.

We forced our way west and a little north as best we could: fatigue

231

and illness had bereft us of the sense which would have told a clear-minded person to lie down and die.

Although we followed the course of the river we did not often set eyes on its waters because of the vegetation. It was clear that we were in river country though, because each dusk great insects called Moustiques – not at all like the friendly, playful midges of England – came out of their lairs and pierced us with red-hot, poisoned fangs, so that Blanche and I, looking at each other's lumpish face of a morning, would have laughed had we had the strength to do so. I dare say that a true-born Englishman would have found such strength. I do not care. These insects were of a size and voracity which cannot be exaggerated: I am convinced that, had they mastered the rudiments of communal discipline, any six of them could have carried me off to devour at leisure, piecemeal or even wholemeal.

As the ground grew wetter and we sploshed through the *ambash* reeds for much of the day, the leeches came. They were revolting, also enfeebling: we must have lost a pint of blood to them each day.

There came a day after God knows how many days when Blanche and I, emaciated and rotten with disease, staggered into a village on the banks of a distributary river, accompanied only by three porters. All that remained to us were a box of clothes and medicines, my chest of arms and several thousands of pounds value in carefully-packed Ming and Kang H'Si porcelains. We cared nothing for the political or religious beliefs of the savages there; our need to rest wiped away all such thoughts. Blanche collapsed and began to snore charmingly. The porters, encouraged by my little hippopotamus-hide *karbash*, laid down their burdens with great care, next to Blanche. I too lay down then, against the chests, snoring, I fancy, before my head touched the earth.

A gentle, courteous kick up the arse awakened me when the sun was low. I rubbed my eyes and looked about me. A dozen of elderly black men surrounded me. Their expressions were hard to read for their faces were fancifully etched with cicatrices; these were unpleasing to my untutored eye. I rubbed my eyes and yawned; this must have been a courtesy of sorts because they all smiled at me. I wished that they had not, for each smile revealed a row of teeth filed to needle-points. I stirred Blanche gently with the toe of my boot and enjoined silence upon her when she opened her eyes. Raising

232

myself to a dignified squatting posture, I stared them all out of countenance then, selecting my words with care, I said:

"Hrrumph!"

This caused agitation in their circle; they jabbered at each other as though discussing protocol.

"M'Gawa!" the eldest said at last. Thinking this to be a greeting I civilly replied "M'Gawa!" I was *wrong*. The old man – the chief, evidently – clapped his hand loudly onto his belly and some twenty young warriors, hitherto unnoticed by me, stepped into the circle, rubbing their thumbs against the edges of their spears with a rasping noise which I could not believe was friendly. I was in a debilitated state but the desire for survival filled me. I stood up, fixing the chief with my eye and a pointing forefinger, and ranted out some twelve or twenty lines of Shakespeare's *Hamlet* in the Dutch translation. He cowered. I turned to Blanche, snapping my fingers. "Absolute alcohol!" I snapped. "Surgical rubbing-spirit! In the medicine chest; *quickly*!" While she rummaged I cowed the simple sons of nature with a few more selections from the Swan of Avon, at the same time indicating by signs that they should bring water, lest worse befall them.

When the calabash of water was drained I slipped into it a little of the absolute alcohol and set it alight. This created a great amazement but when I dipped my fingers in the flaming liquid and flourished them they either ran for their lives or prostrated themselves on their bellies, according to taste.

From that moment we were treated as guests and demi-gods. A hut or *giddah* was allotted to us, also an old woman to attend to our needs. We were feasted regally that night on delicious tender pork or perhaps veal, stewed in a peppery sauce. I confess that I gorged myself, out of politeness and against my will, for I have always been a sparing and delicate eater. Appetite was enhanced by the dancing in firelight of some two dozen nubile – *palpably* nubile – maidens of the tribe: their swinging, sweat-glistening breasts and rotating bellies made a most agreeable sight, although Blanche, inexplicably, found the performance vulgar and unartistic. I have often noticed that women's minds are closed to some of the finer things which life offers us.

After eating, and then drinking many a calabash of toddy fermented from the tender heart-leaves of a certain palm-tree, I remembered my Englishness with a guilty start and enquired whether my bearers had been housed and fed. I had to do this by sign-language, naturally, and it was a little while before I could make our hosts understand. At last they signified assent by smiling, nodding and rubbing their hands upon their distended bellies. I was well content, my duty done. As I accepted yet another calabash of palm-toddy, Blanche suddenly rose and ran frantically from our circle around the fire. I was vexed at this breach of manners but no one else seemed to care and it was not until an hour later, when I joined her in the *giddah*, that I understood that her intuitive grasp of sign-language was better than mine. I assured her that what we had been eating was young goat, but she could not be appeased: she had eaten goat. Goat is not nearly so tender and tasty.

CHAPTER NINETEEN

During our two-month sojourn in the village we convalesced well and replaced much of the flesh which hardship had stripped from our bones. The savages, in their primitive kindness, seemed *concerned* to make us fat, they were forever pressing food on us. Blanche had developed a morbid dislike for meat but she fared pretty well on *cassava* (which is tapioca), sweet potatoes and plantains baked or cooked in red palm-oil or pounded up with *karta* (which is pea-nuts) into a delicious *purée*. She passed her time, when not sleeping, in repairing what was left of her wardrobe.

For my part I ate heartily of whatever was put before me: monkey, for instance, is very good once one has recovered from the first sight of the little creature roasted. My pastime became that of learning the tribe's simple tongue – they had a vocabulary of less than one thousand words but the placement of some of these words was hard to master – and I fell into the habit of meeting the elders of the tribe each day and questioning them about their rites and customs, funereal, marital, festive and so forth. Their habits of thought and language were strange; for instance their adjective for "eatable", I recall, was the same as their noun for "member of another tribe" while, if one added the word for "crocodile", the compound word meant "elderly lady".

The notion grew in my head that perhaps I might one day write a book, displaying the manners of these simple children of God to civilised men as an example to wonder at. (The science of this is now called Anthropology: those of you who are too idle to enter our business House, or incapable of being supple to your benign grandfather, might well go to a University and master this simple science. You could perhaps earn fame thereby, for the world is

235

foolish – but not, I think, fortune, for the world is not wholly foolish.)

One night, tossing feverishly in our bed, which was rendered almost intolerable by the heat of Blanche's perfervid bottom, I occupied myself by making a mental summary of the strange, cruel but infinitely civil behaviour of this tight-knit society of savages whose obliged guests we were. Of a sudden, I had a stroke of insight: there was one piece missing in the almost-logical puzzle of their system of life! One question, which I would pose the very next morning, would decide forever whether they were near-apes performing a meaningless, ritual dance or truly human beings observing a sensible code of behaviour no more different, in essence, from that of us Jews than our code is from that of Christians.

So exhilarated was I at my cleverness that I felt the need to communicate with someone, however hot and moist the night. I slid down into the sagging centre of the bed, so that Blanche's incomparable bottom – hotter and moister than the night – fitted into the concavity of my belly. We were like spoons in a canteen of cutlery – such as we give to old porters who are past their work but not eligible for a pension. My loins stirred. She was deeply asleep but you will learn one day that there are few women, however deep their sleeps, who do not awaken at feeling that particular stirring. She wriggled languidly and muttered something through sleep-sticky lips. I reached around her body and imprisoned a breast: the light muslin of her shift, sweat-soaked, clung to it like a second skin. The nipple – she was gifted as to the nipples, gifted – sprang up so that her pretence at sleep was no longer plausible. She adapted her posture a little and soon I was expressing my pleasure, silently, vehemently. She, too, expressed pleasure, not silently.

I went out on to the platform in front of the hut and kicked the old woman awake, demanding a bucket of water to be thrown over me. She looked at my person closely when pouring the water and tittered impudently, so I made her fetch another bucket.

When I went back into the *giddah*, Blanche seemed again asleep but was now on her back in a posture so abandoned that I felt constrained to pleasure her again, this time more thoroughly. Then, I must confess, I fell into a deep sleep, for, although I was young and vigorous, the night was hot and the climate enervating, you understand.

236

I was up betimes the next morning, adroitly avoiding Blanche's questing hand. I was full of my great and visionary question, the key which would unlock the secret of the tribe's whole way of thought. So soon as I had eaten I lurked by the matting of my door until all the old men of the village had taken their places under the mango-tree. Then I sauntered towards the circle and stood a little way off, gazing at the heavens and scratching myself at the groin. This was courteous, you see; whereas to scratch an armpit would be a shameful act in that village.

After a certain, civil interval I addressed them in the formal fashion which I had learned, speaking slowly because although I had mastered their tongue I knew that my Jewish accent made it difficult for them to understand me.

"Oh, great bulls!" I said to the withered old men. "Oh you with horns of buffaloes and testicles like ripe mangoes! Oh you whose ears still ring with the shrieks of the countless virgins you have deflowered! You whose wives are so fat with your plenty that they cannot stand upon their feet! You who permit the sun to rise and, at your pleasure, bid him hide his face! How sweet would be the inside of my belly if you could but see me!"

The eldest of the elders fumbled vainly in the tobacco-gourd which hung about his neck. I absently dropped four inches of black pigtail-twist on the ground and continued to gaze at the heavens. A pot-bellied child with a great umbilical hernia scampered up and took the tobacco to the chief, who looked at it curiously, then absently cut off a generous half and passed it to the next elder. When the youngest elder had glumly received the shaving which remained for him another silence fell, broken only by the sounds of groin-scratching and the picking of noses.

At last the second-eldest elder – for this was beneath the dignity of the chief – said "We see you, man with the red face, cousin to the son-in-law of a chief; you who service your woman a hundred times in the heat of the night. There is a stool for you here, why do you stand?"

I sat.

A few more civilities were exchanged, interspersed with as many silences. At last the chief looked at me. I cleared my throat, assembled my knowledge of the tongue.

"Father of penises," I began diffidently, "you know that I love you so much that my bowels loosen each time I dare to look at your beauteous face." He opened his mouth; this meant that I was to continue.

"A great thought came to me in the night," I said.

A courteous titter was heard.

"*Twice* this great thought came to you in the night, the old woman tells me," said the chief. The tittering became a guffaw. I remained composed.

"Oh Chief," I said, "I do not speak of pushing babies into women's bellies, I speak of things in a man's mind. Hear me."

The chief raised his hand and all laughter stopped.

"Great King," I said in a dignified voice, "you whose power is felt from sea to sea, you who have long lost count of the children squirted from your wonderfully symmetrical loins, last night I had a thought. During the time that a woman would have two courses of the moon I have eaten your salt and drunk your beer. I have learned to love you and your subjects: the ways of your mighty nation have taught me much. Each day I have asked both hands and both feet" – this meant twenty – "of questions about your ways of life, of feeding, of religion, of marriage. You have taught me much, answering these many questions of mine. The thought that came to me last night was this: in all that time you have never asked me once about my land, my people's customs. Are these of no matter to you?"

There fell a silence which seemed almost to be of embarrassment. At last the chief gestured to the second elder, who spoke.

"You are wrong, man with the face of a setting sun: our bellies are sour with longing to know these things. But amongst our people, if you must know the truth, it is thought a filth and shame for a man to ask questions after he has grown his first pubic hair."

My face, I could feel, grew more than ever like a setting sun. No one spoke; they all gazed politely at the little fire of M'Gawa (bull-dung) smouldering in the centre of their circle. I scanned their faces, which were solemn – no hint of a smile. I pulled myself together.

"Why then," I asked indignantly, "did not you, whose bellies burst with wisdom, tell me of this thing at the outset?"

"You did not ask," he replied blandly.

This ended my excursion into the science of anthropology.

To restore my dignity I regaled them with many an account of Europe and its wonders; our customs and laws, our buildings, our new iron ships which were propelled with the smoke of boiling water, our wars and the blessings of gunpowder. They listened raptly, their mouths open in full politeness. When I drew to a close they clapped their cupped hands against the inside of their thighs, making a noise greater than a London opera audience. One or two of the younger ones allowed themselves to fall off their stools. This was the highest compliment, I knew, which could be paid to a truly gifted liar. Such a man was much prized by that tribe for few savages had mastered the art of lying. Now, as I write, they are surely more civilised in such matters, for their land will be full of traders and missionaries.

Foolishly, I allowed myself to become vexed, for I had spoken nothing but the truth: we Jews only lie in a ritual way when conducting business with our equals. I stalked back to the hut and unlocked the chest of arms. My battery was but a pair of percussion pistols, a heavy rifle, a light flint-lock fowling-piece and my beautiful revolving-pistol. I decided upon the heavy rifle – an old East Indian Company "tiger-gun" with two barrels. I loaded and primed it carefully, re-set the flints, wiped the frizzen dry and marched back to the circle of elders, who were still rocking back and forth, repeating phrases I had used, much as people leaving Gatti's Music-hall bandy the inane jests of the latest *Lion Comique*.

They fell silent, eyeing the strange object cradled in my arms.

"If I have lied to the bull-elephant," I said in an important voice, "then I could not kill the fat goat tethered outside my *giddah* without rising from this stool."

"But there is no fat goat outside your *giddah*, O red-faced teller of stupendous lies!"

I waited, staring without expression at the bull-dung fire.

"Tether a fat goat outside the *giddah* of the teller of tales," said the chief at last.

This done, I drew back the hammer and levelled the rifle at the goat's head: it was an easy shot, perhaps twenty-five paces. There was a great roar and a cloud of smoke; I rocked back on my stool with the recoil. When the smoke cleared, the goat's head was a mere vestige of its former self and those around the circle who had run away were creeping back to their places. The chief, to his great credit, had not budged. I handed him the piece, explaining its use in simple terms, reserving only the intelligence of how to load it.

He was quite ravished with the gift. The old woman of our *giddah* was shrieking loudly and rhythmically, for she had been but a foot away from the goat I had slain. This was vexing after a while. The elders, too, were vexed, because the *lokali* drums were talking from the village ten miles down-river. The king sent for the old woman, who squatted deferentially before him as though about to urinate: the paucity of her clothing made this an unpleasing sight to behold. The king playfully poked the muzzles of the rifle at her nose: she sniffed them, looked down the barrels. The chief pulled the trigger. The heavy ball, scarcely slowed, smashed into the fire with a pyrotechnic effect and screamed over the heads of the elders opposite. The old lady's brains spread themselves most copiously upon those present: this caused much merriment, as you can imagine. I was about to protest on humane grounds but the chief's happy face quite disarmed me. A moment's reflection taught me that goats were edible wealth while old women were more than plentiful, also raucous and of little use after they had lost their teeth and only esculent to crocodiles.

The king – or chief – then turned the gun affably in the direction of the fourth youngest elder, who owned one of the most desirable women in the village, and pulled the trigger. There was a shower of sparks from the frizzen but no explosion, of course, for both barrels were now expended. Again, everyone fell into a paroxysm of merriment except the fourth youngest elder, and the chief. The latter scowled at me. I explained that the weapon had to be filled with more magic after each discharge and that this could only be done at the full moon (we were in the first quarter) or on the departure of an honoured and well-feasted guest. The chief muttered like a sulky child, snapping the locks of the rifle petulantly. I was explaining to him that this would wear out the flints when all fell silent, for the distant *lokali* had stopped speaking and our own hollowed tree-trunk boomed out a response. "*Vroom*, da-da, *vroom* da-da, *vroom* dá-da," it roared, over and over again. This was not a message, I knew that much; it meant only "I hear you." Presently an old man crawled into the circle and licked the chief's feet with every sign of apparent relish. He was older than many of the elders but his position as *lokali*-talker made him a mere intellectual, a Postmaster-General if you will, or, better, an Oxford don to whom a Prime Minister may listen but must not deign to speak. The chief listened benignly to his mutterings.

Extending his other foot to the pleasing lavage of the old person's tongue, he told me that the savages down-river had two pieces of news: first, they had heard two great trees snap although there was no hint of thunder; second, at the mouth of the river, a great canoe was lying, longer than a village and with trees growing from it and monstrous pieces of cloth upon the trees.

We collogued. The chief then dismissed the *lokali* man with a benevolent kick, telling him to talk with the drums up and down the river, saying that he, the progenitor of all elephants, had broken the two trees with his thumb and forefinger out of impatience because the monthly tributes of goats and virgins had not arrived. The second message was to be drummed down-river from village to village: he, whose walls were built of the skulls of those who had displeased him during the last score of scores of years; he who possessed nightly each of his one hundred wives – none thinner than a hippopotamus – bade all the people of the river to guard and cherish his beloved children – to be known by their fiery faces – who would be travelling down-river next day to the great canoe which he, whose very excrement was treasured by all the world, had commanded to appear in the estuary.

This seemed to me a comprehensive *laissez-passer* but the chief, flushed with the possession of his rifle, wished to make assurance doubly sure. He snapped his fingers and an ancient, dirty person, wearing a necklace of nameless things, crept forward. The chief handed me his own ebony wand and bade me go thrash the god. I followed the dirty old person a few hundred yards into the forest; we entered a stockade inside which there stood an idol crudely shaped from the stump of a tree, sheathed with gold and stuck all over with nails. I belaboured it with the staff until a grunt from the witch-doctor told me that I might exercise compassion. Something else then took place within the stockade which was nasty and which I shall not relate in case your daughters might one day see this narrative.

Blanche had five petticoats left and two pair of drawers. I coaxed one of each from her and that evening used them to purchase a quantity of dance-masks, straw-and-shell skirts, gaily-plaited penis-sheaths and other gew-gaws. I opened my chest of porcelains and took out some of the packing-stuff, replacing it, chiefly on the surface of the chests, with this smelly anthropological trash. Then we went to bed, where I explained to a sulky Blanche that the loss of her drawers was of little importance to a woman with an ardent young husband. I brought her round to my way of thinking at last, for she was not unreasonable.

In the morning, before we set off, the chief came to our *giddah* and reminded me that it was now meet to restore the magic to his rifle. With many an incantation I poured quite four ounces of powder into each barrel, then a leather wad, two inches of stiff clay, two lead balls, then more clay. He asked for a further supply of powder but I assured him, truthfully, that the weapon as now loaded would last him the rest of his life. I gave him a little paper of priming-powder and adjured him not to discharge the piece until the moon was full. By then I would be on the high seas, you understand. I had never liked the old woman he had shot, but justice must be done, must it not, and savages must be taught not to play with inventions they have not invented for themselves. Nevertheless, I am glad that I was not present when the chief pulled the triggers, for I am a compassionate man and he had been kind to me in his own way.

Indeed, his kindness was not yet exhausted: as our little procession wound down to the river bank, where two capable dug-out canoes awaited us and our goods, a strange and hideous ululation smote our ears. It was somewhat like an Italian tenor practising his scales and gargling with unpleasant medicine at the same time. This sound was intermingled with the merry laughter of little children. Clearly, some farewell entertainment had been arranged for us, for the chief urged us onward with many a nod and smile and hospitable gesture. When the river bank came into view I must confess I was vexed at the *mise-en-scène*: the fourth youngest elder – he who owned the most desirable wife in the village, you recall – had been tied wrist and ankle and seated upon the point of a five-foot stake planted in the ground. He was not meeting his end with anything of the stoic complacency which is supposed to characterise the Noble Savage; indeed, the hordes of little children were diverting themselves with clever imitations of his antics, encouraged by their admiring mothers.

I applauded politely, for this was clearly expected of me, but I cannot pretend that I found the spectacle at all droll. With the most perfunctory farewells I hurried our party into the canoes. Blanche, I recall, was sick over the side as soon as we were under way: she had probably eaten her breakfast too quickly.

I remember little of our journey down the great river, for, at our first noon-tide pause for food, Blanche and I were persuaded to eat some fresh-water mussels, which grievously afflicted our bowels for the whole of the three days. I recall only the all-pervading, sickly smell as of dead marigolds, the eternity of mangroves and the prodigious number of kingfishers of every size and colour which flashed across our bows like streamers of fire. Yes, and a frightful afternoon when we scorched on a naked sand-bank while a monstrous bull-hippopotamus raved and roared in the shallows, daring us to come into the water and fight with him. My hands shook too much with fever to risk a shot at him, for, had I not hit him lethally with the first shot, he would surely have rampaged ashore and gnashed and trampled us all to death. The canoe-paddlers explained, with many a lewd gesture, that he was in rut.

The last stage of our canoe-journey was through a thick and stinking forest of enormous reeds, following channels which were tortuous and, to me, invisible. I urged the paddlers on with promises of rum, for I was near-frantic at the thought that the ship might sail before we reached the anchorage. When at last we burst out of the reeds onto the open water of the estuary our eyes were blinded by the glare of sky and sea but soon we could descry, at about a mile's distance, the beautiful, blessed ship: a barquentine and with her sails still furled. I shed some feeble tears of relief.

The canoe-men would take us no further than a tumble-down trading post near the shore – and indeed, I would have been reluctant to risk my life and porcelain and Blanche on the sea in those clumsy little crafts. The agent at the trading-post looked as though he might once have been European but he was rotten with fever and stupefied with drink and could by no means be awakened. I rousted out a fat Parsee clerk who sold me rum for the paddlers and then dashed my spirits to the ground by saying that there was only one surf-boat and that it was alongside the ship, loading the last of the cargo. The ship, he added, would then set sail immediately. Indeed, he could now see the boat returning. I snatched the old brass spy-glass from his hands and saw that he was speaking the truth; a boat was heading for the shore in a leisurely fashion and there was unmistakable activity on the ship's yards.

"How long for the boat to reach us here?" I snapped.

He shrugged his shoulders as only a Parsee can.

"Half an hour?"

243

He spread his hands out as though feeling for rain-drops.

It was clear that by no means could we reach the ship before she sailed.

"When will the next ship call?"

"Next season."

Again I shed tears but this time they were tears of bitter chagrin. Robinson Caruso himself could have felt no more desolate a castaway than I.

"Ve could fire signal-gun," said the Parsee nonchalantly, "but gunpowder is werry costly and every ounce is accountabled."

A few minutes later I had bought half a pound of the costliest gunpowder in the world and the little brass gun by the flag-post was banging out three shots. I watched the ship agonisedly until I was sure that activity had ceased: some irritated officer had uttered the blessed cry, "Avast all that!"

The surf-boat was manned by the most curious people: whilst they were in their boat you would have thought them giants, for their chests were like barrels and their arms like thighs, but ashore they presented an extraordinary appearance on little, spindly bowlegs. They were of a tribe called Kroo-men, who are to be found all up and down the West Coast wherever there are boats to be worked. They sped us to the bar of the estuary; there was a flurry of spray and a corkscrewing motion then all of a sudden we were on the beautiful sea itself and pulling through the swell to the barquentine.

We were not welcome on the barquentine.

The captain was an uncouth fellow from Lancashire or perhaps Yorkshire and spoke a kind of *patois* English which was strange to me, but his meaning was clear: on no account was he permitted, or able, to take passengers. I pled, but to no avail.

"Gunpowder is werry costly," I murmured under my breath – and gave him a shameful number of guineas, which made him recall that a Captain had discretion in these matters when saving lives was concerned. In a twinkling a whip was rove to a yard, my goods and Blanche were hove aboard and the anchor was weighed. The breeze was from the south-west, so it still bore the heavy scent of Africa, but I snuffed it with rapture.

The scent of the ship herself was not so rapturous to snuff, for much of our cargo was palm-oil, which stinks. She had come out laden with trashy Preston cotton-goods, Batley shoddy-cloth and some bales of old uniforms from the Napoleonic wars. (These last had made the ship – otherwise cleanly – to be infested with fleas at which Blanche complained bitterly until I explained to her that it was a privilege to give board and lodging to a flea whose ancestor might well have bitten the Duke of Wellington himself. Like all women, she was something of a snob, an attitude now fashionable since Queen Victoria herself took it up at the instigation of the man Albert.)

I signed the ship's papers as Professor Mortdecai, occupation anthropologist. The captain was concerned about our lack of papers until I reminded him of the voracity of the termites on that Coast.

CHAPTER TWENTY

━━◦━━

Neither Blanche nor I was in a condition to remark on the food until we were north of the Cap Verde Isles. When at last we were able to dine regularly with the Captain we did not regret the wasted days, for he kept a poor table. I recall the diet with hateful clarity: one day there would be Lancashire hot-pot, which is a thick, muddy mess of the worst bones from the neck of a starveling sheep, seethed with potatoes and onions to disguise, one supposes, their loathsome appearance. This horror would alternate with Irish stew, which is the same as Lancashire hot-pot but contains much more water, and Lob Scouse – a Liverpool dish of stewed vegetables and crushed ship's biscuit, enriched with gobbets of fat meat. Each Friday there would be Blind Scouse, which is the same but without the gobbets, for the Captain, inexplicably, was a Roman Catholic. On Saturdays there was fat salt pork boiled with pickled cabbage and on Sundays there was, at an unconscionable hour, the weekly feast: a roast of beef from some elderly cow who was more to be congratulated on her longevity than her succulence, served with roast potatoes bobbing about in a sea of warm grease and segments of a firm, yellowish custard called Yorkshire batter. The Captain and his cloddish officers ate ravenously of this harmful ordure and seemed puzzled that Blanche and I preferred to staunch our stomachs with stale bread, rancid butter and what I suppose I must call cheese, for that was what they called it. My respect for those who build the British Empire grew at each meal: " 'tis from scenes like this that Britain's greatness springs," as Lord Byron has said. Dyspepsia is the spur. With such a dinner inside him, it would be a strange man indeed who could not face the charge of Fuzzy-Wuzzy undauntedly; a strange

246

missionary who could not preach the fiercest Old Testament passages with burning eloquence.

Thanks be to God – *any* God who chances to be thumbing through this essentially moral tale – our water-casks had become impossibly foul and so full of animalcules that even these iron-livered North Country men could not drink it, so our Captain put in to the Gran Canaria, at the mole called Las Palmas, so as to complete with water and, no doubt, bargain for more beasts of canonical age. For my part, I laid out a guinea on fresh fruit, a crock of butter, certain crusty loaves and a long, hard garlic sausage. I kept an eye open for the young person I had met there on my outward voyage – how long ago it seemed! – not with any lust in my heart, for I was now a married man and, moreover, too undernourished – but simply to reproach her for the infestation she had ungratefully rewarded me with and to press upon her a cake of the incomparable mercury soap. She was not to be seen; I like to think that she was in the confessional box.

This sausage, coupled with these fruits – I speak figuratively, of course – so restored our well-being that before we weathered Ushant I found myself once again able to reassure Blanche of the vigour of my devotion towards her; this, in turn, gave us both the appetite to warm ourselves in the increasing cold by eating a little of the hot and greasy messes of the Captain's table, which now proved less offensive than they had seemed in the Tropics.

Nonetheless, it was with a great gladness that we heard the anchor-chain crashing through the hawse-hole in London River and our thanks and farewells to the Captain and his officers were, I fancy, not much more than perfunctory.

I had pasted great labels on my chests of porcelain, bearing the words "BRITISH MUSEUM", and these, along with a sudden inability to speak anything but the most broken English, soon cleared me and our goods through the customs with no more than a half-sovereign tactfully laid out here and there. The cases, I, and Blanche were soon on a tax-cart, bumping towards St Botolph Lane. At Mr Jorrocks's warehouse we were greeted by the M.F.H. himself. He peered at me amazedly, cried "Dash my vig!" from a full heart and indeed pulled off the very wig itself and dashed it upon the grocery-encrusted floor.

"Never hoped to see you alive again, Mr Dutch, my dear young cock! And wot's this, wot's this? Your lady wife? Charmed, I'm sure: 'none but the fair deserves the brave' as Nimrod himself has said. You shall come home with me this werry hinstant to meet Mrs J., who I do not doubt will find some scrap of a snack to furnish us out until dinner-time." We did so. Mrs J. burst into tears at the sight of me: for a moment I feared that she would fold me to her bosom. Luckily, Mr Jorrocks presented Blanche to her at that moment, so that it was Blanche who received the enfolding, the kindly, copious tears and the maudlin sayings of "there, there" and "you poor thing, you," etc., while Mr Jorrocks and I stole away to where the good, strong Marquess of Cornwallis lay in black bottles under the dining-room sideboard.

I did not see Blanche again until dinner, when she plied almost as lusty a knife and fork as I did, for she had rested, you see. It was a frugal dinner, Mr Jorrocks explained, because we were but four at table and there had been no time to arrange "made dishes". A tureen of gravy-soup and a stuffed pike were "removed" by a round of boiled beef at one end of the table and a crown-roast of mutton at the other; the corner dishes were but a brace of green geese and another of Aylesbury ducklings; nevertheless, we fared well for we were used to worse, and the black puddings, ragoût of kidneys and pigeon pie which came with the sweet things as second course were barely touched.

When the women had retired to drink those potent, sticky drinks which women drink in drawing-rooms, Mr Jorrocks fetched out two decanters of a port which he himself had only once before broached, he vowed. The two decanters were because he professed himself too old and tired to push decanters the length of a table: it was easier to have one each. It was capital port. Later, Blanche and I slept between lavender-scented linen sheets, smothered luxuriously in feather beds. There was never so happy a man as me that night and Blanche, too, gave every sign of contentment with her lot.

There was, of course, no question of taking such another little shop as I had once kept – so many centuries ago, it seemed – near Strand Street and the Convent Gardens Cabbage Exchange. In those days I had been but a poor, ignorant Dutch Jew; I was now a *rich*, ignorant Dutch Jew, for I owned the finest stock of porcelains in Europe as well as the modest amount of gold I had thoughtfully rescued from the specie-room of the *John Coram*. For running expenses I went to a Dutchman in Hatton's Garden – which is a street, not a garden at all, and where you could linger a week without hearing a word of English spoken – and sold my splendid baroque pearl. I was robbed, of course, robbed, but £485 (plus a sovereign with which to buy sweet-meats for my non-existent children) shewed a good profit on my purchase price from the base of the base Indian, and in any case it has always been my philosophy to leave a profit for the next man.

Not only had I to seek out a more grandiose shop but also one with elegant living-quarters, for I now had a wife and, as everyone knows, wives require drawing-rooms, water-closets and many another fal-lal and folderol. At last we found an ideal place: Mr Jorrocks advised me that an acquaintance of his ("for 'friend' vould be stretching the Henglish language a leetle," he said) had recently gone to Queer Street. This "Queer Street" is an affectionate term used by Londoners to denote Carey Street, where the Commissioners in Bankruptcy sit magisterially the live-long day, striving to teach debtors and creditors to live together in amity. It is a strange, *British* institution and many a fortune has been founded by prudently resorting there. I have heard it said that a sensibly-planned bankruptcy can be as profitable as a well-insured fire.

Be that as it may, Mr Jorrocks's acquaintance, a Mr S. Sponge, had "failed" in his business, which was called the SPONGE CIGAR & BETTING ROOMS, by advertising that he had £116,500 to lend at three and one half per centum – a madness which only a Gentile could perpetrate.

The cigar divan, which we went to inspect that very day, was furnished in the most gentlemanly taste: replete with crimson plush, gilt plaster simulating carved wood, ottomans in bottle-green velvet; red mahogany and crystal chandeliers: one might have thought oneself in Waddesdon itself. It was going for a song and I snapped it up in a trice; that is to say, after little more than three hours' bargaining with the agent for the creditors. It was situated in a quiet, not too dirty little street called Jermyn which runs parallel to the unfashionable end of Piccadilly (where the more genteel whores ply their trade) and is in the Parish of St James's. But why do I tell you this, for have I not often taken you to see where our House was founded, and where it throve until, needing more space, I bought the Duke's house at the Corner of Hyde Park?

The upstairs apartments were spacious and elegant for such a seedy neighbourhood and Blanche declared herself well pleased. Then, at her insistence, we went a-shopping. Our first call was at the

Foundling Hospital, where I bought another bastard, explaining that Orace had ungratefully run away to sea. The new boy seemed sturdy, willing and with clean fingernails. He was happy to leave the Hospital, for his work there was to scrub floors for ten hours each day, except on Saturdays when he was leased out to a "Sabbath goy", who is a man who contracts to light fires for orthodox Jews on that day and to do other tasks forbidden in Leviticus.

I was generous with Blanche and I am bound to admit that she laid out the money well on bedding, furnishings, wall-papers and clothes for herself. Her taste in drawers, stays and smocked petticoats I found exquisite and she discovered an innate gift for removing them in my presence in the most charming way. It was interesting to observe that, as her store of finery increased, so did her saltiness; indeed, there were nights when even I was hard-pressed to match her salacious inventiveness. I believe it was at about that time that I bought her, as a sentimental present, a charming little terrier-whip, the lash bound with green velvet and a silver fox's head on the handle. She had, it proved, not quite out-grown such toys.

I think that, on the whole, I am glad that I shall never understand women. There are some areas of knowledge which we men are better without.

My mother had sent, in care of Mr Jorrocks, a couple of chests of excellent Delft and other wares; these, along with some of the less important items from my cases of Chinese porcelains, furnished forth the still-shuttered windows of my new establishment against the day when I should open for business and astonish the London connoisseurs.

There came a day when the new clothes which I had ordered were delivered and the modest, but not quite tradesmanly, carriage was promised for the morrow. I sent a note to Lord Windermere craving, in a dignified way, permission to wait upon him the following day. The note came back with a scribbled."Pray do, but you'll find me bedridden" on it.

Before this visit, something upsetting happened: when signing the papers for the new bastard I had noted that his first name was "Hugh" and had, accordingly, been addressing him as *"Hooch"*. He came to me and explained, most respectfully, that this name was in fact pronounced "You" in English. I was quite taken aback and told him that this would never do. He admitted to owning a second name – Thomas – and we agreed on this – an excellent name for a bastard.

When the new carriage, drawn by a fine half-bred Hackney bay, was delivered, Tom walked around it in the most knowledgeable way and gentled the horse like any ostler (which is short for oat-stealer, of course). He shyly claimed that he knew how to drive such a conveyance and I allowed him, with some trepidation, to prove his skill. He was, indeed, gifted in the art and I sent out forthwith for a suitable hat and leggings for this capable little dandi-prat.

That afternoon, I found Lord Windermere in a piteous state. It appeared that, some few nights before, he had drunk two bottles of port more than was his wont and had awakened in the night with the frightful kind of thirst which will drive a man to drink water. He had made his own way to the butler's pantry and drunk quite a pint of the stuff. Now, everyone knows that to drink the water of London is to invite disaster, and disaster had indeed descended upon his essential tripes: one could hear them gurgling like Fleet-ditch. He perked up considerably when I produced the little present I had brought him from China: a minute, exquisite scribe's screen in the purest mutton-fat jade and a matching brush-pot in the most unflawed spinach-colour; a colour only to be found in the fabled Jade Mountain which lies somewhere in Shan-Si, is guarded day and night and whose location even the Celestial One has not been told.

He was right to prize this present, for old Jim Christie would have squeezed out quite a hundred guineas for it in his auction rooms. But Windermere was no fool and knew that I too was nothing of the sort.

"Uncommon kind of you," he murmured, just audible over the Vesuvian noises from his innards, "*uncommon* kind. Dare say you've something to sell me, eh? Eh?"

I explained to him that, amongst my new season's stock, I had the incomparable ox-blood piece, bought in Canton, which I have spoken of before, and that I could not exhibit it publicly because no true connoisseur would have eyes for anything else in my shop if it were there; I had to be rid of it, even at a sacrifice. Windermere's eyes glazed with disinterest as he stared abstractedly at a corner of the painted bedroom-ceiling, where some precocious cherubs were disporting themselves in *adult* ways. I uttered, in a flat voice, some seven more words describing the piece. His eyes remained disinterested but I was watching the quickened respiration of his chest.

"How much?" he asked, languidly.

I told him. He sat bolt upright.

"Oh, burst and rot me!" he cried in a frenzy. "If I'd not the squitters already I'd have 'em now! Are you insane?"

"I do not think so," I said carefully, "except, perhaps, in the matter of women."

"Pull the bell-rope!" he yelled. "No, not that one, the other: I need a bedpan, not the butler."

When I re-entered the room, some minutes later, an effete and pallid Windermere begged me to trifle no more with a man trembling, as he was, on the edge of the very grave.

"What's the *real* price?" he asked. "Come now, the real one, eh? Damme, you've had your joke, turned me bowels inside out, let's talk sense now. *Guineas*. Things like that."

"Lord Windermere," I said, gravely as any high-priced doctor, "the real price would blench the cheek of anyone but Nathan Meyer Rothschild" – I repeated this name carefully – "but the price I named to you was but a token of friendship, you understand."

He ranted a little but used no language more dirty than was customary with him. At last, sulkily, he said that he would look at the pot.

"Tomorrow," I said. "Today, if you will forgive me, your eyes are a little tinged with bile and not perfectly able to appreciate the colour of this piece. So, until this time tomorrow, my Lord. . . ?"

"Very well," he rasped in tones of defeat. "On your way out, tell that woman to bring the bedpan again – and tell the butler to give you a glass of whatever you please. I can recommend the *water*, heh heh."

There is a peculiar pleasure in knowing that you have made a sale before the customer has seen anything but the price.

CHAPTER TWENTY-ONE

───◆───

I sprang out of bed the next morning with a song on my lips and the world at my feet. Blanche had, during the night, given me yet more proof of her talents and inventiveness in the field of love and had shyly promised to surprise me deliciously, next bed-time, with a truly remarkable piece of naughtiness which she had been saving up for a special occasion. Moreover, I was rich; I had a glistering new carriage, a splendid emporium ready to startle London with, an ensured sale to Lord Windermere that evening which would bring enough to keep an unambitious man for life and – here I rubbed my hands with glee – Mr Jorrocks was bidden for dinner at two-thirty sharp and I had arranged such a feast as would daunt even his magnificent appetite. He had made me cry "*capivi*" at the Margate breakfast and I had long thirsted for revenge. At this dinner I meant to make him repeat the legendary episode when he had had to beg his friends to lift him up, tie him into his chair and fill his glass.

There was a barrel of oysters dripping in the cellar; an incredible salmon with the sea-lice still clustering on it, brought express from the sandy deserts of Wales itself; a tureen of soup made from a prodigious turtle, the gelatinous meat and gobbets of green fat swimming so thickly in it – both calipash and calipee – that it was a puzzle to find the liquor; Aylesbury ducklings as big as geese; half of a stag's bottom cooked in pastry and many another kickshaw – but the prime remove, the dish to defeat even Mr Jorrocks, was a round of boiled beef. Plain fare, you say? Ah, but this round of beef was from an ox among oxes, an ox which would have made an elephant cringe; moreover, it had been dressed according to the receipt of Signor Francatelli, the pupil of Carême himself and the new *chef de cuisine* to her new Majesty. The receipt alone had cost me a guinea and now, as I write (when I have to count every penny so that I can leave a substantial sum to the Foundling Hospital), it makes me shudder to think of the cost of the cocks'-combs, palates, crayfish and other rarities which were called for. (I shall perhaps append the receipt to this memoir of mine, but I know how you love these little legacies *en souvenir*.)

It was, then, a wonderfully happy Van Cleef or Mortdecai who sat down to dinner that afternoon.

"Wot a werry helegant little repast, Mr Dutch," said Mr Jorrocks, as oyster after oyster flew down his throat. "Can't take my eyes off that salmon. Yes, pray help me, do." A little later: "Vy, wot's this? Haven't seen finer turtle soup on the Lord Mayor's table, swears I don't know where you gets it, unless you've a friend in the Mansion House." And so it went on without a flaw or pause in the arrangements; Tom was trotting to and fro with fresh plates and more bottles, Blanche was beaming and winking at me and old Mrs Jorrocks's great red face was steaming with pleasure as she gobbled.

I passed the ox-blood Ming bowl around as a loving-cup, filled with champagne, then the round of beef was brought in with great *éclat*. I begged Mr J. to take the honours of the carving-knife and he had heaped every plate before he dropped, from a full mouth, the words which were to change my life.

"Almost forgot, Mr Dutch. A person came to the varehouse on Friday, claimed to be a friend of yours."

"Really?" I said, from an equally full mouth. "Did he give a name?"

"Believes he did. Elderly, skinny chap, brown in the face, werry short of teeth and a little the worse for liquor. Ragged pea-jacket buttoned up to the neck to hide his no-shirt, but spoke like a gent – and I means the genuine harticle."

"I do not think I know anyone of that description, Mr J.," I said, reaching for another oyster or two to help the beef slip down. "Do you recall the name?" This question seemed to have the most alarming effect:

"Fetch my hat, Binjamin!" he roared over his shoulder. I gaped.

"Surely, Mr J., you're not going?" asked Blanche, distressed.

"Going, *going*; vy should I be going just ven my happetite is properly tickled? No no, just wants my hat, lid, tile – calls it Golgotha, 'place of the skull' you know, haw haw! – it's my portable scrutoire."

He fumbled in the lining of the great beaver and after turning out a raffle of bills of exchange, promissory notes and notices of the meetings of fox-dogs, finally found and handed to me a scrap of paper with his great blotted scrawl on it. The words were *"P. Stenegave DA PM"*.

I shall not pretend that the oyster turned to ashes in my mouth: such extravagances are bred only in the heated minds of female novelists, but I recall that I gulped at the little bivalve with some difficulty, for it was clear that, against all odds, my dear messmate Peter was alive.

So intense was my emotion that I found it difficult to speak until I had emptied my plate and Mr J. was refilling it.

"Yes, please," was what I said, "and a few of those cocks'-combs and other tid-bits, if you please. Thanks. By the bye, what does 'DA PM' mean?" He inserted his fork under his wig and scratched reflectively. "Can't say as I recalls now," he said, wiping it on his napkin (the fork, not the wig), "but 'PM' must signify 'post meridgium' or afternoon, must it not? My vord, 'ow beautifully laced this beef is with delicate yellow fat, thinks I'll take a touch more. 'Well bred, well grown, well killed, well 'ung, well bought and well-dressed' as the old King used to say. Ah yes, 'DA' signifies the place where you might find this hacquaintance of yours. Yes, that's it, 'Dirty Annie's' is the place he named. Any arternoon, or p.m. Vould have said he was a longshoreman, shy of the price of a pot of ale, but for 'is woice."

I would not have been able to contain myself had Mr J.'s carving not reached, at that very moment, the rich, red centre of the beef. In the event, it was not more than ten or fifteen minutes before I felt constrained to rise to my feet and beg the company's forgiveness, saying that I had reason to think that an old friend was in grave distress. Blanche gave me a puzzled but loving look; Mrs Jorrocks was too deeply – and noisily – involved in victuals to have heard; John Jorrocks gazed at me curiously, for, when wiping my lips with the napkin, I had also cleared part of my face from perspiration with a gesture which Captain Knatchbull would certainly have recognised. There was a chinking noise under the table – Mr J. had his purse out and was proffering it to me. I smiled and shook my head.

"I should be back within the hour, dearest," I said to Blanche, "pray keep our guests here until I return." With that I was off, bounding down the stairs without a thought for my digestion, seizing my hat and hailing the first four-wheeler. The owner of the "growler" had no wish to go to the India Docks but my will was stronger than his.

Outside Dirty Annie's there was the usual scattering of loiterers, hands deeply pocketed. As I passed a little, old, nut-brown man a dear and familiar voice said "Too proud to recognise your old mess-mate, Karli?" I scanned the line of loafers suspiciously, but no, the voice came from the old man. It was Peter; toothless, hairless, wizened and shabby but undeniably Peter.

His smile was not the same, because of the lack of the teeth, but it was as warm as ever, and as wry.

"You, too, have changed, Karli, but losing your puppy-fat suits you."

We fell into each other's arms and I fancy we danced a little jig of delight. No one spared us a glance, for such sights are a commonplace in every great port. Then I said, lying tactfully, that I was starving and that he must come and eat with me, for dinner was on the table.

"Not in these clothes. I mustn't shame you before your fine friends. And, just at present, I have no others. And to tell the truth I would much prefer a drink, it keeps a fellow warm, d'you see." It was a warm day, but I did not point that out. I hurried him away to the nearest decent tavern – that is to say, I tried to hurry him but his gait was uncertain and plunging as though the cobbles of the street were covered deep with feather mattresses. With sinking heart I recognised this gait: it is a sign of *locomotor ataxia*, a disease which visits those who are in the last stages of syphilis.

The nearest tavern to the Docks was empty and dirty; the fat, blubber-lipped landlord who stood at the door had a shifty look. But I did not think that Peter could walk much further; it would have to do.

I ordered a bottle of brandy, lemons, hot water and sugar, such as I knew he loved; also a cold fowl in its broth.

He retched and gagged over his first glass, then his face gained a little colour – although not a colour I would like to see on my own face – and his hand was steadier when he filled the next. Little by little, between potations, I coaxed a disjointed story from him. He was in the mood to drink toasts to the most improbable people and occasions: he made me drink to long life for the odious Captain

Dogg who, pistol in hand, never sleeping, had navigated the open boat like an insane genius, doling out water and biscuit in sips and bites over the countless sea-miles before they made a miraculous landfall on the south east coast of Ceylon.

We drank to the Booby-bird which Peter had caught one dawn in his bare hands and which they had torn apart and gobbled, raw and bleeding, two mouthfuls to a man.

We drank to the marvellous fact that large fishes, when you can catch and boat them, have eyes full of sweet, fresh water.

We stood and drank bumpers, solemnly, to the man who had drunk seawater at midnight and died at noon, and to the old coxswain who had seen his mother walking on the burning water and had stepped over the side to meet her.

We drank to Peter's teeth which, he said, had been rattling loose as castanets by the end of the voyage and which he had given, one by one, to the kindly Sinhalese natives who had guided them (at the point of Captain Dogg's pistol) across the swamps and quagmires to where a Royal Navy frigate had been lying, licking her wounds after a storm-battering.

When I called for the next bottle the landlord thoughtfully coaxed us into the inner "snug" where, he pointed out, we could sing undisturbed by the curious crowd which had gathered about us.

There we toasted the Second Mate, whose hair had turned pure white overnight after a tropic rainstorm. "I swear it's true, Karli," Peter giggled, "you could see the hair-dye all over his face and chest!"

It was at about that time that we determined to become a little drunk. "But first," I said owlishly, "first we must see about you, Peter, for – forgive me – you do not seem to be in good case."

"Pray do not fret, Karli, it's of no importance, I assure you. The pox, d'you see, is up to my eyebrows now. . ." He lifted his cap and sure enough, just below the hairline there was the *corona Veneris*, the crown of Venus, the circlet of pustules which tells the pox-ridden that there is no hope.

"Cheer up Karli," he cried merrily – a merriness made hideous by his naked gums – "my navigation is still adequate; I'll get a berth in some foreign-going bucket and that'll see me through the rest of my allowed time."

I cleared my throat, frantically searching for some way of offering help.

"Your wife . . . ?" I muttered.

"Let's drink to the bitch. Found her in bed with her lover. I offered to thrash him. He thrashed me."

"Your father . . . ?"

"Married his nurse on his deathbed. I'm a Marquess now, the poorest and poxiest Marquess in Great Britain. Let's drink. . ."

I decided to be practical.

"Peter," I said firmly, "the first thing is to get you into a suit of decent clothes; you know you cannot hope to get a berth looking as you do now."

He glared icily, then grinned a travesty of his old mocking grin. "Of course, Karli; it would be churlish to refuse a little temporary help from an old mess-mate. But first, there is the small matter of getting drunk, you recall."

Later we sang a lugubrious ditty called, I think, *"Here's to the dead already – and three cheers for the next man to die."* We sang it again and again, for there was some disagreement about the tune and key.

Later still I recall enjoying the wonderful coolness on my cheek as I rested it in a puddle of brandy, for it seemed to me that I could see Peter more clearly from that angle, you understand.

I must have slept, for wonderful dreams came to me: I was a little, naked child again, I was being carried and rocked in strong arms; I had wet myself. All around me I could hear good Dutch voices shouting. I wept happily. As I floated to the surface of sleep I was puzzled, for the Dutch that was being shouted was not the Dutch of my native Gelderland but the harsh accents of Rotterdam; it made my head hurt. I opened my eyes to utter blackness. The shouting went on and there was a din above my head of stampings and bangings. I was sick.

A door opened and blinding sunlight made me blink. Black against the sun I made out the shape of a huge man.

"Get up," said a voice I thought I had heard before.

I rose to my feet and staggered towards the figure, rubbing my eyes and trying to focus. There was a snake-like thing dangling from its hand.

"Where am I?" I whimpered.

258

"You're in the *Rose of Boston*, loading for Sydney, New South Wales. And you call me 'Sir'," said Lubbock.

I gaped. The rope's end flicked out and my groin jumped in agony.

"Aye aye, Sir," I said.

ACKNOWLEDGMENTS

"In our trade we be all felons, more or less" (R. Kipling).

The men from whom I have stolen most freely (in this book, I mean) are dead: Basil Lubbock who wrote *The China Clippers* and Robert Surtees who created the immortal John Jorrocks, M.F.H. I hope that when my time comes I shall be able to look them in the face. My thanks are due to Commander Hanson, R.N.(Retd) of Jersey and formerly of the China Station, who first pointed my bows in this direction. No one could write about the Treaty Coast without the aid of Maurice Colliss's classic *Foreign Mud*. Commander Kemp's *Oxford Companion to Ships and the Sea* was published just in time to kedge me off some dangerous lee-shores. As to the rest I can only say, like the little girl who spat at Nursey, "I'm afraid that was my own invention."

My thanks are due to my former wife Margaret, whose patience would shame Griselda and whose loyalty certainly shames me.

Last, I must thank all my new friends in County Cavan, whose unquestioning kindness to their new neighbour has carried me through a long, dark winter: the fact that I cannot list their names here is a measure of their number.

KYRIL BONFIGLIOLI

THE FIVE MORTDECAI NOVELS

'I am Charlie Mordecai. I like art and money and dirty jokes and drink. I am very successful'

Don't Point That Thing at Me

The Hon. Charlie Mortdecai is up to his earlobes in trouble. A Goya painting has gone missing and the authorities seem to think he knows something about it. He does. If he and his thuggish manservant Jock are not very careful, some very nasty men with guns are liable to make them very dead.

After You with the Pistol

It's been made clear to Charlie that he has to marry the beautiful, sex-crazed and very rich Johanna Krampf. The only fly in the ointment is that she seems determined to involve him in her crazy schemes of monarch-assassination and heroin smuggling. Perhaps it's all in a good cause – if only he can live long enough to find out.

Something Nasty in the Woodshed

Charlie has decamped to Jersey after a spot of bother in London, and is hoping to lie low with his manservant and his new bride. But then a friend's wife is attacked, and for once he takes on the role of pursuer rather than pursued.

The Great Mortdecai Moustache Mystery

Charlie's main excitement in Jersey is cultivating an exuberant moustache, even though it endangers conjugal relations. Things perk up when he's invited to Oxford by his old tutor to investigate the cruel and unusual death of a lady don. He uncovers the culprit – but not before coming across enough villains to shoehorn into a stretch limo.

All the Tea in China

After an act of lechery that anyone but a close relative might forgive, Karli Mortdecai Van Cleef, a distant relative of the Hon. Charlie Mortdecai, throws in his lot with an opium clipper bound for China. So begins a staggering adventure. It runs in the family . . .

He just wanted a decent book to read ...

Not too much to ask, is it? It was in 1935 when Allen Lane, Managing Director of Bodley Head Publishers, stood on a platform at Exeter railway station looking for something good to read on his journey back to London. His choice was limited to popular magazines and poor-quality paperbacks – the same choice faced every day by the vast majority of readers, few of whom could afford hardbacks. Lane's disappointment and subsequent anger at the range of books generally available led him to found a company – and change the world.

'We believed in the existence in this country of a vast reading public for intelligent books at a low price, and staked everything on it'
Sir Allen Lane, 1902–1970, founder of Penguin Books

The quality paperback had arrived – and not just in bookshops. Lane was adamant that his Penguins should appear in chain stores and tobacconists, and should cost no more than a packet of cigarettes.

Reading habits (and cigarette prices) have changed since 1935, but Penguin still believes in publishing the best books for everybody to enjoy. We still believe that good design costs no more than bad design, and we still believe that quality books published passionately and responsibly make the world a better place.

So wherever you see the little bird – whether it's on a piece of prize-winning literary fiction or a celebrity autobiography, political tour de force or historical masterpiece, a serial-killer thriller, reference book, world classic or a piece of pure escapism – you can bet that it represents the very best that the genre has to offer.

Whatever you like to read – trust Penguin.